"What's so funny?" she asked.

Still chuckling a little, he turned to look at her. "Cletus knows a joke or two."

"Care to share?"

"Sorry. They're not fit for a lady's ear."

"Now, Alex," she said quietly, "you know I'm no lady."

His broad smile faded to a softer one. "I don't know any such thing."

Alex continued to stare at her, and slowly something seemed to come alive between them. His gaze was sure and steady, focusing on her face as if it were the first time he was seeing it.

"What?" she whispered.

"You look beautiful tonight."

Her heart jolted hard, then settled into a maddening rhythm.

"It's the tiki torches. Every woman looks good by the light of a tiki torch."

"I don't think the torches have anything to do with it. . . ."

By Jane Graves
Published by Ivy Books

I GOT YOU, BABE

Wild at Heart

Jane Graves

IVY BOOKS • NEW YORK

An Ivy Book
Published by The Ballantine Publishing Group
Copyright © 2002 by Jane Graves

www.ballantinebooks.com

ISBN 0-8041-1969-4

Manufactured in the United States of America

First Edition: October 2002

OPM 10 9 8 7 6 5 4 3 2 1

To Barbara Dunlop and Pam Baustian,
for your wit, your friendship, and
for talking me off the ledge a time or two.
What would I ever do without you?

chapter one

It was nearly eight o'clock before the massive front door of the colonial mansion opened and Shannon Reichert stepped onto the front porch. Halfway down the block, Valerie Parker snapped to attention, adjusting the side mirror of her van just enough that she could watch the woman sashay down the sidewalk toward her late-model Lexus. She wore her red hair upswept in a wild, cascading style, complemented by a skimpy scarlet dress that was so hot it practically set the shrubs on fire.

Red dress, red heels, red lips, red hair. *Bingo.* A man-hunting ensemble if Val had ever seen one.

If only Shannon's husband could see her now.

Shannon got into her car and started it. As soon as she pulled away from the curb, Val waited a few moments, then made a U-turn with her van and followed at a discreet distance.

The Lexus made its way down Augusta Drive, a swirling ribbon of road that ran through the heart of posh Waverly Park. They passed one extravagant home after another, all testimonies to just how lavishly one could live if one could swallow the price tag that went along with the lifestyle.

Shannon turned left onto Russell Road and headed east. The Friday-night traffic in Tolosa, Texas, made surveillance in a moving vehicle a challenge, but the bumper beeper Val had slipped onto the Lexus, while not the world's most accurate apparatus, would at least help her zero in on the direction the car was traveling if she happened to lose it along the way.

Every mile Shannon drove took her out of her home territory of exclusive shops and four-dollar cups of coffee and moved her closer to a neighborhood that Val swore she would have avoided at all costs. White collars became blue, Porsches became pickups, and the ethnic mix became obvious because there actually was one.

To Val's surprise, Shannon pulled into the parking lot of a bar called the Blue Onion, one of those working-class establishments with a red neon sign out front, a trashy alley out back, and a considerable amount of after-hours relaxation going on in between. Val had been there only once, tracking down a deadbeat dad who was known to spend his child-support money on alcohol and women. She knew people came to places like this for three reasons only: to play pool, to get drunk, and to get laid. By the way Shannon was advertising herself tonight, Val could only assume she was heavily focused on number three.

Yes, Shannon was definitely going slumming. But for what purpose? To meet a current boyfriend, or to find a new one? That remained to be seen. Val hadn't recorded calls to anyone except Shannon's manicurist and yoga instructor. If she was planning a rendezvous with a lover, she hadn't used her home phone to confirm it.

Val cruised along behind the Lexus, following its driver into God-knew-what situation. The games rich people played were positively amazing. Of course, Shannon was rich only by the grace of Jack Reichert, her fifty-four-year-old husband. She had exactly the kind of hot little body that would trip the trigger of a man who had enough money to buy just about anything he wanted except his youth back. Marrying a twenty-something woman was his way of reassuring himself and the rest of the world that his equipment was still intact and functioning, since the Porsche 911, the big-game hunting, and the hair-replacement surgery hadn't done the trick. And for Shannon, marrying a rich older man was her way of reassuring herself that she'd always have plenty of what she wanted most in the world: money.

Then two days ago, Reichert coughed up some of that hard-earned wealth—a thousand dollars, to be exact—and instructed Val to find out what kinds of activities his young wife was engaging in whenever he was out of town on his frequent hunting trips. Reichert, like most men with gold-digging wives, felt he had a right to know if she was handing out to other men for free what he'd bought and paid for.

In her relatively short life, Val had discovered that people betrayed each other right and left, and she found it more than a little ironic that she'd ended up in a career that threw her right into the heart of the very thing she hated the most. But, at least most of the time, she had the satisfaction of ensuring that morally deficient people paid for what they did to those who trusted them. If there was dirt to be had, she never stopped digging until she came up with it. Tonight, as always, failure was not an option.

Shannon slid her Lexus into a parking space and stepped out. She turned on the charm as she headed for the bar, and by the time she reached the door, three men who had just arrived were fighting over who got to open it for her.

Val could either stay out here and wait for Shannon to emerge with the man of her dreams, or she could go inside and observe the process up close and personal. She opted for the latter. Even if Shannon didn't stray from her wedding vows tonight, she still might exhibit the kind of bad behavior that would keep her husband shelling out more money to keep the case alive.

Val waited for a minute or two, then stepped out of her van. She was dressed in faded jeans and a T-shirt, wearing almost no makeup, with her long spirals of dark hair hanging loose around her shoulders. She'd blend right in with the crowd.

Shannon, on the other hand, was clearly out to be noticed.

Once inside, Val spotted Shannon on a stool at the bar, so she moved across the room and found a secluded table along the wall beneath a neon Budweiser sign. People were laughing too loudly, drinking too hard, and smoking as if the surgeon general had never even addressed the subject. The twang of country music filled the air.

A waitress approached her, a tall, busty woman whose coarse blond hair showed an inch of dark roots.

"What can I get for you, sweetie?"

"A beer. Whatever you have on draft."

"Coming right up."

"Tell me something," Val said. "That redhead over there. Does she come here often?"

The waitress turned toward the bar and eyed Shannon. "Nope. Never seen her before."

Okay. Shannon was new around here. But Val still couldn't say for sure why she'd chosen to come to this particular place.

"Do you know her?" the waitress asked.

"No. But it's hard to miss her, isn't it?"

The waitress leaned in. "Just between you and me, I wish she'd pick some other place to strut her stuff."

"Really? Why?"

"Peacocks like that one always cause problems. The women customers hate them because the men won't stop looking at them, and the waitresses hate them because the men get all hung up with the view and forget to tip."

Val gave her a phony sigh. "I hear you. I'm meeting my boyfriend for a few beers. If he gets an eyeful of her, I might as well not even be here."

The waitress shook her head sadly. "What is it with men, anyway? They can have good, quality women like ourselves, and instead they make fools of themselves over ones like that." She huffed with disgust. "Morons."

"Yeah," Val agreed. "Morons."

"I'll get your beer so you can drink to that. And believe me, sweetie, if I wasn't working, I'd be drinking to it right along with you."

A moment later, the waitress brought Val her beer. Val left it untouched in front of her and settled back in her chair, waiting for Shannon to make a move.

An hour and a half later, she was still waiting.

Shannon's antennae seemed to be up and fully operational, but all she did was watch the crowd, turning away the countless men who tried to buy her a drink, sipping the one she'd bought for herself instead. She did glance toward the door occasionally, though, which led Val to believe that maybe she was supposed to meet somebody here and had gotten stood up. Then again, she didn't look the least bit annoyed. If the average woman had waited an hour and a half for a man who hadn't bothered to show, she'd be in a major snit by now.

In the meantime, Val had been forced to fend off a few guys herself, ones who weren't drunk enough yet to think they could approach a showstopper like Shannon. Fortunately, they'd been easily dissuaded by her "I'm waiting for my boyfriend" line.

A couple of times in the early days of her career, she'd tried "No, thank you, I'm a lesbian," hoping to shut down any male hormone activity in the vicinity, only to discover that instead of discouraging men, it turned them on. The last time she'd said, "No, thank you, I have gonorrhea," the guy got a big smile on his face and said, "So do I." That had been it. She'd sworn off the smart-ass remarks forever.

Okay. So every profession had a few built-in hazards.

Actually, Val could put up with the negatives as long as enough positives flowed her way. Unfortunately, tonight it looked as if the positives were going to be few and far between. Evidently Shannon had painted on her red dress, teased her hair, slipped into stiletto heels, then planted herself on that bar stool because she needed a drink or two and enjoyed breathing secondhand smoke. It was the only explanation for her presence there, because it sure didn't look as if she intended to cheat on her husband.

Or maybe she was just an old-fashioned girl. One who didn't cheat unless she found Mr. Right.

Since the waitress thought the guy Val was supposedly meeting hadn't shown up yet, she reiterated her opinion that men were morons and offered her something even stronger than beer. Val bitched a little about her imaginary boyfriend to make things look good, but, since she was still on the job, she declined the drink. She sighed with disgust, feeling absolutely certain that her surveillance tonight was going to be a complete bust.

Then Alex DeMarco walked through the door.

For a long, tense moment, Val sat frozen in her chair, staring in disbelief. Her heart kicked wildly, then settled into a hard, thudding rhythm.

Alex.

Her reaction to him was swift and unrelenting, putting every one of her senses on alert. For several seconds she held her breath, feeling as if the world had suddenly jolted to a halt. It had been five years since she'd seen him, but he hadn't changed one bit. He was still six feet four inches of rock-solid cop, who looked as if he could take on the entire criminal element of Tolosa, Texas, with *both* hands tied behind his back.

Tonight he was dressed down in jeans, boots, and a denim shirt. Tall and broad-shouldered, he was still in top-notch physical condition, radiating an aura of superiority that only a man with such a physically imposing presence could. And seeing him now made her feel as if the last five years had never happened.

She remembered the first day he'd walked into the police academy classroom and stood at the podium. Her visceral reaction to him then was just as she was having now—a breathless, heart-stopping feeling that he was a truly extraordinary man. And now, for just a few moments, she forgot everything that had happened between them and succumbed to that attraction one more time. No matter how much she resented the inner man, she'd admire the outer one until the day she died.

He stood by the door for a moment, scanning the bar with an intense, vigilant expression that said he could instantly become more dangerous than any situation he found himself in, a characteristic that made other men instinctively wary of him, while at the same time it made women swoon. When he moved through the crowd in the direction of the pool tables, women's heads turned like dominoes falling. And Alex wasn't one of those self-deprecating men who didn't realize the impact he had on the opposite sex. He knew. With every move he made, every breath he took, he knew.

Once he glanced vaguely in her direction, and Val ducked her head. She waited until he turned away again, then reached into her purse, grabbed a barrette, and pulled her long, dark hair into a low ponytail. Then she pulled out a pair of amber-tinted glasses and put them on. She wasn't taking any chances that he might recognize her. She wished she didn't give a damn one way or the other, but she'd never been one to lie to herself. Alex DeMarco was the last person on earth she wanted to talk to.

When he reached the pool tables, one of the three men standing there lobbed him a cue. He said something to a waitress, who immediately handed him a beer, giving him a smile that said the special this week was a free waitress with every drink. Alex merely nodded his thanks for the beer and racked up the balls.

The men he was with actually smiled and even laughed

once in a while, displaying none of the intensity Alex radiated with every heartbeat. Were they friends of his? Other cops? Val didn't know. She didn't know anything about him at all anymore, except that he was a totally uncompromising man with a code of behavior that was impossible for any mortal to live up to, and that she'd once been foolish enough to think she was desperately in love with him. He'd had more power over her than any man ever had—the power to shatter her dreams and break her heart all in one swoop.

He'd done both.

Of all the gin joints in all the towns in all the world . . .

Oh, stop being so melodramatic, will you?

It was behind her now. Said and done. Ancient history. And if she still couldn't be in the same room with him after all this time without coming unglued, she had more problems than she'd ever be able to deal with.

Then Val realized a good five minutes had passed during which she'd failed to glance even once in Shannon's direction. She turned and looked toward the bar, and she almost wished she hadn't.

Whatever ambivalence the woman had shown only minutes before had vanished. She'd turned on her stool and was gazing across the room toward the pool tables. She was quite a distance away, but still there was no question which man had finally gotten her attention. She sat up straighter, eyeing Alex with the tense, hyperaware look of a sleek, hungry leopard who'd spotted its prey and was preparing to attack.

Val had been on the right track. Apparently Shannon never cheated unless she found Mr. Right.

And Mr. Right had just walked through the door.

"Hey, DeMarco," Botstein said. "Blaylock says he can pick up that redhead at the bar. I told him to put his money where his mouth is. You wanna get in on some of that action?"

No. What Alex wanted to do was play a few games of pool, have a couple of beers, then go home and forget this god-awful day had ever happened. But curiosity made him turn to check out the woman in question.

Blaylock didn't stand a chance.

Blaylock was a nice guy, after all, and when it came to

women like that, nice guys finished last. She sat at the bar wearing a nearly nonexistent dress, and the pose she struck— her body turned outward toward the crowd, her legs crossed provocatively, and her breasts thrust forward—indicated that she was looking for something more tonight than meaningful conversation with a member of the opposite sex.

A man-eater if he'd ever seen one.

He started to look away, then realized that she was looking back at him. She held his gaze for one second, two, then shifted casually on her stool to allow her skirt to inch farther up her thigh. She looked away for a moment, running her fingernail around the rim of her glass, then flicked her gaze back toward him again. This time she raised her chin a notch and tilted her head, indicating that she was looking for a response.

Subtle, but to the point. And Alex wasn't the least bit interested.

Not that she didn't make him think twice before discarding the idea. Women who dressed to thrill generally made sex a breathtaking experience without a lot of strings attached. When he was younger, that had worked for him. Often. But now that he was well past the thirty mark, he was more discerning about the women he kept company with. Quick rolls in the hay with predawn departures didn't hold the same appeal for him as they once had, especially with women who had razor-sharp edges like that one.

He turned away from the woman and reached for the rack so he and Ford could get a game of pool under way.

"If I were you," he told Blaylock, "I'd let that one go."

"Are you kidding?" Botstein said. "She's the hottest piece of ass ever to walk into this place!"

It usually didn't take long for Botstein to grate on Alex's nerves, but tonight he'd set the record.

Alex liked Ford and Blaylock just fine. Ford was a balding guy in his mid-forties, a steady cop who dug in deep to the job and wore it like a second skin. Blaylock was younger, in his late twenties, friendly and congenial, but he didn't have a problem getting serious fast when the situation called for it. They were guys Alex could depend on, guys he'd trust with his life, guys who could shut up long enough to play a decent game of pool.

Botstein, on the other hand, never shut up. He'd finally retired a few years ago at the age of sixty-two, which was a real plus for the city of Tolosa, since he hadn't done an honest day's work in years. If only he'd do everybody one more favor and move to Florida, Alex would help him pack his bags. Instead he stuck like glue to the cop hangouts, telling stories about those glorious days when police officers got respect, as if he'd ever actually earned any himself.

"Don't listen to him, kid," Botstein told Blaylock. "No guts, no glory, right?"

"If you get tangled up with that one," Alex said quietly, "you'll get a whole lot more than you bargained for."

"*More* than I bargained for?" Blaylock said with a smile. "Sounds good to me."

The other men laughed along with Blaylock, but in the end he listened to Alex. He kept his money in his pocket, ordered another beer, and contented himself with admiring the woman from a distance.

Alex racked up the balls for a game of nine-ball. Ford won the lag for break, then fouled right off the bat by missing the one ball, proof positive that he'd already had a couple of beers too many.

Alex started his inning by quickly sinking three balls in a row. Playing Ford right now was like shooting fish in a barrel, but given how his day had gone, a little mindless entertainment was fine by him.

The morning had begun in fine fashion. He'd found out that the crime lab had lost a semen sample from a rape case he'd investigated. Just lost it, as if it were a set of car keys. All Alex had left now was a little he-said/she-said testimony that was never going to cut it, and one more rapist was going to walk.

Then around noon he'd learned that Richard Murdock, a murderer he'd arrested six years ago, had walked out of prison last week on parole. The guy had ended up with a manslaughter conviction, and after six years of incarceration, the parole board had apparently decided that he was no longer a threat to society.

Yeah, okay. I killed somebody. But you can trust me. After

*all, I haven't stabbed another inmate or taken a swing at a
guard in over two years now.*

Alex banked the four ball off the head rail. It smacked the
side pocket so hard that it nearly bounced out again, but he
felt the need to take out his frustration on something. Pa-
roling a murderer for good behavior. Good God—what kind
of logic was that?

Blaylock came up beside him. "Heard you had a little problem with a shooting down on Carver Street this afternoon."

Alex frowned. That was the third thing that had happened
to really make his day.

"Damn rookie didn't secure the crime scene," he said. "By
the time I got there, a couple of reporters had stomped all
over it. I handed the kid a roll of yellow tape and told him
where the next one was going to go if he didn't learn how to
use it."

Actually, he'd wanted to take the kid by the collar and kick
his ass all the way down the street, but of course that wouldn't
have been professional.

"I suppose you've already written him up," Ford said.

"First thing tomorrow." Alex leveled his cue and sent the
six ball into the corner pocket with a resounding clatter. An
official reprimand. Now *that* was professional.

"Why don't you give the kid a break?" Ford said. "We all
had our screwups in the beginning."

"DeMarco didn't," Botstein said, tossing a handful of pea-
nuts into his mouth, then talking as he chewed. "From what
I hear, he's Superman. X-ray vision, flying, superhuman
strength—the whole nine yards."

"No kidding," Ford said.

"It's true," Botstein said. "You guys notice that whenever
we see Superman, DeMarco's never around?"

Blaylock turned to Alex with a grin. "I think he's got you
there."

That was just what he needed right about now—for Ford or
Blaylock to start agreeing with Botstein. Alex just shook his
head. Why the hell did he keep coming to this place? It was a
bad habit he was going to have to try real hard to break.

A few minutes later, Alex sank the nine ball into a corner
pocket, then informed Ford that he owed him ten bucks.

Playing him was really no sport at all. Even when he was sober, he didn't give a damn about the outcome, while Alex never played any game he didn't intend to win. He collected his money, downed the rest of his beer, then decided he'd call it a night.

"It looks to me like you need some *real* competition."

He turned at the sound of the female voice, only mildly surprised to find a certain redhead standing behind him. She was holding a pool cue, twirling it lightly between her fingers. Her red dress was even more spectacular up close, a glittery sheath with a zipper from her cleavage to her navel. And judging by the way her nipples protruded through the clingy fabric, she didn't find undergarments to be the least bit necessary.

"I'm not looking for anything right now," Alex said. "In fact, I was just leaving."

"Actually, I lied," she said. "*I'm* the one who's looking for some real competition." She pulled a hundred-dollar bill out of the side pocket of her purse and laid it on the edge of the table.

"And I think you're just the man who can give it to me."

chapter two

The redhead's words said she wanted to play pool. The way she spoke said she wanted to play a different game entirely. Alex had a feeling she was a master of both, and he really wasn't up for either one.

He glanced at the other guys. Blaylock's eyes were popping out of his head as he stared at her, and Botstein's tongue was practically dragging on the floor. Ford simply looked amused. She'd also caught the attention of other people in the vicinity, mostly men, and they eased closer to see what was happening.

"No, thanks," Alex said. "As I said, I'm on my way out."

"Of course. I understand. I suppose it *would* be rather embarrassing for you."

"Excuse me?"

"It's always a blow for a man when he gets beaten by a woman. Even at a game like pool."

Alex heard a few snickers from the crowd. He knew she was merely pushing his buttons, but at the same time he'd never been one to back down from a challenge, no matter where it came from.

"That assumes, of course, that you expect to win," he said.

"We won't know until we play, will we?"

"I'd hate to take your money."

"I'd love to take yours."

That generated a few catcalls from the crowd. They eased in closer. Excitement was hard to come by around here, and they didn't want to miss out on any of the fun. At the same time, the redhead continued to stare at him. *With a flick of my cue,* her expression said, *I can take you out.*

What the hell, Alex thought. He could always use an extra

hundred bucks. He flipped through his wallet, then laid a pair of fifties on top of her hundred. "Nine-ball?"

"Fine by me."

Alex discovered very quickly that she hadn't been bluffing. She won the lag, broke, then wasted no time in sinking six balls in quick succession. And every time she leaned over the table to take a shot, her skirt rode up, the fabric stretching so tightly over her ass that anything she wore beneath it would have clearly shown through. Alex found himself wondering what every man in the place had to be wondering, too: Did she have anything at *all* on under that dress?

Then, miraculously, she missed a relatively simple bank shot off the foot rail, setting him up to drop the final three balls. She backed away from the table. Somebody handed her a drink, and she sipped it slowly, never taking her eyes off Alex.

He sank the four ball, then the seven. Then he rose, leaning on his cue to study the final shot. He glanced over at the redhead. She placed the glass she held just beneath her collarbone and rolled it gently back and forth, blinking languorously, and a second later a bead of condensation slithered down her chest in a skinny rivulet and disappeared between her breasts.

So much for subtlety.

Alex turned his attention back to the pool table and took his shot. Unfortunately, his brain remained more attuned to that droplet of water than to the nine ball he was trying to sink. It got caught in the jaws of the corner pocket, ricocheting back and forth three or four times before coming to rest an inch away. He stepped away from the table, automatically holding his expression steady and unconcerned, even though he'd just set up a shot a blind man couldn't miss.

The redhead handed her drink to the man standing beside her, then moved around the table. With a flick of her cue, she sank the ball. A roar went up from the crowd. She laid down her cue and picked up the money, and as the crowd dispersed, she drifted over to Alex.

"You're a good player."

He eyed her up and down. "When I'm not distracted."

"Yes," she said. "The music *is* a little loud in here, isn't it?"

Music. As if that had a thing to do with it.

Then she leaned so close to him that he could smell her perfume, an exotic, musky scent that penetrated the air between them. "I know a place where the music's just right. I'd love a little company."

To his surprise, she slipped the hundred-dollar bill into his hand. He saw an address written across it—1834 Augusta Drive.

Augusta Drive. Waverly Park. The high-rent district.

It was just as he'd imagined. She was rich and bored and looking for a playtoy for the evening, but it wasn't going to be him. He sensed that an evening with her would be far from a relaxing experience, not to mention the fact that she appeared to have a pale, narrow indentation around the ring finger of her left hand, where he was pretty sure a wedding band usually resided.

He took her hand, turned it palm up, laid the hundred in it, then closed her fingers over it. "You beat me fair and square. It wouldn't be right to take your money."

The redhead raised her chin slightly, as if trying to decide whether or not to get offended by his brush-off. Then she slipped the hundred inside her purse. She gave him a very clear "you don't know what you're missing" smile, then turned and walked out the door.

Botstein watched her leave, then came up beside Alex. "So what was that all about?"

"She was looking for a little company for the evening."

Botstein's jaw dropped. "And you turned her down? Are you nuts?"

"Yeah, Botstein. I'm nuts. But that means she's free tonight. If you hurry, you can still catch her."

Ford and Blaylock hooted at that. Botstein gave them a "go to hell" look, even though it was a generally known fact that he hadn't had a nonprofessional sex partner since the Nixon administration.

Alex handed Ford a twenty. "I'm calling it a night. Settle up for me, will you?"

"Sure, DeMarco. See you later."

Alex left the bar, the country music becoming dim and muffled as the door closed behind him. The night air was hot and stagnant. He strode across the parking lot to his car and opened the driver's door. Then he heard a woman's voice behind him.

"Hello again."

He turned to see the redhead sitting on the hood of a black Lexus across the parking lot, one red stiletto heel hooked over the front bumper. She motioned for him to come over.

Damn. He did not need this.

He shut his car door and approached her, wondering what she had in mind this time. "Is there a problem?"

She held out her hands helplessly, giving him a self-deprecating smile. "Yes, I'm afraid so. I just did the silliest thing. I broke my key right off in my door lock. Can you believe it?"

He glanced at the driver's door of her car and saw part of a key protruding from the lock.

"I would have thought a late-model Lexus would have keyless entry," Alex said.

"It's not working. That's why I used the key." She gave him a sweet, innocent look as she spun her story, even though they both knew there was nothing sweet or innocent about her. "I don't suppose I could beg a ride home, could I?"

If there was one thing Alex hated it was manipulation, and this woman used it at every opportunity. For some reason, the image of a spider slithering along a web came to mind.

"Why don't you call your husband to come pick you up?"

She stared at him evenly. "I don't have a husband."

"Your boyfriend, then."

"I don't have one of those, either."

"Then I'll call you a cab."

"I don't trust cabdrivers. Not in this part of town. They prey on defenseless women."

She was right about this part of town, though her suggestion that she was defenseless was something he'd take issue with. He didn't think this woman had a defenseless bone in her body.

"But you trust me? A man you've never met?"

She slipped off the hood of the car and walked toward him, her dress clinging to her breasts and hips like a coat of red paint. "One of the waitresses in there told me you're a cop."

She stopped in front of him. "Is there any reason I shouldn't feel safe with a cop?"

"Of course not. I'll call a patrol unit. They'll be happy to see you home."

"Oh, but that would be such an inconvenience for them, when you're right here to handle the situation." She cocked her head imploringly. "It's getting late, and I'd just like to go home. Is a ride really too much to ask?"

His sister Sandy told him he always went for dumb women because smart women intimidated him. That wasn't true at all. He loved smart women. What he hated was shrewd women— shrewd, unpredictable women with so much baggage it would take a team of skycaps thirty minutes to drag it across a room. And he had a feeling that this woman fit that description perfectly.

Alex started to parry one more time, then decided to give up the game. Her house wasn't too far out of his way. He could pull up to the curb, drop her off, and that would be that.

They got into his car, and during the fifteen minutes it took to drive to her house, she didn't say a word. No small talk. No humming along with the radio. Nothing. She merely crossed one leg over the other and ran her fingertips up and down her thigh, relying on body language to remind him of exactly what she had to offer. And he still had no intention of buying.

He pulled up next to the curb at 1834 Augusta Drive, a house so big it could hold three families and they'd never even come close to each other. He left his car running.

"Is this the place?"

"Yes," she said. "Thank you so much. You don't know how much I appreciate—" She stopped short, her hand flying to her throat. "Oh, my God."

"What?"

"The light in my bedroom. It's off."

Alex looked toward the house. "So?"

"I always leave it on when I go out at night." She turned a panicked gaze toward Alex. "Somebody's in my house."

"Do you live alone?"

"Yes. And I know I left the light on. I *know* I did."

"The bulb probably just burned out."

She swallowed hard, fear clouding her eyes. "Do you think you could . . . would you please come inside?"

Her persistence amazed him. She was smart enough not to try a direct come-on again, but she had no shortage of other ploys she could call into action. Was there anything this woman wouldn't do to get him into her bedroom?

"I'm sure you just forgot you turned off the light," he said.

"No. I didn't. I swear to God I didn't."

"Look," he said sharply. "I have no intention of going into your house. Now if you'll just get out of the car—"

"So this is the kind of help I can expect from the police?" she said, her voice ringing with indignation. "I'm afraid to go into my own home, and you won't even check things out for me?"

Alex wanted to beat his head against the steering wheel, because she'd just given him no choice in the matter. If she went into that house alone, and by some stretch of the imagination she happened to end up on the other end of an intruder's gun, she'd tell the world that she'd requested police assistance and had been ignored. Did he really want to deal with that possibility, no matter how remote?

"Okay," he said with a disgusted sigh. "I'll check it out."

He killed the engine, got out of his car, and followed her to her front door. Once inside, she turned and punched a code to disarm the security system.

"Was it still on?" he asked.

"Yes," she whispered.

"Does anybody else have the code?"

"No. No one. I can't imagine how someone could have gotten in."

That's because they couldn't have.

Leaving the front door ajar, he scanned the foyer, then glanced into the living room. The sheer size of it was amazing, with gleaming wood floors and ceilings that soared to at least fifteen feet. If all the stuffy antique furniture and Oriental rugs were cleared out and hoops were put at either end, it would have made a great basketball court.

"Which way to the bedroom?" he asked.

She pointed down the hall. He walked in the direction she indicated, the woman following tentatively in his wake. On the way there, they passed double doors leading into a large room with dark paneling. He paused a moment and looked inside. It appeared to be a den, with a leather sofa, a pool table, and walls filled with hunting trophies. Exotic ones. Leopards. Buffalo. Wildebeest. A zebra skin was stretched across the floor in front of the fireplace.

The room, without a doubt, had *man* stamped all over it.

It was just as he'd figured: she was married, or at least living with a man, because any guy who went to the trouble to shoot that many exotic animals would never have left his hard-won trophies behind. He might be out of the house right now, but it was clear to Alex that he still lived there.

Just go through the motions and get out of here.

He turned the corner and went into the bedroom. He flicked the wall switch, and muted light illuminated the room. Oak floors. More Oriental rugs. A king-size four-poster bed. Art on the walls that was probably worth more money than he made in a year.

"See," he told her as he entered the room, his gaze circling the area. "Nobody's here. You must have just forgotten—"

That was when he heard the zipper.

He turned around just in time to see that hot little dress fall off her shoulders. It hesitated at her hips, and she shimmied a little to send it the rest of the way to the floor. Now he finally knew what she was wearing beneath it.

Absolutely nothing.

Jesus. What had he done to deserve a day like this?

"I thought I'd put your mind at ease, Officer," she said, kicking the dress aside and walking toward him on those red stiletto heels, an innocent smile on her face. "You know. In the event you thought I might be carrying a concealed weapon."

Weapon? No worry there. She couldn't have concealed a postage stamp under that dress.

She reached around, punched a button on the stereo, and hip-hop music poured out. She eased closer and gave him a seductive smile. "But maybe you'd better frisk me just to make sure."

"Let me guess," he said. "Your key problem wasn't accidental."

"No. It wasn't."

"Locksmiths don't come cheap."

"No. They don't."

"And it appears you didn't suspect an intruder, either."

She gave him a smile of mock apology. "I'm afraid not. But it's certainly nice to know just how gallant the members of the Tolosa Police Department can be."

With that, she slipped up next to him, wrapped her arms around his neck, and kissed him.

The moment he sensed her coming in for the kill, he put his hands on her arms to push her away, but the sheer wantonness with which she attacked him, moving her tongue and her lips and her hands in ways that defied the laws of nature, made resistance a little tougher than he'd anticipated.

Damn. This woman had talent, and lots of it. She also had a husband out there somewhere, and that was a line he absolutely refused to cross.

Finally he took her by the shoulders and pushed her away, only to have her grasp his shirt on either side and yank it apart. The buttons snapped off and plinked against the hardwood floor, baring his chest and abdomen all the way to his waist.

"What the hell do you think you're doing?" he shouted, looking down at his ragged shirt. "Are you *crazy*?"

"I wanted you from the moment you walked into that place tonight," she said, sliding her hands beneath his shirt to roam over his chest, "and I *never* take no for an answer. Before the night is out, you're going to be very glad that I'm a persistent woman."

She shoved his shirt aside, dropped her lips to his chest, then dragged them downward, leaving a trail of ruby-red lipstick in their wake, ending near his belt buckle with a tiny nip of her teeth.

Holy shit.

He grasped her by her upper arms and yanked her back up. She responded by leaning into him and pressing her breasts against his bare chest. A strand of bright red hair fell across her forehead. Her cheeks were flushed, her eyes heavy-lidded with a look of sheer sexual hunger.

"Don't tell me you don't want me," she said. "I'll know you're lying."

He was male, and he was breathing. To say he didn't want a gorgeous naked woman who was ready, willing, and obviously able would have been slightly disingenuous. But actually to go through with it would be slightly insane.

He pushed her away to arm's length, in spite of the fact that the majority of his blood supply was already on its way to his groin. "No. I don't want you. Not now, not ever. I don't like deception, and I don't like games. And I sure as hell don't mess around with married women."

"I told you I'm not married."

"That den we passed on the way back here says otherwise."

She started to speak, then closed her mouth again, apparently deciding that adding one more lie wasn't going to get her anywhere.

"Okay. So what if I'm married? So are you."

"Me? I'm not married."

"Yeah. Right." She eased closer to him again. "Look. My husband's out of town. What he and your wife don't know won't hurt them." She reached for his belt buckle, giving him a seductive smile. "Now, come on, baby. Let's have a little fun."

"No way. I'm out of here."

He brushed past her and started to leave the room, when all at once he felt a sharp prick in the back of his right hip. He thought for a moment that he must have been stung by an insect. He reached around blindly to brush it away, but suddenly he felt dizzy. He stayed on his feet as long as he could, but his balance went haywire, knocking him to his knees.

What the hell . . . ?

His vision started to swim, and the walls went in and out of focus. He tried to rest back on his heels to regain his balance, but his head was spinning and he couldn't get his bearings.

He'd had a beer or two, but not nearly enough to—

A wave of nausea hit him hard, and he weaved a little, sure he was going to be sick. He squeezed his eyes closed, but it only intensified the dizziness. He fell forward onto the rug, his muscles weak and useless, his mind going dark.

What the hell had she done to him?

It was his last thought before he blacked out.

chapter three

He's in there having sex with her.

Val sat in her van two doors down from the Reichert house, trying to ignore that obvious fact, but still the images of Alex and Shannon together filled her mind. She picked up the newspaper from the seat beside her and fanned herself. It was hot tonight. So hot. And thoughts of Alex naked raised her body temperature even more.

When Shannon left the Blue Onion, Val had followed her out to the parking lot, relieved that she seemed to have finally given up for the evening. Then Alex had come out, and the moment Val realized that Shannon had finally hooked him, the most awful feeling of dread had swept through her.

But how could that be? After all this time, how could he still affect her like this? She resented him. Hated him, even, for what he'd done to her. Yet here she was, rattled by the fact that he was having sex with another woman. Of all the men in that bar tonight, why did Shannon have to choose Alex?

Because she's not blind.

And Alex. Why was he messing around with a married woman? While Val doubted he knew Shannon was married when he agreed to go home with her, he had to know by now. The very nature of his profession said he could read people in a heartbeat, so she couldn't imagine him not being able to discern Shannon's marital status thirty seconds after entering her house.

And he wasn't coming out.

Twenty minutes passed. Then thirty. Finally Val got up the nerve to grab her binoculars and turn them toward the bedroom window, thinking the curtains might be open just a bit and she could see inside. They weren't.

She tossed the binoculars aside and sat back with a sigh of disgust. *Stop being such a masochist. You don't really want to see them together, do you?*

She wished now that she'd never taken Jack Reichert's money, never tailed Shannon tonight, never seen Alex walk into that bar. And if she were smart, she'd get the hell out of there and simply tell Jack Reichert that his wife was an angel and he could stop worrying about her cheating on him, because she didn't want to deal with any of this.

Damn you, Alex. Damn you for getting in the middle of this and making me think about you all over again.

A myriad of emotions whirled around inside her mind, erasing the present and plunging her back into the past, making her remember what had happened between them, when all she'd ever wanted to do was forget.

Five years ago, she'd felt every emotion, every desire in her life as if they were fires burning inside her—the pursuit of a profession she wanted desperately, the pursuit of a man she thought she'd die if she didn't have. Those two things had gotten inextricably bound together until she couldn't possibly have separated them, until she couldn't sit through one of Alex's classes at the academy without her mind wandering into uncharted territory. Every move he made seemed sexual to her, every word he spoke a verbal caress. Sometimes she'd sit there pretending to take notes, but all the while she'd be wondering what he'd be like as a lover. Cool and calculating? Warm and sensual? Hot and dangerous? She had a feeling he could be all those things, and more.

Then she'd found out. One incredible night, she'd found out. Afterward he'd held her in his arms. He hadn't said a word. He'd just held her tightly, as if he never wanted to let her go, and in her youthful ignorance she thought that meant something. She thought it right up to the moment she awoke the next morning and found him gone.

Later that day she found out she was being dismissed from the academy.

It was a blow that had shaken her all the way to her bones. And when she found out who had recommended she be dismissed, the pain of it had been more than she could tolerate.

Alex had known the whole time he was making love to her that he'd put the wheels in motion for her dismissal.

He was the reason she wasn't a police officer today, and the reason that even now she examined a man's motives with a microscope before she let him get within shouting distance. Alex had given her a lesson in the difference between love and lust, attraction and admiration, then thrown in a primer on the advisability of trusting a man whose loyalties lay elsewhere. They were all very thorough lessons she'd never forgotten.

Or forgiven.

Val already had photos of Alex talking to Shannon outside the bar, along with photos of them getting into his car together and going into her house. Photos could disgrace a person like nothing else, and if that person needed disgracing, she never hesitated to take dozens of them.

The one thing she didn't have this time was video evidence. Jack Reichert had told her that it was unnecessary for her to set up video surveillance equipment or even a bug in the bedroom, insisting that his wife would never have the audacity to bring a lover into their home. He'd been dead wrong, of course, but now Val was glad she hadn't pushed the issue. If she were true to her client, she'd have to preview such a video to ensure its quality before giving it to him, and she hated the thought of actually seeing what she'd already pictured so clearly in her mind.

But in this case, video didn't matter. She had plenty of evidence to prove to Reichert the identity of the man his wife was seeing. And if she let him have that information, Alex could be humiliated.

She pondered that for a moment, then thought, *So what?* She had nothing to feel guilty about. If Alex had no qualms about screwing around with a married woman, she had no qualms about passing that information on to the woman's husband. It would be up to Reichert to decide what to do with it. If his plans included a little public embarrassment, so be it. Alex had handed her enough humiliation to last her a lifetime. Maybe it was time he was forced to experience firsthand exactly what it felt like.

Sorry, Alex. This is what good boys get who mess around with bad girls.

She picked up her camera again, adjusted the telephoto lens, then zeroed in on the license plate on Alex's car. But before she could click the shutter, she heard a noise coming from her phone-tap receiver. A dial tone. Music in the background. Then only three numbers were dialed.

Nine, one, and one.

She sat up suddenly and jacked up the sound. The operator came on the line. Then she heard Alex's voice, controlled panic flooding every word.

"I'm at the scene of an attempted murder, and I've got a woman who's not breathing. Get someone over here *right now.*"

Val froze. What did he say? Attempted murder? Woman not breathing?

What the hell was going on in there?

Throwing open the van door, she leaped out and hit the ground running. She raced across the lawn, reached the sidewalk, then hurried up to the front door and found it ajar. She flung it open and scanned the foyer. No one was in sight. Loud music was coming from the back of the house.

She hurried down the hall, looking right and left through doorways. Den. Guest room. Bathroom. Then the hall took a right turn, and suddenly she was standing at a bedroom doorway. From the look of it, it was the master bedroom.

Alex was on the bed beside Shannon. His hand was beneath her neck, tilting her head backward. He was dressed. She wasn't. Her naked body lay sprawled on the bed, those red heels still strapped to her feet.

She wasn't moving.

Alex bent over her, and for a split second, Val had the surreal impression that he was kissing her. Then he dropped his ear against her chest.

CPR.

"Alex?"

He snapped his head around. For a long, suspended moment, he just stared at her, clearly not believing what he was seeing.

"Val? What in the *hell* are you doing here?"

She just stared at him, then at Shannon. The woman's face was a sickly shade of gray. A deathly shade of gray.

"What are you doing here?" Alex demanded. "Tell me!"

"Surveillance," she said finally. "Jack Reichert suspected her of cheating and hired me to tail her."

"Her husband?"

"Yes. And I heard your nine-one-one call."

"You had her phone tapped?"

"Yes."

"God, I don't believe any of this." He started chest compressions, a sheen of sweat breaking out on his forehead. "Damn it! Where's EMS?"

EMS. CPR. Acronyms that frequently led to DOA.

"They're coming," Val said. "I hear the sirens. Is she—"

"I don't know," he said, dropping his ear to her chest again. "I can't hear a thing, and I'm not sure about her pulse, either. Damn it! Will you smash that stereo?"

Val ran over to the stereo and poked at the multitude of buttons, finally locating the on/off switch. Silence fell over the room. Alex listened to Shannon's chest again while Val crawled onto the bed from the other side and reached for her neck to feel for a carotid pulse.

"Oh, my God!"

She recoiled sharply, yanking her hand away. A bruise circled Shannon's neck, with a horizontal ribbon of blood just beneath her chin.

For a moment Val thought she was going to be sick, and she swallowed hard to suppress the sensation. Alex breathed twice into Shannon's mouth again, then did more chest compressions, his jaw clenched, shoving so hard against her that the bed shook. Val's gaze traveled from Shannon's neck down to her left arm. A red welt encircled her wrist, standing out in sharp relief to her pale porcelain skin. She had a matching wound on her right wrist.

Then Val noticed the scarves.

Dangling from the bedposts were a pair of knotted silk scarves, their ends tattered, fluttering softly with every move Alex made. And on the pillow next to Shannon's head was a man's belt, the end still looped through the buckle.

Alex wasn't wearing one.

A sick sensation crept through Val's stomach. Shannon had been tied to those bedposts. Alex's belt had been around her neck. And somebody had pulled it tight.

Erotic asphyxiation.

The term came to her in a fuzzy, out-of-focus memory, one of those lurid things she'd read about somewhere or seen in a documentary and filed away, thinking she'd never have to access it again. And certainly never in conjunction with Alex DeMarco. He was a man she'd once admired. A man who could do no wrong. A man whose lofty ideals she'd never been able to live up to.

A man who got his sexual kicks in ways she never could have imagined.

"What happened here?" Val asked, her voice choked. "Tell me what happened!"

"I don't know."

She blinked with surprise. "You don't know? How could you not know? You were here all the time!"

"Yes," he said, suddenly looking a little confused. "I was. But I was out—"

"Out?"

"Unconscious," he said sharply. "Passed out. I was drugged or something. When I woke up, she was tied to the bed, and . . . and the belt was around her neck."

Unconscious?

Then she noticed his shirt. It was hanging open. Threads dangling. Ripped in places where buttons had once been. And a smear of something red trailed down his chest. Without even getting closer, Val knew what it was: lipstick.

Something had gone on between them tonight, something wild and out of control, something that had shoved Shannon right to the border between life and death.

And Alex had pushed her over.

He slowed his efforts at resuscitation, then stopped completely, his breath coming hard, staring down at Shannon's lifeless body as if he'd finally realized he was trying to resuscitate a woman who wasn't coming back.

The sirens grew louder.

He put his hand against his forehead and squeezed his eyes

closed as if he had a severe headache. His breathing was still harsh and heavy, echoing through the silence of the bedroom.

Val had never seen him with a hair out of place. A wrinkle in his clothes. A speck of dust anywhere. He'd always had the shipshape, spit-polished look of a man who was in control of every aspect of his life.

Now he looked weary. His hair was mussed, his shoulders sagging, his shirt torn. And there was an unmistakable glimmer of panic in his eyes.

He looked like a man who'd just committed murder.

"Alex," she said, her voice barely above a whisper. "What have you done?"

His gaze snapped up to meet hers. "Me? You think *I* did this?"

"Alex—"

"You actually think I *strangled* her?"

"I know it was probably an accident," Val said quickly. "You probably didn't mean for things to get out of hand, but—"

"Val!" he shouted. "Goddamn it, listen to me! I had *nothing* to do with this!"

How could he deny it? By saying he didn't remember? No. That was impossible. The evidence was right there in front of her, all of it pointing to Alex.

She backed slowly off the bed until she was standing beside it, the most gut-wrenching feeling overtaking her.

He was lying.

Run. Get the hell out of here. You do not *want to be in the middle of this.*

She whipped around and headed toward the bedroom door.

"Val!"

Alex leaped off the bed, and in three strides he caught her wrist and spun her around to face him. He clamped his hands onto her upper arms and yanked her toward him, staring down at her with brutal intensity.

"You were outside. Did you see someone coming into or out of this house?"

"No! I didn't see anybody!"

"Anything strange? Out of the ordinary?"

"No! I'm telling you, I didn't see anything!"

"Val!" he shouted, giving her a hard shake. "You must have seen something! Think! *Think!*"

His fingers dug into her arms, his eyes wild with desperation, and she had the horrible feeling that he was on the verge of completely losing control. Could he be one of those frightening people who could fool the world? Straight as an arrow on the surface but twisted like a labyrinth underneath?

She had to get out of there. *Now.*

She thrashed against him and finally slid from his grasp. She lost her balance and almost fell, then came back to her feet and spun around to leave the bedroom.

And met the cops coming in.

Alex watched as the patrol cops came through the door, trying to get his bearings, trying to make some sense out of a situation that made no sense at all. Every move the officers made seemed hazy and exaggerated, every moment long and drawn out, like a slow-motion sequence in a movie. His pulse pounded in his head in sync with his heart, feeling like machine-gun fire.

Both officers had had their weapons drawn. They glanced at the body and knew the woman was dead. One of them went for Alex, the other for Val. They were shouting.

"Turn around!" one of them shouted at Alex. "Facedown on the ground!"

He felt hot and disoriented, unsteady on his feet. He stumbled to his knees, then lay facedown on the carpet. He knew this drill. Knew it by heart. But he'd never expected to be on the receiving end of it.

Oh, Christ. This can't be happening.

The officer grabbed his left arm and snapped a cuff around his wrist, then pulled his other arm around and did the same, until his hands were bound behind his back.

The officer stood him back up. Alex wavered a little. The officer nudged his foot, moving his legs apart, then frisked him. He extracted his wallet from his pocket, then flipped it open.

"You're a cop?"

Alex didn't say a word.

He looked over to see that Val was receiving the same treatment, and when their gazes met, he'd never seen anger like he saw on her face right then.

Then the cop grabbed Alex by the arm, escorted him out of the house, and put him into the back of a police car. Swirling red lights from emergency vehicles fanned around the neighborhood, lending a surreal feel to the already bizarre situation. Alex put his hand to his head, feeling as if somebody were beating on it with a hammer. If only he could clear his mind and *think*.

He tried to remember what had happened in there. Something for them to go on. Something that would prove that they had the wrong man in custody.

He had a vague, dreamlike memory of the woman kissing him. Teasing him. He remembered pushing her away, telling her to stop, then trying to leave the room. He remembered being dizzy. Falling. Then . . . nothing. Until he'd woken up to a gruesome scene right out of a snuff film.

The moment he'd awakened, he'd stumbled over to the bed, fumbling for his pocketknife to slice through the scarves that bound her wrists. Then he pulled the belt from around her neck and felt for a pulse. He thought maybe he'd found one, a tiny glimmer of life, even though her skin was ashen and her eyes empty. Wishful thinking? Maybe, but her body had still been warm, and miracles did happen, so he'd done everything he could to bring her back.

But this time, no miracles. And all he could think was, *Who killed this woman? And why don't I remember any of it?*

And then there was Val.

To look up and see Valerie Parker standing in that bedroom had practically knocked him unconscious all over again. Val, who undoubtedly still hated him with every breath she took. A wild, willful woman who'd been a thorn in his side from the day he'd met her.

Alex looked up to see them bringing her out of the house. She glanced at the car where he sat, and their gazes met. The expression she wore right now bore a striking resemblance to the way she'd looked as she stormed away from him that day five years ago. Confused. Hurt. Angry. Accusatory.

How could you have done this, Alex? How?

In her mind, he'd betrayed her back then, and he'd committed murder now. That left the odds of her wanting to help him at exactly zero. Yes, they were bringing her in, but they'd find out soon enough that instead of being a suspect, she was a hell of a good witness. All she could do was incriminate him, and after what had happened between them, she'd take great joy in doing it.

She was put into another patrol car at the same time an officer got into the driver's seat of the car where Alex sat. Briefly, he glanced back at Alex, and in that moment, it didn't matter that Alex was a cop. It didn't matter that he'd had nothing to do with this. Alex knew that look. It wasn't officer to officer.

It was officer to suspect.

Alex had always liked the feel of interrogation rooms. They were simple places, with hard chairs, a bare table, empty walls. Not unlike a prison cell. There was nothing in any of them to distract from a detective's task, which was to extract as much information from an individual as quickly as possible with a minimum of fuss. It was a place designed to be uncomfortable, solitary, and intimidating. How many times had he used this very room? A hundred? Two hundred? He had no idea.

The longer he sat there, though, the clearer his head became. The situation didn't feel nearly as ominous as it had when he'd been standing at the scene of the crime. When he looked at things logically, he realized they were just going through the motions. Playing it by the book. When all of the evidence at the scene of a crime points to somebody standing right there looking guilty as hell, you bring him in. If he'd been those cops, he'd have dragged his ass down here, too. They had to, no matter how laughable it was that he could have committed murder. But all this would get straightened out soon enough.

The only thing that kept him from rationalizing everything away was Val.

A detective would be questioning her. Separately from him, of course, so they couldn't share the same story in the event that the two of them had conspired to commit murder. But as soon as they figured out she'd had nothing to do with it, what would she be telling them? She was a loose cannon. A wild card. And just like five years ago, he couldn't begin to predict what she'd do. She was the kind of hot-blooded, passionate, go-for-broke woman who could get a man in trouble just for thinking about her. The kind of "look but don't touch" woman he avoided at all costs. He could intimidate the rest of the world to keep them at arm's length, but he'd never been able to intimidate Val. She'd always been able to crawl right under his skin, to blast apart whatever barriers he threw up in her way. And even though he knew now just how misguided he'd been five years ago, still the memory of that last night they'd spent together made him lie awake sometimes, wondering what might have been.

Stop it. You don't need to be thinking about her. Not like that. Christ, hasn't that gotten you into enough trouble?

He decided that no matter what happened here tonight, he was going to tell the truth, and he was going to do it so calmly and professionally that they'd see what a huge mistake they'd made in focusing on him when the real murderer was out there roaming free, possibly thinking about killing again.

He leaned back in his chair. Took a deep breath, then another. Calm and cool. That was what he needed to be.

Then he heard footsteps outside. As the door swung open, he sat up in his chair again, ready to answer any questions they wanted to throw at him. But when he saw who walked through the door, he knew this night had only begun to go downhill.

Ray Henderson.

Henderson was about fifty. Balding. He wore pants a size too small for the spare tire they were trying in vain to harness, and a tie that contained enough polyester to clothe an entire army of used-car salesmen. He was one of the dangerous ones, not because he was overtly negligent, as Botstein had been, but because he was insidiously so, and that attitude trickled into everything he did. Incomplete reports. Loose-ended investigations. He knew about the extra mile, but had no interest in going it. He was the kind of guy who got under Alex's skin like no other—the kind who just didn't give a damn whether he did things right, did them completely, or sometimes did them at all. Average. Adequate. Did enough on the job to draw a paycheck, but not enough to truly earn it.

Alex knew the man had always felt that disdain and didn't like him. For the briefest of moments, fear trickled through him. He needed the truth here. Needed it desperately. And this was the man designated to search for it?

Henderson sat down in a chair across from Alex, displaying an overly nonchalant attitude that irritated the hell out of him. Then he read him his rights in a deadpan voice. Alex indicated that he understood, and that he waived the right to have an attorney present. He simply intended to tell the truth, and nothing but.

Henderson tossed the yellow pad he was carrying onto a nearby table, letting out a theatrical sigh. "Sorry that officer had to drag you down here like this, DeMarco. But it's his job, you know? He busts into a murder scene, and there you are, looking guilty as sin. What else is he to do?"

Alex was silent. The bastard was loving this. *Loving* it.

"Now, I know you couldn't possibly have murdered that woman, but I gotta tell you"—he sighed again—"it doesn't look good for you."

Alex leaned forward, slicing the man with a no-nonsense stare. "Look, Henderson. We can dance around this if you want to, or we can cut to the chase. You choose."

Henderson's lip curled into a subtle sneer. He sat back in his chair and tapped his pen against the table. "Well, by all means—let's cut to the chase."

"I never met that woman before tonight," Alex said. "She told me she had a problem with her car and asked me to take her home from the Onion. When we got there, she told me she thought she had an intruder and wanted me to check out her house. Once we got to the bedroom, she came on to me. I told her to forget it. I turned to leave, got dizzy, and passed out. Somebody must have drugged me. When I came to, she was tied to the bed. The belt was around her neck. I called nine-one-one and tried CPR, but she was already dead. I have no idea who did it."

Henderson gave him a deadpan look. "You're kidding, right?"

Alex held his temper. Barely. "It's the truth."

"You're saying this woman drugged you."

"Somebody did. I want a drug test. Urine, blood, all of it."

"Sure, DeMarco. I'll have them suck out every bodily fluid you've got and run them through every test in the book. But in light of the physical evidence, it won't make a damned bit of difference. Drugged or not, you were the one holding the smoking gun."

"Somebody else was in that house. They had to have been."

"Valerie Parker says no. In fact, she had a lot of interesting things to say."

"And I suppose you're going to tell me all of them."

"Just thought you might be interested."

"You mean you just thought maybe you'd try to strong-arm me into a confession. You think I don't know the drill?"

The smug look on Henderson's face told Alex he'd hit the mark. This was the kind of recreation the bastard enjoyed above all else—being able to stick it to somebody who was bigger, smarter, and a whole lot more competent than he could ever hope to be.

"You can save your breath," Alex said. "I don't give a damn what Valerie Parker told you. It doesn't change what *I'm* telling you."

"Did you have sex with the victim?"

"I told you I gave her a ride home. That's all."

"How'd your shirt get torn?"

"She did it. I told you she came on to me."

"But you didn't have sex with her."

"No. The autopsy will prove that."

"Not if you used a condom."

"Did you find a used condom in the house?"

"The investigation isn't complete yet. But no. Not so far."

"What does that tell you, then?"

"That you flushed it?"

Alex lurched forward, his voice low and full of fury. "God-damn it, Henderson! I did not have sex with her!"

Henderson sneered. "Listen to me. You're in deep shit here. You were found at the scene with your shirt practically ripped off. Her lipstick was all over you. A belt was found on the bed that looks as if it matches the bruises and laceration on her neck. You weren't wearing one. And you've got no plausible explanation for how most of that happened. If you were me, what would you think? That maybe you had yourself a pretty good suspect?"

"I gave the victim CPR!"

"So Ms. Parker said."

"If I murdered her, why was I doing that?"

"Killer's remorse?"

"What?"

"Look, DeMarco," Henderson said, assuming that hush-hush, buddy-buddy kind of voice that really pissed Alex off. "We both know what happened here. She was a really hot piece of ass. She wanted to get a little kinky, and of course you were going to go along with it. Give the lady what she wants, right?"

Alex couldn't believe this. Anger shot through every nerve in his body.

"I'm not saying you meant to kill her," Henderson went on. "That PI tells me she was really putting the moves on you. Maybe she was a little kinky, and you thought, Hey, why not, if it gets her off, and then you looked down and realized things had gone a little too far—"

"I did not murder that woman!"

"Don't worry. I think we're talking manslaughter here. I'm sure I can get the D.A. to take it easy on you. No problem."

No problem?

Alex lurched forward, his voice low and threatening. "Listen to me, you son of a bitch. I had nothing to do with that woman's death. *Nothing!*"

"And I've got a shitload of evidence that says you had *everything* to do with it!" Henderson's face twisted into an ugly sneer. "You think I like this, DeMarco? You think I like seeing you get yourself into a mess like this?"

"Yeah, I do," Alex said. "I think you like it a lot. I think every time a guy like me goes down, it makes you look like not quite so much of a fuckup. That's what I think."

Henderson's lip curled with disdain. "You're so god-damned self-righteous. You've always looked down on the rest of us, like you're so perfect and we're the scum of the earth. But you know what? You step out of line, you get slapped just like everybody else. And buddy, you've really stepped out of line this time."

He stood up, giving Alex a look of total contempt.

"You're under arrest for the murder of Shannon Reichert."

chapter four

What followed was Alex's worst nightmare.

Mug shots were taken. Fingerprints. Samples were taken for urine, blood, and DNA tests. And the humiliation he felt was overwhelming. He was being dragged around like a common criminal, like some lowlife who would be dangerous if he were let out of restraints. And all of it happened with the officers and employees working long nights trying real hard to look the other way.

Alex knew the only way he could get through this was to make no eye contact. Say nothing. Pretend that nobody was witnessing his humiliation. Still, he could hear the buzz of gossip, undulating like a tidal undertow. And by tomorrow that whispered gossip would become a flurry of speculation, with everyone tossing in an opinion about whether he was guilty or not.

Finally he was returned to a holding cell, escorted by an officer who clearly wished he were doing anything else but incarcerating another officer. He looked the other way as he shut the cell door, never meeting Alex's eyes. And that was fine with Alex.

He sat down on the bunk. The tiny room had walls of concrete blocks, with a solid metal door that had only a small window of unbreakable glass. The only allowance they'd made was to put him in a cell by himself, and for that he was thankful. The last thing he wanted to do was rub shoulders with the scum who really belonged in here.

He rested his elbows on his knees and dropped his head to his hands. His head still throbbed—whatever he'd been drugged with had been powerful stuff. He only hoped that whatever it was, it was still in his system and the drug tests he took would reveal it. He rubbed his hands over his face and let out a long, weary breath, wondering how in God's name all of this had happened.

When they'd taken his badge away, they might as well have severed one of his limbs. Being a cop was in every nerve synapse in his body, every drop of blood, every speck of DNA. He'd been heading in that direction ever since his father took him down to the station when he was four years old, sat him up on the watch commander's desk, and told everyone within earshot that he was a chip off the old block. And that meant that right now he was supposed to be on the outside of this cell looking in, not the other way around. It was as if somebody had played some kind of a weird cosmic joke on him, only he'd missed the punch line.

And that bastard Henderson was laughing his head off.

It had been about half an hour since Alex had made that one phone call granted to anyone who was arrested. And if only he'd had a family like everyone else's, the decision of who was going to receive that phone call might not have been so difficult. But no. He had a family full of cops. And those who weren't cops were connected to law enforcement in one way or another. For the most part, they were prone to over-reaction, and by coming down here they'd probably only make the situation worse.

Alex's brother John was also a detective, but he and his wife, Renee, were on their honeymoon in the Bahamas. That was probably a good thing. When he was pissed off, John didn't always do a lot of thinking before acting. He'd demand to know what the hell they thought they were doing arresting his brother, then stomp so loudly into the jail that they'd consider arresting *him*.

If Alex called his sister Sandy, chairman of the Tolosa Crime Watch Council, she would probably tell him that getting caught up in this was his own damned fault, that it wouldn't have happened if he'd gotten married years ago and went home to a wife every night instead of hanging out in sleazy pool halls. Then she'd give him a big, useless hug and tell him everything was going to be all right, and he could certainly do without that.

His grandfather was likewise out of the question. He was

an ex–prosecuting attorney who would first express total out-
rage that somebody thought his grandson had shifted to the
wrong side of the law, then start spewing legal crap left and
right that Alex was in no state of mind to try to decipher. And
his aunt Louisa—was the solution to his problem really a
plateful of double-fudge brownies and a good night's sleep?

Then there was his cousin's wife, Brenda. Oh, Lord—what
if she got wind of this before he could get the hell out of here?
Brenda was a gung-ho patrol cop and sharpshooter for the
SWAT team, whose idea of justice frequently bordered on the
bizarre. Within five minutes, she'd be arranging to meet Henderson in a dark alley, then swear later that she wasn't respon-
sible for the twisted mass of flesh that used to be his face.

In the end, his brother Dave had been his only real option.
Two years ago Dave had lost his wife in a car accident,
leaving him alone to raise their baby daughter. It was a
tragedy that would have paralyzed most men, but somehow
Dave had picked up the pieces and moved on, making both of
his jobs—as a patrol cop and as a father—look easy. Even
though he was the youngest brother, he had a way of taking
care of things. Making them right. Making even the worst
crap that life could throw at a person seem a little less grim.

Alex had awakened Dave from a sound sleep and given
him the facts of what had happened. True to his brother's nature, he didn't overreact. He didn't ask any questions. He
merely said he was going to drop his daughter off at Aunt
Louisa's house, then come down to the station. And Alex was
thankful for that.

Twenty more minutes passed that seemed like two hundred. Then Alex heard footsteps, and the sound of a key in a
lock. The door swung open and his brother was allowed into
the cell. Alex found he could barely look him in the eye. He
hadn't done anything wrong. He was innocent, for God's
sake. So why did he feel so guilty?

Dave sat down beside him. "How are you doing?"

"How do you think I'm doing? I've been accused of
murder."

"Okay. Tell me all the details. Start from the beginning,
and don't leave anything out."

Alex did as his brother asked, trying to speak as calmly and rationally as he could, but there were a few times, especially when he talked about Henderson, that he was on the verge of losing it. But his brother calmly took it all in, asking a few questions here and there and nodding occasionally to encourage him to go on.

"I know it doesn't make sense," Alex said when the story was finished. "I can only tell you what happened."

"Okay. Tell me again about this PI who was tailing the victim. Did she see anything suspicious while she was watching the house?"

"She says no. But once the cops got there, I couldn't talk to her anymore."

"Surely she was questioned."

"Yes. She was."

"And she saw nothing?"

"I'm not sure what she saw." He closed his eyes. "There are a lot of things concerning her I'm not sure about."

"Like what?"

Damn. Why Valerie Parker? Why? "This particular woman . . ." Alex sighed. "She might have a bit of a grudge."

"You know her?"

"Yes. Five years ago she was a cadet at the academy. I was instrumental in having her dismissed."

Dave's gaze faltered. "Oh, boy. So she's a PI now?"

"Yeah. And let's just say she may not be inclined to speak kindly on my behalf."

"You really think she'd still be out to get you for having her dismissed? A lot of time has passed. Surely she wouldn't—"

"There was a little more to it than just her being dismissed from the academy."

"Oh?"

"Yeah. It was . . . personal."

"Personal? How personal?"

"As personal as it gets."

Dave held his gaze steady, but Alex could tell he'd gotten the gist of the problem, and he didn't much like what he'd heard. "Did this personal stuff take place before or after her dismissal?"

"Before." Alex paused. "The night before."

"Shit, Alex. Are you telling me—"

"I don't want to go into it," Alex said sharply.

Dave let out a long breath. "Okay, then. How vindictive do you think she's inclined to be?"

That was a loaded question. Whatever Val did in life, she did it for all she was worth. Did that include hating him?

"I'm not really sure. But I'm innocent. In the end that's all that's going to matter."

"Wrong," Dave said. "If the truth were all that mattered, you'd be walking the streets right now."

"It'll all get resolved soon enough, even with Henderson on the case." Alex made a scoffing noise. "Bastard never should have arrested me in the first place."

"From what you've told me, it was a solid arrest."

Alex looked at him with disbelief. "Whose side are you on?"

"Yours. And that's why I'm telling you that before this thing goes any further, you need a lawyer. Innocent people go to jail every day. Most of them have crappy legal counsel. That's not going to happen to you."

Alex hated this, but Dave was right. He needed a lawyer to help him untangle whatever legal mess this situation was creating. Anybody would, innocent or not.

"Any suggestions?" he asked Dave.

"Ethan Millner."

Alex jerked to attention. "Millner? Are you crazy?"

"He's the best."

"He's an asshole!"

"Listen up, Alex. You're not part of the prosecution's team here. You need a defense attorney. A good one."

"Ethan Millner is underhanded. Manipulative. He bends the law—"

"But he never breaks it, and he wins practically every case he takes."

"That's right! Criminals are running loose all over this city because he got them off!"

"If he can get guilty people off, then he shouldn't have any trouble with an innocent person. He's your best bet."

"I said no!" Alex stood up and paced toward the wall. "You *know* how much I hate him!"

Dave rose and followed him. "But you hate him for the

very reason you need him now. Because he's good enough to have decimated you a time or two on the witness stand."

Alex whipped around. "No! I'd rather go to prison for twenty years than deal with that money-grubbing bastard!"

Dave sighed. "Look, I know how you feel about him, but—"

"No, goddamn it, you *don't* know how I feel!"

"Alex—"

"If this is the best you can do for me, then why don't you just get the fuck out of here?"

In an instant, Dave slapped his palm against Alex's chest and backed him against the wall, his face tight with restrained anger. "Listen to me, big brother, and listen good. This is *murder* we're talking about. With the right spin by the prosecution, you could end up frying for this no matter what the truth is. If it takes Ethan Millner to make sure that doesn't happen, then that's who we're bringing in. Do you understand?"

Fury and frustration tore through Alex. He tightened his hands into fists, desperate to lash out at something. But his brother? Good God, what was he doing?

Acting like a fool.

He consciously relaxed his fists, only to realize that his hands were shaking. Shit, he was losing it.

Dave backed away, and Alex sat down on the bed and dropped his head to his hands. "I'm sorry, Dave. Christ, I'm sorry. I shouldn't have said that. It's just that I don't know what to do here. How to handle this." He gave a humorless laugh. "A murder accusation. That was pretty much last on my list of things I thought I'd ever have to deal with."

"Forget about it."

Alex rubbed his eyes, feeling as if he hadn't slept in two days. He'd hoped that somehow this would blow over. He'd hoped that Dave would scoff at the charges and tell him not to worry. Instead he wanted to bring in Ethan Millner, a man who made Johnnie Cochran look like an amateur. A man who, if the price was right, wouldn't think twice about bringing Hitler up from South America to convince a jury that the Holocaust was just a big misunderstanding. A man who Dave thought just might be the only thing between him and a guilty verdict.

"Millner," Alex said wearily. "We've clashed too many times. He probably won't even take the case."

"He's on his way over here right now."

"You called him?"

"Right before I left the house."

"Figured you'd be able to talk me into it?"

"Figured you'd flip out, then eventually come to your senses. As usual."

Alex liked to think he was the levelheaded, intuitive one in the family, but Dave had him beat in that category by a mile.

"Just talk to Millner, then go from there. One way or the other, he'll have you out of here tomorrow."

"I don't want you getting dragged through the mud with me, Dave. You or anyone else in the family."

"Will you forget the family? They're not the issue here."

"And Dad. God, can you imagine what he would think about this?"

"He's dead. He's not thinking a damned thing."

But it never really felt that way to Alex. He'd always felt as if his father were watching him, whether in this world or the next, ready to pat him on the shoulder if he toed the line and knock him senseless if he didn't.

His father had been invincible. A towering icon of everything that was upstanding and upright. A man whose life had been like an arrow leaving the bow and finding the center of its target—traveling without a single deviation along the way. Right was right, wrong was wrong, and anyone who thought otherwise was either a degenerate or a Democrat.

Ruthless.

Alex had heard the word tossed around a time or two by people who didn't know he was within earshot. But they just didn't understand a man whose code of behavior was so finely tuned, so sharply honed, so ingrained in his everyday life that he wasn't swayed by anyone or anything. And it was true that if somebody crossed Joseph DeMarco they lived to regret it, but not once in his life had he been anything but above reproach, because he'd never stepped off the straight and narrow. He merely expected everyone else in his midst to live up to the same standards. Particularly his three sons.

Yes, he'd enforced those standards with the business end of a belt more times than Alex cared to think about, because his father believed wholeheartedly in corporal punishment. And that punishment had grown more intense the older he and his brothers got, with a whole lot more power behind the old man's punch, but only because he couldn't get through to his big, rambunctious, hardheaded boys any other way. It had been the best thing for him. His father had taught him right from wrong, because he'd had the guts to slap him back in line whenever he stepped out.

And what Alex had never told his brothers, never told anyone, were the words their father had spoken to him once when it was just the two of them alone: *John and Dave. They're my sons, and I love them. But you're the one, Alex. You're the one I'm the most proud of.*

Well, there wasn't a lot for his father to be proud of right now.

"Now, listen to me," Dave said. "When you get out of here tomorrow, I want you to lie low. Let Millner handle things. Let the investigation proceed—"

"Investigation, my ass. Do you really think Henderson is going to go out of his way on this one? He's got his suspect, and he's loving every minute of it."

Alex could deal with anything but this. Anything but being dragged through a court battle with the whole world looking at him as if he'd committed murder. Every second that ticked by made the anguish he felt seep right down to his bones.

"The rest of the family," Alex said. "I can't see them right now. I need a couple of days to get a handle on this."

Dave nodded. "They won't like it, but I'll put out the word."

"And whatever you do," Alex said, "don't tell Brenda."

"I have to. If she hears it through the grapevine, she really will be pissed. But don't worry. I'll keep a tight hold on her choke chain."

"She's not the only one who's going to go nuts. You'd better put a leash on John, too."

"He and Renee won't be back from their honeymoon until Thursday. I'll tell Renee first. She'll keep a lid on him."

Renee. If anyone would understand how he was feeling right now, it was her. She'd once been accused of an armed robbery she didn't commit. John had risked his career to help her clear her name, even when everyone, including Alex, thought she was guilty. Somewhere in the midst of all that, to Alex's utter astonishment, John and Renee had fallen in love. They'd gotten married just last weekend, and Alex was thankful for that. Marriage would eventually call a halt to the kind of nauseating kissy-kissy stuff the two of them had exhibited nonstop over the past several months.

But even as Alex felt obligated to give them a hard time about that behavior, he felt twinges of jealousy that John had found somebody who loved him as much as Renee did. Alex had never even come close to that kind of relationship with a woman. Not that there hadn't been candidates over the years, women who would cheerfully have accepted a ring and a wedding date, but it had never taken him very long to find fault with them and lose interest. How strange was it that the only woman who'd ever held his attention for longer than a couple of weeks was the one who'd ended up hating him?

Valerie Parker.

Dave had warned him to lie low, but he had to talk to her. The moment he got out of here tomorrow, he intended to go see her, even though there was a better than average chance she'd slam the door right in his face. He had to find out what else she'd seen at the Reichert house, something she might not even realize she saw, something locked away in her mind that Henderson hadn't bothered to go in search of.

Right now, it was his only hope.

chapter five

Val woke Saturday morning at eleven o'clock with the king of all headaches. She got up, took a shower, got dressed, and when the headache didn't subside, she took four aspirin, then poured a glass of orange juice. That made her sick to her stomach, so she followed it with an oatmeal-raisin bagel, which didn't help in the least.

At the police station the night before, they'd quickly realized that she was a far better witness than she was a suspect. She'd answered every question as truthfully as she could, knowing all the while that every word she spoke pushed Alex one step closer to jail.

But what she couldn't seem to get out of her mind was the look Alex had given her as the police came through the door of the Reicherts' bedroom.

No matter what happens now, no matter what you hear, no matter what you see, I did not kill that woman.

He'd hurt her in ways that had gone bone-deep, yet she still didn't want to believe that he could have done anything as terrible as murder. If she did, then she'd have to feel even more ridiculous that she'd ever loved him in the first place.

No. You didn't love him. Infatuation is not love. Admiration is not love. And lust is most certainly not love.

She'd kept the TV on just long enough after she got home last night to watch a late-breaking report on Channel 6 about the murder. The reporter who came on the screen was one of those seasoned, hard-nosed, vulturistic few who stayed up late listening to the police band, hoping to be first on the scene of a sensational story.

This one was right up her alley.

Behind the reporter, neighbors had milled around on the

sidewalk near the street. Lights and cameras appeared as if from nowhere, along with police cars and emergency vehicles, with the patrol cops marking the area with black-and-yellow tape.

Val knew the reporters wouldn't stop until they'd squeezed every bit of loud, irresponsible, in-your-face journalism out of this story that they possibly could. And what a headline they were going to come up with for this one: *Woman strangled by cop in sex-related murder.*

Val considered herself fortunate that nobody appeared to have released her name to the press. Still, chances were excellent that sooner or later somebody would be knocking at her door and sticking a microphone in her face, and she certainly wasn't looking forward to that.

She really wished that the moment Alex had shown up at that bar, she'd closed up shop and gone home, so she wouldn't have to deal with any of this. Up until last night, she'd succeeded in pushing Alex to the back of her mind. It had been a long time since an hour couldn't pass without her thinking about him, and now she was back in that place all over again.

Enough.

She got up off the sofa, collected dirty laundry from her bathroom hamper, and threw it into a pink plastic basket. She'd always felt as if there was nothing in life she couldn't put into perspective if only she took a load of clothes to the Laundromat. She'd resisted getting a washer and dryer all these years, because doing laundry was just the kind of mindless activity she needed sometimes to get her out of her apartment, to keep her from brooding, to clear her head.

When she was growing up, laundry had been a task for the hired help, always performed out of sight of the family, with clean clothes appearing in drawers and linen closets as if little laundry fairies had stolen the dirty things away in the night and replaced them with clean ones. Now Val took great joy in doing the dumb little mundane tasks of life, even though her mother would have stroked out at the very thought of it.

Val decided that after she finished at the Laundromat, she'd head over to her office to do a little research. She had a missing-person case where a wife was sure her husband had run away with another woman three months ago, but since there appeared to be no foul play involved, the police wouldn't touch it. Actually, the woman didn't want her husband back, but she desperately wanted the Lhasa Apso he'd taken with him. A little computer research would probably help pin down the guy's whereabouts. Missing husband, missing dog—it didn't matter to Val.

Anything to keep her mind off Alex.

Alex had dreaded the humiliation of standing in the court-room in front of the judge, entering a plea, having bail set, with all eyes in the vicinity focused on him, wondering how a cop could possibly have ended up with a murder accusation against him. Fortunately Millner made quick work of get-ting him released. The bail that was set was reasonable given the extent of the crime he was accused of committing. But even though Millner was working effectively on his behalf, Alex was still disgusted at the very thought of having to deal with him.

He told Alex he'd be in touch, picked up his briefcase, and walked out of the courtroom as if encounters like this were all in a day's work. Even though the two of them had clashed in the past, Millner was all business—one of those guys who didn't seem to care who his clients were or what they'd done. If you had the money, he had the time. Dave told Alex he should consider himself lucky in that regard. Instead, it made Alex hate him even more.

After posting his bail, Dave drove Alex back to his apart-ment, where three reporters lay in wait for him. He shoved his way past them, went inside, and took a much-needed shower, feeling as if he had to wash that holding cell out of every pore in his body. As the water rained down on him, he made a vow to himself that he intended to keep: he wasn't going back to jail—under any circumstances. He was an innocent man, and he'd be damned if anyone on this planet was going to lock him up again. And he'd be damned if he was going to sit back and let guys like Henderson and Millner determine his fate.

When Alex went back outside, the reporters were still wait-ing for him, shouting stupid questions and rolling tape that was probably going to end up on the evening news. One guy got a little too close, and Alex came within an inch of inserting his camera in a place where there was not nearly enough light to get a clear picture of anything. Their lack of rational behavior astonished him. Did it make any sense at all to approach a man you knew had been accused of murder, stick a microphone in his face, and start yelling at him?

Bloodsucking bastards.

He got into his car, refusing to say a word. Even though one of the reporters tried to follow, all it took was a little bit of creative driving to lose him. Then he headed for Val's apartment.

Ten minutes later, he entered her neighborhood, an area near downtown that was neat and clean but ugly as sin, with bland prewar architecture and storefronts that were still firmly rooted in the mid–twentieth century. Weird people lived in neighborhoods like this one—people on the fringe who wore strange clothes, had excessive tattoos, and didn't think twice about piercing body parts that were best left intact. The neighborhood was still home to a few older people who'd been there since time began and were loath to leave, even with the influx of bizarre neighbors, but mostly it was a haven for the alternative crowd. Val called it home with a smile on her face.

He parked his car in the only place he could find—a parallel spot a block away from his destination. He got out and started toward Val's building, only to see her through the smudged plate-glass window of a nearby Laundromat.

She wore a tight pair of jeans slung low on her hips, a T-shirt, and tennis shoes. She flicked a long, dark strand of hair over her shoulder, then started pulling laundry out of a washer with the single-minded intensity that was so much a part of her personality. Five years hadn't mellowed her in the least. As cool as he was, that was how hot she ran. And always—always—she had to do things her way, whether her way was best or not.

Alex remembered a shoot/don't shoot scenario she'd undergone in training. There had been a crowd of people behind her target, yet she'd still opened fire. He'd reprimanded her for it. She'd countered that she'd hit the suspect dead center. Six times. What she'd never understood was that her marksmanship didn't matter in the least. Yes, she was one hell of a shot, but it was easy to be off a few inches in a real-life situation, so she had to learn to follow procedure to avoid getting innocent people killed.

Follow procedure. Val didn't even know the meaning of the words. She couldn't toe the line if her life depended on it. She insisted on moving the line, erasing the line, drawing another line entirely. She'd irritated the crap out of him nearly every time she opened her mouth. She soaked up everything he said, then challenged all of it. And good God—if she'd said *why* one more time, he would cheerfully have smacked her.

Then there was that day in the park.

One relentlessly hot July afternoon, he'd run into her on the jogging trails that wove through Cottonwood Park, a public facility that consisted of acres of fields and forest adjacent to the police academy. Seeing her there didn't surprise him—she prided herself on physical fitness, and he had no doubt she could kick the ass of ninety percent of the other cadets, male or female. He'd met men who could chew iron and spit bullets, but not one of them had the guts Valerie Parker had. Unfortunately, she did something that day that told him she also had an unhealthy dose of insanity thrown in.

She challenged him to a footrace.

"Come on," she said, injecting a taunting tone to her voice as she danced from one foot to the other. "Two miles. I'll leave you in the dust."

Alex hadn't been able to believe it. She stood five-foot-six, while he was six-foot-four with a stride that outmatched hers by a mile, which meant he was predestined to be able to outrun her anytime, anyplace.

"Okay, then," she said. "One mile, if you don't think you can go two."

Thinking it wouldn't hurt to knock her down a notch or two, he'd said sure, that he could stand to put in another couple of miles at a nice, leisurely pace.

They took off. She pushed—God, how she pushed, her legs pumping wildly just to stay within shouting distance of him. Then she surprised him by closing some of the distance between them, and he'd actually had to kick it up a notch in order to stay ahead of her. But still the outcome was hardly in question. He heard her panting behind him, taunting him, even when she could barely breathe for the effort she was exerting.

Then he'd done something he'd never done in his life, and to this day he wasn't completely certain what had made him do it. Maybe he'd sensed something in her that needed to win, that was desperate to win, something beyond claiming victory in a little footrace. Maybe he just wanted to see her reaction. Whatever the case, he'd lightened up. He'd imperceptibly shortened his strides as they reached the cluster of crape myrtles that marked the end of the second mile, allowing her to huff past the trees only a few strides ahead of him to win the race.

She came to a halt and leaned over, her hands against her knees, her breath coming in great, gulping gasps. When she looked up, he saw sweat pouring down her face, plastering golden-brown spirals of hair against her temples.

"Told you I could take you," she said. "Guess it's true what they say, huh? The bigger they are, the harder they fall?"

Humility had never been one of Val's strong suits, a quality that had pretty much prevented her from carrying on a nice, cooperative relationship with her fellow cadets. And right now, it wasn't endearing her to him, either.

"Might want to spend a little more time on the old cardiovascular workout," she went on. "I mean, you just got beaten by a girl." She shook her head sadly. "What *will* the other cops think?"

If she hadn't gloated, maybe he wouldn't have said a word. He'd have just let her think she'd beaten him and gone about his business. But he'd always had a competitive nature himself, and the words were out of his mouth before he knew it.

"They'll probably think I was an idiot to let you win."

She blinked with surprise. "You *didn't*—"

She froze as the truth struck her.

"You *bastard*!"

She hauled off and belted him. Hard. With every ounce of energy she had, she smacked him on the upper arm, then drew back to do it again. Before she could throw that second punch, he grabbed her by the wrist, spun her around, and pinned her against him, his arm clamped around her chest.

"Val! Cut it out!"

"Damn you for patronizing me! If I beat you, I want to *really* beat you! Now let me *go*!"

"Are you going to hit me again?"

"Are you going to be a pompous, condescending *ass*?"

She punctuated that last word with an elbow to his ribs. He recoiled in shock, the breath momentarily knocked out of him. When she spun around to face him, he grabbed her by the shoulders.

"Are you aware that you just struck a superior officer?"

She made a scoffing noise, and that was when he knew: she was never going to make it. Never.

It wasn't as if she couldn't cut it academically. In that regard she was at the top of the class. Hell, she was a better shot than any of the other cadets. She exceeded the minimum physical requirement by a landslide. But her attitude would make her a danger to any officer she worked with. A harsh, abrasive disciplinary problem somebody was going to have to deal with on a regular basis. A competitiveness that just wasn't healthy for an officer in the field. And a temper . . . God Almighty, what a temper. How would she respond to citizens who got crossways with her? With suspects who gave her crap? Would she haul off and belt them, too?

There was a part of Val that would never fall in step with the rest of the world. She had an outlook on life that was so radically different from his own that it should have instantly repelled him.

It didn't.

Instead, the strangest feeling had overcome him. The cool, methodical way he negotiated his life suddenly seemed to fade into the background, and he'd had the most incredible urge to grab onto that energy of hers, to draw from it, because just being around her made him feel alive in a way he never had before.

They stood there staring at each other for a long time, both of them still breathing heavily. Slowly something shifted, expanded between them. It was as if the hot summer air had become electrified all around them. She licked her lips, a smooth, sensual movement of her tongue, and all at once he'd found himself thinking about what it might be like to kiss those lips.

And the look on her face said that for maybe the first time since he'd met her, their thoughts were in perfect alignment.

He dropped his gaze to her lips, tracing their fullness with a slow sweep of his eyes. It was an involuntary action, and the moment he realized he was doing it, he yanked his gaze back up again. He hadn't moved fast enough. Those lips he'd just been admiring curved into a knowing smile.

Damn.

She gave him a look that said she'd finally cracked his code and she could get under his skin anytime she wanted to. And he had the most uncanny feeling that it was the truth.

He released her and backed away, horrified that his thoughts had had nothing to do with her as a cadet and everything to do with her as a woman. And that was absolutely unacceptable.

He forced his face into a stoic expression. "Learn your limitations, Val. Don't challenge somebody twice your size to a footrace. You'll lose every time."

She gave him a knowing smile. "I don't think there are any limitations. None at all."

There were so many meanings to that comment that he couldn't begin to sort them all out. She backed away from him, one step, two, then turned and jogged away. She never looked back, but somehow he knew that she was aware that he was watching every stride she took.

And now, five years later, as he watched her through the window of the Laundromat, he felt the same way he'd felt back then. No matter how wrong he knew it was, he just couldn't take his eyes off her, which brought him right back around to thinking about that one night they'd spent together.

And he had to stop it. Right now.

If there was something she was forgetting about last night, anything that could point to someone else who might have been in that house, he had to find out what it was. He did not need to be thinking about sex with this woman, no matter how unforgettable it had been, because it had led to nothing but grief for both of them. She had frustrated him and fascinated him all at the same time, and that was a dangerous combination—one he needed to steer clear of at all costs. She was a witness. Nothing more. And undoubtedly she'd be a hostile one.

Keep your cool, or she'll make you lose it. Bank on it.

He shoved the glass door open and stepped inside. Humidity hung heavily in the air, mingling with the scent of laundry soap and dryer sheets. Rows of rusty-edged washers hummed and squeaked. On a red vinyl couch at the back of the room, an old lady in a blue-flowered dress and a hair net sat reading *People* magazine.

"Val."

She spun around, her expression shifting to one of surprise, then suspicion. In the span of a single second she seemed to grow two inches, her spine straightening like that of a soldier facing inspection. She pushed a strand of long, curly hair behind her ear and gave him a wary frown, as if he were the last person she'd expected to see and the first person she'd go to war with if she did.

She turned to one of the dryers, rested the pink laundry basket against her hip, and started fishing out towels. She was the only person on the planet who could make doing laundry look like a mission from God.

"I see you're out on bail," she said.

"We need to talk."

"No, we don't."

"What did you see when you were outside the Reichert house?"

She sighed with disgust. "We've been through this already."

"Last night was not the best time to discuss it."

"Oh, yeah? Well, you seemed pretty hell-bent on discussing it anyway. I have the bruises to prove it."

He glanced down at her arm and saw that she wasn't lying. A faint, purplish bruise circled her left arm just above her elbow. A quick glance told him she had a matching one on the right. If she was out to make him feel guilty, she'd succeeded.

"I need some answers here, Val. The detective on the case has already got me convicted."

"Really?" She slapped the laundry basket down on the counter and plucked out a worn bath towel. "Whatever happened to solidarity in the ranks?"

"I drew the biggest bastard in the department. And you know it's even worse for a cop. Everybody assumes we get cut slack, so we get no slack at all."

She flicked the wrinkles out of the towel and started to fold it, which told Alex she didn't give much of a damn about that. His hope that maybe she'd become just a shade less hard-headed in the past five years flew right out the window.

"What do you know about the Reicherts?" he asked. "Do you know of anyone who might have had a motive to kill Shannon?"

She faced him with a look of exasperation. "Has it escaped your attention that I'll probably be the chief witness for the prosecution? Testifying *against* you?"

"All I want you to do is think about what else you might have seen that night. No matter how insignificant it seems."

"I'm a private investigator. If I'd seen anything else— *anything*—I'd have documented it, insignificant or not. It's my job, and I'm damned good at it."

Private investigator. Alex had to fight to erase the derisive expression he felt settling over his face. Not that it surprised him that she'd turned out to be one of those. Shoot from the hip, skirt the law, answer to no one, with the concept of coop-eration not even an issue. If ever there was a profession tailor-made for Valerie Parker, that was it.

"You know as well as I do that sometimes people don't remember details until later," he told her. "All I want you to do is think for a minute. Try to remember."

She slapped the folded towel down beside the laundry basket. "Do you think I haven't? Do you honestly think I haven't gone over last night in my mind at least a hundred times already?"

"Then you need to go over it a hundred and one."

"A *thousand* and one won't tell you any more than you know right now."

"What exactly did you tell the police?"

"The truth. And nothing but."

"And what do you consider to be the truth?"

"You know what I saw last night. That's what I told them, and what I'll continue to tell them. I'm not lying for anyone, including you."

"You mean especially me."

She gave him that look he thought he'd forgotten—that stern, tight-jawed, dug-in expression that said she wasn't about to be swayed by anyone or anything. She returned to her towel folding, pointedly ignoring him.

He didn't know how to get through to her. Other people were easy to deal with because intimidation always worked when nothing else did. But trying to intimidate Valerie Parker was like threatening a grizzly bear—it only made her mad.

"Can we just go somewhere and talk about this?" he asked.

"It's pointless. I can't help you."

"Can't, or won't?"

She raised her chin, her jaw tightening with anger. "Do you really think I'd deliberately withhold evidence that might prove you didn't do it?"

Yes. That was exactly what he thought. He didn't care how many years had passed. That unholy anger she'd unleashed on him back then couldn't possibly have dimmed to the point of rationality, and she might not think twice about taking it out on him now. The irony was unbelievable. If she was looking for revenge, the perfect opportunity had just landed squarely in her lap.

"I'd like to think you wouldn't," he said, "but I know we've got history here. If you let that get in the way of—"

"My God." She recoiled, giving him a look of utter astonishment. "You really do believe I'd let you go to prison just to settle some old score, don't you?"

What was he supposed to say to that? After what had happened between them, it was possible that not only would she nail his coffin shut, she'd grab a shovel and bury it six feet under.

"Look, let's just forget I said that, okay? Of course you wouldn't do that."

"You're patronizing me, Alex. I can hear it in your voice a mile away, so don't even try it."

He expelled a harsh breath. "What do you want me to say here, Val? Do you want me to beg? Is that what you want?"

"All I want is for you to leave me alone."

"You really believe I killed her, don't you?"

She didn't answer for a long time. Finally she shrugged indifferently, refusing to meet his eyes. "I don't know. I wasn't in the house at the time. I have no way of knowing whether you did it or not."

"Come on, Val! Do you really believe I tied Shannon Reichert to that bed and strangled her?"

"You're strong. Very strong. And if you got involved in something with Shannon that went a little beyond the norm and you both got carried away, you might not have realized—"

"I didn't get *involved* with her at all!" He clenched his teeth, wishing he could put his fist right through one of these crappy old washing machines, but then somebody might accuse him of having a violent temper, and he sure as hell couldn't afford that right now.

"No one believes that I'd murder someone in cold blood. No one. But having kinky sex with a stranger and strangling her—nobody has *any* problem believing that."

"So you didn't have sex with her?"

"No!"

"Come on, Alex. She looked plenty naked when I got there."

"That was her own doing, not mine. And I was dressed, wasn't I?"

"You had time to put your clothes back on."

"Things were not what they looked like. If you knew what really happened—"

"Don't you get it?" she said. "It doesn't matter what really happened! All that matters is that you look guilty. So damned guilty that even if you're not, you're *never* going to prove it. I don't care if I saw an army of serial killers outside that house last night. You were the one in there. You were the one with the torn shirt and her lipstick all over you. It was your belt around her neck. And nothing I say or do is going to change that!"

She piled the folded towels on top of the unfolded ones in the laundry basket and picked it up off the counter. He grabbed her arm, forcing her to set it down again.

"Val. Don't go."

She let out a sharp breath, closing her eyes in a gesture of frustration.

"Look at me," he said.

She turned slowly, and for the first time, the look of accusation seemed to disappear from her eyes. He met her gaze without blinking, offering her the one and only thing he had left: the truth.

"I had *nothing* to do with Shannon Reichert's murder."

In that moment he felt that old connection between them, a connection so powerful and so elemental that he couldn't deny it any more now than he'd been able to deny it five years ago. But just as quickly she severed it again, her expression becoming cold and indifferent.

"Then get yourself a really good lawyer, Alex. You're going to need one."

She pulled her arm from his grip, picked the basket up, and strode out of the Laundromat. And his best hope for some kind of explanation for what had happened last night walked right out the door with her.

For the first time since he woke up on the Reicherts' bedroom floor, Alex felt powerless—totally powerless to stop the legal machine that was going to smash him like a steamroller. He'd thought maybe she could help him, that maybe a memory would suddenly appear that would lead him to discover who else had been in that house. But that was never going to happen.

As the glass door shut behind her, Alex slammed his fist down on the lid of a nearby washing machine. The metal rattled wildly. The old lady reading her magazine looked up at him with a shocked expression. She got up off the sofa and shuffled over to sit in a brown plastic chair on the other side of the room, watching him suspiciously the whole time.

Christ, he was falling apart. Right now when he needed to keep his cool, he was losing it.

The next time he saw Val would be in court. He would be forced to sit there and listen to her recount the events of last night calmly and coolly, as if there had never been anything between them. She would tell the jury how she'd rushed into that house to find him half-crazed, disoriented, his clothes torn, and Shannon Reichert naked. Dead.

And the worst part of all was that she wouldn't be lying.

He watched through the window as Val walked half a block up the street, the afternoon breeze swirling her hair wildly around her head. Then she turned and strode across the street toward her apartment building. Jaywalking, of course. Did she ever do *anything* according to the rules?

Then he heard a loud crack. Instantly he knew what it was. Gunfire.

In the same moment, Val spun hard to one side, the laundry basket slipping out of her hands and hitting the ground, spilling towels onto the street.

And then she crumpled to the pavement beside it.

chapter six

Alex yanked the Laundromat door open and raced out into the hot summer afternoon. Cars ground to a halt, their drivers getting out and gaping at Val lying in the street. Alex felt a jolt of foreboding that by the time he got to her, he was going to be holding a dead woman in his arms.

He leaped off the curb and into the street, shoving people aside before finally kneeling down beside Val. He felt a flush of relief when he saw she was moving, then a rush of panic again when he saw her clutching the side of her head and blood oozing between her fingers.

She was conscious. At least she was conscious.

He knocked the laundry basket out of the way and grabbed one of the towels. He tossed it over his shoulder, then swept Val into his arms and headed back toward the Laundromat. Whoever had pulled the trigger might be waiting to pull it again.

"Call nine-one-one!" he shouted to onlookers. "Tell them there's been a shooting!"

After seeing several people dive into pockets and purses for cell phones, Alex carried Val into the Laundromat and laid her on the red vinyl sofa away from the plate-glass window in the front. He knelt beside her, pried her hand away from her temple, and immediately pressed the towel to it. She sucked in a quick, sharp breath, hissing with pain.

"I know it hurts," he told her. "Just hold on."

After a few seconds he pulled it away again and saw, to his immense relief, that the bullet had only grazed her temple, going just deep enough to bleed like crazy. Blood had never bothered him. Lord, he'd seen enough of it to last him a lifetime. So why was his stomach churning at the sight of it now?

"Alex," she murmured. "What happened?"

"You were shot."

"Shot?"

She held her hand up in front of her, and her face blanched. "Blood. Oh, God. I'm not very good with blood."

"It's okay. The bullet just grazed you."

"Feels like it went a foot deep."

"I know it hurts, but it's not bad. Head wounds just bleed a lot. You're going to be okay."

"I can't look at the blood. I mean it, Alex. I can't—"

"Close your eyes."

She did as he said, taking a deep, shaky breath. Alex continued to hold the towel to her head, his palm against her opposite cheek. He heard a siren in the distance.

"Did you see anyone?" he asked her.

"No. No one."

Blood seeped through the towel, and Alex pressed harder. Val grimaced with pain. "Somebody wants me dead."

"No. It was probably just a random shooting. You were in the wrong place at the wrong time. There are a lot of nuts out there."

Alex heard the siren come closer, then the plaintive downward spiral of it falling silent. A moment later he looked over to see two officers coming through the door. One he didn't recognize. Thank God the other one was Ford. He wanted somebody competent to deal with this. To find out who had pulled that trigger and find out *now*.

Ford came up beside them, a startled look on his face. "Alex? What are you doing here? What's going on?"

"I don't know. She was shot while she was crossing the street. I carried her in here to get her out of the line of fire."

"How bad is it?"

"Flesh wound. Deep, but it just grazed her. Another inch to the left . . ."

Jesus. He couldn't even say it. Another inch to the left, and she'd be dead right now.

Ford knelt down beside them. "What's your name, ma'am?"

She blinked her eyes open. "Valerie Parker."

A flicker of recognition lit Ford's eyes. He turned back to Alex. "Does this have anything to do with last night?"

So he'd heard. Of course he had. By now everyone had.

"I don't know."

Ford turned to Val. "Do you have any idea who did this?"

"No. I didn't see anyone. Came out of nowhere."

"Do you know of anyone who might want to take a shot at you?"

"No. No one."

Another siren wailed in the distance. Ford turned to the other officer. "Check out the situation outside, will you?"

The officer nodded and left the Laundromat.

Ford turned to Alex. "You need to clear out of here."

"What?"

"Getting in the middle of another situation that looks fishy isn't going to help your case any. Just get out of here, okay?"

Val reached her hand up and grasped Alex's arm. She looked up at him plaintively, her face ashen. "Don't go."

She was scared. She'd nearly been killed, and she was scared to death, even though he couldn't imagine that Val Parker would be scared of the devil himself. He'd always thought of her as a woman with a coat of armor over her coat of armor. But not now.

Suddenly all the animosity between them seemed to have disappeared. His hand still rested against her face, opposing the towel he was holding against her temple on the other side. Without even thinking, he stroked his thumb lightly back and forth across her cheek. She tightened her hand against his arm, letting her eyes drop closed again, and he knew that nothing on earth could make him leave her now.

"You'd better secure the area," he told Ford, his gaze still fixed on Val. "And make sure you find that bullet. Will you let me know when you do?"

"Alex—"

"Just go."

He stood up. "Yeah. Okay. I'll let you know." He started to walk away, then turned back. "Just so you know, I was going to come by and see you today. That murder accusation is bullshit. I don't know what really went on, but I do know that redhead was a disaster looking for a place to happen."

"It looks bad for me. I wouldn't blame you if you kept your distance."

"No way. I'm with you a hundred percent, buddy. If there's anything I can do for you, let me know."

"Thanks, Ford."

As Ford left the Laundromat, Val's eyes came open again. "Last night. This has something to do with last night, doesn't it?"

"Shh. Don't think about that now."

He wanted to believe that it was a random attack. Tried to believe it. But he didn't buy coincidences. He had the nagging feeling that Ford had hit on it right away—whoever had pulled that trigger had done it because he'd found out that Val had been outside the Reichert house last night. The gunman had been trying to eliminate a possible witness to a murder, and he'd come within an inch of succeeding.

When the paramedics finally showed up and took Val to the ambulance, Alex walked alongside her, ignoring the curious stares of the other officers who'd arrived on the scene. In the end, they took Ford's lead and acted as if his being there were nothing out of the ordinary. Alex knew the gossip would start the moment he left, but for now everybody was keeping their mouths shut.

As they loaded Val into the ambulance, Alex headed for his car. She hadn't asked him to come to the hospital, but he was coming just the same.

He got into his car and paused a moment, thinking about those few seconds after the shot had been fired, when he didn't know if Val was dead or alive. He'd felt a gut-level reaction that had nothing to do with the usual response he'd have to a shooting victim. It had everything to do with the fact that the victim was Val.

No.

He brushed off the feeling, reminding himself that Val was nothing more to him than a momentary temptation he'd given in to at a highly inopportune time. It had brought both of them nothing but grief. He'd known what was right that night, and he'd ignored it at his peril. He wouldn't be making that mistake again. He had to keep his hands off her. He had to keep his distance.

But he had to keep her alive.

Ten minutes later he reached Tolosa Medical Center, a

sprawling complex consisting of a hospital, a research center, and a pair of seven-story towers that housed doctors' offices.

Alex hated the sight of it.

Anytime he'd been there in a nonofficial capacity, something had always been wrong, something he couldn't fix, something that made him feel helpless. His mother had died at this hospital years ago after finally losing a long battle with cancer. He'd been only ten at the time. Her death had been painful beyond description for him, but at least he'd been prepared for it.

His father's death had been another story entirely.

On that cold winter day eight years ago, Joseph DeMarco had had no idea that the guy he'd pulled over on a routine traffic stop had a body in his trunk that he didn't want discovered. The moment he walked alongside the car, he'd been gunned down. A single bullet to the chest, right there at the side of the road.

Alex and his brothers had been called to the hospital. Alex still remembered the profound anger and helplessness he'd felt when he went to his father's bedside. All three of them had been there—he, John, and Dave—but it was Alex he reached for, the favored son, the one he knew had followed in his footsteps so closely. In a raspy, breathless voice, he spoke his dying words.

Get the bastard.

Two days later, bone-tired from lack of sleep, Alex had finally located the guy in a run-down cinder-block house on the south side. When he barricaded himself inside, Alex called in SWAT to help pull him out, and somehow he'd managed to refrain from personally doing the job of the judge and the jury right there on the spot.

Alex's hands tightened against the steering wheel. He was experiencing the same kind of anger now that he'd felt back then. Instead of fading as the minutes passed, it grew with every breath.

But why? It had been his father back then, for God's sake. Not a woman who drove him crazy with every word she spoke, who just might be the person whose testimony would send him to prison for a very long time. Still, he kept thinking about the look in Val's eyes as she stared up at him in that Laundromat, grasped his arm, and begged him not to go.

She wanted you with her. You.

No. She'd acted out of fear. That was all. She'd have clung to anyone at that moment, anyone who she thought could protect her. And he had no doubt that when she came to her senses, she'd never even consider touching him again.

An hour and a half later, Val lay on an emergency room bed, a hard, white-sheeted platform with a rocky pillow that would have been right at home in a medieval torture chamber. She'd bumped her head on the pavement when she fell, but since her neurological exam had been normal they hadn't deemed a CT scan to be necessary. Still, she had strict instructions from the nurse that she wasn't to leave until somebody returned to check her out.

One of the patrol cops had dropped by to question her about the shooting, but it had been a brief interview. What could she possibly tell him beyond what she'd told the other cop she'd talked to at the scene? No, she hadn't seen anything. And no, there wasn't anyone she knew of who might want her dead.

Except maybe Shannon Reichert's killer.

She'd mentioned that as a possibility, and the cop dutifully made a note of it, though he didn't seem particularly convinced that it was even a viable scenario. Neither one of them mentioned the fact that if what she speculated was true, it meant that someone besides Alex had killed Shannon. And with the mountain of evidence against him, who in the world was going to believe that?

Val sighed impatiently, wishing the nurse would return so she could get out of here. Her headache had been reduced to a dull throb, courtesy of the pain medication the woman had insisted she take, but she didn't think much of the loopy feeling she was starting to get as a result of it. Then she touched the gauze bandage on her temple and wondered if the stitches would leave a scar.

Dumb thought. She didn't give a damn about a scar. Not when she could have been in the morgue right now instead of the ER.

She closed her eyes, remembering the blast of gunfire, followed by a sharp, searing pain. She'd fallen to the pavement and strangers had surrounded her, staring down at her, and her head had hurt so much. Only seconds passed, but every one of them had seemed hours long.

Then the crowd had parted, and she'd looked up to see Alex beside her. He'd picked her up, carrying her as if she weighed nothing, moving her out of harm's way. And then he'd laid her on that vinyl sofa in the Laundromat, his hand against her cheek as he held the towel to her wound, touching her firmly but gently. In that moment, the most indescribable feeling had swept over her. *You're going to be all right. As long as Alex is here, you're going to be all right.*

Then she remembered how she'd clung to him like a scared kid. Embarrassment shot through her.

It was because of the blood. She hated blood. The sight of it made her light-headed and sick to her stomach, making it hard for her to think straight. That was why she'd acted so completely helpless.

She'd calmed down now, though. Taken stock of the situation. She decided she was going to believe that whoever shot her was just some random wacko. Alex had said so, hadn't he? She'd been in the wrong place at the wrong time.

Nothing to worry about.

A young dark-haired nurse swept back the curtain that surrounded Val's bed. "How are you feeling?"

Val sat up, weaving a little. The nurse put her hand against her shoulder. "Why don't you stay put for a minute more? We don't start collecting rent unless we send you upstairs."

"Nah. I've got places to be. Home, for instance, getting out of this bloody T-shirt."

Val waited for the dizziness to subside, then slid off the bed, trying not to look down at herself. Her stomach was none too stable right now, and looking at blood was not going to help any. She teetered a little as she stood up, her head starting to pound all over again.

"Do you have somebody to drive you home?" the nurse asked her. "That Percocet I gave you is going to kick you hard in a minute. You'd better make sure you're sitting down."

Val thought about calling her friend Darla. Darla owned the nail salon next door to Val's storefront office on Fourteenth Street. They had breakfast or lunch together almost every day that Val was in her office, trading off on paying the tab. Once Darla had even nursed her through a particularly nasty case of the flu. But this wasn't something that a big pot of chicken soup was going to solve. As much as she loved Darla, she wasn't in any mood to answer questions, to hear mindless reassurances, or to have somebody "taking care" of her. She sorted through her mental short list of other friends, then decided she'd rather tough this one out on her own.

"If you can just give me the phone number of a cab company," she told the nurse, "I'll be fine."

"Sure. Just come on out to the front desk. But take it easy, okay?"

She followed the nurse out to the reception area. She glanced through the sliding glass doors leading outside to the portico and the parking lot beyond them. Her heart kicked up a little. She had no idea who had pulled that trigger. Was he out there right now, waiting for a chance to get off another shot, hoping this time he found his target?

No. It had been a random shooting. Or somebody had been aiming for somebody else and she'd gotten caught in the line of fire. The guy was long gone. Nothing to worry about.

Then her gaze traveled over to the waiting area, and when she saw who was there, her heart skipped. Alex was sitting on the edge of a chair, his elbows on his knees, tapping his fingertips together impatiently.

How long had he been there? She checked her watch. If he'd followed the ambulance, he'd been sitting there over an hour and a half.

He turned and saw her, suddenly coming to attention. Their gazes met, and he rose to his feet. The nurse handed her the phone numbers of a couple of cab companies, and by the time she started to dial, Alex had reached the desk.

"Val," he said. "What are you doing?"

"Calling a cab."

He took the phone from her hand and replaced it in its cradle. "No. I'm taking you home."

"Excuse me?"

"A cab isn't safe. The guy who shot at you may still be out there."

Val felt a little tremor of apprehension, but managed an offhand shrug. "That's nonsense. It was just a random shooting. You said so yourself."

"I don't think so." He inched closer and dropped his voice. "I didn't want to say anything earlier, but I think Ford was right. Whoever killed Shannon found out that you were watching the house last night. He's afraid you saw something you shouldn't have."

"The other cop who came by here didn't seem particularly convinced of that."

"Forget him. What do you think?"

She had the most terrible feeling that Alex was right. This was no coincidence. But if that was true, if Shannon's murder and the shooting today were indeed related, then she was forced to reach another conclusion she hadn't wanted to deal with, either.

She looked up at Alex. She had to say it. He deserved to hear it after how she'd gone on at him in the Laundromat, but it didn't make it any easier to say.

"You didn't have anything to do with Shannon's murder, did you?"

He stared at her a long time, his gaze steady. "Did you ever really believe that I did?"

Despite everything she'd said to him, despite all the evidence to the contrary, despite all the well-founded animosity she'd carried with her all these years, she knew in her heart that the world would come to an end before Alex DeMarco would commit murder. Suddenly his insistence last night that he was innocent seemed as irrefutable as the sun rising in the east.

She turned her gaze away, finding it hard to look him in the eye. She'd all but called him a murderer not two hours ago, when she'd known in her heart that it couldn't possibly be true.

"What I said to you earlier, about not knowing if you did it or not—"

"Forget it."

She let out a soft sigh. "So you think that whoever killed Shannon thinks I might be a witness he needs to get rid of."

"That's what I think."

"Well, that's news I'm not exactly thrilled to hear."

"We can talk about it later. After I take you home."

It was hard to say which she feared more at that moment—a murderer with a gun, or Alex DeMarco stepping inside her apartment one more time. She'd managed to dodge the gunman today. Five years ago Alex had hit her squarely in the heart, and she didn't know if she was up to dealing with him again—under any circumstances.

She thought about the Beretta she kept strapped around her ankle, the one she never left home without. Now that she was on her guard, the guy wouldn't get the drop on her again.

"I don't go anywhere unarmed," she told Alex. "You know I can take care of myself."

"Under normal circumstances, I don't doubt that. These are not normal circumstances. What kind of pain medication did they give you?"

"Just Percocet."

"One or two?"

She paused. "Two."

"Well, that ought to improve your aim. What are you planning on doing? Walking right out the front door of the ER?"

She hadn't really stopped to think about that yet. "You have a better idea?"

"Yes. I parked my car around the corner of the building by a side entrance. Chances are he won't be waiting for you there."

"Aren't you being a little dramatic?"

"Aren't you being a little careless?"

"You're just trying to scare me."

"Hell, yes, I'm trying to scare you! Whoever shot at you knows he missed. With a little more luck than he had the first time, he could get off a solid head shot instead of a flesh wound."

"I doubt that's going to happen."

"Val? Just once would you say, 'Okay, Alex. That sounds good. Let's do it your way'? Just one time?"

"Alex—"

"Just once. Humor me."

"But—"

"You can't do it, can you? You can't agree with me on anything. You can't just say—"

"Will you *stop* trying to tell me what to do?"

There had been a time when verbally sparring with Alex had been one of her favorite sports. But this was another situation entirely. She didn't want to fight with him. Didn't *feel* like fighting with him. Damn, her head felt goofy—the nurse hadn't been kidding about the drug kicking in. Her thoughts suddenly felt weird and disjointed, as if she hadn't slept in days, which allowed images of angry, faceless gunmen to sweep through her mind. She took a deep, ragged breath, her gaze turning involuntarily to the double glass doors leading to the parking lot.

"It's okay," Alex said. "I know you're scared. Anybody would be right about now."

She turned back. "Don't try to be sympathetic, Alex. It doesn't suit you."

"Don't try to lie to me. I saw your face when we were in the Laundromat."

"I don't like blood. I panicked a little. That's all. Don't make more out of it than it really was."

She hadn't intended to dwell on that, but at least it offered some explanation for her childish behavior. But now she realized he was probably going to say, *You don't like blood, huh? Then you'd have made a hell of a police officer.*

She almost wished he would. If he made a snide remark right now, it would be a lot easier to go on hating him.

"Just let me take you home," he said.

His voice was calm. Gentle. And so damned tempting.

"I don't need you."

"Tonight I think you do."

Oh, Lord, Alex. Don't do this. Don't be nice. I can deal with you when you're being arrogant and demanding, but I can't deal with this. Give me something to fight against here.

She looked up again and met his gaze, and all those feelings came rushing back again, those feelings of attraction, of need, of desire that had been trapped inside her all this time, like slow-burning embers that had never been extinguished. And the way he was looking back at her—as if he could read every one of her thoughts—made her suddenly feel stark naked.

He knows. He knows you can't even look at him without getting hot all over again.

No. She was giving him way too much credit. Those damned painkillers were making her think dumb thoughts. Dumb thoughts that centered around throwing herself right back into his arms again.

He'd betrayed her, and what she really needed to be doing was running away from him as far and as fast as she could. But if she did, would she be running right into the path of a killer?

He was right: she *was* scared. But he was the last person on the planet who was ever going to know it.

"Fine," she said. "You win. Take me home. I suppose it beats a smelly old cab. And at least you speak English."

To her surprise, he smiled. "Why, Val, I do believe that's one of the nicest things you've ever said to me."

Good heavens. She'd forgotten how he looked when he smiled: warm and handsome and very, very charming. There was a time when she would have cheerfully drowned in that smile, and just one glance at it now put her on the verge of diving right back into it again.

"You say there's a side door to this place?" she said, brushing past him, wishing her legs didn't feel so wobbly, wishing the medication hadn't made her so shaky that she had to concentrate just to put one foot in front of the other.

"Down the hall," Alex said. "Right by that exit sign."

Despite her efforts, when she turned into the hallway, she stumbled a little, and Alex caught her arm. She tried to shake loose from him, but she succeeded only in tangling her feet together even more. He wrapped his arm around her shoulders to keep her from falling.

"Alex—*don't.*"

He pulled her around, grasped her by her upper arms, and stared down at her admonishingly. "Val? Will you cut out all the tough-girl crap? You're a pharmaceutical basket case right now, and if you fall, you're liable to crack your head open and end up staying here all night. Is that what you want?"

Without another word, he wrapped his arm around her again and headed for the exit.

Damn it. Why had she let that nurse talk her into pain medication? Her head had hurt like crazy, but she certainly could have toughed it out. The Percocet made her bleary-eyed and tremulous and a little nauseated, and right now it felt too good to be leaning on Alex. He was a solid wall of strength and steadiness, and she had the feeling that as long as she held on to him, nothing could touch her.

No. You're forgetting what he did to you. You may think you can trust him now, but you'd better keep your eyes wide open.

She decided she'd let him take her home, but that was it. Any talking they needed to do about this god-awful mess they could do tomorrow, and someplace besides her apartment. And once this damned drug wore off and she returned to her right mind, she'd never let Alex get near her again.

chapter seven

By the time they arrived at Val's apartment, Alex could see that she was practically asleep on her feet, though she did everything she could to hide that fact. He pulled her keys from her hand to open her apartment door.

She shot him a look of disgust. "You want to give me back my keys?"

"Come on, Val. You couldn't even find the keyhole right about now."

He swung the door open and stepped aside for her to enter. She did. He followed her inside, closing the door behind them.

"Alex, I don't want you here."

"That guy could decide to finish the job he started this afternoon. And if he does—"

"See this door?" Val said. "A handle lock, a dead bolt, and a chain. Three very nice barriers against the bad guy. I'll deploy every one of them just as soon as you're gone."

"You really think those locks are going to stop him?"

She swayed unsteadily, as if a gentle breeze might blow her right over.

"Val? Why don't you lie down before you fall down?"

She closed her eyes and put her hand to her forehead. "I can't fight you right now, Alex. I can't. So will you please just do as I ask and go?"

"Lie down, and I might consider it."

"You're lying."

"Yes, I am."

"Do you have to be so pushy?"

"Yes. Evidently I do."

Finally she spat out a breath of disgust, then turned and headed through her living room toward the hall.

"Where are you going?"

"To get out of this bloody T-shirt and wash up a little."

Okay. At least she'd stopped arguing with him. That was half the battle won.

Alex glanced around her apartment. It was just as he remembered it, and that surprised him. Not that it was the same, but that he remembered that it was the same, from the scarred hardwood floors to the rough plaster walls to the thrift-store furniture. He'd been with women whose names he couldn't even remember, much less their décor, but he remembered this apartment as clearly as if he'd been here yesterday.

He looked at the bookshelves that lined one wall of her living room, filled with an assortment of books so eclectic that anybody on the planet could have found something to keep himself busy. Stephen Hawking's *A Brief History of Time* sat right next to a hardcover edition of *The Shining*, which was next to a tattered copy of *Dorland's Medical Dictionary*. The older books contributed to a faint musty smell in her apartment, which mingled with the scent of vintage oak woodwork. People who lived in places like this were generally a little quirky. That described Val perfectly. He'd always wondered why a person like her would want to become a police officer. It seemed an unlikely career for somebody with her unconventional approach to life. Why had she even pursued it in the first place?

And then he looked at her sofa, and memories came flooding back.

He remembered the surprised expression on Val's face when she opened her door that night five years ago and saw him standing in the hall. He came inside, sidestepping her questions as to why he was there. He asked her to sit down on the sofa, still looking for the right words to use to break the news to her about the dismissal that was coming the next day. Not once in his life, under any circumstances, could he remember being unable to say something that needed to be said, but this time everything he came there to tell her had gotten stuck in his throat.

Being a police officer wasn't the right profession for her. In

the end, she was going to see that he'd done her a favor by rec-
ommending that she be dismissed. She was still young. She
still had a hundred opportunities out there to find a direction
for her life. He was doing the right thing.

But if he truly believed that, then why were the words so
hard to say?

He knew just how much his being there that night knocked
her off guard, because as they sat down on the sofa, her eyes
narrowed warily, and she refrained from the usual teasing
banter she tossed at him. He said something stupid about the
weather, or something that had been in the news that day, the
kinds of things people say when they can't think of anything
else. Then she tilted her head questioningly, tucking a strand
of dark hair behind her ear. Her fingertip seemed to move in
slow motion as it curled around her ear, then grazed her neck
as she dropped her hand back to her lap. That innocent gesture
had made his mouth go dry as parchment.

Just tell her.

He must have silently repeated that to himself at least a
hundred times. Getting himself to listen—that had been the
problem. But why?

In his younger days, he might as well have installed a re-
volving door in his apartment for the parade of women he'd
dated. But only part of him had shown up for those relation-
ships. They'd been surface kinds of involvements requiring
little emotion, emotion that he could turn off and on like a
light switch. But something about Val reached right inside
him, bone-deep, until he felt as if he couldn't even *find* the
switch.

She irritated him. She challenged him. She aggravated him
so much sometimes that he wanted to throttle her. And still, it
got to the point that every minute he wasn't with her, he
was thinking about her, wondering how he was going to stay
one step ahead of her next time. Wondering what off-the-
wall thing she was going to do to make him pull his hair out
tomorrow.

Wondering what it would be like to kiss her.

The thought of having all that energy she exuded with
every breath directed specifically at him was just about the
sexiest thing he could possibly imagine. And that night in her

apartment, it was the only thought he seemed to be able to grasp. That should have been his cue to get up off the sofa and put as much distance between the two of them as he possibly could within the confines of her apartment.

Instead, he eased closer.

Alex?

That softly spoken word had been a question. Actually, several questions all at once: *What are you doing? Why are you here? What's happening between us?* And that was when he should have told her. He should have told her that the profession she wanted so badly she couldn't have, that by this time tomorrow she'd be out of the academy.

Instead he leaned even closer, sliding his hand along the top of the sofa behind her head.

She swallowed hard. Her gaze dropped to his lips, then came slowly back up again, her eyes suddenly alive with anticipation. From one second to the next, they went from cadet and superior officer who clashed at every turn, to a man and a woman who wanted each other more with every breath they took. His pulse thundered inside his head.

Stop it. Back off. You have to tell her, and you have to do it now.

But he couldn't. Instead, he did what he'd been thinking about doing for weeks.

He kissed her.

The moment he touched his lips to hers, there was no going back. That first contact was like a spark setting off a forest fire, and their lovemaking turned out to be just as hot and exciting as he'd always believed it would be. And through it all, he deliberately ignored the truth: he knew something she didn't, and that something was going to rip her heart out.

Later, after she'd fallen asleep, all he could think about was how much she was going to hate him tomorrow for what he'd done tonight. For what he *hadn't* done tonight. After what they'd just shared, he couldn't bear to see that look of betrayal on her face. And that was why he'd left.

It had been a gutless decision, one of the few he'd ever made in his life, and one he'd lived to regret. He should have stayed until morning and tried to explain what was going to happen. Tried to find some way to make her not hate him for what he'd done. Tried to tell her how sorry he was that things had turned out the way that they had, even though he'd been the one to make it happen.

Tried to tell her that even though he couldn't see her as a police officer, he had no trouble seeing her as a woman.

Over the past five years, somehow he'd managed to make himself believe that she'd been just one in a long line of women who'd meant nothing to him. But now, faced with the very real possibility that somebody was out to kill her, he knew just how much he'd deluded himself.

"There. If I do any bleeding in this, at least it won't be so obvious."

Alex looked over to see Val walking back into the room wearing a red T-shirt. She sat down on the sofa with a heavy sigh, and to his surprise, he won the rest of the battle without firing a shot. After giving him a token look of disgust, Val laid her head down and pulled her feet up onto the sofa. And damned if he didn't have the urge to go over there and make history repeat itself.

"You're not gone," she murmured.

"I told you I was lying about that."

She closed her eyes, as if to pretend he wasn't even there. That was fine with him. Maybe she'd fall asleep.

He pulled a book off her bookshelf, a leather-bound volume that was a little tattered around the edges.

"Alex?" Val murmured drowsily, unable to see him over the back of the sofa. "What are you doing?"

"Looking at your books. *Winnie the Pooh?*"

"Be careful with that. It's a first edition. Worth a bundle."

He set it back down on the shelf and picked up another one. *"Secrets of Tai Chi?"*

"Eastern mysticism. It's intriguing. Now, will you put it down?"

He picked up another book. *"Sweet Savage Love?"*

"Damn it, will you get your hands off my books?"

"Nope. This is interesting."

"I'm armed, Alex. And I'm a damned good shot."

He had to admit she was right about that. At the academy, she'd outperformed every other cadet at the firing range, as well as any seasoned officers who happened to show up. Including him.

"Maybe," he said. "But right now you'd be lucky to hit the broad side of a barn."

"You're a pretty big target. Don't push me."

He put *Sweet Savage Love* back on the shelf. Sounded like an interesting book. Or, at least, it was interesting to picture Val reading it. At night. In bed. Wearing nothing.

"Alex, sit down. As long as you're here, I've got a couple of questions."

"Just rest. We can talk in the morning."

"Sit."

He shook his head. She really *hadn't* changed a bit.

He came around the sofa. He had a choice between a rattan rocker and a fluffy, overstuffed chair covered in a fabric that looked like an explosion in a flower store. He chose the fluffy one. He sank halfway to China.

"Nice chair," he muttered.

"Thank you." Val put her arm behind her head, looking as if she could barely keep her eyes open. "Why did you go home with Shannon last night?"

He excavated himself from the depths of the chair and sat on the edge of it. "Why do you think I went home with her?"

"To get laid?"

"Wrong. Did you see her sitting on the hood of her car outside the Onion?"

"Yes."

"She told me she broke her car key off in the lock. I agreed to take her home."

"But you went inside her house."

"When we got there, she saw the light off in her bedroom and she swore she'd left it on. She said she thought she had an intruder. I knew it was a ploy to get me into her bedroom, but as a cop, I had no choice but to go along with it."

"So you weren't planning on getting up close and personal."

"Not for one moment. You were in the Onion, right? Watching her?"

"Yes."

"That hundred-dollar bill from the pool game. Did you see her give it to me?"

"Uh-huh."

"Did you see me give it right back to her?"

"Uh-huh."

"She'd written her address on it. Her subtle way of suggesting I come home with her. I had no intention of having anything else to do with her."

"When I came into the house, she was naked."

"Her doing, not mine. It was amazing how fast she could get out of that dress."

Val nodded. He assumed he'd convinced her, because she wasn't exactly one to keep her opinion to herself.

"You said you were drugged. Forgive me, Alex, but—"

"I know. It's the flimsiest story ever, and if I were on the other side of it, I'd call it bullshit, too. But it's the truth. I'd tell you more if I knew more. But I don't."

"Do you think somebody drugged your drink at the Onion?"

"I don't think so. The dizziness came on suddenly, and I was out in seconds. I have no idea what could have—"

He froze. Yes, he did. How could he possibly have forgotten?

It was a fuzzy memory, but just before he'd started to feel light-headed, he remembered thinking that maybe he'd been stung by something. An insect, he'd thought at the time. But no. Not an insect.

"It was a needle," he told Val.

"A needle?"

"Yes. Right before I got dizzy and blacked out, I felt something in my hip. Something sharp. I thought at the time that it must have been an insect, but it was more intense than that."

"And you're just now remembering it?"

"It was a powerful drug. It's hard for me to focus on anything that happened around that time."

"So Shannon stuck you with a needle?"

"She had to have. There was nobody else in the room."

"This makes no sense. She sticks you with a needle, knocks you out, and then she's murdered?"

"I never said it made sense. I can only tell you what happened."

"Are you sure she was the only one in the house?"

"I didn't see anyone else."

"Someone could have been in the bedroom."

"But she was the only one close enough to stick me. I had just turned around. She was right behind me, and that's when I felt it."

"But no needle was found."

"No. But the drug screen didn't rule out that I might have been drugged."

"You had a drug screen?"

"I insisted on it. They found an unidentifiable substance, but they said it could be anything."

"Why didn't they know what it was?"

"When they do a drug screen, they have to know what they're looking for. They can only compare my samples to those of known substances. If something shows up that's outside the bounds of those substances, it's impossible to say what it is."

"But if you had the actual drug, they could match it, right?"

"Right. But there's also the possibility that the drug I was shot with had left my system by the time they did the test, and the unknown substance is something else entirely."

Val shook her head. "I don't understand any of this. Even if somebody was in that house, even if you were drugged, the question is, why?"

Alex sighed. "I have no idea."

"So what are we supposed to do now?"

"We're supposed to hope they find the bullet. Hope they can eventually match it to something. Hope we can find out who shot you before he tries it again, and before I go to prison for a murder he committed."

"So it's as simple as that?"

"Yeah," he said wearily. "It's as simple as that."

Val shifted on the sofa, grimacing a little. This time she put her hand to her stomach.

"When's the last time you ate?" he asked.

"I don't know. Maybe ten o'clock this morning."

"You took Percocet on an empty stomach? No wonder you're nauseated."

"I'm not nauseated."

"You're holding your stomach, Val. That's what we in the detective business call a 'clue.' "

"I'm fine."

"I'll fix you some toast."

"I don't want toast."

"Yes, you do."

She glared at him. "You really piss me off sometimes, do you know that?"

"Only when I'm right. Butter?"

She stared at him a long, deadpan moment, then turned away with a sigh. "Dry. I don't think I could handle anything else."

Alex got up and went to her kitchen. He fished through half a dozen cabinets before finally finding the bread in the refrigerator. He stuck two slices in the toaster, which looked like one his mother had used when he was a kid.

He glanced around the room. Along a wall near the kitchen table was yet another bookshelf. The top shelf held framed photos, and as he moved closer, he saw one that surprised him. It showed a girl of maybe fifteen, whom he recognized as Val, with an older man dressed in a police uniform beside her.

He blinked with surprise. Who was that man?

He looked closer for a clue that it had been taken at some kind of police "meet the public" function. But it had clearly been shot in a private home.

The officer looked too old to be her father. He appeared to be Hispanic, with a uniform unlike those worn by Tolosa officers. Val's dark hair, dark eyes, and deep complexion said she could possibly have at least one relative who was Hispanic. But if she had a relative who was a cop, why had she never mentioned him? Maybe he should ask her.

Maybe he shouldn't.

He pulled the toast out of the toaster, put it on a plate, and brought it into the living room. Val's eyes were closed.

"Val?"

She didn't respond. Her hands were folded over her chest. She was breathing softly. Rhythmically.

He set the toast down on the coffee table, then went to her bedroom. He flipped on the light in the adjoining bathroom and closed the door halfway, just so he'd have enough light to see what he was doing, then pulled back the covers on her bed. When he went back to the living room, she was still asleep, her fist pulled up to her chin, the bandage on her temple making her look like a wounded angel.

Since he intended to be the one sleeping on the sofa, he took a chance that she wouldn't wake up and scooped her into his arms, took her to her bedroom, and laid her down gently. She never woke. For about half a second he considered undressing her, then decided it wasn't worth facing her wrath when she woke up in the morning to find herself half-naked. Then he glanced down at her ankle and caught sight of a holster peeking out from beneath the hem of her jeans. She hadn't been kidding about being armed.

He gently slid the leg of her jeans up to her knee, then peeled back the Velcro of the ankle holster as quietly as he could and removed it along with the weapon it held. He laid them aside, then started to pull the leg of her jeans back down again.

He stopped. Stared. God, she had pretty legs.

A woman as tough as Val should have had legs that looked like redwood trunks, but hers looked more like willow saplings. He remembered being in this very room, running his hand from her thigh down to her calf and back up again, feeling skin that was warm and soft and satin smooth. That night had been a hot, hazy, intense experience that was going to dwell in his mind for the rest of his life and probably well into his next one.

Still, the last thing he should be doing was looking at her now. Not just because she'd be pissed as all get-out if she woke and caught him staring, but because he wasn't completely sure he could continue to look without touching.

Face it. You want her. Hell, you'd take her right now if only she was cognizant enough to let you.

Who was he kidding? If she were cognizant, she'd boot him right out of her bedroom and slam the door behind him.

Just then she stretched a little, throwing her arm back over her head, the motion pulling her T-shirt tight across her breasts, outlining them so distinctly that what little was left to his imagination was filled in by his five-year-old memory of seeing her in the darkness of this bedroom, naked and willing. For a long, unguarded moment he let himself think about that. Touching her. Kissing her. Doing more than just touching and kissing. Long hours of passionate sex when neither of them had even come up for air.

Then he thought about Val's fist connecting with his face the moment he laid a hand on her. Did he really need that kind of complication?

That was the problem with Val. Just being around her made him think stupid thoughts, do stupid things. It was as if her outrageous behavior was contagious, and there was no way for him to immunize himself against it. Right now he wanted nothing more than to crawl into this bed beside her. And Jesus—if he thought he'd done something stupid five years ago, that would make him look positively brilliant by comparison.

He pulled the covers up over her and reluctantly left the room. He'd sleep on her sofa tonight and catch hell for it from her tomorrow. Then maybe she'd settle down and the two of them could try to figure out who was trying to frame him and kill her.

That he was in Val's apartment was unbelievable. That he was staying the night in her apartment was mind-boggling. He had the strangest feeling that they were two people destined to cross paths from now until the end of time, with each new encounter stormier than the last. If so, he couldn't even imagine what tomorrow might bring.

chapter eight

Val blinked her eyes open to the pale rays of morning sun that eased through her bedroom window. A little disoriented, she rolled over and checked the clock on her nightstand. It was almost seven-thirty.

Then she remembered what had happened. She touched her fingertips to the gauze bandage still stuck to her temple. It hadn't been a bad dream after all. She had most definitely gotten shot.

She got out of bed, her head throbbing a little, and walked gingerly toward her bedroom door. On the way, she caught sight of herself in her dresser mirror and almost screamed. Her hair was going in a dozen different directions, even more so than usual, and the bags under her eyes drooped halfway to the floor. She ran a hand over her hair a couple of times and succeeded only in making it stick up more.

Then she thought about Alex.

Her heart skipped a little. How had she gotten to bed last night? Had she been so out of it that she'd walked in here and not even realized it?

Or had he carried her?

She went to the living room. He wasn't there. Then she smelled coffee.

She walked to the kitchen. Her bare feet made no sound on the hardwood floor, but still he turned the moment she reached the doorway. His eyes, usually so sharp and focused, were still sleepy, taking the edge off their usual intensity. His hair was mussed, but in a way that looked warm and sexy and totally engaging, as if he had just awakened after a night of particularly good sex. He was wearing his shirt, but it was un-buttoned down the front, revealing just enough of his broad, muscled chest to remind her of what the rest of it looked like. What it felt like. What it *tasted* like.

She remembered the fantasies she used to have about making love with Alex long before it had actually happened. Every one of those fantasies had ended the same way, with the two of them together in her kitchen the next morning, drinking coffee, eating breakfast, laughing, kissing, then pushing the breakfast dishes aside and making love all over again.

That part had stayed a fantasy.

She walked into the kitchen. "Good morning, Alex. You look like hell."

He ran his hand through his hair with a grimace. "Gee, thanks."

She came up beside him and reached into the cabinet for a coffee mug. "Didn't I tell you to go home last night?"

"Yeah. So?"

"So you didn't have to stay. I told you that."

"Now, Val, you know it's really not in me to be a nice guy. Better take it when you can get it."

Nice guy. She wanted to argue about that one—strongly—but she couldn't. Because that was exactly what he'd been. Taking her home. Staying with her because he was afraid the gunman would come for her again. Waking up and making coffee this morning. It was a contradiction she really didn't understand right now, and it made her more than a little wary.

"How long have you been up?" she asked, pouring a mug of coffee.

"An hour or so. I've been checking into some things."

"Such as?"

"I called Ford. They found the bullet."

"And?"

"It was a seven-millimeter Remington Ultra Mag."

"Rifle ammunition?"

"Yeah. Used in the Remington seven-hundred series. That kind of ammo is very weapon-specific." He paused. "You were shot with a bullet that could bring down a five-hundred-pound antelope."

Val felt a swirl of nausea at the thought of that. Whoever shot at her hadn't been messing around. If she had been leaning just a little to the right, then . . .

She didn't even want to think about it.

"No wonder you didn't see the gunman," Alex went on. "Nobody would have. He was probably a hundred yards away."

"You're joking."

"The angle of your wound shows that the bullet had a slight downward trajectory. I'm betting somebody was shooting from a second- or third-story window. If other people had been shot, then maybe we could attribute it to some lunatic picking people off at random. It happens. But no. One shot." He paused. "Meant just for you."

Val sat down in one of her kitchen chairs, her mind spinning. Alex sat down beside her. "But who, Alex? I can't imagine who—"

"Reichert."

She looked at Alex with surprise. "What?"

"I saw that den of his. He's a hunter. Did you know that?"

"Yes, but—"

"I think he's the one who tried to kill you."

Val stared at him dumbly. This just wasn't computing. "We already decided that whoever shot at me was the one who killed Shannon. That means—"

"That Reichert killed his own wife."

Val felt a cold chill. Reichert had always struck her as a hard man, one who took what he wanted out of life and didn't give a damn who he screwed in the process. But was he capable of murder?

"What was his motive?" she asked.

"Come on, Val. It's pretty clear he suspected her of cheating."

"Well, yeah, but—"

"I think he wanted to nail her *and* the guy she was cheating with. He kills her; then I wake up and take the rap. He wanted not only to take out his wife but frame the man she was sleeping with at the same time."

"Now wait a minute. It couldn't have been Reichert. He was out of town the night Shannon was killed."

"Maybe he was, and maybe he wasn't."

"But why in the world would he have me watching a house where he intended to commit murder?"

Alex pushed his coffee mug aside. "Okay. Let's suppose

instead of staying and calling nine-one-one, I'd left the scene. He'd have nobody to pin the murder on. If he had you watching the house, you could tell the police that I was at the scene at the time the crime was committed. It was his way of making sure someone else took the fall for the crime, with the added benefit of punishing the man his wife was sleeping with. And under those circumstances, nobody would even consider him a suspect."

Val felt a little breathless. Could that be what happened? Was it possible that Reichert was that devious?

"But if what you say is true, then Reichert wants my testimony. Why would he try to kill me?"

"Maybe he realizes now that he slipped up somehow. Maybe he thinks you saw too much, that you'll remember something later that he said, or be able to place him at the scene. At this point you've given your statement to the police, a statement that implicates me. You've already accomplished exactly what he set out for you to accomplish, even if you don't actually testify in court."

"You said you saw no one else in the bedroom. How did he get close enough to stick you with a needle?"

"I don't know. There must be some explanation. We just have to find out what it is. Ford's going to check out his alibi, then talk to Henderson about getting a search warrant for the Reichert house to try to find that rifle."

"Do you actually think he's going to have it lying around the house? If I were him, I'd have dumped it in a lake by now."

"I'm betting he still has it."

"A weapon he attempted murder with?"

"I know the type of guy he is. With all that hunting he does, he's clearly a man in love with his arsenal. I've known guys who would junk a gun about as quickly as they'd junk their firstborn son. I'm betting he'll just hide it until any heat is off. He has no idea anyone suspects him at all."

"But there will still be nothing to actually tie him to Shannon's murder."

"No. But I don't think it'll be much of a leap for somebody to consider the possibility that if he shot you, he might also have killed his wife."

Then Val thought of something else, and her heart nearly stopped. "Alex. Oh, God."

"What?"

"I talked to Reichert before I put Shannon under surveillance. I told him I wanted to set up a hidden camera in their bedroom in case she brought a man there. He flatly refused. He told me there was no way that Shannon would have the audacity to cheat with another man in their own home."

"If you'd set up video equipment—"

"I'd have caught the murder on camera." She hadn't wanted to believe it, but maybe Alex was right. Reichert was starting to look like a very good suspect.

Suddenly she heard three loud raps on her front door.

"Are you expecting anybody?" Alex asked.

"No. Nobody."

Alex rose from the table and went to the door. Val followed, watching as he looked out the peephole.

"What the—"

To Val's surprise, he flipped the locks and opened the door. A man strode into her apartment. Tall. Dark hair. Jeans. Royal blue T-shirt stretched across a broad chest. And he was almost as handsome as Alex.

"Dave?" Alex said. "What are you doing here?"

"Ford called me. Told me what was up." He turned to Val with a smile. "Hi. I'm Dave DeMarco, Alex's brother."

Another five seconds and Val would have come to that conclusion all by herself. The family resemblance was indisputable. Dave wasn't quite as tall and muscular as Alex, but if he'd been standing next to anyone but his brother, he'd have looked pretty impressive. But while Alex radiated an aura of intensity, Dave's expression was pleasant and outgoing.

"I'm Valerie Parker," she said. "Val."

Dave nodded, and she got the feeling that his knowledge of her extended beyond her name and address. She wondered just how much he knew about her relationship to Alex.

"How did you know where to find me?" Alex asked.

"Ford said you were here."

"How did you know Val's address?"

"I looked it up in the phone book."

Alex turned to Val with disbelief. "Your home address is in the stinking *phone book*?"

She shrugged. "So what? These days with the Internet, anyone who wants my address can find it with a couple of mouse clicks."

"That doesn't mean you should publish the damned thing!" Alex shouted. "You're a PI, Val. A lot of your business is catching people doing crap they shouldn't be doing! Suppose one of them has a grudge and decides to act on it?"

"You don't have to yell."

"Do you have any idea how dumb that is?"

"You think everything I do is dumb. Tell me something new."

Alex glared at her. "Just make sure you have it taken out of the phone book next time."

Val turned to Dave. "Has he always been this bossy?"

"Yes," Dave said. "Always."

Alex shot Dave a nasty look, which thoroughly delighted Val. She'd known Dave for only two minutes, and already she liked him.

"Ford called you?" Alex asked Dave. "Why?"

"Because he figured I was the only one who could keep you from beating the crap out of Henderson."

Alex frowned. "Why am I going to feel the need to beat the crap out of Henderson?"

"Ford filled me in on what's been going on. Val getting shot, finding the bullet. But Henderson isn't even interested in questioning Reichert about it. And since he refuses to connect the two crimes, he won't ask the judge for a search warrant to look for the rifle."

"That bastard," Alex muttered, pacing toward the sofa. "He wouldn't know how to conduct an actual investigation if his life depended on it."

Dave turned to Val. "Nice place you've got here."

Val smiled. "Thank you."

"He's had it in for me for years," Alex said, "but he's never been able to do anything about it. Now the second he has a chance—"

"I like the plaster walls," Dave said. "And the original hardwoods. You don't find those much anymore."

"That's why I like it," Val said. "It's quaint."

"I have to do something, Dave," Alex said, his voice growing angrier by the moment. "I'm not going to let him get away with a half-assed investigation. I have to go talk to him."

"You've sure got a lot of books," Dave said.

"Yeah, I can't seem to stop collecting them. Every time I go to a used-book store—"

"Hey!" Alex said. "Will you two cut out the small talk? We've got a problem here!"

"Uh-huh," Dave said. "And we're going to talk about it. Just as soon as you cool off a little."

Alex's mouth was set in a rigid, angry line, his fists in tight knots. He glared at his brother for a moment, then closed his eyes, took a deep breath, and let it out slowly. "Dave?"

"Uh-huh?"

"Is there anything on this planet that rattles you?"

"Oh, yeah. I get rattled every time one of my brothers is on the verge of doing something stupid and I think maybe I'm going to have to knock the snot out of him to keep him from doing it. I just don't bother to let him know that until it becomes necessary. And it's not going to become necessary, is it?"

Alex shook his head slowly, then looked at Val. "See the crap I have to put up with from my family? And do you know the scary part? Dave's the normal one."

Val didn't see any crap at all. She saw two brothers who loved each other a lot, who'd probably go to the mat for each other no matter what. Alex was understandably upset, since it was his neck on the line, so right now it was Dave's job to keep a handle on things.

"Okay, Val," Dave said. "A couple of questions. First of all, how are you feeling? Is your head all right?"

"I'm doing okay."

"Second, I want you to tell me if there's any part of you—any part—that still believes that Alex might have killed Shannon Reichert."

This guy really got to the point. Val shifted her gaze to Alex and found him staring at her. She could tell he still wondered what her answer might be.

"No," she said quietly. "There's not."

"Okay. Now number three. Who do *you* think killed her?"

"Well, Jack Reichert's looking pretty good to me right now, except for the fact that he was supposedly out of town on the night of the murder. I don't know if he can prove his whereabouts or not."

"If he's not a suspect, he doesn't have to prove it," Dave said.

"Another thing," Alex said. "Before you got here, Val told me that when Reichert first hired her to tail Shannon, she offered to set up video equipment in their bedroom to document Shannon's cheating. Reichert refused."

Dave turned to Val. "What reason did he give for that?"

"He said she'd never be shameless enough to bring another man right into their home."

"Or maybe he was afraid of getting caught on camera killing his own wife," Alex said.

"Okay," Dave said. "I'll tell Henderson that. I don't know if he'll listen, but I can try."

"I'm betting he'll still tell you to go to hell," Alex said.

"Maybe not. I'm the only one in the family who's never pissed him off."

"I'm still not holding my breath."

"You'll have to for a little while. Henderson is on vacation for a couple of days. He won't be back until day after tomorrow."

"Oh, that's great."

Alex's face looked tight and drawn. Weary. All at once Val could see just how much of a toll this was taking on him, though she knew the world would come to an end before he ever admitted it.

"The rest of the family," Alex said. "How are they taking all this?"

"I'll leave that to your imagination."

"In other words, pandemonium."

"Oh, yeah. But they're behind you, Alex. They know you want them to butt out for now, and they're okay with that."

"Really?"

"Of course not. But they'll stay out of your way. And you know they're ready to help just as soon as you need them."

Alex nodded.

"I've got to get going," Dave said. "But I'll let you know what I find out tomorrow." He turned to Val. "Will you remind

Alex every once in a while that maybe he ought to stay away from the police station? From Henderson in particular?"

"In case he forgets?"

"Right. He's been known to have episodic amnesia."

"How tragic. Does that run in your family?"

"No. It's just Alex, thank God. The rest of us were spared."

"Beat it, Dave," Alex muttered.

"Nice to meet you, Val," Dave said. "You be careful now."

"I will."

Dave headed for the door. Alex stepped outside with him, motioning to Val that he'd be back in a moment, then pulled the door closed behind him.

Val edged toward the door, wondering what they might be saying. But they were speaking too softly for her to hear, and she decided that if she had her ear glued to the door when Alex came back into her apartment, she'd only get another lecture, and she could certainly do without that.

Dave was nice. An interesting contrast to Alex. She couldn't help wondering what the rest of his family might be like. If they were anything like Dave, Alex was a lucky man. The very idea of having a huge family waiting in the wings as Alex had, ready to help him through the darkest of times, was something so foreign to Val that she almost couldn't grasp the concept. She only knew that it would have to be a beautiful thing, for once in her life, to feel bedrock beneath her feet instead of sand.

Out in the hall, Alex pulled Dave aside.

"Val," he said in a low voice. "She's too careless. Reichert could be anywhere, and I'm afraid she's going to get her head blown off. So I'll probably be staying here with her, at least for now."

Dave just stared at him.

"What?" Alex asked.

"Tell me what's going on between you two."

"What are you talking about?"

"You said there was something years ago. Is there something now?"

"No. Absolutely not."

"Looks like you've been here all night."

"They gave her pain medication yesterday at the hospital. She couldn't have protected herself if that guy had come after her again."

Dave looked at him critically. "There's more to it than that."

"No, there's not."

"I think there is."

"Why?"

"Because you yelled at her."

Alex blinked. "What?"

"I've never seen you yell at a woman before. Not once."

"Sure you have."

"Nope. Never."

Alex narrowed his eyes. "Let me get this straight. You think there's something going on between us because I *yelled* at her? Does that make any sense at all?"

"It's this thing you've got, Alex. Even if you're pissed off, with most people you're in complete control as you're ripping them to shreds. You never actually yell, no matter how angry you get. Unless it's somebody you care about."

Alex was pretty sure his brother had completely lost his mind. "How did you arrive at that conclusion?"

"By watching you for thirty years."

"Will you stop with the psychoanalysis? Christ, you're a know-it-all sometimes."

"And I'm a pretty good judge of character, too. I like Val. If not for this situation, I'd tell you to go for it. But just be careful about getting tangled up with her again under these circumstances. If we can't get this mess straightened out, she could be the one to put you in prison. And that's going to be a damned hard thing to face if you're in love with her."

"If I'm—" Alex gaped at his brother with total disbelief. "You are way, *way* off base here, Dave."

"Not that I've ever known you to actually fall in love, but there's always a first time."

"That's enough. Just shut up and get out of here, will you?"

Dave regarded Alex for a few more moments, then nodded. "Sure, Alex. Just watch yourself, will you? That's all I'm asking."

Alex nodded.

"I'll be in touch."

Alex watched his brother disappear down the stairs. Dave really did piss him off sometimes, thinking he knew what was in everybody else's head before they knew it themselves. But he was wrong about this one. Dead wrong.

He came back into the apartment, but when he looked around, he didn't see Val. He checked the kitchen, then went down the hall and found her in her bedroom sitting at a desk, punching away at a computer keyboard.

"Your brother's nice," she said.

"My brother's a know-it-all."

"Yeah, but you love him anyway."

What was with the two of them? How could they possibly be in collusion when they'd known each other only five minutes?

"What are you doing?" Alex asked.

"Question," she said, her gaze focused on the computer screen. "Do you think Dave can get Henderson to change his mind and go for a warrant?"

"Nope."

"You're absolutely sure about that?"

"Henderson's out to get me. He's not about to back down under any circumstances."

"Okay," she said. "Then we have to go to plan B."

Oh, Lord. Her plan A's were scary enough. The more she moved down the alphabet, the more frightening it got.

She clicked the mouse, waited a moment, then looked closer at the screen. "Just as I thought. There it is."

"There's what?"

Alex came around to look at the screen. He recognized the Web site as a subscription-only site used for background checks. Val had pulled up information about Shannon Reichert.

"See?" Val said, pointing to one of the fields. "March eleventh, 1974. Or 31174."

"Shannon's birthdate. So?"

"The first time I met with Reichert about putting Shannon under surveillance, I went to his house. I arrived there at the same time he did. I remember three of the five numbers he punched to turn off his security system. Three, one, and one. All I needed were the last two."

"Surely Reichert isn't stupid enough to use something that obvious as a security code."

"Sure he is. People do it all the time. The most common things they use are birth dates and the last digits of their social security numbers."

"You're still only assuming—"

"It's a safe assumption. Believe me."

Val had a knowing look on her face that was starting to make Alex very nervous. He sat down on the edge of her bed and skewered her with a sharp stare. "Val? What are you planning on doing with that information?"

"Oh, I don't know." She shrugged. "I thought maybe I'd take a little stroll through his house, maybe look around for a certain rifle—"

"Are you *crazy*?"

"And I'll plant a bug, too. If he says anything incriminating, we'll nail him."

"No!" Alex said. "No way! Get that out of your head right now. That's breaking and entering!"

"Only if I'm caught."

Alex bowed his head, letting out a long breath. "All you have is the code for the security system. It won't get you past the locks."

"Like those would be hard to pick?"

Her cavalier attitude astonished him. "Do you realize you're talking about breaking into the house of a man who may have just tried to kill you? He's probably armed to the teeth in there. If he finds you in his house, he could blow your head clean off and be justified in doing it."

"It's not nearly as risky as it sounds. All I have to do is find a time when I know he won't be there."

"You'll be breaking the law!"

"If I find something that incriminates Reichert, nobody's going to care about that."

"And if you don't—"

"I will."

"No, damn it! You're not going within a mile of that house!"

Val narrowed her eyes. "Do you like the idea of prison, Alex? I hear cops get real good treatment in there."

"Forget it, Val."

"But Alex—"

"Good *God*!" he shouted. "You haven't changed one bit! You're still just as wild and reckless as you ever were! This is exactly the kind of crap that got you thrown out of the police academy!"

As soon as the words were out of his mouth, he regretted them, but he couldn't take them back now. Val's eyes slowly narrowed, her expression hot with anger.

"No, Alex. It's *you* who got me thrown out of the police academy."

He did not want to deal with this. "I had no choice. You know that."

"You had plenty of choices." She paused, looking at him pointedly. "About a lot of things."

He knew exactly what she was talking about, and he didn't want to touch that issue, either. "No matter what you think, the only reason I came to your apartment that night was to break the news to you. That's all."

"No. You came to my apartment that night because you wanted to get laid."

Alex felt a surge of anger. "I don't want to talk about this." He stood up quickly and headed for the door.

"Of course you don't," Val said. "Because it makes you sound like a colossal son of a bitch."

Alex stopped, then turned slowly back around. Val was staring up at him, wearing that fierce, defiant expression that made him absolutely crazy.

"If you'll remember," he said, his voice low and angry, "I tried to talk to you afterward. Tried to explain. But you wouldn't let me."

"Oh, yeah? And what would you have said? 'Sorry, babe, but if I'd told you what was coming down, you might not have put out last night'?"

"Damn it, Val! It wasn't like that!"

"Sure it was. The whole time we were together, you knew you were going to kick me out of the academy the next day!"

"It wasn't just me. There were other officers—"

"But your opinion was the deciding one. You made the difference. Once they knew you didn't approve of me—"

"Not of *you*! Of you as a police officer, and there's a big difference between the two. It just wasn't the right profession for you."

"Oh, yeah! You're so damned high and mighty, telling me what's good for me and what isn't! You could have given me a chance, Alex. Half a chance. Hell, I'd have settled for less than that!"

"I gave you more chances than you ever deserved," he said, jabbing his finger in the air. "You were a wild card. You wouldn't follow procedures. You always had a better way. And forget following orders. You thought the chain of command was a joke. How is an officer in the field supposed to trust somebody like you? Anyone who was depending on you to watch his back would have ended up with a bullet in it!"

Val glared at him. "I already know what you think of me. You made that quite clear the day you kicked me out."

"Then I guess we don't have much else to say to each other, do we?"

Alex went into the living room. He grabbed his socks and boots, sat down on the sofa, and pulled them on. She'd baited him. Baited him into losing his temper so she could continue to believe that he was exactly what she thought he was. Baited him into saying terrible things to her so she could go on hating him. And he wasn't going to take it anymore. He didn't need to stay here any longer. Now that she'd slept off the painkiller, as long as she was careful, she could take care of herself just fine.

As long as she was careful. Who was he kidding?

It didn't matter. She wasn't his problem. She clearly wanted him out of her life, and that was just where he wanted to be: out of her life.

He stood up. Turning, he saw Val standing at the doorway leading from the hall, probably gearing up to berate him all over again.

"Lock your door when I leave," he told her, "and keep a weapon handy. And for God's sake, whatever you do, don't go near Reichert's house."

She folded her arms over her chest. "I've survived quite nicely all these years without your advice, Alex. I expect I'll survive a few more."

This woman was never going to change. Never.

He put his hand on the doorknob, then stopped and turned back. "What happened that night was a mistake. I wish I could take it back, but I can't. You can think what you want to, but I never meant to hurt you."

She lifted her chin. "Then I'd hate to think what you could do to me if you really set your mind to it."

Alex yanked the door open and stepped into the hall, and only through a Herculean effort was he able to keep from slamming the door behind him.

He headed toward the stairs, anger rolling through him. Shannon Reichert had stood stark naked in front of him, offering him a body that was beyond belief, and still he hadn't had the least bit of trouble telling her no when he smelled trouble. So why was it that he hadn't been able to keep his hands off Val? Why was it that whenever he was around her he misplaced every bit of common sense he'd ever possessed? And why was it that she was so adept at getting under his skin even now? Hell, he couldn't remember ever spending more than an hour with her that they didn't end up in some kind of argument.

But despite his anger, when he reached the stairs, he stopped and turned back. Listened.

He heard Val's dead bolt click. Then the twist of the handle lock. And a second later, the rattle of the chain as she slid it into place. Of course, none of the three would be worth the metal they were made of if Reichert decided to come after her again, but still, it made him feel better to know they were there.

But why did he give a damn? She hated him for what had happened between them. It was going to stay that way from now on, and there was nothing he could do to change it.

Absolutely nothing.

chapter nine

Val collapsed on her sofa, still shaking with anger, but now that anger was punctuated with tears. *Tears.* She thought she'd cried her last tear over Alex DeMarco, but it looked as if she wasn't through yet.

Damn him.

It was a mistake, Val. That was how he characterized making love to her. A mistake.

I never meant to hurt you.

That was a lie. How could he think that she'd be anything but hurt when she found out what he'd kept from her?

She'd been so shocked to wake up that morning and find him gone. She'd searched her apartment for a note he might have left, or for some indication that he'd just stepped out for a moment and he'd be back. Nothing. When she tried to call him at his apartment, she got his answering machine.

She shrugged it off at first, telling herself he'd get in touch with her later in the day. But when noon came, then one o'clock, an ominous feeling crept through her. Something had made him leave before she woke, and she had a feeling she knew what it was.

Regret.

He was probably wishing that he'd never come to her apartment last night. He was probably thinking up ways to avoid her, because to him, it had been just sex and nothing more. She thought that was the most awful thing that could possibly happen.

The reality turned out to be much, much worse.

About two o'clock, she received a phone call from the lieutenant, asking her to come to his office. She couldn't imagine why he would want to see her, and her stomach was in knots all the way there. When she arrived, he motioned for her to enter the room.

And that was when she saw Alex.

He was sitting in a chair beside the lieutenant's desk, wearing a perfectly pressed suit, a starched shirt, and a silk tie. He looked official. Businesslike. And when she met his eyes, she saw nothing.

Absolutely nothing.

He seemed to stare right through her with an emotionless demeanor that was agonizing. In his gaze she saw not a hint of the heated passion or the desperate desire to make love to her that he'd shown the night before. Instead, his dark eyes were cold, his lips caught in a firm, unyielding line of detachment. Her stomach clenched with apprehension.

And then came the dismissal.

At first she wasn't certain she'd heard the lieutenant right, but glancing at Alex, seeing his stony stare, she knew she had.

We believe you'd be better suited to another profession. One with more flexibility. More latitude. One where you're not required to take orders from a superior officer.

We. As if anyone else's opinion had been needed once Alex had spoken.

Disregard for authority. Unconventional approaches to assignments. Refusal to follow procedure. It had all been in the report, signed and sealed. And with that, she was out. And through it all, Alex just sat there, his arms folded, saying nothing, staring at her as if she meant absolutely nothing to him. As if he hadn't come to her apartment the night before. As if they hadn't made love for hours.

He'd known. The entire time he'd been with her, he'd known what was going to happen. And he hadn't said a word.

The lieutenant started expressing his regret over the situation in one of those patronizing tones people use when they want to appear as if they have a heart but they really don't. Val wanted to scream. She turned midspeech and left his office, knowing she had to get out of there because tears were welling up in her eyes and she was *not* going to cry in front of Alex.

She ran out of the building, the heat of humiliation burning her cheeks, tears finally breaking through and cascading down her face. She reached her car, fumbled for her keys, dropped them on the ground. She tried to pick them up, but tears were clouding her eyes so badly that she couldn't even see to do it.

She finally located her keys. Stood. Tried to fit the key into her car door. Then she felt a hand on her shoulder. She whipped around to find Alex standing behind her.

"Val. I wanted to tell you last night, but—"

She slapped him. With every ounce of energy she had in her, she slapped him right across the face, her hand stinging with the effort. She doubted that anyone else on earth could have done that to Alex DeMarco and lived to tell about it. But he took it. And that made her even more furious.

She started to hit him again. He caught her wrist and just held her there, staring at her with the one thing she didn't want to see on anyone's face.

Pity.

She yanked her arm from his grasp. "How could you have done this to me? How could you have come to my apartment last night, knowing about this, and then—"

"Val, you don't understand. Just let me explain—"

"Don't ever come near me again!"

She fumbled her key into the lock and yanked the door open, desperate to get out of there, to put as many miles between her and Alex as possible.

She spent the next several hours in a daze, sure that her entire world had come to an end, feeling as if she wanted to crawl into a hole and pull the dirt in after her.

And that was remarkably how she felt right now.

No. Forget him. He means nothing to you. And you clearly mean nothing to him.

She had to get herself together. She might have forgotten momentarily what Alex was, but she certainly remembered now. He could hurt her only if she let him. And she wasn't going to let him.

Tomorrow was Monday. Under normal circumstances, she'd be going to her office, then heading off to do surveillance work on a couple of insurance-fraud cases she was working on. She hated to admit it, but she'd felt secure when she was with Alex. Now she didn't.

She took a deep, calming breath. All she had to do was

keep her eyes and her ears open. Refrain from walking in big, open areas. Stop taking elevators. Scan the area before she stepped out of her car.

Hide in the shadows and pray Reichert didn't try to shoot her again.

Then she got angry. Let Reichert come after her. If he did, he just might be surprised to find a gun in his face and a very pissed-off woman on the other end of it.

She didn't need anyone. Least of all Alex DeMarco.

Dave had held Brenda at bay all weekend, not yet prepared to deal with her special brand of input on Alex's situation. But now that it was Monday morning, he knew his hours were numbered.

He dropped Ashley off at Aunt Louisa's house so he could go to work, then headed back out to his car, hoping to make his escape before Brenda showed up.

No such luck.

He'd just swung his car door open when he saw Brenda's Hummer coming around the corner. She buzzed down the street and brought the vehicle to a halt in front of Aunt Louisa's house, deliberately blocking the driveway. Dave sighed. Unless he wanted to drive his car across the lawn and jump the curb, he was stuck.

Brenda leaped out of the Hummer along with her six-year-old daughter, Melanie, who also stayed with Aunt Louisa during her summer break from school. Melanie was a tiny blond girl with an angelic face and hair like spun gold, with a sweet little disposition that reminded him of Shirley Temple without all the mugging. That Brenda had actually given birth to her was something the family might have questioned if a few of them hadn't actually witnessed the event for themselves.

Melanie started to skip into the house, but Brenda stopped her on the driveway.

"Mellie, do you remember what I told you about watching TV?"

Melanie rolled her eyes. "Yes, Mama." She took a deep breath. "June Cleaver and Donna Reed are oppressed females in a male-dominated society who bear no resemblance to the modern women of today."

"And?"

"Mary Ann is a better role model than Ginger."

"And?"

"And *Xena: Warrior Princess* is on at three o'clock."

Brenda gave her a big smile and a kiss on the cheek. "Good girl. Now go on inside. I need to talk to Uncle Dave."

Melanie gave Dave a smile and a wave, then trotted off. Dave turned to Brenda. "Did I tell you I'm getting her an Easy-Bake oven for Christmas?"

"You do, and I'm getting Ashley a G.I. Joe. Complete with miniature Stinger missiles and a functional latrine."

Dave had no doubt that Brenda would make good on that threat, even if she had to commission Mattel to create a new toy just for her.

Brenda yanked off her sunglasses. "So what's going on with Alex?"

"I told you he wants you to stay out of this."

"Alex doesn't know shit about what's good for him right now. I know Henderson's being a pain in the ass. I can help with that."

"Brenda, your kind of help results in emergency room visits and prosthetic limbs."

"I'll be subtle. I swear."

"Like a bulldozer is subtle."

"Hey, I don't want to see Alex go down for this any more than you do! The worst he's ever done to a woman is not return her phone calls. I imagine he could drive one to suicide or something. But commit murder? Never."

In Brenda-speak, that was a huge show of support.

She continued to stare at Dave like an attack dog just waiting to be unsnapped from its leash. And surprisingly, the more Dave thought about it, the more he realized that she might be just the catalyst he needed to get Henderson to see things his way, especially since he'd be there to ensure that Brenda wouldn't get out of hand and bring a second homicide into the family. Henderson hated John and Alex. He was scared of Brenda.

Big difference.

A lot of people thought Brenda was mildly deranged, and Dave couldn't say he hadn't wondered that himself a time or two. But mostly she was merely gung-ho in a way that put George Patton to shame. Ex-military, she'd done a tour of duty during Desert Storm. She was happy they'd won the war, but terribly disappointed that she hadn't been able to personally gouge out Saddam Hussein's eyeballs.

"Okay, Brenda. Maybe I do need your help. Good cop, bad cop." He gave her a sly look. "Which one do you want to be?"

Brenda gave him that thin, calculating smile that always seeped onto her lips whenever she smelled blood. "Which one do you think?"

At nine o'clock, Val pulled her car into a parking space outside her office, a small storefront on Fourteenth Street. Looking through the window of the nail salon next door, she saw Darla getting ready to open up. Val noticed that she'd switched from being a blonde to being a redhead over the weekend, which wasn't a big surprise except for the fact that Darla was black. She always said that hair was no big deal. If you did something you hated, you could just shave your head and start all over again.

Val waved to Darla as she got out of her car, and then unlocked the door of her office and went inside. She stopped. Listened. She heard nothing, but did that mean somebody wasn't hiding in the bathroom, or in her small storage room in the back?

Damn it. She hated this. She wasn't going to be afraid. She wasn't. She fired up her computer, then hauled out a few files. An hour or so later, she'd started to relax, convincing herself that it was dumb to be scared. After all, what kind of idiot would murder somebody at their place of business in broad daylight, then expect that nobody would see him leave the scene of the crime?

She went to the bathroom. As she was coming out, she heard somebody on the sidewalk outside. Adrenaline surged through her.

She ran to her desk, yanked her drawer open, circled her hand around the weapon she kept there, and hauled it out— just in time to see Darla come through the door carrying a McDonald's sack in one hand and a newspaper in the other.

Val let out a silent breath of relief. She stuck the weapon

back in the drawer and managed to close it before Darla realized that she'd been only a few moments away from getting her head blown off. Her friend barging through her door about this time of morning was a commonplace event; yet Val had practically jumped out of her skin.

Darla turned and saw the gauze bandage on Val's temple, and her eyes widened.

"What happened to you?"

"It's nothing. I just scraped it on one of my kitchen cabinet doors."

"Pretty big bandage for a little scrape."

"It was the only size I had."

She eyed Val critically. "You okay? You're looking a little peaked."

"I'm fine."

"Uh-huh. And I'm Madonna."

"Really?" Val said, sitting back down in her chair. "You've got a new look, Madonna. I like it."

"Yeah, I gained twenty pounds, aged ten years, and turned black."

"The hair's nice."

"You like it?" Darla said, patting her newly tinted hair. "Melvin begged me to go back to red. Says it turns him on. Of course, he thinks I ought to dye *all* my hair red, if you know what I mean." She rolled her eyes. "There's only so much I'll do for fashion's sake."

"Or for Melvin's sake."

"Whatever."

Darla slapped the sack and the newspaper down on Val's desk. "Well, if something's ailing you, Mac here will fix you right up."

Give Darla a choice between five-star cuisine and Chicken McNuggets, and she'd pick the Chicken McNuggets every time.

Darla hauled the food out of the sack. "Egg McMuffin or sausage biscuit?"

Val's stomach was still in knots, and she didn't think she could eat a thing.

"Egg McMuffin."

Darla handed her the Egg McMuffin, then sat down in the

chair beside Val's desk and opened up the sausage biscuit for herself. Then she flipped open the newspaper. Glancing across her desk, Val saw yet another story about Shannon's murder, and she hoped her friend would pass right over it.

"Oooh, look at that," Darla said. "Another story about that rich woman's murder."

No such luck.

"Did you read about it?" Darla asked.

"Yeah. I read about it."

"It really was something. Strangulation. A sex thing. And a cop as a suspect, of all people." Darla raised an eyebrow. "So what do you think? Did he do it?"

On most days, Val didn't mind Darla's constant chatter, her excessive gossiping and her endless questions, because basically she was good at heart. Today, though, she really wished Darla would go back to sculpting nails, particularly when the questions she was asking were about Alex.

"I have no idea," Val said.

"Well, I'm betting he's guilty. I mean, who else would have done it? He was right there."

Val opened up the Egg McMuffin and took a bite. Chewed. Swallowed. Barely.

"It says right here that the dead woman was only twenty-eight. Her husband was fifty-four." She made a scoffing noise. "What some women won't do to get their hands on a hefty bank account. I guess he's really rich, huh?"

"They say he has a dollar or two."

"Says here they're burying her at ten o'clock tomorrow morning. Resthaven Memorial Garden—that ritzy cemetery on the north side. Shoot, her husband's probably spending more to put her in the ground than I make in a year. You know, buying her one of those classy marble headstones, or maybe even a mausoleum vault. And don't you know that every flower shop in town is bought out? And here I got my birthday coming up tomorrow." She shook her head with disgust. "Now Melvin will have an excuse not to bring me flowers. I can hear him now: 'I woulda brought you three dozen roses, Darla, sweetie, but there was that rich woman's funeral. Not a flower was left in the city.'"

The progression of Darla's thought process had always

amazed Val. Let her go long enough, and she'd turn a discussion of *Sesame Street* into a diatribe on nuclear war.

Val pictured Reichert at that funeral, crying over his dead wife, as if he hadn't been the one to put that belt around her neck. That infuriated Val. The only good thing about his presence there was that she'd have at least a couple of hours when she wouldn't have to worry about him pointing a gun at her.

Wait a minute. A couple of hours? When he wouldn't be at home?

"When did you say the funeral is?" she asked Darla.

"Ten o'clock tomorrow morning."

"At Resthaven?"

"Yeah."

If Reichert wasn't guilty, he would be saying good-bye to his dead wife. If he was, he'd want people to *think* that was what he was doing. Either way, he'd be there.

And Val would be at his house.

She'd disarm the security system, then pick the lock. Then she'd look for the kind of rifle that matched that bullet, and if she couldn't find it, she'd scour the house for evidence that Henderson hadn't bothered to search for, some other tangible indication that maybe Reichert had a motive to kill his wife in addition to the fact that she was cheating on him. Financial records reflecting large amounts of money being moved for some reason. Recent insurance policies. Something. Anything. And if she found some evidence, at least she'd know for sure Reichert was the culprit, and then she could come up with a creative way to take him down. And even if she found no evidence, at the very least she could bug the house. Sooner or later he'd say something incriminating, and she'd nail him.

Wait a minute. Dave was going to talk to Henderson sometime tomorrow. Should she wait to see what he found out about getting a search warrant?

No. She couldn't wait. Shannon was going to have only one funeral. Val knew she wouldn't get this chance again. She had to strike now while the case was still fresh and Reichert would be certain to be out of the house.

She decided she'd swing by the cemetery around ten o'clock tomorrow morning, spot Reichert's car just to verify that he was there, then make her way over to his house.

"Uh-oh," Darla said. "You've got that look on your face."

"What look?"

"The same one you had when that weird guy you dated once kept coming by your office. The pushy one. You got that look when you were thinking about how to get rid of him."

Val grinned. "It worked, didn't it?"

"Oh, yeah. Of course, now he thinks you're a CIA operative who kills people for a living. So what is that devious little mind of yours up to now?"

"Just a little business I have to take care of."

"I pity the poor soul who's gonna be the recipient of that business."

"Now, Darla," Val said with a smile, "I think I resent that."

"No way, honey. You're my hero. Most women put up with way too much crap, me included. But not you."

Damn right, Val thought. She wasn't about to sit around waiting for something else to happen. She was going to make something happen. She didn't care what Alex had said about breaking into Reichert's house. He wasn't the one walking around with a bull's-eye on the back of his head, just waiting for Reichert to take another shot at him.

But he *was* the one who'd be going to prison if the real murderer wasn't found.

There had been many times in her short career as a private investigator when she'd bent the law, when she'd gotten information she wasn't entitled to, using means that were a little underhanded, when she'd misled people into believing one thing when the reality was something else entirely. But she'd never actually broken the law. Then again, she'd never faced a situation where, if she didn't, she herself was in danger. And even now, in spite of everything, the last thing she wanted was for Alex to go to prison for a crime he didn't commit.

Then she thought about how she'd lashed out at him yesterday, tossing all those old accusations in his face.

Think what you want to, but I never meant to hurt you.

His words had whirled around in her mind since yesterday, nagging at her, making her feel a little less righteous in the resentment she felt toward him. A part of her wanted to go on hating him forever, while another part wanted to believe that there was a way for them, after all this time, to finally reach an understanding.

And maybe more.

What's the matter with you? How can you still have feelings for that man? How?

Because when she thought about how he'd brought her home from the hospital, watched over her and tried to make sure she was safe, she wasn't completely certain he was the rotten person she'd made him out to be, no matter what he'd done to her in the past.

Breaking into that house was a risk. A big one. Even though she'd suggested it offhandedly to Alex, she wasn't stupid enough to believe that there weren't dangers involved. It might be the only way to save herself from another one of Reichert's sniper shots, but she wasn't certain she'd chance doing it for herself alone.

For both of them, she would.

On Tuesday morning, Alex sat in the living room of his apartment, surrounded by silence. He checked his watch for approximately the hundredth time that morning. It was ten minutes after ten—exactly four minutes later than the last time he looked.

Why did he even bother? Time wasn't going to move any faster than it already was, which was at a snail's pace. But then again, what difference did it make? He had absolutely nowhere to go. If this had been any other Tuesday, he'd have been at work by now. But not today. And maybe never again.

If Monday had been excruciatingly boring, Tuesday was turning out to be even worse. What did people who didn't have jobs do all day? Stare at the four walls? Wear their fingers down to the knuckle hitting the buttons on the remote control? What kind of a life was that?

Doing nothing gave a man way too much time to think. To reflect. To worry. To dwell on things that were better left untouched. Like what had happened with Val.

Yes, there were kernels of truth in all the accusations Val had made. He'd known what was going to happen the next day, and still he'd slept with her. It didn't take a genius to figure out that she was going to hate him for it.

But there had been more to it than that. Exactly what, he wasn't sure. All he knew was that his motives were nothing like Val had alleged. If he'd just been looking to get laid, he could have found a hundred other women to be with that night who wouldn't have hated him in the morning.

That night, at that moment, it had to be Val. But how in the world could he ever make her understand that, particularly when he didn't completely understand it himself?

It was time he stopped trying to understand. Every time in his life when he'd gotten within shouting distance of her, something negative came of it. And right now, considering he was facing a murder charge, more negative was something he could really do without.

If he were convicted of Shannon's murder, he'd serve time. If he survived that, he'd be back out on the street. Jobless, because a felony conviction meant he'd never work as a police officer again. What would he do for a living? Just applying for a job with a record like that would be a nightmare.

He thought about how Dave was going to talk to Henderson this morning. Maybe his brother could make him reconsider the warrant.

Maybe pigs would fly.

For lack of anything better to do, Alex flipped on the TV and ran the dial. A cooking show. An infomercial for a weight-loss product. Some crappy talk show full of degenerates talking trash to each other. A moldy old sitcom. He flipped the TV off and tossed the control to the sofa beside him.

He picked up the newspaper from the coffee table, thumbed through it, then wished he hadn't. Unfortunately, certain reporters thought Shannon's murder deserved daily coverage even though absolutely nothing new had happened. The press was treating this as an open-and-shut case, and since he was a cop, they were doing it with as much sensationalism as possible. People loved that kind of thing. A cop goes bad, has wild, kinky sex, commits murder. Alex scanned the article and found out that he was right. There was nothing new, except the fact that Shannon's funeral was today.

Alex froze. Funeral?

For a full ten seconds, he stared at the words on the page,

the implication of them coming to him in bits and pieces. Funeral. Ten o'clock. Resthaven Memorial Gardens.

Reichert would be there.

All I have to do is find a time when I know he won't be there. . . .

Alex checked his watch. It was almost ten-fifteen.

He tossed down the newspaper, yanked up his cordless phone, and dialed Val's number. The phone rang three times, four, five. She didn't answer.

She was probably just in the shower. He told himself he'd call her back in five minutes. Three minutes later he tried again. No answer.

He called directory assistance and got her office number. Three rings, voice mail.

He laid the phone back down. Okay. He had to get a grip here. She'd just been talking big. Surely she wouldn't be stupid enough to break into Reichert's house. For about fifteen seconds, he talked himself into that possibility, only to talk himself right back out of it again.

He jumped up from the sofa and grabbed a gun, ignoring the fact that he no longer had a license to carry it. He snagged his car keys and tore out of his apartment. As he got into his car, he glanced around quickly to see if any holdouts from the press were still dogging him. When he saw no one, he decided that they'd given up camping on his doorstep and had gone on to bother somebody else. He got into his car and started the engine, then stopped for a moment, letting it idle.

He shouldn't be doing this. Val wasn't his problem. He'd told her not to do it, so if she got caught breaking in, it was her own damned fault and she'd have to pay the price for it.

Then he pictured Reichert coming home early. Picking up a rifle. And this time hitting his mark.

Alex jammed his SUV into gear, pulled out of the parking lot, and headed for the Reichert house, hoping that Val wasn't in the process of doing the stupidest thing imaginable.

Who was he kidding? Of course she was. He only hoped he could get there in time to stop her.

Ten minutes later he was rounding the corner onto Augusta Drive. He looked up the street and didn't see her van. Then he swung around the end of the block and headed down the alley, holding out hope that she wasn't as insane as he'd thought.

She was.

Her van rested on the shoulder of the alley drive two doors down from the Reichert house. He swung around it, then pulled up directly behind the Reichert's backyard. A wood fence prohibited him from seeing the back of the house.

Leaving his engine running, he rolled down the window and surveyed the area. *Damn.* Why hadn't he anticipated this? Why hadn't he stayed one step ahead of her, knowing she'd strike during the funeral?

Because staying one step ahead of Valerie Parker was a full-time job and then some. And because it wasn't his job in the first place.

Reichert had murdered once. He probably wouldn't hesitate to do it again. Only this time he'd have cause to do it— she was an intruder in his house. He wouldn't have to justify it. Wouldn't have to pay for it. Shannon was dead. Val would be dead, too, and he'd be able to walk away from both crimes.

Alex wanted to go in there and drag her out of that house by her hair, then slap her senseless for even thinking of breaking in. But he couldn't. The last thing he needed to do was get caught inside the house of the woman he supposedly murdered. He'd just have to sit here and hope that she came out of the house before Reichert went in.

And then, faintly but distinctly, from inside the Reichert house, he heard a woman scream.

chapter ten

Alex flung his car into park and killed the engine. He leaped out, sure that the worst had happened, just as he'd feared. Reichert had found Val. He'd caught her in there. He had her cornered in his house, and God only knew what he planned to do with her now.

Alex ran up to the gate leading to the backyard and found it locked. He leaped up, grabbed the top of the fence, and pulled himself over. He hit the ground on the other side at the same moment another scream came from inside the house.

He raced around the swimming pool, leaped over a low hedge, and ran up to the plate-glass patio door. He yanked on it and found it locked. He spun around, picked up a clay pot full of red geraniums, and hurled it through door. The glass shattered, flying in a wild spray in all directions. He kicked the remaining shards away from the frame and stepped through the scattered soil and smashed flowers into the house, his gun drawn.

More screams.

"Val!" he shouted. "Val, where are you?"

When she didn't answer, fear raced through him. If Reichert had hurt Val, he'd kill him. He'd drop him right where he stood and not think twice about it.

Just then a woman came around the door from the kitchen, a short, stout Hispanic woman with a cordless phone pressed to her ear. She took one look at him and screamed.

What the hell. . . ?

"Alex!"

He spun around to see Val standing at the doorway between the hall and family room. In a rush of understanding, he knew what he'd walked into, and it wasn't good. The screams hadn't been from Val.

The screams had been *because* of Val.

The woman chattered wildly into the phone in Spanish, her eyes wide with fear. Alex couldn't understand a thing she was saying, but he got the gist of it in a hurry. She was probably Reichert's housekeeper. And she was calling 911.

He just stood there, absolutely dumbfounded. What in the hell was he supposed to do now?

Val rushed to his side. "Come on. We have to get out of here!"

She grabbed him by the arm and pulled him toward the patio door, dirt from the flowerpot and broken glass crunching beneath their feet. Alex could hear the woman still prattling on to the 911 operator in a wild flurry of Spanish, which meant they were only minutes away from having the entire Tolosa police force at the door.

He stopped and looked back. Val yanked on his arm. "Alex! Let's go!"

He stepped through the broken patio door behind Val. She started around the swimming pool. He caught her arm and spun her back around.

"Wait! We can't run away from this!"

"What?"

"We have to stay. Explain what happened."

"Explain? Are you out of your mind? Your explanation will include the fact that I broke into that house!"

"That's *your* problem, not mine!"

Val swept her windblown hair away from her face. "Listen to me, Alex. The last time you hung around and tried to *explain*, you got arrested for murder. If they find you here now, you'll be thrown right back in jail until your trial and have no chance of proving that Reichert is guilty. Is that what you want?"

"Did you find something in the house to nail him?"

"Maybe. Eventually. But nothing we can hand the cops right now. We have to go!"

He looked back at the house. He shouldn't have any reason to run. All he'd been trying to do was save Val from being a victim. But would anybody believe that?

Hell, no.

He'd never be able to come up with an explanation for why he'd hurled a flowerpot through that glass door and entered Reichert's house. Nobody would believe that he thought Val was in danger, because nobody thought Reichert was a threat in the first place.

Sirens wailed in the distance.

"Alex! Let's get out of here! *Now!*"

In a split second, a series of images flashed through his mind. Henderson's face, leering at him, secretly thrilled to be able to throw him in jail again. The cold faces of the jury members, turning the mountain of evidence against him into a guilty verdict. Prison walls surrounding him, closing in so tightly that he couldn't breathe. And the second they snapped cuffs on him again, prison was exactly where he was going to end up.

"Get in your van," he told Val. "Meet me at the abandoned drive-in movie theater just off Highway Four. Don't speed or run any lights, or you'll get picked up for sure. Now *move!*"

He gave her a leg up and over the fence, then climbed over it himself. Val took off toward her van. Alex got in his car. He started the engine and drove down the alley, then turned onto the street. The sirens grew louder. He went the opposite direction.

He clasped the steering wheel so tightly his knuckles whitened. For one of the few times in his life, he felt truly angry. Not just pissed off, or annoyed, or even infuriated. He felt a soul-deep anger reserved for only the most monumental of injustices. First he'd been arrested for murder when all he'd done was try to save the victim's life. And now, because he'd tried to save Val, he'd ended up getting burned again.

Hell, not burned. Incinerated.

And as of right now, he had absolutely no idea how to put out the fire.

It was almost ten-thirty before Dave and Brenda managed to locate Henderson. He was taking his usual hour-long morning break at a diner near the station, eating a doughnut.

Make that four doughnuts.

When they came into the diner, Henderson's gaze snapped

up. He looked at Dave questioningly. He looked at Brenda as if he wished he were wearing riot gear. They sat down next to him at the table.

Henderson looked at them warily. "What do you two want?"

Dave struck a nonchalant pose. "We want to talk to you about Alex."

"Nothing to talk about."

"Sure there is. He's been accused of murder."

"Look, Dave. I know it's hard to swallow that your brother did something like this. The odds were that sooner or later one of the many women he seems to attract would get a little kinky and things would get out of hand." He shrugged and took another bite of doughnut. "It happens."

"I don't know, Henderson. All that kinky stuff doesn't sound like Alex to me."

"Men do a lot of stupid things to get laid. You think he's exempt?"

"Oh, give me a break," Brenda said. "You think a guy like Alex has to work to find a willing woman?"

"Maybe he was losing his touch."

"Maybe you'd like to lose a few teeth."

Henderson turned to Dave. "You want to tell her to shut up?"

"Actually," Dave said, "I've been doing a lot of thinking. If you find out who shot Valerie Parker, I bet you'll find out who killed Shannon Reichert. And I'm betting that person just might be her husband."

"Yeah, Ford was yapping about that, too. Sorry. Don't see the connection. People are shot in this town every day."

"With a high-powered hunting rifle?" Brenda said. "Put two and two together, will you? Or is simple math out of the question?"

Dave gave Brenda a warning stare. She huffed with disgust and looked away.

"She's a PI," Henderson said. "Have you ever known one of those not to piss somebody off eventually? I bet she's got a dozen people right now who'd like to blow her away."

"A woman was murdered," Brenda said. "Valerie Parker was watching the house at the time. Connect the dots, you moron!"

Dave looked at Brenda admonishingly. "Brenda? Let's have a calm, rational discussion here, okay?" He turned back to Henderson. "Reichert knew his wife was cheating on him. There's your motive."

"He says he wasn't even in town."

"Can he prove that?"

"He doesn't need to. He's not a suspect."

Nothing like a circular argument to really make a case, Dave thought.

"All I'm asking you to do is get a warrant," Dave said. "If you don't find a rifle that matches that bullet, we can all cross Reichert off our lists."

"He was never on my list."

"Hey!" Brenda said, rising from her chair. "Get the damned warrant!"

Dave put a hand against Brenda's shoulder and pushed her back down. She folded her arms across her chest, fuming silently.

"Sorry, Henderson. Brenda's just a little upset. Alex is family. You understand."

Henderson's gaze shifted nervously to Brenda, as if he expected her to leap up and bite the head right off his shoulders. "Yeah. Right."

"There's more. When Reichert hired Valerie Parker to tail his wife, she offered to set up a video camera in the Reicherts' bedroom just in case Shannon brought a man home with her. Reichert refused. Just present that fact to the judge along with everything else, and let him make up his mind about probable cause."

"I told you I'm not going after a warrant. Now the two of you get out of here!"

Moving with the stealth of a cobra, Brenda rose from her chair. She leaned forward, placing both palms on the table in front of Henderson and skewering him with a deadly stare.

"Dave," Henderson said a little nervously. "Tell her to get out of my face."

Dave leaned away and held his palms out helplessly, as if he'd tried his best but the matter was now entirely out of his hands.

Henderson shoved his chair away from the table and stood up. "If the two of you don't clear out of here, I'm going to—"

"What?" Brenda said. "What are you going to do? Call the cops? We *are* the cops!"

"I don't have to put up with this!"

Brenda leaned in again. "Yeah, I think you do. And do you know why?"

"Why?"

"Because I happen to know that it wasn't just Botstein involved in that New Year's Eve incident a few years ago."

Henderson froze, his eyes widening. "I don't know what you're talking about."

"Sure you do, you degenerate. The one with the hooker and the Doberman."

Every ounce of blood seemed to drain from Henderson's face. "Shit." He wiped his hand over his mouth, glaring at Dave. "It was that brother of yours, wasn't it? John couldn't keep his big mouth shut!"

"You know, I think I do recall hearing something about that," Dave said. "Interesting story. It's been filed away in the DeMarco Family Blackmail Repository for quite some time now. And damned if it didn't come in handy."

"You wouldn't say anything about that to the chief. You wouldn't—"

"Try me."

Sweat popped out on Henderson's forehead, those dark, birdlike eyes of his shifting back and forth.

"I always liked you, Dave. You know? Your brothers can be such bastards sometimes, but not you. And now you go and give me shit like this."

"You mess with one of us, you mess with all of us. Don't you *ever* forget that."

"Come on! You know that the judge will never buy the warrant! The guy supposedly wasn't even in town. And what's his motive for shooting at Valerie Parker, anyway? He hired her to follow his wife. Do you hire somebody to watch a person you intend to kill? The judge will laugh in my face."

"Do it anyway."

Dave grew hopeful at the sight of Henderson standing between a rock and a hard place. He knew the guy was only a few seconds away from giving in, because even though he was a degenerate, he really didn't want the whole world *knowing* he was a degenerate.

Henderson's cell phone rang. He yanked it off his belt. After a few moments of cryptic conversation, his expression slowly shifted.

He hung up the phone, then sat back down in his chair. "Well. Looks like a search warrant is pretty much out of the question now."

"Oh, yeah?" Brenda said. "And why is that?"

"Because Alex just took an unauthorized tour of the Reichert house."

Dave felt a stab of foreboding. "What?"

"The housekeeper caught him breaking and entering. He and Valerie Parker. They were in there together. Kind of interesting, don't you think?"

"That's impossible. Alex would never have—"

"Don't tell me what he never would have done! Not when I've got an eyewitness who says he broke into that house!"

"Come on! That makes no sense! Would he be stupid enough to get caught inside the house of the woman he supposedly murdered?"

"Maybe he left something behind the night of the murder that he needs to retrieve," Henderson said. "Ever thought about that?"

Brenda sneered. "Or maybe he's looking for the rifle you won't get a search warrant for!"

Dave could tell Henderson was trying to keep from smiling, but it was clearly a hard-won battle. Good thing he was keeping it in check, though. Brenda was skewering him with those bulletlike eyes of hers in a way that said that if his mouth so much as turned up a single millimeter, she was going to gnaw right through his jugular.

"I don't give a shit what they were looking for," Henderson said. "They were in there. I don't know any judge who's likely to consider the husband a stronger suspect than your brother in light of that."

"Where is Alex now?" Dave asked.

"He seems to have fled the scene," Henderson said. "Really racking up those charges, isn't he?"

That sarcastic little smile finally made its way to Henderson's lips, and Brenda started toward him. He recoiled, and Dave managed to grab her arm and yank her back before she actually made bodily contact.

"There's more to this than meets the eye," Dave told Henderson, as he dragged Brenda toward the door. "And you'd better not stop until you find out what it is."

"Is that a threat, DeMarco? I mean, you could go to the chief with whatever you've got on me, but what's the point?" He held out his palms. "My hands are tied."

He sat back with a self-satisfied smirk, and Dave decided his advice earlier to Alex had been extremely faulty. He'd like nothing more at this moment than to see his brother beat the crap out of Henderson and leave nothing but a pile of broken bones behind.

He pulled Brenda out to the sidewalk in front of the diner.

"Smug little bastard," Brenda muttered. "I ought to knock every one of those tobacco-stained teeth right down his throat. I can do it, too. One doubled-up fist in just the right place—"

"Forget him. He's not going to be able to help us."

"Wonder how he'd look with his nose shoved up into his sinus cavity?"

"We had him. He was going to get the warrant, or at least try. Damn it! I told Alex I'd talk to Henderson. So what was he doing in that house?"

"Maybe I could perform a little sadistic dentistry," Brenda mused. "Like in *Marathon Man*. A highly underrated movie, in my opinion."

"I've got to talk to Alex. Find out what's going on."

"Or maybe I'll just rip out his tongue. I read once in *Soldier of Fortune*—"

"Brenda! Will you spare me the bodily torture fantasies for just a minute?"

Brenda sighed. "Well, Alex is in deep shit now, no matter what the answers to all those questions are."

She was right. And there was nothing they could do now. All they could do was wait until Alex surfaced again, and hope to hell he had some kind of an explanation for all this that might keep him out of jail.

"By the way," Dave said, "what was the deal with the hooker and the Doberman? I must have missed that one."

"Ask John to tell you about it. He can do the sound effects."

Oh, that sounded entertaining. He'd be sure to bring it up at the next family lunch.

"Something else is going on here," Brenda said. "There must be a reason Alex broke into that house."

Maybe, but Dave couldn't imagine what that might be. He had a feeling that as of right now, there wasn't a thing he could do to help Alex. He was on his own.

Alex pulled into the abandoned drive-in theater, the tires of his SUV crunching against the gravel drive. He wheeled around behind the boarded-up concession stand and got out, trying to keep his cool. Val had done a lot of really stupid things since he'd known her, but this one topped them all.

With every moment that passed, his situation grew more dire. He'd committed a crime. Then *left* the scene of the crime. Throw all that on top of a murder accusation, and he was really sitting pretty.

And where the hell was Val, anyway?

A few minutes later he saw her van in the distance. She pulled into the drive-in. She got out of her car tentatively, as if she thought he just might snap her right in two. *Good.* It was about time she was afraid of something, and it didn't bother him in the least to have that something be him.

She held up her palm. "Look, Alex. Before you start in on me, I had nothing to do with your ending up in that house. That was your doing."

"I heard screams, Val! I thought it was you! What was I supposed to do? Just sit out there and let Reichert have at you?"

"That's what you thought was happening?"

"Yes!"

"You came in to save me?"

"Yes!"

"Well, that was stupid as hell."

"What?"

"For future reference, let me assure you that I can take care of myself. The last thing you needed to do was get caught breaking into the house of the woman you supposedly murdered."

Alex looked at her with total disbelief. "Would you tell me how I got to be the stupid one in this scenario? You should be thanking me for trying to keep you from getting your head blown off!"

"Either way, we're sunk now. The housekeeper knows who both of us are, and she was quick to fill the nine-one-one operator in on that fact."

"How do you know that?"

"Because she was screaming into the phone that the man who killed Mrs. Reichert had broken into their house."

"You understood what she was saying?"

"I speak Spanish. Enough, anyway. My mother was Mexican."

"Oh, that's just great."

"Don't you want to know what I found in the house?"

Alex took a deep breath and expelled it slowly. "Is it something that's going to get us out of this mess?"

"Not exactly. Not yet, anyway."

"I assume it wasn't the rifle, then."

"No. The man has a good-sized arsenal, but none of his rifles were in the Remington seven-hundred series. A search warrant wouldn't have helped us. And I was interrupted before I could get a bug planted. Not that it would have done us any good, anyway, since my receiver has to be within three hundred meters to pick anything up. I doubt we'll be getting that close to the Reichert house again."

"Then what *did* you accomplish?"

"I played back his answering machine messages. There was one dated this morning at nine-thirty. To Reichert. From a woman named Angela."

"Who was she?"

"I don't know. She was calling from his ranch."

"Ranch?"

"He has a ranch in southwest Texas, about thirty miles outside a little town called Tinsdale. It's northwest of San Antonio, not far from the Mexican border. This woman told him that everything would be ready at the ranch by the time he got there tomorrow morning."

"Ready for what?"

"She said that all eighteen guests had confirmed and would be arriving for the hunt tomorrow morning, and that she'd be sure that the barbecue was set up for the party tomorrow night."

"Hunt? What kind of hunt?"

"I went through Reichert's files. Get this." She opened the door to her van and dug through a backpack on the front seat. She handed Alex a brochure, and after looking over it, he saw that Reichert had quite a profitable business going. For a rather staggering fee, a hunter could come to Reichert's ranch and be guaranteed to shoot the animal of his choice. And what a choice Reichert offered him.

Wildebeest. Water buffalo. A dozen different kinds of exotic deer and antelope. And whatever Reichert didn't have, he assured his clients he could get it, whether or not it was indigenous to Texas or even to the United States. If they had the money, he had the means to bring in any animal a man wanted to shoot.

"Kind of turns your stomach, doesn't it?" Val said. "Do you know if it's legal?"

"It's legal, at least in the state of Texas. It's called canned hunting. I was involved in a murder case years ago that touched on it. Reichert can bring in almost any animal he wants to."

"But where does he get them?"

"Probably from zoos."

"Zoos? He steals them?"

"Nope. They sell them. It's a good source of income for some zoos. Of course, the ones who do it would prefer the public didn't know about it."

"Yeah. I can see why."

"The only animals he can't legally use are big cats. But if he can find a way to get a rhinoceros out there, it's within the bounds of the law."

Val grimaced. "That's really sickening."

Alex had to agree with that sentiment. Hunting had never been his thing, even fair hunting. He couldn't fathom what kind of man would get his kicks by shooting a penned-up animal.

"She also told Reichert that the girls would be there at nine o'clock."

"Girls?"

"Entertainment, evidently. She said that Lorena was sending over at least a dozen. What do you think? Dancers?"

"Maybe more. I bet Reichert knows how to show his guests a *really* good time."

"This man is getting more disgusting by the minute."

"What else did the woman say on the phone message?" Alex asked.

"She asked him to call her when he got home from the funeral." Val raised an eyebrow. "And get this. She said, 'I know you had to go to the funeral to make it look good. But by the time you hear this message, it'll all be over with.' And then she said she was *dying* to see him, and to please get out there as quickly as he could."

" 'Make it look good.' Do you think she was in on the murder?"

"I think she at least knows that he did it. And it's pretty clear that Shannon wasn't the only one in that marriage who was cheating."

"So Reichert didn't kill Shannon because she was sleeping with other men," Alex said. "He wanted her out of the way so he could have another woman."

"And maybe she knew he was having an affair and was going to take him to the cleaners in a divorce."

"Then why would he want to take out the man she was cheating with if it wasn't revenge?"

"Because he was a handy person to take the fall no matter what."

Alex felt a prickly sensation on the back of his neck, as if they'd suddenly taken a quantum leap closer to the truth.

"And I had another thought," Val said. "It would be a little dangerous for Reichert to move all those wild animals around. Do you suppose there would be occasions when he'd want to sedate them?"

"Probably."

"You were shot with a drug that they couldn't identify on standard tests. Could it have been an animal tranquilizer?"

Alex considered that for a moment and realized that it made perfect sense. "That could explain a lot."

"Maybe it wasn't a needle after all," Val went on. "Maybe it was a dart gun. Suppose Reichert hid and waited for Shannon to bring a man home. Then he used a dart gun to hit you with an animal tranquilizer. You passed out, and he killed Shannon. Then you took the fall."

A dart gun. That explained how Shannon could appear to be the only one in the vicinity when he was shot.

"I think we're on to something, Alex. Something we can actually pursue."

"Pursue?"

"We need to get out to that ranch."

Alex closed his eyes, willing himself to remain calm. "You didn't cause enough trouble here? You want to go out to his ranch and cause some more?"

"Hey! If I hadn't broken into his house, we wouldn't know all this stuff. So I think it's about time you shut up about how stupid it was and admit that it was the only way to get us something we could use."

"So the end justifies the means?"

"Hell, yes! When it's the only way to find the truth!"

"And if we can't eventually pin the murder on Reichert, I'll end up with another charge against me!"

"And if we *do* manage to pin it on him, you get to stay out of prison, and I get to go on living!"

Alex ran a hand through his hair, his jaw tight with frustration. He hated this, mostly because Val was starting to make sense.

"So what do you propose we do if we go to the Reichert ranch?"

"Bug the house. Hope he says something incriminating. Personally, I think the woman he's screwing is in on the murder, or at least knows he did it. No telling what the two of them might say when they're four hundred miles away from Tolosa and they think nobody could possibly be listening."

"How do you propose we get into the house to plant a bug?"

"We'll have to figure that out when we get there."

As much as Alex hated to admit it, Val was right. At least

now they had something to go on. And staying in Tolosa meant that sooner or later he'd end up in jail, and that was a place he vowed he'd never go to again.

"Reichert isn't due to be there until tomorrow morning," Val went on. "If we leave now, we can beat him there. With luck, it'll be just this woman in the house and maybe only a couple of other people. Then we can find a way to get inside."

Alex couldn't believe what had happened in the past two days. He swore to himself that he'd have nothing more to do with this woman. Now he was seriously considering taking a four-hundred-mile road trip with her to break into yet one more house. Was he crazy?

Unfortunately, it appeared that the answer was yes.

"Okay, Val. Here's the deal. From here on out, I'm calling the shots. Every damned one of them. If I tell you to do something, you do it, no questions asked. I don't want you to so much as sneeze without asking my permission. Do you understand?"

He didn't even bother to wait for her answer, because he knew any yes she gave him today could easily turn into a no tomorrow. Warnings were pointless with Val, but it made him feel better that at least he'd issued one.

He strode over to his car and opened the door. He grabbed his sunglasses and his cell phone, then opened his glove compartment to get a Texas map. He shut the car door and locked it.

"I'm leaving my car here. It can't be seen from the road, so I doubt anyone will find it. But it doesn't matter even if they do, because we'll be long gone. How well equipped is your van?"

"I've got surveillance equipment, cameras, flashlights, binoculars. Transmitters, receivers. All kinds of bugs. A costume or two when I need to go undercover. You name it, I've got it."

"Weapons?"

"Two. One on me and one in the van."

"Give me your keys."

She did.

"Get in the van."

"You're driving?"

"Don't argue."

They both got in the van. Alex started the engine.

"I guess this means we're going to Reichert's ranch," Val said.

"Yes. And it's a crapshoot. Before it's all over with, we could both end up a hell of a lot worse off than we are right now."

"But we could also pull it off and walk away. Knowing what we know about Reichert, the odds look pretty good to me."

Alex had never been a gambler. Never had any desire to fly to Vegas, join a poker game, or even buy a lottery ticket. Questionable outcomes made him tense. Edgy. He'd spent his whole life trying to reduce risk rather than asking for more.

He started the engine. "Ever been to Vegas?"

"What?"

"Vegas. Ever been there?"

"Sure. Hasn't everybody?"

"Ever play poker?"

"I like blackjack."

"The jackpot in the Texas state lottery is fourteen million this week. How many lottery tickets did you buy?"

"Only one for the big jackpot. But I won twenty bucks on a two-dollar scratch-off ticket."

He just stared at her, shaking his head in disbelief.

"What?"

Alex put the van in gear, wheeled it around in a one-eighty, and headed out of the drive-in. He'd vowed that he would do anything to stay out of prison. He'd just had no idea it would be something like this.

chapter eleven

It was early afternoon in the town of Tinsdale, Texas, where the sun beat down on Cedar Street with the intensity of a blowtorch. The pavement was hot enough to melt shoe leather if a person were to linger too long, and anyone who ventured out without the proper precautions was subject to a heavy-duty case of heatstroke. But even the fires of hell couldn't deter Deputy Stanley Obermeyer from his appointed rounds.

On the sidewalk outside the sheriff's office, he took a deep breath and tugged on his belt, adjusting his weapon on his hip. Then he touched the brim of his Stetson, cocking it downward until it dipped along his forehead at just the right angle. He pulled his mirrored shades from his pocket and slid them on.

Yeah. It felt just right. He was definitely looking *good*.

He started down the sidewalk of Cedar Street, the main drag of Tinsdale, a town so small that it occupied only a faint dot in the southwest portion of the map of the great state of Texas. But size wasn't everything. He told himself that looks were deceiving, that anything could happen at any time, so he had to stay on his toes. A bank robbery. An assault. A murder, even.

At least he hoped for one of those someday.

He patrolled this dinky little town, all the while wishing it were New York or L.A. or Chicago. He'd always dreamed of working the mean streets, where murder happened as often as petty theft everywhere else. A place where cops spent their days and nights chasing down the bad guys, then went for a beer afterward and swapped stories.

That was being a police officer. Handing out parking citations and chasing down stray dogs wasn't.

He lengthened his stride, hoping he looked like a man on a mission, a man with places to be, a man who was charged with keeping Tinsdale, Texas, safe from the bad guys. As he passed Darnell's Hardware, he gave his reflection a sidelong glance in the grimy plate glass and decided that maybe he was getting the hang of it. He kept his gaze cocked in that direction as he walked, noting that the saunter he'd practiced, kind of a John Wayne/Clint Eastwood combo, was starting to look pretty good on him. He pulled his shoulders back, setting his mouth into a badass frown, and was pretty sure that if he encountered a criminal right about now, that particular deviant might just think twice about messing with a man like him.

Then he looked farther down the street and saw Glenda McMurray coming his way.

His heart skipped wildly, and it was all he could do to maintain his professional demeanor. Glenda had come to live in Tinsdale three months ago to be near her aging grandmother, and from the first day he saw her, Stanley hadn't been able to think about much else. He was only five-foot-five, so most women either looked him dead in the eye or towered over him. Not Glenda. She was a tiny little thing, barely five feet tall and lucky if she weighed a hundred pounds. For one of the only times in his life, a woman made him feel big.

As usual, wire-framed glasses framed her pretty brown eyes, and her long brown hair was pulled back in a silver barrette. She was wearing the same kind of long, loose, gauzy skirt and strappy little sandals that she always did, and it seemed to Stanley that one day she just might go floating right up into the clouds. He knew that most of the other guys in town thought she was a little plain, but to him she looked like an angel.

Glenda worked as a reporter for the *Tinsdale Weekly*, which of course wasn't anywhere near a full-time job, so she also worked part-time at the Quick Mart. Stanley had taken to dropping by for more cups of coffee and soft drinks and potato chips than he ever had before, and Glenda always had something nice and cheery to say. Still, he tried to play it pretty cool, because he knew that the last thing a woman wanted was to feel as if she were being chased. He hoped maybe his offhand attitude would eventually draw her in for a closer look, though he had to admit that he didn't seem to be making a lot of headway in that direction.

She stopped in front of him. "Hello, Stanley."

Oh, boy. Be cool, he reminded himself. *Be very, very cool.* "Glenda."

He said her name matter-of-factly, keeping his chin up, his shades on, and his face impassive, trying to refrain from grinning like some stupid junior-high kid.

"I'm afraid those kids are at it again with the fireworks," she told him.

Stanley sighed inwardly. The few days before the Founder's Day Celebration were always such a pain in the ass—every bit as much as the Fourth of July. Kids around here didn't have much of anything to do in the summer. Setting off fireworks qualified as high-quality entertainment, and shoving lit black cats into the mail slot of the front door of the newspaper office and then running like hell was the most entertaining of all.

Stanley folded his arms across his chest. "Well, I expect I'll have to have another word with them, then."

"Thank you, Stanley. I'd appreciate that."

Truth was, he hadn't had a word with them the first time around when old man Grimstead, the editor of the newspaper, griped yesterday about Tony, Roy Jr., and the other boys and their own special form of vandalism. When those same boys were eleven or so, Stanley had been able to intimidate them, but now that they were fourteen, they were all swagger and arrogance, and about half of them were taller than he was.

But now that it was Glenda asking and not old man Grimstead, he'd have to take a stab at putting them in their places. He couldn't let her down, because a woman like Glenda would expect any man she'd consider dating to act like one. A big, bad one who could kick some ass whenever the need arose.

He'd found out long ago that women didn't give a flip about brains or sensitivity in their men, no matter how much they protested to the contrary. Give a woman a choice between a smart, sensitive man and a brainless, demanding Neanderthal and they went prehistoric every time. And since he was tired as hell of losing out to that, he'd finally given in to the old adage: If you can't beat them, join them.

"Glenda," he said suddenly, before he lost his nerve. "You. Me. Movie. The Meridian. Saturday night. Yes or no?"

She blinked with surprise. Then her pretty face eased into a warm smile. "Stanley? Are you asking me out?"

Be cool. Don't let her see you sweat.

He gave her an offhand shrug. "I've got a free night."

Her smile faded. "A free night?"

"Yeah. Now that I've cut my evening workouts down to four nights a week"—he cracked a knuckle—"I think I can spare a few hours."

She raised her eyebrows. *Yes.* Now he'd gotten her attention.

"I see," she said, nodding slowly. "Well, then. I guess I know how I'm going to be spending my evening now."

Stanley brightened, hope gushing through him. "You do?"

"Yes. Watching a *Brady Bunch* marathon and doing my nails."

"But—"

"Good-bye, Stanley."

She gave him a sweet little smile, then turned and walked away, that long skirt swishing around her ankles. She stepped lightly off the curb and crossed the street, looking, as always, as if she were walking on air.

He slumped with disappointment. If he lived to be a hundred, he'd never understand women. What in the hell did they want, anyway? He knew for a fact that being himself didn't work, but he wasn't completely sure just who else he was supposed to be.

And now he was going to have to talk to Tony and Roy Jr. and try to get them to cut out the vandalism. Unfortunately, they were exactly like the guys he'd known in high school, the ones who'd called him a wimp and a weenie and snapped towels at his ass in the locker room.

High school. Four years of his life he'd just as soon forget. He'd been a walking, talking cliché—a hundred-pound weakling who'd had far more brains than brawn. And he'd have gladly traded all of those brains for a body that girls couldn't wait to get their hands on, retaining only enough gray matter to enable him to run a post pattern on the football field or hit a baseball out of the park. He would cheerfully have lived in blissful oblivion, never knowing anything but glory on the sporting field and even more glory between the sheets.

After high school, things hadn't gotten a whole lot better. He knew the only reason he'd gotten this job was that Sheriff Dangerfield had a thing for Stanley's aunt Thelma, which meant that most of the citizens of Tinsdale didn't have a whole lot of faith in him, which meant his dream of becoming sheriff when Dangerfield retired in a few years was pretty much impossible.

He dragged himself through the rest of his rounds, finding the town pretty quiet because nobody wanted to venture out in the hundred-and-three-degree heat. He came back into the sheriff's office, flipped on the portable TV sitting on the credenza, then collapsed in a chair behind his desk to look over some citizen complaints. A lawnmower theft. A noisy dog. An abandoned car.

Damn. Did anything interesting *ever* happen in this town?

Then he heard familiar music coming from the TV. He checked his watch. Yep. Time for *Gunsmoke*.

Stanley would never have admitted it to anyone, but in his favorite daydream, he was one of those guys in old westerns who rode into a lawless town and cleaned it up, making it a place where decent people could live. He was a man the young widows in town came to for protection against gunfighters and Indians and other assorted bad guys, then threw themselves at him in gratitude for his strength and fearlessness and deadeye marksmanship. And most of the time he imagined one of those women was Glenda.

Still reeling from his failure with her, he needed a little pick-me-up. Something to let him know he was making progress somewhere in his life. Some indication that he wasn't the great big screwup everybody in this town seemed to think he was.

Just him and Matt Dillon. One on one. He'd always had the feeling that if he could ever outdraw TV's most famous marshal, his life just might take a turn for the better.

He looked at the television. It was time.

Stanley stood up, teasing his fingertips over the handle of his revolver, waiting for Matt to go for his gun. The instant he did, Stanley whipped his weapon out of its holster. Matt pulled the trigger.

So did Stanley.

In a reflex action, his finger clenched the trigger and a shot exploded. A bullet flew dead center into the television screen, obliterating Matt, Matt's weapon, and every storefront, hitching post, horse, and pedestrian on Main Street in Dodge City. Television parts sprayed all over the room, sounding like a bomb going off, slinging shards of glass against the walls and pinging to the floor.

"What the *hell* do you think you're doing?"

Stanley whipped around. Sheriff Dangerfield. And boy, did he look pissed.

Dangerfield, a big man with a lazy walk and a rapidly receding hairline, slammed the door of the sheriff's office and walked over to what used to be an intact television, giving it a deadpan look of utter disbelief.

"Boy? You mind telling me why you shot the television?"

"I-I didn't mean to. It was an accident."

"Shit. It was *Gunsmoke* again, wasn't it? Didn't I tell you to cut that out?"

Stanley swallowed hard. "I kinda pulled the trigger by mistake."

Dangerfield buried his head in his hands in utter frustration, and Stanley wanted to shrink down to mouse size and disappear into a hole. Forever.

"I ought to fire your ass," Dangerfield said. "And if you weren't Thelma's nephew, I would."

"It won't happen again, Sheriff. I promise."

"Boy, when are you ever gonna learn? I mean, it's not that hard a job, is it? This is Tinsdale, Texas, not one of those hellholes like Los Angeles or Chicago. Just quit trying to act like Bruce Willis and Clint Eastwood and all that other shit and just do the job, okay?"

"Yes, sir."

"Now, I'm leaving in a couple of hours for Wichita Falls. I'll be there for three days. And during that time, I don't want that gun of yours to leave that holster. Do you hear me?"

"Yes, sir."

"If I come back and see a window blown out or a hole in the side of the building, not even Thelma's wheedling will save you. You got that?"

"Yes, sir."

"That set cost three hundred dollars. It's coming out of your paycheck."

"Yes, sir."

"I'm going over to the diner to have a little lunch, and then check out the setup for the celebration tonight. Then I'll be getting on the road. You'll be the only law enforcement there tonight. Think you can handle that?"

"Yes, sir."

"Get this mess cleaned up, and then I want you out on patrol, you hear me?"

"Yes, sir."

The humiliation Stanley felt at that moment was probably one of the worst of his life, and he had a lot to compare it to.

As the sheriff walked out the door, Stanley picked up some of the bigger pieces of the decimated television, piling them together, then headed to the back room for a broom. On the way, he passed the bathroom and caught his own reflection in the mirror.

Even though he was twenty-seven years old, he still looked like a kid. He'd tried growing facial hair, wishing he could have one of those sexy five-o'clock shadows women seemed to love, but all he'd gotten were a few scraggly hairs and people laughing behind his back at the pitiful attempt.

Maybe someday he'd leave here. Maybe he'd try to become one of those cops he admired so much. But first he wanted to be sheriff of Tinsdale, Texas.

He grabbed the broom, sighing with resignation. Unless he woke up tomorrow morning six inches taller, fifty pounds heavier, with the ability to kick a major amount of ass and shoot only those things that required shooting, that was never going to happen.

chapter twelve

Val decided there was nothing worse than riding in a van for three hours on a state highway that felt as if it hadn't been resurfaced in fifty years. It ran dead center through the middle of nowhere right into the afternoon sun, which was so strong that even her sunglasses and the sun visor did little to counter it.

They'd stopped at a Wal-Mart in a small town about two hours outside Tolosa. Alex told her to go inside and buy a couple of changes of clothes and any toiletries she wanted, while he did the same. They checked out at different registers so nobody would put the two of them together. Val was glad for the stop—she had no idea how long they'd be gone, and wearing the same clothes for days on end and not even being able to brush her teeth held very little appeal for her.

"It's going to take us forever on these back roads," Val said to Alex. "Are you sure we can't chance the freeway?"

"We've already been through this twice."

Val sighed. "Okay. So what are we going to do when we hit San Antonio?"

"Highway Twenty-one intersects Highway Forty-six, north of town. We'll swing around the city, then head up through Kerrville and then west from there."

She looked at the map, at the route he had outlined. By the time they got where they were going, her insides would be mush.

Then Alex's cell phone rang. He picked it up off the seat and looked at the caller ID.

"Dave."

He laid the phone back down.

"Guess you don't want to talk to him, huh?"

"No. The less he knows about what I'm doing, the better. I don't expect it'll be the last time he calls, though. Just don't answer it."

Alex leaned back against the armrest of the driver's door, one wrist draped over the steering wheel. Even though he wore sunglasses, she still could see his watchful, tense expression, full of controlled intensity. He was a cop, through and through. To a certain extent, all cops were immersed in their jobs, and she could spot one in a crowded room in a heartbeat. Their stances. The looks on their faces. The way they watched their surroundings as if they expected all hell to break loose at any moment. But with Alex, it was more than that. She knew this murder accusation had shaken him to his very core, a core that would be true blue until the day he died. If he ended up in prison, if he had that taken away from him, what kind of man would he emerge as years later?

She didn't even want to think about it.

Alex glanced down at the dashboard. "We're getting low on gas. I need to stop."

To Val's surprise, a few miles later he bypassed a fairly decent-looking truck stop with a restaurant attached and turned into a beat-up gas station/convenience store that was so outdated that it wasn't even equipped to allow a customer to pay at the pump.

"Alex."

He killed the engine. "What?"

"I need to go to the bathroom."

"So go."

She looked back over her shoulder. "They might actually have a clean one back at that other station."

"That other station is crawling with people. We can manage just fine here."

"You mean *you* can manage just fine. I'm the one who has to sit down to pee." She sighed. "Imagine that. My first case of penis envy."

He gave her a warning look. "Just keep a low profile. Keep your sunglasses on, and don't talk to anyone."

Val got the key to the bathroom from the attendant, a room that turned out to be one of the more disgusting ones she'd ever encountered. The mirror was grimy, the walls were filled with graffiti, and it looked as if it hadn't been cleaned in . . . well, *ever*.

A minute later as she was finishing up her business, she saw something out of the corner of her eye, skittering across the floor.

A roach. *Yuck.*

And it wasn't just any roach. It was a Texas-size roach, huge and black and ugly as hell, and she had no doubt it had brothers who were hiding in the woodwork, ready to join the battle.

She stomped her foot to try to get it to go the other way, but that only confused it, and it turned and came right for her. She heaved a roll of toilet paper at it, missed, then picked up another roll and managed to cripple the creature just long enough to make her escape. Once she was outside, she realized she'd left the key in the bathroom.

Too bad.

Alex was already back in the car. She yanked the door open and got in.

"Don't you *ever* stop at such a god-awful place again," she said, slamming the door.

"What's wrong?"

"I thought they grew roaches big only in east Texas." She shuddered. "I just saw one the size of a Shetland pony."

Alex shook his head. "What is it with women and bugs, anyway? Just stomp the damned thing and move on."

"Stomping it would only have made it mad. *Shooting* it. Now, that might have stopped it."

"Good, Val. Nobody would pay any attention to us here if you pulled out a gun and shot an insect."

He started the van. "I got some food. We may get into a situation where we can't risk going someplace public. At least we'll be able to eat."

Val looked into the sack behind the seat. Crackers, granola bars, potato chips, cookies, snack cakes. In another sack were two dozen bottles of water.

"Not exactly health food," Alex said, swinging the van back onto the highway. "The selection was a little limited."

"Works for me," Val said, extracting a package of Ding Dongs. "Want anything?"

"I'll wait awhile to clog my arteries, thank you."

"Oh!" she said. "I almost forgot."

She set the Ding Dongs on the dashboard, reached behind her seat, and hauled out the small backpack she'd taken into the Reichert house with her. Zipping it open, she pulled out a notebook computer.

"What's that?" Alex asked.

"Shannon's computer."

"What?"

"Or at least I think it's Shannon's. I found it in her underwear drawer."

"Are you telling me there was a notebook computer in that room and Henderson didn't take it as evidence?"

"That's right," Val said. "I didn't know if it would tell us anything, but I thought it couldn't hurt to grab it."

"Val—"

"No!" She pointed a finger at him. "Don't you dare yell at me for stealing! Don't you do it! This could tell us a lot, and I wasn't about to leave it behind!"

"Val," he said gently. "I was just going to tell you to check the charge. See how much juice it's got left. I'm way past worrying about a little petty theft."

"Oh," she said a little sheepishly. "Sorry. Conditioned response." She turned it on and found the little battery icon. "Looks like it's almost fully charged."

"What else do you see?"

Val ran her finger over the touch pad, then clicked on "My Documents." "Not much, really. Hmm. Beef Stroganoff?" She opened the file. "A recipe. I guess Shannon liked to cook someplace else besides the bedroom."

She looked down the rest of the file names. Chicken Cordon Bleu. Teriyaki beef. Peanut butter cookies. Thai salad. Lemon squares. She clicked a few open. Definitely recipes.

"It looks as if that's all she used this for. To catalog recipes. She's got some drink recipes, too."

Val read down the list. Velvet Hammer. Fuzzy Navel. Zombie. Alabama Slammer. Screaming Orgasm.

Screaming Orgasm?

She smiled furtively. "Alex? Have you ever had a Screaming Orgasm?"

He glanced at her, then turned his eyes back to the road. "Sure I have. Just not the kind you drink."

Val blinked. "Did you just make a joke?"

"Does that surprise you?"

Actually, it flabbergasted her. "Of course not. You're one of the funniest people I know."

"And you're one of the most sarcastic people I know."

"Wonder what's in a Screaming Orgasm," Val said. She clicked. The document popped up on the screen, and her heart skipped. It wasn't a recipe. It was a letter. She scanned it, and excitement raced through her.

"Alex. I think we hit the jackpot."

"What?"

"It's a love letter. And I don't think it's intended for Reichert."

"Who is it addressed to?"

"It's not."

"Read it."

" 'I've missed you so much, my darling. I know we can't be together now, but I'm counting the days until we can.' What do you suppose that means?"

"I don't know."

She continued reading. " 'J is still as unreasonable as ever, and I don't know how much longer I can go on. The days seem to drag by.' "

"I assume J is Jack Reichert?"

"Probably. 'The only thing that keeps me sane is my memory of the last time we were together. I remember how I—' " Val stopped short.

"How she what?" Alex asked.

"She's reminding him what she used to do to him. It's lewd, graphic, and vulgar." Val scanned the paragraph, wondering how the computer had kept from bursting into flames as Shannon wrote. "Interesting. Shall I read it out loud?"

"Does it clearly indicate that they were having an affair?"

"It clearly indicates that they were having wild, animalistic sex. Does that count?"

"Just tell me what else it says."

" 'I'm so glad you'll be free soon and we'll be together. J is giving me a hard time about the divorce, but only because of the money.' "

"Shannon had filed for divorce?" Alex asked.

"I don't think so. I always check those things out before I take a case, because sometimes clients don't tell the whole story, and I like to know what I'm getting into. She may have asked him for a divorce, but no papers had been filed yet."

"Is there more?"

Val read on. " 'He doesn't love me, but I know you do, and that's what keeps me going. Stay safe, and always remember that I love you, too, and I'll see you soon.' "

"That's it?"

"Yeah."

"Did she sign it?" Alex asked.

"No."

" 'I can't wait until you're free.' Sounds as if her boyfriend was getting a divorce, too. Apparently he decided that it was too risky to see her again until it was final. What date was that file created?"

"April twenty-second."

"Four months ago. Wonder what's happened since? Are there any more letters?"

Val clicked on "White Russian." It was a recipe for a White Russian. She scanned the other drink names. Whiskey Sour . . . Singapore Sling . . . Tom Collins . . . Sex on the Beach . . .

"Aha," she said. "Sex on the Beach. I'll just bet . . ." She clicked. "Yep. Here's another letter."

"Any indication who this one's to?"

"No." She read through it quickly. "It says pretty much what the other one did: 'I can't wait until you're free' . . . graphic sexual description . . . 'love you, love you, love you' . . . no signature."

"Any other suspicious drink names?"

Val found two more letters under "French Tickler" and "Between the Sheets." The last one actually mentioned a date.

" 'I'm counting the hours until August second,' " Val read, " 'when we'll be together again.' "

"Must have been the date his divorce was final."

"And I'll bet you anything that Reichert knew about him, and that's why he had me follow Shannon." Then Val had another thought. "Wait a minute. If Shannon was so hot after this guy, then why did she pick you up the night of the murder?"

"I don't know. Either the relationship fizzled quickly, or she was cheating on him, too."

"Huh?"

"I doubt one man was enough for Shannon. To tell you the truth, I doubt *five* men would have been enough for her."

Val scanned the rest of the file names. "I don't see any more drink names that are suspect."

Well, nothing sexually suspect, anyway. But she had to wonder about any drink called Mexican Death Wish. She clicked. Equal parts tequila and Southern Comfort. Shake and swallow. *Yuck.*

Alex shifted in his seat, clearly feeling as stiff as she was after four hours in the car. "Okay. This is good. We know for a fact that Shannon was having an affair, and that she wanted a divorce, and that she was going to be fighting with Reichert over the settlement. That's a pretty strong motive for murder on his part."

Val clicked around for a few more minutes, seeing nothing but program files. Then she saw "My Pictures." She clicked it, and her heart skipped when she saw three file names: AD1, AD2, and AD3.

"Here's something," Val said. "She has some image files." She clicked the first one, and she couldn't believe what came on the screen.

"My God," Val said.

"What?"

"Pull over."

Alex pulled over onto the shoulder of the road and put the van in park. Val turned the computer around so he could see the screen. His eyes widened with surprise.

"A picture of me?" he said.

Val couldn't believe it. That was exactly what it was.

She clicked the other two. More shots of Alex. They all looked candid, as if he didn't even know they were being taken. When she looked closer, she could see where he'd been at the time—in the parking lot of the Blue Onion.

"I don't get this," Val said. "Why would Shannon have pictures of you?"

"I have no idea."

"She knew your name, too. AD1, AD2, and AD3." Val shook her head. "This is so weird. Do you hang out at the Blue Onion a lot?"

"More than I should." He continued to stare at the picture on the screen. "Looks like it was no accident that Shannon picked me up that night."

"I don't think so, either. She was there for a good hour and a half before you showed up. She turned down every other man who tried to buy her a drink and came straight for you." Val flipped back and forth from one picture to another. "It's almost like she was stalking you. Took pictures of you on the sly, then decided to go after you that night."

"Shannon was a little sex-crazed. Obsessive. I wouldn't put that past her."

"I don't know. Shannon didn't strike me as the type who'd obsess over a man before she went after him. She seemed like the type who would just walk right over and throw herself at the first one who looked good to her."

"I can't imagine what else it would be," Alex said.

"Well, keep thinking. We have letters that say she was obsessing over a guy who's on the verge of divorce, and photos that say she was obsessing over you. There has to be some connection we're missing."

Alex pulled the van back onto the state highway and they traveled for two more hours, swinging north around San Antonio, passing through Kerrville, then heading farther west. They stopped again for gas at a station similar to the first one they'd gone to. Val gave him a dirty look before getting out and heading to the bathroom. When she returned a few minutes later, that dirty look had morphed into one of total disgust.

"That's it," she said, slamming the door. "Next time I'm peeing in the bushes."

"What's the matter?" Alex asked.

"Damn roaches," she muttered. "I've seen creatures in horror movies that weren't as grotesque as what I just saw in that bathroom."

He shook his head. "You and my sister Sandy. She used to flip out over bugs, too."

"So did you squash them for her?"

"Hell, no," he said, pulling the van back out onto the highway. "I terrorized her with them."

"That's awful!"

"Actually, when you're about thirteen years old, it's pretty damn funny."

"Yeah, right." Then Val's eyes widened, as if a truly unspeakable thought had just occurred to her. "I'm warning you, Alex. If you ever come near me with one of those disgusting things, forget shooting the bug. I'm shooting *you*."

He grinned. "You're giving me all kinds of ideas."

"Alex!"

"Come on, Val. You've got nothing to worry about. I quit scaring girls with bugs . . . what? Two or three years ago?"

Val rolled her eyes. "You told me how much crap your family gives you. Sounds like you dish out plenty yourself."

"Only in self-defense. Or retaliation." He paused. "Okay. Sometimes just for the hell of it."

"From what Dave said, you must have lots of relatives to choose from."

"Two brothers and a sister. Aunts, uncles, a couple of cousins. Grandparents. My parents are both dead."

"I'm sorry. Recently?"

"It's been a while. My mother died from cancer when I was ten. My father was killed in the line of duty."

"Your father was a cop?"

"Yeah. Shot during a routine traffic stop about ten years ago."

"That's terrible."

"It's the chance a cop takes every day. The Tolosa Police Department lost one of its best, believe me."

"So you and Dave followed in Dad's footsteps."

"John, too. All three of us are cops. So is my cousin's wife, Brenda."

"I sense a family tradition."

"You don't know the half of it. It's what my father was, and my father's father. I can't imagine anything else."

"So you've lived in Tolosa all your life?"

"Yeah."

"Where did you go to high school?"

"Tolosa South."

"Let's see . . . captain of the football team. Am I right?"

Alex gave her a wry look. "How'd you know?"

"Come on, Alex. It's written all over you. What position did you play?"

"Running back."

"Bet you played basketball, too."

"Yeah. My team won the state championship my senior year."

"Baseball, too, I'm sure. I'll bet you could jack a ball right out of the park."

"I think I still hold the single-season home-run record."

"Track?"

"Decathlon. Silver medal, Junior Olympics."

"Wow. What happened to the gold?"

"I had an off day."

"Swimming?"

"Nope. No swim team."

"Or you'd have probably mastered that, too."

He smiled a little. "Probably."

"The ultimate jock. Gee, who would have thought it?"

"What about you, Val? Who were you in high school?"

"Me? Let's see. I was the smart but weird girl in the back of the class with the extremely bad attitude who wanted to be anywhere else, and very often was." She gave him a humorless laugh. "I spent a lot of time looking at guys like you, wondering what you saw in those brainless, big-breasted cheerleaders."

"You just summed it up. Big breasts, no brains. Easy score. This is going to come as a shock to you, but teenage boys think about sex a whole lot more than they think about having meaningful conversations."

"But they sure didn't think about doing it with girls with orange hair."

"You had orange hair?"

"When it wasn't blue. My mother and stepfather hated it."

"Which is why you did it."

"Oh, yeah. It was why I did a lot of stupid things."

"So your home life wasn't the best."

She shrugged. "It was the same old story you've heard a million times. My mother married a man I hated. I rebelled; they flipped out. And so it goes."

"Where was your real father?"

"He left when I was two. Never came back."

"Why did you hate your stepfather?"

"It came with the job." She looked away. "Aren't all stepfathers evil?"

He was on the verge of asking her to elaborate on that, because clearly there was more to the story than what she was telling him. Then he decided that he really didn't want to know. The last thing he needed was to get emotionally tangled up with Val when he had a murder accusation hanging over his own head.

Still, he was curious.

He glanced over at her to see her staring out the passenger window, and he couldn't help wondering what she was thinking. Maybe someday he'd find out. But for now, he needed to focus his attention on keeping himself out of prison.

Where Val was concerned, though, he knew that was going to be easier said than done.

The landscape grew drearier the farther west they went, and Val swore she'd never seen so much of nothing in her entire life. The two-lane highway was practically deserted. The searing Texas sun seemed to melt the drab landscape into a dreary conglomerate of scraggly trees, sparse grass, and rocky hillsides. Most of the barbed-wire fences were so dilapidated that cattle seemed to be staying within their boundaries by general consent alone.

"We're getting close," Alex said. "We're only about thirty miles from the ranch."

Val checked her watch. It was nearly six o'clock. "Can we pick up a bite of real food somewhere?"

"Maybe. If we can find a place. But it doesn't look like there's much out here."

Val grabbed the map. "Look," she said. "We're only a few miles from Tinsdale. Maybe there will be someplace to eat there."

Alex glanced over at the map. "I wouldn't hold out a lot of hope. It seems to be a pretty tiny town."

"Alex! Look out!"

He jerked his gaze back to the road, immediately swerving hard to the right. He missed the armadillo that had wandered across their path, but when he tried to yank the steering wheel back, he wasn't fast enough. The van plowed over a cluster of rocks on the shoulder of the road, bouncing Val hard against her shoulder belt.

Alex hit the brakes, slowing the van, and Val cringed when she felt the telltale *kathump, kathump* of a blown-out tire. He brought the van to a halt on the shoulder, yanked the door open, and walked around to the right front tire of the vehicle. Val did the same. She didn't even have to look at the tire, though. The angle the van was sitting at told the whole story.

Alex turned his gaze to meet hers. "Why did you yell at me while I was driving?"

"Because you were going to hit that armadillo."

"Val? Which would you rather have? One more armadillo as roadkill, or this van as roadkill?"

She got the point. "Okay. I'm sorry. I didn't think. I just—"

He held up his palm. "Never mind. It's okay."

"It is?"

He took a deep breath and let it out slowly. "Yes. Of course. Everything is going to be just fine." He turned and walked toward the rear of the van. "I'll just get the spare, change the tire, and then we'll be back on the road again."

Spare?

Val felt her stomach drop all the way down to the parched red earth. "Uh . . . Alex . . ."

He turned back.

"There's a little problem."

He walked slowly back toward her, his calm, cool demeanor shifting toward tense, tight, and angry.

"What problem?"

"I had a flat a couple of years ago. It ruined the tire, and I put the spare on, but as far as replacing it—"

His eyebrows flew up. "Are you telling me you don't have a spare tire?"

She shrugged helplessly.

Alex ran his hand through his hair. "I don't believe this," he said, his voice escalating. "I just don't *believe*—"

"Before you get all wound up to chew me out, it's not going to do you any good. It's not going to make a spare tire magically appear, so do me a favor and save your breath."

"Okay, Val. Fine. I'll stay calm, providing you have some brilliant suggestion that's going to get us out of this mess."

"I don't know. Maybe a car will come along."

"We're out in the middle of nowhere! We haven't seen another car for the past twenty minutes! And people don't stop for strangers, particularly out on a deserted road like this one."

"Sure they do."

"Oh, yeah? What universe have you been living in for the past twenty years?"

"The one where cars like that one stop for people in trouble."

Alex spun around to look at the car she was pointing at down the road, the one that was slowing down, looking as if it was going to pull over.

She crossed her arms over her chest, feeling pretty darned smug. Alex's life was so structured that any deviation from dead center made him crazy. She imagined he probably had a spare tire for his spare tire. An extra bottle of catsup at all times. A month's supply of dehydrated food and bottled water in case of disaster. Not only could he not go with the flow, he got all pissed off that there was even a flow in the first place, trying to carry him someplace he didn't want to go.

Unfortunately, all the smugness she was enjoying seeped right out of her when she realized the car that was stopping was black-and-white with a siren on top.

"Uh-oh," Alex said under his breath. "We've got trouble."

chapter thirteen

As the police car pulled up behind the van on the shoulder of the road, Alex immediately went on high alert.

"Oh, boy," Val said. "What do we do now?"

"Just play it cool. He's a local guy. The only reason he's stopping is because it looks like we've got car trouble."

Alex knew that if Henderson had put out an APB of some kind on them, and this guy had seen it, they might have a problem. It would take some fast talking, and maybe some fast acting, too, to get them out of the situation. Alex tried not to think about what that might entail, or just how far he'd go to ensure that they kept moving down the road. He'd just have to play it by ear and hope the guy had no idea who they were.

The officer got out of the car, a skinny little guy wearing a khaki uniform and a cowboy hat that looked a size too big for him.

"What seems to be the problem here?" he asked.

"Flat tire."

The guy stopped and gave his belt an upward tug, jostling his sidearm. He barely had the body to fill out the belt to hold the damned thing in place.

"Need some help changing it?" he asked.

"We don't have a spare."

"Hmm," he said, crossing his arms over his nearly nonexistent chest. "Y'all aren't from around here, are you?"

No, Alex thought, *I'm not. Nor would I ever want to be.*

"See, I can tell because everybody who lives out here knows it's not smart to go gallivanting around inhospitable countryside like this without a spare tire. And a couple gallons of water and a full tank of gas, too." He sniffed. "And a snake-bite kit wouldn't do any harm, either."

He talked as if this were a remote part of the Sahara accessible only by camel and a Bedouin guide. And he also talked as if he had no idea who they were.

"Yeah, well, right now, I'd settle for the spare," Alex said.

"We can pull the tire off and I'll give you a lift back into town. Cletus's station will be open for another half hour or so. He can get you a new tire."

Fortunately, Val at least had a jack. In minutes Alex had the tire off. He heaved it into the trunk of the patrol car.

"Y'all hop in," the deputy said, "and we'll head on back to town."

A quick glance told Alex that the car was standard-issue, with a hard plastic seat in the back to simplify cleanup after messy arrests, such as driving while intoxicated. It also had a cage between the front and back seats and no interior door handles. Alex knew if he rode back there and the deputy got smart about their real identities, he'd be trapped.

Before he could say anything to Val, though, she opened the back door and got inside the car, motioning him to the front seat. At the same time, she gave him a knowing look that said she saw the danger as clearly as he did. One thing about Val—she might be hardheaded, but she was quick on the uptake.

A few minutes later they passed a sign stating that they'd entered the city limits of Tinsdale, Texas. Cedar Street, the main drag, was home to a row of storefronts that looked as if they hadn't been updated since the 1950s.

"What a charming little town," Val said, and Alex thought at first that she was just being nice. Then he thought about her neighborhood and realized that she probably meant every word.

As they approached the service station, they passed under a big red-and-white banner stretched across the street.

"You're having a celebration?" Val asked.

"Yeah. Tonight. This is Founder's Day. It's bigger than the Fourth of July around here."

The deputy pulled up to the service station, which sat right next to a motel called the Bluebonnet Inn. It consisted of a row of eight rooms constructed of cinder block and painted a screamy shade of blue. Alex opened the back door for Val, then pulled the tire from the trunk, and they all went inside.

"Hey, Cletus," Stanley said to the man behind the counter. "Picked these folks up out on the highway east of town. Flat tire. Told them you could fix them right up."

"Sure thing," he said.

"I'll leave you to it, then. I've got to get on over to the celebration."

A woman came through the door from the garage who was maybe in her forties. She was about to pop the buttons on the western-style shirt she wore, and her hair was a color of red that Alex couldn't imagine occurring in nature. Ever.

"Hey, Inez," Stanley said. "Y'all heading over to the celebration pretty soon?"

"Soon as we close up here, we'll be right over."

As the deputy left the station, Cletus came around the counter. He was in his forties, thinning a little on top and thickening a little around the middle. He examined the tire.

"Can you replace it?" Alex asked.

"Yep."

"You have a tire in stock?"

"Yep."

"How long will it take?"

"I'll have it done by tomorrow morning."

Alex felt a jolt of apprehension. "Tomorrow morning? I thought you said you had a tire."

"I do. It's the rim that's the problem."

"The rim is damaged?"

"Oh, yeah. And I don't carry this kind. Gonna have to get one from Ruston in the morning. They got a bigger stock over there."

"You can't go now?"

"Nope. The store'll be closed by now. You folks from around here?"

"No."

"Then you'd better just plan on staying the night."

"Staying the night?" Val said, then turned to Alex. "Uh, we have places we need to be."

Alex didn't like this. Not one bit. He had no idea who might be on their trail. But it wasn't as if they had a choice. Without a tire, they were stuck.

"That motel next door," he said to Cletus. "Do you know if there's any vacancy?"

"Me and Inez run that, too. We're almost to capacity with the celebration and all, but we've got one room left."

Almost to capacity. Seven rooms out of eight. This guy was a regular Howard Johnson.

"Good," Alex said. "We'll take it. If you can just give us a key—"

"Sorry. Can't."

"Can't? Why not?"

"You wouldn't want in one of those rooms right now."

"Why not?"

"Because I set off bug bombs about thirty minutes ago."

"Bug bombs?" Val said.

"Yeah," Inez said. "We fog the rooms once every three months. If we don't, pretty soon the vermin take over. And let me tell you—in these parts, you *never* want to let that happen."

"No kidding," Val said suddenly. "Kill those suckers. Every last damned one of them."

Everyone turned to stare at Val. She gave them a sheepish look. "Sorry. Bug phobia."

"Hey, I don't blame you one bit, sweetie," Inez said. "I hate them, too. Which is why we fog every three months."

"But you said you're almost at capacity," Alex said. "Isn't that a bad time to exterminate?"

"Nah," Cletus said. "It's a perfect time. The rooms will be vacant, because everybody'll be at the celebration. By the time they get back, the fogging will be done, and I'll have the rooms all aired out."

Alex slumped with frustration. Could this experience get worse? Was there any way it could get any worse?

Cletus pulled his cash drawer out and locked it beneath the counter, looking as if he was getting ready to close up.

"Okay, then," Alex said. "Can you direct us to a restaurant where we can get some dinner?"

"Sorry. It's closed."

"It's only six-thirty."

"The evening part of the celebration is starting."

"Anyplace else we can get a bite to eat?"

"Sure."

"Where's that?"

"At the celebration."

Alex felt as if he were on a merry-go-round with no way off.

"You folks are more than welcome to come along," Inez said.

"No, thanks," Alex said.

"There's gonna be a watermelon-seed spittin' contest. And a chili cook-off."

"No, thank you."

"And a dance, too. Live band."

"No. I'm sorry. We can't."

" 'Course, some of the boys have been hunting rattle-snakes all day, and I expect they'll be cooking those up, too."

"We'd love to come," Val said.

Alex shot her a look of disbelief. What did she say?

"I knew the rattlesnake would get you," Inez said with a grin. "The park is just down Cedar Street. If you'll wait just a minute, Cletus and I will close up the station, I'll grab my potato salad, and we'll walk over there with you."

"Sounds wonderful," Val said with smile. "Thanks so much for the invitation."

"We'll wait outside," Alex said.

He grabbed Val by the arm and dragged her out the door, then stopped short and faced her.

"Are you out of your mind? We don't know how wide-spread a net Henderson has decided to cast. Somebody might recognize us."

"I doubt that."

"That's because you're being careless, as usual."

"No, I'm not. I'm being logical."

Logical? Val?

"Look, Alex. If anybody was going to recognize us, it would have been that deputy. He'd have read some kind of APB or something. But as you can see, he didn't have a clue."

"Still, I don't like the idea of getting out in the middle of a bunch of people."

"We've only been gone from Tolosa since ten-thirty this morning. What are the odds that anyone would have heard that a man and a woman are on the run who meet our description?"

"They could have seen a Tolosa paper right after the murder and recognize me."

"Then they'd have to take the Tolosa paper, wouldn't they? And have it delivered by mail. What are the odds of that? Dallas or Houston papers, maybe. Not Tolosa. And in order for them to have seen any TV reports, they'd have to pick up the local stations around Tolosa. They can't do that out here. If by some chance they can, it means they've got satellite and they're watching something a whole lot more interesting than a local news broadcast from halfway across the state. And it's going on six-thirty already, so nobody's going to be home watching TV tonight. They're all going to be . . ."

"At the celebration."

"Very good, Alex. You're catching on."

"This is a bad idea."

"No. It's a great idea. I'm starving. Oooh!" she said, lifting her nose and sniffing. "I can smell the barbecue from here. Can't you?"

"Val—"

"Admit it, Alex. You're just afraid that somebody's going to make you eat rattlesnake."

"Val—"

"I bet if you ask real nice, they'll give you the rattle as a souvenir."

"Val!"

He started to berate her all over again, because God knew he was totally justified in doing it. But then she did something that he considered to be a hit right below the belt.

She smiled.

It wasn't just a regular smile. That he could have handled. This was different. This was a smile so broad and brilliant that it could have lit up the entire landscape of southwest Texas in the dead of night. Instead of making him want to throttle her, it made him want to smile back. And he did. Just a little.

"Well, I'll be darned," she said, staring at him as if he were a scientific oddity. "Alex DeMarco really *can* smile."

"I'm not smiling."

"Then what is it? Gas?"

He sighed with exasperation. "You absolutely wear me out, do you know that?"

"Yeah," she said, still smiling. "I know. Consider it good mental exercise."

Now there was an analogy. Since Val had shown back up in his life, he felt as if he'd run a mental marathon.

"I hope you'll at least try to have fun," Val said.

"Fun?"

"Yes, *fun*. You say the word as if you've never heard it before. Don't you ever have any of that?"

Sure. He played pool. He went to an occasional football game, and usually in the spring somebody got a softball team together. Had lunch with the family—well, that could go either way. But most nights he just went home alone, watched a little TV, had a beer or two, fell into bed, then woke up and did it all over again. Fun?

He pondered that for a moment.

No. Not really.

Cletus and Inez came out the door and locked it behind them.

"I guess it'd be nice if we actually introduced ourselves," Inez said to Val. "My name's Inez Miller, and this is my husband, Cletus."

"It's so nice to meet you," Val said. "I'm Sarah Roberts, and this is my husband, Dan."

Good job, Alex thought with a little bit of surprise. The simpler the names, the easier they would be to remember. He would have expected Val to come up with something slightly more difficult to deal with. Like Bonnie and Clyde.

Ten minutes later they were walking with Inez and Cletus through the park toward a large pavilion. Barbecue pits were set up adjacent to it, and picnic tables were lined with red-checkered tablecloths. Even though the sun was nearing the horizon, the heat of the day still hung in the air, but a nice evening breeze was starting to make the temperature at least bearable.

Stanley came up beside them. "Well, hey there, folks. I see you decided to join the celebration."

"Yeah," Val said. "Smelled the barbecue and couldn't turn it down."

"Don't believe I caught y'all's names back at Cletus's place."

Val introduced them to the deputy by their phony names, and they made nice all around. Alex would have preferred not to give any names at all, even fake ones, but if they were asked, they had to respond with something.

Then all at once a woman hurried up to Stanley. "You'd better get over to the tasting table. Nadine and Raydine are going at it."

"Those two ladies bickering *again*?"

"More likely ready to start tossing chairs around. You remember what happened last year."

"And a sorry sight it was," Stanley said. "Raydine and Nadine are sisters, but you'd never know it when it comes to the chili cook-off. One of them would stab the other in the back to get that blue ribbon. I'd best go break them up." He sighed dramatically, shaking his head. "The things I have to deal with."

And that, Alex thought, was probably the extent of the things he could deal with.

As the deputy strode toward the tasting table, the altercation got louder.

"Because he's your brother-in-law, that's why!" one of the women said.

"Are you suggesting that Odell can't be impartial?" the other one hollered back.

"There's no *suggesting* about it!"

They lunged for each other, and it was all Stanley could do to wedge his skinny body in between their far more substantial ones. He looked like a tiny sliver of lean turkey between two sourdough buns.

"Now, wait just a minute!" he shouted, grasping each lady by a shoulder and shoving them apart. "Nadine! Raydine! I'm warning you! You go disturbing the peace any more, and I'm gonna have to haul you both in. You hear?"

Big words, Alex thought, considering that if either woman chose to throw her weight around a little, she could squash the deputy like a bug.

The two women continued to glare at each other, and the situation was clearly at an impasse. Finally Stanley looked out over the audience, focusing on Val and Alex. "Can y'all come up here for just a minute?"

Alex and Val looked at each other.

"I think he's talking to us," Val whispered.

"Yeah, you two. These two ladies are related to just about everybody in town, so we need somebody impartial to judge this contest. You wouldn't mind doing that, now, would you?"

A low profile. That was what they needed to maintain. But at this rate, that was never going to happen.

"Sorry," Alex said. "We don't know a thing about chili."

"All you have to do is taste each one and tell us which one you like best."

"No, thanks. We can't."

"Sure you can. Eat the chili, make a decision. Simplest thing in the world."

Alex opened his mouth to protest again, but he couldn't think of a really good objection. And since every pair of eyes in the pavilion had turned to them, continuing to say no would be worse than just doing it and getting it over with. And what Val had said was true. The odds of any of these people recognizing them were slim to none. He'd wager that most of them weren't even sure they were in the twenty-first century.

They started toward the tasting table. Val was actually smiling, as if she was looking forward to this, as if a stupid celebration in a hick town was her idea of a good time. He'd never understand her if he lived to be a hundred.

There actually appeared to be three finalists, but from the behavior of Nadine and Raydine, apparently they were the only two who were really in the running. The deputy handed Alex a spoon. He dutifully took a big bite from the first pot and began to chew. He tasted tomatoes, beef, chili powder— the usual suspects when it came to chili. And then something strange and powerful began to happen.

Heat. Painful heat. Blazing heat. It was as if somebody had stuffed a flamethrower in his mouth and pulled the trigger.

Spitting wasn't an option. He had to swallow.

The concoction traveled down his throat, searing every inch of his esophagus along the way. His eyes watered, and sweat popped out on his forehead and ran down his temples. He tried his level best not to gag, but still a few coughs escaped.

"It's the habanero peppers that give it the kick," Nadine said with a grin of pure delight. "Harold calls it my napalm chili. He says it's the hottest thing this side of the jungles of Southeast Asia. He was there, you know."

"Yup," a man in the audience said, who was most likely Harold. "Leaves nothing but scorched earth behind."

Alex took a deep, gasping breath. Somebody handed him a glass of pale green liquid on ice. He took a desperate gulp, only to jerk back, exploding in a fit of coughing.

Holy shit. Was that a margarita? If so, he'd just poured alcohol on a five-alarm fire.

"Weenie," Nadine muttered. "Probably eats chili from a can."

Alex glanced over and found Val smiling. Grinning, actually, as if she thought this was funny. But as soon as this stuff was taking the top three layers of skin off the inside of *her* mouth, he was going to have the last laugh.

"Now it's Sarah's turn," he said, handing her a spoon. To his surprise, she gave him a big smile and dipped a healthy bite of chili out of the pot. Had she not noticed the smoke coming out of his ears?

But as she started to pop the spoon into her mouth, she stopped suddenly, then turned to Nadine with a look of utter distress.

"Oh! Now, hold on just a minute. Did you say this chili is made with *habanero* peppers?"

"Yeah."

"Oh, darn it!" she said, dropping the spoon back into the pot with a dramatic *thunk*. "Wouldn't you know it? I'm *allergic* to habanero peppers. Every time I eat one, my throat closes up and I get all red and I can't breathe, and . . ." She sighed. "Well, let me tell you, it's not a pretty sight."

Alex couldn't believe it. She'd just described his experience perfectly, and allergies had nothing to do with it.

"Oh, that's such a shame, sweetie! You're missing out on one of life's biggest pleasures."

Val shook her head sadly. "I know. A life without peppers. It's a hard cross to bear, let me tell you." She turned to Alex with a sunny smile. "Well, Dan. Guess that means it's all up to you now, huh?" She nodded toward the remaining two pots of chili. "One down, two to go."

He was going to get her for this. He didn't know how, he didn't know when, but she was a dead woman.

He took a bite of Raydine's chili, and within seconds sweat beads were forming on his sweat beads. This contest wasn't about who could make the best chili. It was about who could do the most thorough job of incinerating an intestinal tract. He managed to swallow without coughing this time, but it was a hard-won battle.

Val turned to Raydine with a plaintive sigh. "It looks as if your recipe has habaneros in it too."

"Well, of course," Raydine said proudly, then got a suspicious look on her face. "But if you think I'm telling you what else is in there, think again."

"Nobody gives a damn what's in it," Nadine muttered.

Raydine started toward Nadine again, and while the deputy was breaking up the catfight one more time, Alex leaned over and whispered to Val, "Practical jokes are for small minds."

"Then call me a peabrain, but it's *still* funny."

"Before this night is out, I'm going to force-feed you a whole bowl of this stuff. I'm going to put one knee on each of your shoulders, and it's going down. Every bite."

Val grinned. "Big talk for a man who can't handle his chili. And you didn't do so great with the margarita, either."

"Margarita, my ass. It was six shots of tequila with a drop of lime juice for flavoring. Nitroglycerin doesn't have that kind of blasting power."

"Okay," the deputy said, nodding toward the third pot. "One more to go, Dan." He looked at the ladies, who were glaring at each other like a pair of junkyard dogs. "And make it snappy."

Alex angled the spoon over to the third pot, dipped it in, and took a bite, hoping by now that the nerve endings in his mouth had been permanently annihilated so he'd be spared the pain of actually tasting the stuff. But he got a welcome surprise. He chewed and swallowed, and his mouth didn't burst into flames.

Pepperless chili?

He put down the spoon, picked up the blue ribbon, and slapped it down in front of the pot.

A gasp went up from the crowd. Then silence. It was as if everyone in the tent were holding a collective breath, and for a moment Alex wondered whether he'd just incited a riot. Then the deputy started clapping, and somebody else joined in, and pretty soon the whole tent came alive with applause, whistling, and catcalls. Somebody pulled a young woman to her feet and escorted her up to the tasting table. She wore a long, loose skirt, wire-rimmed glasses, and a very surprised expression. Nadine and Raydine just stood there with their mouths hanging open.

Alex shook the woman's hand and handed her the ribbon. "Congratulations," he said. "The winner, hands down."

More applause. The woman looked very pleased. Nadine and Raydine looked homicidal.

"Way to go, Dan," Val whispered, smiling. "Those two just put out a contract on you. Better watch your back while we eat."

Alex looked around at the crowd, most of whom were moving toward the food tables to fill up plates. His gut feeling told him there was no danger here. That feeling had never failed him before, but still he intended to be on the lookout. All it took was one person to recognize them, and all hell would break loose.

chapter fourteen

Val decided it was the best meal she'd ever eaten. *Ever.*

Barbecued brisket, potato salad, cole slaw, baked beans, and a variety of other salads and breads and all kinds of other good stuff. Alex was sitting across from her at the picnic table, and judging by the speed with which he was clearing his plate, he seemed to be just as taken with the food as she was. Then somebody came by and offered them drinks. She took a Diet Coke, and Alex popped the top on a can of Coors.

"So," Val asked him. "How are the old taste buds? Coming back to life?"

He raised an eyebrow. "I *will* get you for that. Sometime when you least expect it. And you won't even know what hit you."

Val grinned. "Not a chance."

"You see if I don't."

He gave her a knowing look, as if he were already plotting revenge. Little did he know, but she'd have been thrilled if he actually carried it out. If he played a practical joke, it meant he really did have a sense of humor in there some-where. She wasn't holding her breath, but it was nice to think that somewhere, someday, he'd make good on the promise.

He pointed to her plate. "I see you passed on the rattlesnake."

"Had to. Those pesky allergies again." She sighed dramati-cally. "I swear, there's not a single decent thing on this planet that I can eat."

"Don't tell me. You're also allergic to liver and anchovies."

"That's why I like you, Alex. You catch on quick."

She smiled at him again, and this time he smiled back. God, he was beautiful when he smiled. At what point in his life had he decided that a smile was something he could do without?

About halfway through their meal, the winner of the chili cook-off joined them at their picnic table, introducing herself as Glenda McMurray.

"You're a smart man," Glenda told Alex, as she put her plate on the table and sat down. "By picking my chili you kept Nadine and Raydine from killing each other. Of course, now both of them want to kill me."

"Nah. I'm the one at the top of their hit list. But it really wasn't a contest. Yours had the one ingredient I value most in chili."

"What's that?"

"Blandness."

Glenda grinned, then leaned in and whispered, "Don't tell Nadine and Raydine, but I got my recipe off the back of a chili seasoning packet."

"You seem to have forgotten the habanero peppers," Val said.

"Are you kidding? I swear, those things will eat up the inside of a Crock-Pot quicker than battery acid."

After a few more minutes, Inez and Cletus joined them, their plates piled high. Soon the whole table was buzzing with conversation, and even after everybody finished eating, they hung around, chatting until evening became dusk. The whole park came alive with activity. Kids ran relay races on the hillside near the pavilion while women started setting out desserts. As one beer after another disappeared from the coolers, the commotion level kicked up a notch, punctuated by laughter and good cheer.

As Cletus was engaging Alex in a discussion about spark plugs that he couldn't possibly have been interested in even though he was pretending he was, Val glanced over at the deputy, who sat at the next picnic table with another group of people. Every few minutes, he'd look over at them. At first it made her heart skip a little, thinking that maybe he was on to them, but then she realized it wasn't her and Alex he was looking at. It was Glenda.

"You and the deputy," Val whispered to Glenda. "Is something going on between the two of you?"

"Me and Stanley? No. Nothing." But then she glanced over

at him, and Val saw that the moment their eyes met, they both looked away again.

"He likes you, doesn't he?"

Glenda shrugged and took another bite of pea salad.

"Do you like him?"

She shrugged again. "Sometimes."

"Sometimes?"

Glenda sighed. "When he's not trying to be a tough guy."

"What do you mean?"

"Like tonight. He couldn't just talk to Raydine and Nadine. He had to go getting all tough with them, telling them he was gonna toss them in jail if they didn't straighten up. Sounds kinda silly, because everybody knows there's no way he's gonna do that. Those two ladies would end up locking *him* up if he tried."

"So you don't think much of the macho approach."

"I don't know. If it fits a guy, I suppose it's all right." She glanced at Alex. "Like your husband there. If he said stuff like that, you can bet your life people would listen, and it wouldn't sound stupid. But it'd make more sense for a guy like Stanley to rely on what's between his ears and not on the rest of his body. When he finally did that, by getting you two up there to judge the contest, everything turned out just fine. I thought that was a pretty smart thing for him to do."

Val smiled. She was so cute. And Stanley was such an idiot. She decided before the night was over, she was going to have a word with him.

They ate the rest of their meal, making small talk about nothing in particular, and Val noticed that Glenda and Stanley traded several more glances. When Glenda got up to go to the bathroom, Val leaned over to Alex.

"Did you see those two?"

"What two?"

"Stanley and Glenda."

"What about them?"

"They like each other."

Alex just stared at her dumbly. "What?"

"He likes her, but he's always trying to show off, and she hates that, but he probably thinks that's how he's got to act to impress her, but it turns her off, and . . . well, you can see the problem."

Alex stared at her, dumbfounded. "How do you know all that?"

"It's just girl talk."

"I've known some men for ten years and I couldn't tell you that much about them."

"That's because you're a man. I've been known to go into a public bathroom with a total stranger, and in the time it takes to wash our hands, I've heard her entire life story."

"This may come as a shock to you, but men don't do a lot of chatting over the urinal."

"Which is why you don't know a thing about each other."

He rolled his eyes, but ended up smiling anyway, and just the sight of it made another jolt of pure pleasure surge through her. Then she glanced over at the dessert table and saw the deputy reaching for a slice of pie.

"I'm getting some dessert," she told Alex. "Can I bring you something?"

"Anything. As long as it doesn't have peppers in it."

Val went to the dessert table. "Hello, Deputy."

"Mrs. Roberts. Mighty fine barbecue, isn't it?"

"Yes. Mighty fine." She glanced at Glenda, then looked back at Stanley. "Glenda McMurray. She's been talking about you."

Stanley's eyes widened, and he looked as if he'd swallowed a golf ball. "She has?"

"Yes. She's been telling me what a smart man you are."

Stanley looked at her with total incredulity. "That's what she's been saying?"

"Oh, yeah. Women like that, you know. Smart men."

"They do?"

"Well, of course they do."

Stanley just stared, perplexed.

"And later," she said, "when the dance starts?"

"Yeah?"

"I think she'd like it if you asked her to dance."

"Really?"

Val grabbed a pair of double-fudge brownies. She started

to walk off, then looked back over her shoulder with a know-ing smile. "Really."

Stanley's mouth hung open dumbly, and she wondered if maybe she hadn't put him into irreversible sensory overload. It was sure going to be interesting to see if he worked up the nerve to talk to Glenda, much less ask her to dance.

The park had eased into near-darkness, with only a pale or-ange glow remaining around the horizon. Somebody was in the process of lighting several copper tiki torches around the perimeter of the pavilion. A few seconds later the overhead lights in the pavilion were dimmed to a warm, faint glow, leaving the torch flames to provide most of the illumination.

She headed back toward the picnic table and saw that Alex was sipping from his second beer and carrying on a conversa-tion with Cletus and a couple of the other men. It struck her that he actually seemed to be having a good time.

She stopped a moment and watched him, and the sight made her breath catch in her throat. Even when he was re-laxed, he had a commanding posture, always holding that gorgeous body of his in a way that drew her attention like nothing else. Even beneath the dark T-shirt he wore, she could clearly see the outline of his broad, muscular shoulders and chest, along with biceps and triceps that were beyond belief. That he was handsome was a given. It was almost as if God couldn't bear to give him that beautiful body without a face to go with it. Maybe it was shallow of her to respond so com-pletely to a man's physical appearance, but when a man looked like Alex DeMarco, she couldn't imagine a woman on earth who wouldn't wallow around in that shallowness right along with her.

Then she thought about how they'd be staying in the same room tonight. She closed her eyes and took a deep breath, steadying herself before she dropped the brownies. She could only pray there were twin beds.

As she approached the table, Cletus apparently said some-thing funny, because Alex laughed, a deep, rich, hearty laugh that wrapped itself around Val's heart. She put the brownies on the table and sat down next to him.

"What's so funny?" she asked.

Still chuckling a little, he turned to look at her. "Cletus knows a joke or two."

"Care to share?"

"Sorry. They're not fit for a lady's ears."

"Now, Dan," she said quietly, "you know I'm no lady."

His broad smile faded to a softer one. "I don't know any such thing."

Alex continued to stare at her, and slowly something seemed to come alive between them. He'd had a couple of beers, but a man like him didn't fall easily under the influence. His gaze was sure and steady, focusing on her face as if it were the first time he was seeing it.

"What?" she whispered.

"You look beautiful tonight."

Her heart jolted hard, then settled into a maddening rhythm. Alex had never been one to toss around compliments, and it caught her completely off guard.

"It's the tiki torches. Every woman looks good by the light of a tiki torch."

"I don't think the torches have a thing to do with it."

Commotion was going on all around them as the band started tuning up and people moved chairs to circle what was going to be the dance floor, but for that moment in time, Val barely saw them. She had eyes only for Alex.

"It's so nice to get away from everything," she whispered. "Even if it's only for a little while."

His smile faded, and he looked away.

"What's wrong?"

"Nothing, really," he said softly. "It just reminded me of why we're here."

"Don't think about that."

"It's hard not to think about being accused of murder."

She ran her hand gently up and down his arm. "Not tonight you haven't been," she said. "Okay? Not tonight."

His gaze shifted to where her hand rested against his arm. She started to pull away, only to have him take her hand in his. And that simple touch electrified her.

"I'm glad you talked me into coming," he said. "This has been—" He stopped and gazed around the pavilion, then laughed softly. "I don't believe it, but this has actually been fun." Then his smile dimmed. "And you were right. I don't usually have much of that."

"Then maybe you need somebody like me around once in a while to shake things up."

"Yeah. Maybe I do."

The band started to play, some wild-and-woolly country song that had the whole place stomping, but to Val it sounded like white noise. Alex turned to face the band. She did the same. He kept hold of her hand, resting it against his thigh beneath the picnic table, and Val thought her heart was going to jump right out of her chest. Her eyes were on the band, which featured a fiddle player who was clearly the star of the show, but her entire attention was focused on the feel of Alex's strong, callused fingers against hers.

She couldn't look at him. She didn't want to think about what it meant. She just wanted to feel it. He stroked his thumb back and forth against her hand, a soft, gentle motion that mesmerized her. The humid night air still held most of the relentless heat of the day, but right now it felt like a warm blanket that had wrapped around both of them, bringing them together.

The band played a second song, then a third, and still they sat there, holding on to each other, saying nothing. Then the band downshifted into a soft, soulful song with a much slower pace.

Val looked across the pavilion and noticed that Stanley was talking to Glenda. Then she rose, and the two of them went to the dance floor. *Good.* He'd gotten up the nerve to ask her to dance, and she'd said yes. True love in the making.

She leaned closer to Alex. "Look. Stanley and Glenda. They're dancing."

"Interesting couple."

"Just goes to show you that there's somebody for everybody."

"And they just happened to find each other in Tinsdale, Texas. What are the odds?"

"Maybe they're just destined to be together."

Alex smiled indulgently. "Uh-huh."

"What?" she said. "You don't believe in fate? In destiny?"

"Come on, Val," he said teasingly. "You know me better than that."

Val smiled. She did. He was a man who insisted on being in control. The very idea that some unseen force would be pushing him around the universe was something he'd take great exception to.

"Well, can you think of any other explanation for why some people are attracted to each other?"

Alex turned to look at the band again, but she could feel his attention still focused squarely on her.

"I suppose it would explain a lot," he said.

Val had expected nothing but bad attitude from Alex tonight, with lots of pointed frowns to remind her of just how he felt about the mess they'd ended up in.

And now this.

Don't forget, she told herself. *Don't you ever forget what he did to you.*

But as much as she willed herself to remember, the memory was fading fast, until the only thing she seemed to be able to comprehend was what was happening here and now.

Soon the song wound down. Another one began.

"Another slow song," Alex said.

"Yeah."

"Come on."

To Val's surprise, Alex rose from the picnic table. Still holding her hand, he coaxed her to stand, then led her toward the dance floor. She followed as if she were in some kind of trance, her body hot and shaky, her mind muddled, giving her the uncanny, out-of-body feeling that she'd fallen asleep and was dreaming the whole thing.

If that's true, Lord, please let me sleep forever.

When they reached the dance floor, he eased her around to face him. Slowly he slipped his arm around her waist. She rested her palm against his chest. He pulled her closer, until their bodies were pressed together.

Oh, yes.

They didn't dance as much as they simply moved with each other, letting the music flow over them. Val had never really had a sense of just how big and powerful Alex was until she'd found herself in his arms that night five years ago, and she had that same feeling now, as if she were being held by a man strong enough to wrestle a grizzly to the ground. With a soft sigh, she laid her head against his shoulder, then stroked her hand down his back, feeling planes of solid muscle from his shoulders to his waist, wishing she could slip her hand beneath his shirt and feel his bare skin against her hand.

Wished he would take his shirt off altogether.

Alex moved his hand from her waist, sliding it up to her shoulder and finally to her neck. He tucked his hand beneath her hair until his fingertips found the skin at the nape of her neck. He stroked his thumb back and forth there, sending hot shivers all the way to her toes.

Nothing on earth felt better than this. *Nothing*.

But there was something else she felt as he held her, something besides pure sexual feeling. She felt warm. She felt content.

She felt safe.

No. It was a lie. An illusion. She'd trusted him that night five years ago, too, and look what it had gotten her.

But it was only a dance, she told herself. Just one dance.

Then he shifted a bit, and she felt the hard ridge of his arousal pressed against her. Desire sparked hot and heavy inside her, pooling right between her legs.

No. It was more than a dance. Much more. He wanted her. She could feel it.

And she wanted him.

When she woke up this morning, she couldn't have imagined that they would end up in a place like this, talking and laughing together, then dancing in the dark. Or that they'd be sleeping in the same room tonight.

The song slowly wound down. Alex pulled away slightly, and their eyes met. He stared down at her a second, then two. She knew what he intended to do, and the mere thought of it made her heart race like mad. He lowered his head, and she felt as if eons passed before he finally, finally touched his lips to hers.

She leaned into him automatically, and the moment she responded, he tilted her head back and delved deeper, slipping his tongue into her mouth and stroking it against hers. Her breasts felt hot and tingly, her skin suddenly so raw and sensitive that it seemed to sizzle everywhere he touched her..

Yes. Yes. Now she remembered. *Oh, God.* She remembered

exactly what he felt like. What he tasted like. How persistent
his mouth felt against hers, how every soft, scorching movement of his lips and tongue made her muscles go weak.

There had been unguarded moments over the years when
she'd lain awake at night and tried to recall every detail about
the way he'd kissed her, but as time went on, the memories
slipped out of focus, and she knew there were parts of them
that she'd never remember again. But now it all came back to
her in a blinding rush, and she wondered how the memory of
something so incredible could possibly have faded at all.

One tiny part of her was telling her she ought to push him
away, that it could lead to nothing but misery for both of
them, but kissing him felt as natural, as perfect as anything
she'd ever done, and right now she felt as if the only way she'd
be miserable was if she made him stop.

"Well. Looks like I'm just in time."

They pulled apart quickly and spun around. Cletus was
standing beside them, holding a motel room key.

Oh, God. She couldn't do this. She just couldn't. She
wanted Alex with a desperation that bordered on obsession,
but she just couldn't face the consequences. It had nearly
killed her when she'd found out that in the long line of women he'd slept with, she'd just been one more. If things ended
that way tomorrow morning, this time she didn't think she'd
survive.

Fool me once, shame on you. Fool me twice . . .

"Just aired out the rooms," Cletus said. "You folks are free
to go back to the motel whenever you want to. And it looks
like that 'whenever' is probably right about now."

"Yes," Alex said, taking the key. "Thanks."

"No problem," he said with a grin. "No problem at all."

chapter fifteen

As they walked back to the motel, neither Alex nor Val said a word.

Alex had no idea what had come over him, but when they were at that celebration, he suddenly had the feeling that they'd gotten stranded in a foreign land, in a place where all their problems suddenly melted into the background. And he hadn't been lying. Val looked beautiful. As usual, she'd plunged right into the heart of the action, so full of life that people were naturally drawn to her. He thought about reprimanding her for talking so much to Glenda and all the other people when they really should be lying low, but he had a gut feeling that it just didn't matter.

He'd taken her to the dance floor for one reason only: because he wanted to get his hands on her, to touch her again after all this time, to see if his five-year-old memory of her was as accurate as he thought. It wasn't. It missed by a mile. The reality of touching her again put his memory to shame.

And then he'd kissed her. He didn't remember a time in his life when he'd kissed a woman in public. But right out there on that dance floor in front of the entire population of Tinsdale, Texas, he'd kissed Val as if the next step they took would be right into bed.

And she'd kissed him back.

The noise of the crowd and the music faded away as they walked, until all he heard was the soft, hollow sound of their footsteps along the sidewalk. Now that it was just the two of them alone, walking along this deserted, small-town street with no distractions, the prospect of making love to her was so overwhelming that he couldn't think of anything else.

They reached the motel, and he opened the door to room

seven. He stepped aside for Val to enter. She reached for the wall switch, but he covered her hand with his, then pulled it away from the switch before she could flip it on. He drew her around to face him, closing the door behind them at the same time. Nothing but moonlight illuminated the room.

"Alex?" she whispered, a questioning look filling her eyes, just as it had that night all those years ago.

It was almost as if he was getting a second chance to make things right. To make love to her, then wake with her in the morning, and no matter how desperate their situation, to come to some kind of understanding. To show her, finally, that he wasn't what she thought he was at all.

"I hadn't counted on tonight, Val," he said. "Not for one minute. I couldn't have imagined—"

He stopped short, treading softly, wanting to make sure she was with him on this. They had too much history for him to risk making a wrong move now.

"I think you want what I want," he said. "Am I wrong?"

"That depends on what you want."

"I thought I made that clear on the dance floor."

"That was a kiss," she told him. "Only a kiss."

Alex felt a twinge of foreboding. As hot as he was for her right now, he didn't think he'd be able to stand it if she turned around and walked away from him. The way she felt, the way she smelled, the way she tasted—all of it was heaven to him. This was what he wanted for the past five years, whether he'd admitted it or not. Until Val, he'd never had the feeling that he'd walk through fire to make love to a woman, but that was exactly what he felt now.

"Okay, then," he said. "I want more than a kiss. Don't you?"

No denial. Only a long, shaky breath.

Too fast. He was moving too fast. *You've got all night, DeMarco. Use it.*

Or maybe that wasn't it at all. Maybe she was thinking twice about having any kind of relationship with a man who might end up in prison for the next twenty years. Could he really blame her for that?

He smoothed his hands over her shoulders. "I know this is

a strange situation. We're in a hell of a mess, and we don't know what's going to happen tomorrow. So just for tonight—"

"So just for tonight we might as well have sex?"

Startled, Alex leaned away. "No. I didn't mean it like that."

She laughed a little, but it didn't ring true. "But you said it, didn't you? 'Just for tonight.' "

"Val—"

"It's okay, Alex. We're both on the same page now. You want sex; I want sex." She hooked her fingers into his jeans pockets and pulled him back against her. "We're stuck here together, so why not?"

Suddenly all her indecision seemed to vanish, and a thin, cynical smile crossed her lips. What the hell was going on?

It was a monumental effort, but he pushed her away and held her at arm's length. "Val? What are you doing?"

"Gosh, Alex. Of all people, I didn't think you would be somebody I'd have to explain sex to."

Then he knew. She was doing it again. Making huge assumptions about his motives, then baiting him with them to see if he would bite. And if he did . . .

He felt a rush of anger. She was playing a game. Nothing more. She assumed he was merely taking advantage of the situation, just as she thought he had five years ago. She was looking for another reason to go on hating him, and if he took her up on her offer after what she'd just said, she'd have her ammunition.

He was tired of the games. Tired of the accusations she hurled at him. Tired of being treated like the bad guy when he'd never intended to hurt her at all, back then *or* now. And he wasn't going to put up with it anymore.

"Okay," he said. "Fine. You want sex? Let's have sex."

In one smooth swoop, he yanked the hem of his T-shirt out of his jeans, then took it off. He flung it aside, then took a step forward, forcing her to take an awkward step backward until she bumped into the door.

"Take off your clothes."

She blinked with surprise. "What?"

"I said take off your clothes. And move it. I'm not a patient man."

She looked at him with momentary disbelief. Just as

quickly, though, her expression melted into sarcasm. "Gosh, Alex. You're such a romantic."

"It's just sex, Val. Remember? If you want flowers and candlelight, go somewhere else."

He saw the surprise in her eyes, but true to her nature, she didn't back down. After a long pause, she pulled off her T-shirt, striving for an air of nonchalance. She was wearing a lacy blue bra, its fabric so thin he could clearly see the outline of her nipples. Desire flashed through him in an instant, making him so hard so fast that it was all he could do not to rip his jeans off to take away some of the pressure. He wanted to touch her. He wanted desperately to stroke her nipples, to move his fingertips slowly back and forth over them until he felt them harden, until they pressed against the fabric of her bra.

But he couldn't. Not this time.

"Now the jeans."

He saw her swallow hard. "Sure, Alex. Whatever you say."

With a deep, silent breath she ripped open the button fly of her jeans.

"All the way off."

He stood so close to her that she could barely wiggle out of them. Once they were on the floor, he kicked them aside. He lazily appraised her body, moving downward to her waist, then lingering over her blue bikini panties. They were as thin and lacy as her bra, doing little to hide the dark triangle of hair that disappeared between her legs.

And those legs. They were as perfect as he remembered. He had a sudden flash of how they had once been wrapped around him, pulling him deep inside her. He'd felt her hot breath against his ear, saying his name over and over. . . .

He forced himself to look up again, to meet her eyes. He saw a flicker of apprehension, which escalated when he took half a step forward and placed a palm on the door beside her head. She swept her tongue over her lips, her breath coming faster.

Those lips. *Damn.* The kisses he'd given her so far had just been warm-ups. He wouldn't mind spending all night just reacquainting himself with that beautiful mouth of hers.

"So what are you waiting for?" she said breathlessly.

He moved one hand down, and with a casual flick of his fingertips, he opened the front clasp of her bra. She instantly raised her arms and covered her breasts.

"Is there a problem, Val?"

"N-no. Of course not. I was just surprised. . . ."

"Take it off."

After a moment, she slid the straps off her shoulders and let the bra fall to the floor behind her. Before she could cover herself again, he grabbed her wrists and pushed her hands to her sides, then stared down at her. Her breasts were incredible. They were fuller than they seemed to be when she was clothed, and perfectly shaped, capped by rosy-brown nipples that were hardening all by themselves in the cool air of the motel room. For a full ten seconds, all he could do was stare at them, imagining what it would feel like to touch them.

"Like what you see?" she asked.

"Oh, yeah," he said. "That is one *nice* pair of tits."

She closed her eyes at the vulgar remark, letting out a nervous breath at the same time. Her phony enthusiasm was fading quickly, her bravado melting away.

"Come on, Alex," she taunted, her voice a little shaky. "Aren't those jeans of yours getting a little tight?"

"First things first." He backed away from her. "Get on the bed."

She paused a moment, then brushed past him and went to the bed. She'd barely sat down before he pushed her onto her back, taking a wrist in either hand and pinning them against the bed above her shoulders. Her eyes flew open wide, glinting with unmistakable panic, an expression that grew even more distressed when he pressed his knee onto the bed in the space between her legs. She squirmed against him, but she was trapped.

"So is this how you want it?" he said. "Down and dirty?"

"Sure," she said breathlessly. "Why not?"

"Wish I'd known that all I had to do was snap my fingers and you'd get naked. Think of all the fun we could have been having."

He could feel her trembling, but still she looked at him defiantly. "You're all talk, Alex. Where's the action?"

He released her and backed away, catching her panties with his fingertips in one smooth move and yanking them down to her knees. She gasped and tried to sit up, but he pushed her down again.

"Don't move."

He sat down on the bed beside her, splaying one palm against her abdomen. Then he ran his other hand upward from her knee until he reached the junction of her thighs. She closed her eyes, her jaw clenched tightly, and a hot pink flush rose on her cheeks.

He slid his hand over the silky hair between her legs. She gasped and reached for his hand to still it, but he parried with his other hand, pushing hers away. Then he slid his fingers downward and tried to slip them inside her, only to meet with enough resistance that he knew just how much she'd been lying to him. She might be talking as if she were enjoying this, but her body was telling the real story.

"I thought you were ready for sex," he said.

"Alex—"

"You're a tease, Val. Your words are telling me you want it, and your body's telling me you don't. Which is it?"

"I do want it. But I'm not quite . . . I mean, you haven't . . ." Her voice trailed off, and she turned her head away.

"Haven't what? Made love to you?"

"No. That's not what I mean."

"Then what do you mean? I'm just giving you what you asked for. So what's the problem?"

"No problem. I-I just—"

"I thought we decided we'd dispense with all that useless foreplay crap. Was I wrong?"

"Stop it, Alex."

"After all, Val, it's just sex."

"I said *stop it*!"

She sat up suddenly and reached for the bedsheet. Before she could drag it over her, Alex stood up, grabbed her by her upper arms, and hauled her to her feet.

"Of course you want me to stop! And do you know why? Because now you know what 'just sex' feels like and you don't want any part of it!"

She opened her mouth to speak, then closed it again. Tears sprang to her eyes.

"It's pretty damned cold, isn't it?" When she didn't respond, he gave her a shake. "Isn't it?"

"Yes!"

"Does it bear *any* resemblance—any at all—to what happened between us five years ago?"

She blinked several times, her expression wavering. Then she seemed to crumple a little in his grip, and her eyes filled with tears.

"No," she whispered.

"Then don't you *ever* use those words to describe anything between us ever again. Do you understand?"

She gave him a shaky nod.

He released her. She sat back down on the bed. He grabbed her jeans and T-shirt and tossed them to her. He walked over and picked up his shirt from the floor.

"You actually thought I meant to go through with it, didn't you?" he said. "That you were seeing the real me?"

She wiped a tear from her cheek with the back of her hand and turned away again. He pulled his T-shirt over his head and yanked it down.

"That just goes to show that you don't know a damned thing about me." He strode to the door, then whipped back around. "I'm tired of being the bad guy, Val. I know I made a lot of wrong moves that night. But don't you ever again try to insinuate that I was nothing but a hard-hearted son of a bitch who didn't give a damn about you, because you know better. You *know* better."

He yanked the door open and left the room, slamming it closed behind him.

Val pulled the sheet up to her chin, tears staining her face, still feeling Alex's anger radiating throughout the room. She held her hands out and realized they were trembling.

He was right. He'd been a totally different man five years ago. He'd made love to her for hours, kissing her, touching her, coaxing her to peak after peak of excitement, taking pleasure himself only when he'd given it to her first.

Nothing like the man he'd been tonight.

No. That wasn't right. It was exactly like the man he'd been tonight, before she'd accused him of wanting her for all the wrong reasons.

She pulled on her jeans, then peeked out through the curtains. Alex sat on the steps outside, his back to her. He was just sitting there motionless, his elbows on his knees and his hands clasped in front of him, staring ahead at nothing.

Val lay down on one side of the bed and pulled the covers up over her. What had she done, talking to him like that? Everything had been so wonderful, and then she'd said those things, and then . . .

She started to cry again. It felt so strange, so unfamiliar to have all those tears running down her face, and she desperately tried to stop. She never cried. Never. The only times she could remember shedding a single tear in her adult life, Alex had been the cause of it.

Eons seemed to pass before she heard his footsteps on the porch. He opened the door and came back inside the room, then walked to the edge of the bed. Her heart thundered inside her chest.

But he didn't say a word. He merely grabbed a pillow, then a spare blanket from the closet. He tossed them both down on the sofa on the other side of the room.

"Alex. You don't have to sleep on the sofa."

He didn't respond. She turned slightly and saw him taking off his shirt again. Then he lay down on the sofa. She had the most desperate urge to walk over there. To touch him again. But she knew she couldn't stand it if he pulled away from her. And he would. She had no doubt about that.

She lay awake for a long time, Alex's words floating around inside her mind.

Don't you ever again try to insinuate that I was nothing but a hard-hearted son of a bitch who didn't give a damn about you, because you know better. You know *better.*

If that were true, though, it begged the question: If it hadn't been just sex between them, then what had it been?

At eight o'clock the next morning, Stanley opened the door to the Quick Mart and stepped inside, the jingle bells attached to the door announcing his arrival. But Glenda was busy ringing up a customer and didn't look his way.

He circled around to the coffeepot and poured himself a cup. Unfortunately, his hands were shaking so much that when he reached for the creamer, he practically spilled it.

No. He had to get a grip. Everything was cool. Glenda had danced with him last night. He hadn't stepped on her feet or said anything really dumb. And when he walked her back to the table where she'd been sitting, she'd invited him to join her.

Of course, then Tony and Roy Jr. and all their friends had started setting off pop-bottle rockets a little too close to the pavilion. He'd had to leave the table to handle that situation, and then Harold, who'd had about three beers too many, tried to take a swing at Odell for no apparent reason except that the two of them hated each other. By the time he got finished clearing all that up, Glenda had gone home and he hadn't gotten to talk to her again.

But he could talk to her now.

All he had to do was make a little small talk. Shoot the breeze. Then, when he was all loosened up and relaxed, he could try asking her out again. They'd gotten along pretty well last night. Maybe this time she'd say yes.

He fiddled around putting cream and sugar in his coffee until the customer left, then brought the cup to the counter. "Morning, Glenda."

"Morning, Stanley. Nice celebration last night, wasn't it?"

"Yeah. Real nice." He handed her a five-dollar bill. "I'm sorry you couldn't stay longer."

"I didn't realize I'd stayed as long as I had. I had to get home to see about my grandmother."

"Uh-huh."

She punched the register, then put the five in the drawer and handed him his change. And all at once, his mind went totally blank.

Say something. Say anything.

He couldn't think of a damned thing.

He just stood there staring at her as several long, excruciating seconds ticked past, until he was absolutely sure that he looked like a total dimwit.

"Stanley? Is there something else you need?"

"Need?"

"Yes."

"Uh, no. Nothing. Just the coffee. Thanks."

He backed away from the counter. Then he turned and left the store, kicking himself all the way back down the street to the sheriff's office.

Before coming into the store, he'd rehearsed a hundred things in his mind that he could say to Glenda, but when the chips were down, he hadn't been able to remember a single one of them.

Hot outside, isn't it? Gonna be another scorcher.

I see you're getting more kinds of potato chips in now than you ever were. Why is that?

That's sure a pretty blouse you have on today.

Look at that. Y'all got some new bumper stickers. "Keep honking, I'm reloading." That's a good one, isn't it?

Now, how hard would that have been?

Plenty hard, when he looked like a geek and acted like one, too.

Stanley went into the sheriff's office, set his coffee on the desk, and collapsed in the chair. He was crazy about Glenda. Absolutely crazy about her. He couldn't sit still for two minutes without an image of her pretty face popping into his head. Yet even after she'd danced with him last night, still he could barely talk to her, and if he couldn't talk to her, then he'd never be able to ask her out again, and if he couldn't ask her out again . . .

Well, somewhere at the end of all that was marriage and happily ever after, but for a guy like him, taking those steps in the middle would be like climbing Mount Everest.

He glanced into the tray of the fax machine and was surprised to see a document laying there. That was rare. Sheriff Dangerfield had gotten the machine because he thought it was time that they moved into the twenty-first century, but it didn't do much but sit there and collect dust.

He picked up the piece of paper, and a word leaped out at him like a big neon sign.

WANTED.

Stanley came to attention, wheeling around in his chair and sitting up straight. According to the fax, a man named Alex DeMarco had jumped bail and was wanted on a bizarre sex murder charge in Tolosa. Six feet four inches tall, two hundred twenty pounds, brown hair, brown eyes. And, of all things, he was a police officer.

Then Stanley looked at the photo, and if he hadn't been sitting down, he was sure he'd have fainted dead away.

It looked exactly like Dan Roberts.

Stanley blinked. Then blinked again. But there was no mistaking the face. None at all. Dan Roberts was actually Alex DeMarco. And he was a murderer. And a rogue cop on top of that.

The fax went on to say that he was thought to be traveling with a woman, and it gave her description. The description fit Sarah Roberts perfectly. Only her name was really Valerie Parker.

Oh God, oh God, oh God . . .

A hot tingle inched its way through Stanley's body, and his hands began to shake. He laid the fax down on the desk and clasped his hands together, but still they quivered like Jell-O. He took a long, deep breath.

Fugitives. Real live fugitives right here in Tinsdale. He knew who they were. But they didn't *know* he knew.

He could bring them in.

The moment that thought entered his mind, dread shuddered through him. He'd never be able to pull off something like that. Not with a guy DeMarco's size, and a cop at that. Never.

But if he did . . .

They'd talk about him from now on. The man who kept Tinsdale safe from the bad guys. *Tell us the story again, Stan. About how you brought those fugitives in.*

And then they'd buy him a beer and hang on his every word. They'd slap him on the back and ask him how things were going—had he apprehended any more dangerous criminals lately?

His picture would be in the paper. Maybe Glenda herself would put it there, and when she stopped to look at it she'd think about what a brave man he was.

This town needs a man like you running things, everybody would say. *Of course you'll be our new sheriff, won't you?*

But this was scary. Really scary. He knew he should ask for help.

No. Damn it, if he asked for help, then those guys from Ruston and Wendover would take over everything, and everyone would forget that he was the one who'd spotted them in the first place.

He had to do this all by himself.

He'd told the two of them that he'd pick them up this morning at Cletus's station to take them back out to their van. That was when he could make his move.

He sat back in his chair and formulated a plan, thinking that if he could only keep from throwing up, it just might work.

chapter sixteen

"Gotcha all fixed up," Cletus said. "I called Stanley and told him you're ready to go, and he's coming right over to take you back out to your car."

"Thanks, Cletus," Alex said. "Appreciate it."

"Anytime. The next time you folks are passing through, you be sure to drop by."

Alex picked up the tire and took it outside, where he saw Val coming across the parking lot from their motel room, her backpack tossed over one shoulder. He turned his gaze away as she approached.

"I paid the bill," he told her. "Stanley will be here any minute to take us back to the van."

She nodded silently.

Damn. He hated this. He hated that they'd barely spoken this morning. He hated that he couldn't even look at her because of what had happened between them last night. He'd wanted so much to make love to her, to spend the long hours of the night trying to make up in some small way for what had happened between them years ago. And then somehow it had gotten all twisted around. And then he'd lost it. Completely lost it. Damn it, he'd pushed her so hard that she'd had to *shout* at him to get him to stop. Not once in his life could he remember being that angry and that out of control.

And once again, Val had been the cause of it.

Not that he hadn't been justified in his anger. But the way he'd chosen to take it out on her had been completely out of line. Maybe it was time he learned his lesson. He never should have danced with her, never should have kissed her, never should have done anything that would lead to the two of them naked in bed.

Keep your distance from now on. No matter what.

Stanley pulled into the parking lot and brought his car to a halt a few feet away from them. He got out of the car and gave them a smile. "Morning, folks. Are you ready to go?"

"Yeah," Alex said. "We're ready."

The deputy unlocked the trunk. Alex tossed the tire inside it and slammed the lid.

"Oh, sorry about that stuff in the front seat," Stanley said. "My aunt talked me into going down to the fruit market this morning and picking up a few things. I didn't have a chance to drop them by her house."

Alex looked in the front seat, and the skin prickled on the back of his neck. It was piled almost to the ceiling with crates of fruit, with no room for a passenger. Anyone who rode in this car with Stanley would be riding in the backseat.

Something was up.

"It's not far out to your van," Stanley went on. "I thought you wouldn't mind riding in the back with your wife."

He was staring at Alex with a funny little smile that didn't quite reach his eyes, which were widened just a little bit more than they should have been. It was only ten o'clock in the morning, but the man was sweating as if it were already the hottest hour of the day.

Alex didn't know how, but Stanley was on to them. And Alex knew if he got in the backseat, he was a dead man. But the last thing he needed was a confrontation right here on the main drag of Tinsdale.

"Now, Stanley, I know it's a company car and all, but you really should have put that fruit in the back. Those crates are going to mess up that upholstery something awful. Here," he said, opening up the car door. "I'll take care of it."

He grabbed the crates, one by one, and transferred them to the backseat. The deputy just stood there, frozen to the pavement, his eyes shifting back and forth nervously.

"There you go," Alex said, brushing his hands off. "Shall we get on the road?"

"Uh . . . sure," Stanley said. "But, hey, Dan. Why don't you hop into the backseat this time and let that pretty wife of yours ride up front?"

"He can't do that," Val said.

They both turned around to look at her.

"See, he's always had this claustrophobia problem. He can't stand small, closed-in places." She turned to Alex with a look that said she knew what was going on with Stanley as well as he did. "You go ahead and get in the front seat, honey. I'll ride in the back."

She opened the back door and got into the car. Alex closed the door, then waited to see if the deputy was going to get into the driver's seat before he got into the car himself.

Now that his initial plan had failed, Stanley had three choices. Confront Alex now, confront him later, or don't confront him at all. By the way the man was starting to tremble, Alex was betting on number three.

When the deputy got into the car, his hands were shaking so much that it took him three stabs to get the key into the ignition, which told Alex that the odds of his still trying to apprehend them were slim. He was probably just going to take them back out to the van, let them go, then put some real law enforcement on their trail, but still Alex had to be on his guard.

He slid into the seat next to Stanley, and they drove in silence. Stanley didn't know it, but he should have been thanking his lucky stars that it wasn't a real murderer he was dealing with, or he probably would have been dead by the side of the road by now.

A few minutes later, the deputy pulled up behind the van where they'd left it on the shoulder of the road. Alex got out of the car, then opened the back door for Val to get out. Her expression was tense.

"Don't do a thing," he whispered. "Let me take care of this."

The deputy came around the car and unlocked the trunk. Alex reached in and grabbed the tire. When he stood back up, he was looking down the barrel of Stanley's gun.

Well, shit.

He had to hand it to the guy. He'd actually found that one nerve that allowed him to take his gun out of his holster. But pull the trigger? Alex didn't think there was any way that was going to happen, but he had to watch it just the same. He looked at Stanley with an even gaze, holding his voice steady.

"Something wrong here, Stanley?"

"I know who you are," Stanley said, his voice as shaky as his hands. "Both of you. And I'm taking you in."

"I think there's some mistake. Just who is it you think we are?"

"Alex DeMarco. Valerie Parker. You're a cop. You killed a woman in Tolosa."

Alex turned to Val. "Sarah? What's he talking about?"

Val shrugged offhandedly. "Got me."

"Cut it out," Stanley said, his voice escalating. "I know who you are, and you're going to jail."

"I didn't kill anybody, Stanley. You've got your facts screwed up."

"I don't have anything screwed up. You're Alex DeMarco."

The guy clearly was going to pursue this. Alex decided that further denial wasn't going to get him anywhere.

"Yes, Stanley. I'm Alex DeMarco. Now, what are you going to do about it?"

The deputy's eyes widened. "Get in the backseat."

"Sorry. Can't do that."

"You have to. I have a gun. And I'm n-not afraid to use it."

Alex would take issue with that last statement. Clearly he was *very* afraid to use it.

There was only one thing Alex could do here. There was a risk involved, but a small one. Judging from the way the man's hands were shaking, he figured it was a bigger risk that he'd accidentally pull the trigger and blow both him and Val away.

Alex took two steps forward and yanked the gun right out of his hand.

Stanley gasped, then choked a little, staring down at his hands as if Scotty had suddenly beamed his gun back up to the *Enterprise*. He scrambled backward until he hit the squad car with a heavy thud, holding up his palms. If he'd been shaking before, he'd hit 9.5 on the Richter scale now.

"Don't shoot!" he said, his voice as tremulous as the rest of him. "Please don't shoot!"

Alex shoved the gun into the waistband of his jeans, shaking his head with disgust. "You sorry son of a bitch. How many boxes of Cracker Jacks did you have to go through to get that badge?"

Stanley blinked rapidly, his bland brown eyes full of fear. "W-where did I screw up?"

Alex looked at him with total disbelief. The one thing he couldn't tolerate was incompetence, and this guy had the corner on the market. "Where did you screw up? Where *didn't* you screw up?"

"What do you m-mean?"

"First of all, the fruit thing. Just how stupid do you think I am?"

"Alex," Val said, a warning tone in her voice. "I think it's time we got out of here."

"And never let somebody see you sweat. Never. You've got to learn how to bluff. Even if you're scared shitless, you've got to fake the bad guy into believing you're not. If you don't, you're going to end up a dead man. Do you hear me?"

"Y-yes, sir."

"I saw it the moment you showed up at the motel," Alex said. "You didn't have control of the situation. I'm telling you the bad guys can *smell* it. And they'll use it against you every time. You've got to be a man other officers can trust. Personally, Stanley, I wouldn't trust you to take out the trash."

"Alex," Val said sharply. "That's enough. Let's get the tire changed and get out of here."

"And another thing. The second I came at you, the second you were threatened by a known fugitive, you should have pulled the trigger. And you shouldn't have stopped pulling it until the threat was over. Got that?"

"I should have shot you?"

"Hell, yes!"

Alex couldn't believe it. Part of the role of a law enforcement officer was the ability to shoot to kill if the need arose. This guy wouldn't have the guts to swat a fly.

Alex yanked open the back door of the police car and motioned for Stanley to get in. He immediately complied. Alex shut the door, then pulled the jack out of the van and changed the tire. The whole time, Val stood a few feet away from him, saying nothing. He could tell she was pissed about something, but he couldn't worry about that now.

Once the tire was on, he threw the jack into the van, then opened the back door of the patrol car.

"Get out."

By the look on the deputy's face as he emerged from the car, he was absolutely certain that he was about to draw his last breath. *Good.* That meant he probably wouldn't try anything stupid.

"Take it easy, Stanley," Val said. "I know what you're thinking, but Alex has never killed anybody his life, and he's not about to start now."

Alex turned to Val with disbelief. "Val? You want to shut up?"

"I mean it," Val went on. "He didn't kill that woman. And even though he's trying to show you what a badass he is, there's no way he's going to hurt you. So don't worry, all right?"

"Wrong, Stanley," Alex said, filling his voice with as much malice as he possibly could. "You'd better worry. You'd better worry a *lot*. And you'd better keep worrying the whole time I'm talking to you. Do you understand?"

Val spat out a breath of disgust and turned away.

Stanley looked back and forth between them, as if he didn't know which one of them to believe. What the hell did Val think she was doing? Once this situation was over, he was going to have a word with her about this. A very loud, very threatening word, and for once in her life, she was going to listen.

"Is there another way back to town besides the main highway?" he asked Stanley.

"Uh . . . not really. Except if you cut cross-country. Across that pasture is a dirt road that heads back toward town."

"A dirt road, huh? About how far do you figure it is on that dirt road back to town?"

"Six miles. Maybe seven."

"Much traffic on that road?"

"Pretty much none at all."

"So it might be kinda tough to pick up a ride."

Stanley looked at him as if he were out of his mind, but he was way too scared to say so. "Yeah. I guess it would be."

Alex nodded. "I'll give you one thing, Stanley."

"What's that?"

"Your uniform looks good. Nice polish on the shoes. And the slacks. Nice sharp crease. I like that."

"Uh . . . th-thank you."

"Take them off."

Stanley's eyes shot open wide. "Huh?"

"I said drop your pants."

Stanley stared at him dumbly. "You want me to take my pants off?"

"Didn't I just say that?"

"Don't, Stanley," Val said, then turned to Alex, her voice tight with anger. "Don't make him do that. It's not necessary."

Stanley glanced back at Alex, his gaze hopeful, as if he thought maybe he'd change his mind. Alex responded by leaning in closer to the deputy, lowering his voice to a malicious drawl.

"Now, Stanley, Val's spent a lot of time here trying to convince you that I'm a real pussycat. But just between you and me, I'm not the kind of man who puts up with a whole lot of crap. And the minute anybody hands me any, I start to get pissed. Really pissed. Now, it's up to you. Do you really want to mess with me?"

Stanley swallowed hard, then began to unbuckle his belt. Val buried her face in her hand, shaking her head. Stanley stepped out of the pants, revealing blue boxers with tiny white polka dots. Alex yanked the car keys out of one of the pockets, stuffed them into his pocket, then took the deputy's pants and tossed them into Val's van.

"Okay, Stanley. Tell me what tipped you off. How did you know who we really were?"

Stanley reached into his shirt pocket and pulled out a folded piece of paper. Alex took it from him and opened it up, and he realized immediately that staying out of the hands of the authorities might be a lot tougher than he'd anticipated.

Henderson had done a fax blast, probably to every law enforcement agency in the state, something Alex definitely hadn't expected. The man's grudge against him was even more powerful than he thought, so much so that he intended to turn over every single rock he could in order to find him.

Alex folded the fax back up and stuck it in his hip pocket. *Okay.* At least now he knew what they were up against.

"Just so you know," Alex said, "there's no use trying to put anyone on our trail. Before you can even make it back to town, we'll already have crossed the border into Mexico." He turned to Val. "Let's go."

He left Stanley standing there and went to the driver's door of the van. Val opened the passenger door, but instead of getting in, she reached behind the seat and grabbed two bottles of water.

"What are you doing?" he asked.

She didn't respond. She turned around and walked back to Stanley.

"You'll get thirsty in this heat," Alex heard her say.

Stanley took the bottles from her. "Thanks."

"Glenda. I think she really likes you. Just be yourself, okay? That's all she wants."

"That's because she doesn't know me very well."

"No. She does. Trust me on that, okay?"

He nodded.

"Sorry about the pants. Alex can be so unreasonable. He's not a killer, though. Really. Just a jerk sometimes."

"Val!" Alex shouted.

"Gotta go." She sighed a little. "I really hate the thought of going to Mexico, but if we don't, Alex is going to end up in prison for something he didn't do. I guess it's a good thing I speak some Spanish, huh? It's going to come in handy." She gave him a smile. "*Adios,* Stanley."

Stanley waved a little, as if they were two good friends parting ways. Val trotted back to the van and got inside. Alex put the vehicle in gear and hit the gas.

"What in the *hell* was all that about?" he asked.

"What? Giving him water so he doesn't drop dead in the heat?"

"No. All that other crap. Right now that man is the enemy, and you're treating him like he's your best buddy. And you've got the nerve to tell him that I was being a jerk?"

"You were. You didn't have to humiliate him."

"He pulled a gun on us! Did you want me to just let him take us to jail?"

"No! But you didn't have to tell him he isn't fit to wear a badge and all that other stuff!"

"He *isn't* fit to wear a badge!"

She fumed silently, wearing that stern-jawed, narrow-eyed expression again that said she wasn't half-finished with him yet, though he sure as hell didn't know why.

"Val," he said, speaking slowly and distinctly so she wouldn't miss his meaning. "He allowed a suspect to take the gun right out of his hand. He's a danger to any other officer he works with."

"You're always so damned righteous. Not everyone can be as picture-perfect as you are."

"He's wearing a badge. He shouldn't be. That pisses me off."

"He's a Barney Fife in a one-horse town! Will you cut him just a little bit of slack?"

"He wanted to take us to jail!"

"He was just trying to do his job, and you had to go and humiliate him. Telling him what a breeze it would have been to take you in if only he'd done it right. Well, that's bullshit. I don't give a damn what that poor guy did, he didn't stand a chance against you."

Alex just stared at her. "Whose side are you on?"

"All you had to do was take his car keys. You didn't have to take his pants. That was gratuitous."

"Gratuitous? I do something to make sure we get enough of a head start that maybe he won't be able to put *real* law enforcement on our tails, and I'm being *gratuitous*?"

"Is that in some police handbook somewhere, Alex? The more you humiliate a man, the less likely he is to give you trouble? It's got to be written down somewhere, because I know how you like to go by the book."

"It was the best thing to do, and you know it," Alex said hotly. "Without his pants, he'll walk back to town on the dirt road instead of the highway, trying not to be seen. He'll stand no chance of getting picked up. Hell, he'll do everything he can *not* to get picked up. That'll buy us at least a few hours before he tells everybody he knows that we were here."

Val glared at Alex. "Can you imagine how that made him feel? Can you even *imagine*?"

"I don't give a damn how he feels!"

"No. You don't, do you? You never think twice about how anyone feels."

Val turned to stare out the passenger window, her arms folded across her chest. Alex couldn't believe this. If he'd ever wondered if he'd made the right decision to recommend her dismissal from the academy, he damned sure wasn't wondering now. Not only was she reckless, she was a bleeding heart, and that kind of attitude would have gotten her killed within a year.

"Val, if I had to worry about the feelings of everybody I deal with every day, I'd never get my job done."

She turned to glare at him. "If you worried about *somebody's* feelings just once in your life, you might actually prove you have a heart."

Alex gritted his teeth, willing himself to stay calm. A heart. Was that what she wanted him to have? Did she want him to be sweet and sensitive and all that other crap, so much so that he let his guard down? That he considered somebody's *feelings* over their ability to escape?

He'd handled the situation with Stanley exactly as he should have, to minimize their chances of getting arrested. If he went looking for that heart that Val swore he didn't have, both of them were going to be in big trouble. Connecting with people in a personal way, as Val was so prone to doing, only caused problems when the time came to lay down the law. He'd learned that lesson with Val herself, hadn't he? If he hadn't gotten so close to her, if he hadn't made love to her that night, then when he was forced to dismiss her from the academy it wouldn't have been nearly as traumatic for either of them.

Keep it impersonal. That was what he should have done then, and what he was right to do now. But just because he was right didn't mean that proclaiming it was the smartest thing to do. Val was so pissed at him that she wouldn't be in any state of mind to get to work once they reached the Reichert ranch. He had to fix that. Right now.

"Maybe I was a little hard on Stanley," he said.

Val turned slowly, a disbelieving look on her face. "What did you say?"

"I probably didn't have to say all that. If I had it to do again, I wouldn't."

Val shifted around in her seat and stared at him. "You wouldn't tell him how incompetent he is?"

"No. I wouldn't."

"Or tell him he could have taken you in, if only he'd done it right?"

"I wouldn't do that, either."

"Or taken his pants?"

"Now, I still would have done that. It was absolutely necessary to slow him down, and that's about the only way there was to do it outside of shooting him. If you'll think about it, you'll know it's true."

Val looked away, then nodded. "Okay. I see your point."

Alex let out a silent sigh of relief. He'd met her in the middle in a nice little compromise, and now maybe they could stay away from each other's throats and get on down the road.

"Alex?"

"Yes?"

She sighed. "Look, I know I flipped out and said some nasty things to you. And I know I undermined your authority in front of Stanley, and I promise you I'll never do anything like that again. But I just wanted you to see . . ."

She paused, as if searching for words.

"I know you don't have any idea what a guy like Stanley goes through, because you've got it all. You're smarter than he is, you're way better-looking, you've got tons more self-control, and you're about a thousand times more capable. Stanley doesn't have any of that to fall back on. So when you start hacking away at him the way you did back there, it doesn't take long before there's nothing left."

All at once, Alex was hit with the memory of Stanley's face when he told him how incompetent he was. It was the look of a man who could probably count the things he'd done right in his life on the fingers of one hand. A man who'd reached for a moment of glory and had gotten humiliated instead. A man who had no trouble living up to his potential because he didn't have any.

To his surprise, Alex felt an odd, thorny sensation begin to eat away at him, making sharp little stabs right into his conscience. He tried to brush the feeling away, but as he played back in his mind the things he'd said to Stanley, it only intensified. How much of that had actually been necessary?

You sorry son of a bitch. How many boxes of Cracker Jacks did you have to go through to get that badge?

The fruit thing. Just how stupid do you think I am?

Personally, Stanley, I wouldn't trust you to take out the trash.

Val was right. It had been gratuitous. He hadn't had to say any of those things to get the job done, yet still he had. He'd systematically kicked the shit out of a man who was already down and couldn't have gotten back up if his life depended on it. And Alex couldn't believe the feeling that came over him.

Shame. He felt ashamed.

Christ, he hated this. Since the day he met Val, she'd made quicksand out of things in his life that he'd always assumed were rock-solid. Made him feel things he'd never felt before. And here she was doing it again.

Stop thinking about it. It's nonproductive. You have a job to do, and you need to get your head on straight.

They rode in silence for miles, drawing closer to their destination. The terrain was hilly with dry grassland, the forested areas limp and water-starved.

Then they came up over a hill, and suddenly the scraggly barbed-wire fence they had been following gave way to a white wooden one that stretched as far as Alex could see. In the distance, a narrow paved road led off the highway onto the property and disappeared into the trees. As they drew closer, they came to a heavy metal gate flanked on either side by brick columns. Small concrete slabs were inset into the columns, and carved into each one, in heavy block lettering, was the name REICHERT. He slowed the van, then came to a halt near the gate.

"Looks like we've arrived."

chapter seventeen

Stanley trudged along the dirt road, every step he took a little wearier than the last. Sweat poured down his face. The breeze had kicked up a bit, swirling dust all around him until it adhered to every inch of his bare skin. He took off his hat, wiped his brow with the already-drenched sleeve of his shirt, then put it back on again. The sun was frying his legs, and he knew they'd be beet red by the time he got to town. Actually, that didn't matter much, because nobody would be noticing the fact that his naked legs were sunburned. They'd only be noticing his naked legs. And with his luck, the sunlight would probably go through his boxers and give him a polka-dotted ass.

He took a swig of the water Val had given him, wondering how in the world a nice woman like her had ever gotten tangled up with a bastard like DeMarco. He'd been terrified when the guy told him to get out of the car, sure that anybody who'd murdered once wouldn't hesitate to do it again. But Val had been right. DeMarco's trigger finger hadn't gotten itchy after all, and except for the fact that he was going to be humiliated beyond all recognition when he came back into town, he'd emerged relatively unscathed.

In a way, though, he wished the man had just gone ahead and shot him.

DeMarco's words echoed through his mind over and over as he walked down this road, and every one of them was true. He was a screwup. A complete and total screwup. DeMarco might be a murderer, but he'd also been a cop, and he was certainly in a position to know how cops were supposed to behave. And what Stanley had done this morning evidently wasn't it. He'd finally had the opportunity to do something really big. Something worthwhile. Something that would make the rest of the world sit up and take notice for once in his pitiful life.

And he'd screwed it up.

When he got back to town, the first thing he should do was notify the Tolosa police that he'd seen their fugitives. But he knew if he did, that sometime, somewhere, some way, word would get back to the people of Tinsdale exactly what had happened out on that highway this morning, and he couldn't bear the thought of that. It was one thing to show up pantless. It was another thing for people to know just how badly he'd had to mess things up in order to make that happen. The two of them were going to Mexico, anyway, which meant that the Tolosa cops couldn't pick them up under any circumstances. So he decided he'd just keep his mouth shut and hope that sometime in the far, far future, people might start to think that they'd just imagined that one day Deputy Obermeyer had walked into town half-naked.

And then he heard a car on the road behind him.

He spun around, feeling a jolt of mortification, only to realize that maybe it was a way to minimize the damages. He could beg a ride, and then get whoever it was to drop him off at his house. Yes, they'd tell the story, laughing their heads off well into the next decade, but at least the number of people who actually observed his humiliation firsthand would be limited to one. Hearsay was a whole lot better than having eyewitnesses. He decided this was a good thing.

Until he saw who was driving the car.

Glenda slowed her Toyota as she approached him, rolling down the window at the same time.

No, no, no!

He glanced around furtively, but he had no place to hide. There wasn't so much as a tree nearby to climb or a shrub to squat behind. He was stuck right out there in the open for Glenda McMurray to laugh at.

He spun back around and kept walking, feeling his face flush as red as his legs. She pulled up beside him, driving as slowly as he was walking. Out of the corner of his eye, he saw her looking at him with utter disbelief, her gaze focusing far too long on what was below his waist. Or what wasn't.

"Stanley? What happened to your pants?"

"Keep on driving, Glenda," he said, still walking purposefully, still refusing to meet her eyes. "Just drive right past me and keep on going."

"No! I'm not going to leave you here like this!"

"Why aren't you at work?"

"My grandma dropped her glasses behind the dresser, so I had to run home for a minute. I was just heading back."

"Why did you take this road?"

"It's a shortcut to her farm if I come in from the back. I drive this way all the time."

And if he'd known that, he'd have taken his chances on the highway.

"You're not going to tell me what happened to your pants, are you?"

"Nope."

"Why you're walking instead of driving?"

"Nope."

"Why you don't have your gun?"

"Nope."

"Stanley, why don't you get in the car and let me take you home?"

He kept walking, wondering what in his life he'd done so awful that God would be punishing him like this. He'd tried to live a good life. He went to church. Tithed ten percent of his pitiful deputy's salary even when he didn't have it to give. Helped people out whenever he could. And now look what had happened. He thought he knew what humiliation was, but he'd never even scratched the surface until now.

"I suppose you're going to tell everybody about this," Stanley said.

"Now, why would I go and do that?"

"Because making fun of me is the number one sport in this town. That's why."

"I don't believe that."

"That's because you haven't lived here long. Pretty soon you'll get the hang of it, right along with everybody else."

"Stanley. You can't just go walking back into town like that. Please. Just get in the car and I'll take you home."

God, what a decision. He could ride with Glenda minus his

pants so she could see up close and personal what a screwup he really was, or he could walk home minus his pants and let the whole town witness his humiliation.

He'd already hit rock bottom with Glenda. Was it even possible to sink any lower?

He stopped. Turned to face her car. She brought it to a halt, and he opened the passenger door and got in. He pressed himself against the door without saying a word, turning his attention out the window.

She drove on, tapping her fingertips on the steering wheel. After a few minutes, she flipped the radio on to a country-and-western station.

"Oooh, I like this song. Don't you?"

He just stared out the window, feeling hot and smelly, knowing that he had to be leaving a butt-shaped sweat stain on the velour upholstery of her car.

"You're going to have a pretty nasty sunburn there," she went on. "Be sure to put something on it when you get home."

Great. She was looking at his legs. His naked, hairy, skinny legs that were currently the color of a ripe tomato. He couldn't imagine anything a woman would find less attractive.

"We've got a couple of new magazines at the store," she went on. "I don't think you saw them when you were in there this morning. You might want to take a look—"

"Glenda," he snapped. "I'm half-naked here. The last thing I want to talk about is songs, sunburns, and magazines."

"I wish you'd just tell me—"

"Hush."

"But—"

"Just drive me home. And don't say another word." *And then I'll pray I never run into you again.*

They drove in silence the rest of the way to town. She pulled up in the alley behind his house and he got out, slamming the door behind him. He heard her say good-bye, but he never turned around, knowing that the last look she was going to have of him featured his backside in a pair of blue-and-white boxers. He was never going to be able to face her again, pants or no pants.

Never.

*   *   *

Val sat in the van with Alex as the engine idled, both of them staring at the narrow paved road that led from the highway onto the property. She assumed it must lead to the house, but the road disappeared into the trees with no house in sight.

"Okay," Val said. "What now?"

"First of all," Alex said, "we have to assume that Stanley will call Henderson. With luck, he believed the bit about us going to Mexico, and what you said there at the end to him should cinch it. I think the most Henderson will do is alert law enforcement in this area that we've been spotted and tell them to be on the lookout. As long as we can get the van hidden, nobody should know we're anywhere near here."

"Can you find out what Stanley ends up telling him?"

"I'll phone Dave later, once Stanley has had a chance to get back to town and spill his guts."

"Is it smart to call Dave? Couldn't he trace a cell call?"

"Some carriers can actually triangulate and pinpoint the position of a caller. Sometimes they can just check signal strength and see how far away the caller is. But it doesn't really matter."

"Why not?"

"Because I trust my brother. He won't even try it."

"Okay. How do you suggest we approach the house?"

Alex eyed it for a moment. "I don't want to go blindly into those trees, not knowing what's on the other side of them, particularly when we're within sight of the highway. We need another vantage point so we can check out the place. Maybe we can find another road through it or around it."

Half a mile down the highway they found a tiny dirt road full of potholes that appeared to run along the western perimeter of the ranch. Driving north, they found that the road led up a hillside. Val rolled down the window, then pulled out a pair of binoculars. She looked to the east, watching for the house to come into view.

"Alex. Stop."

He brought the van to a halt. Val hopped out and looked through the binoculars again. Down in a shallow valley across the treetops, she saw the clay tile roof and stucco walls of a sprawling ranch house, but the summer foliage prevented her from getting a clear look at it.

"There it is," Val said as Alex came up behind her. "It must be half a mile off the highway."

"And we're at least that far away from it where we're standing right now. Guess he's a man who likes his privacy."

"Yeah. Just him and about eighteen other guys who pay big bucks to shoot things." She peered around the area. "Nothing seems to be going on down there. There are a couple of barns behind the house. I can see the roofs of several cabins, too."

"No people around the barns or cabins?"

"Not that I can see. But the view is pretty obscured."

"The hunt has probably been under way since early this morning. It should go on most of the day. This will be a good time to get close to the house and take a look."

Then they got back into the van and drove a little farther until Alex found a place to pull it off the side of the road, deep into some heavy foliage, where it was almost completely hidden from view. He cut the engine.

"Okay. Let me see what you have in the way of bugs."

Val climbed into the rear of the van, dug through a storage bin, and extracted something that looked like a pen. "Fully functional writing instrument, fully functional listening device. No one would ever be able to spot it for what it is."

"Perfect. How many do you have?"

"Three."

"What about a phone tap?"

"No problem." She held up what looked like a telephone adapter. "Plug the phone into this, then plug it into the wall, and we can listen in loud and clear."

"What about receivers?"

She handed him something that looked like a small walkie-talkie. "Tune these to different frequencies, and they'll pick up everything."

"They have recorders, don't they?"

"You bet. Voice activated. We have to be within three hundred meters to pick up a signal, but there's plenty of foliage around the house. We should be able to find cover within that radius."

"How about a camera? We need photos of Reichert and his girlfriend."

"I have three. You can take your pick."

"Okay," Alex said. "Let's proceed as if we're going to be able to get into the house on our first trip down there. Maybe we'll be able to, maybe we won't, but let's be prepared."

"What do you think? Bugs in the master bedroom, the kitchen, and the living room?"

"Sounds good. That should catch most of the conversation going on in the house. And as soon as everything is in place, we'll make a phone call to the ranch. We'll tell Reichert that we know he committed the murder. That should get him and his girlfriend talking."

Val took a deep breath of satisfaction. "It's a good plan. We'll get what we're after, Alex. I know we will."

Alex shoved the gun he'd appropriated from Stanley into the waistband of his jeans. "Okay. Let's get going."

Val stuffed the equipment into her backpack, then slung it over her shoulder. They crossed the road, climbed over the board fence onto the Reichert property, then started down a long, sloping hillside through a fairly dense wooded area. The trees helped block some of the intense afternoon sun, but still the heat was oppressive. The landscape was part rocky, part grassy, and Val's tennis shoes crunched on crumbled granite beneath her feet. Scraggly mesquite trees formed most of the vegetation, with occasional live oaks and junipers sprinkled in. Soon they approached a small clearing, where several antelopelike creatures raised their heads from grazing.

"Good heavens," Val said. "Look at them."

They stopped and stared at the animals, who appeared to be of several different species, with some of the oddest stripes and horns that Val had ever seen. The sight was almost zoo-like in its incongruity, one type clashing wildly with another. But looking beyond the antelope, Val saw something even weirder—a shallow pond with half a dozen creatures that looked like water buffalo milling around it.

"You sure we're still in Texas?" Val asked.

Then she heard something in the brush. She turned to her left to see a horselike creature not twenty feet in front of her. Her gasp of surprise made Alex whip around. His sudden movement sent the creature spinning around and galloping away, his black-and-white–striped haunches disappearing into the foliage.

"Was that a *zebra*?" Val said, her heart still hammering in her chest.

"Looked like one to me."

"God, what is this? The plains of the Serengeti?"

"Reichert's brochure said he could get anything anybody wanted to shoot. I guess he wasn't joking."

Val couldn't believe this. All these beautiful animals, and the only reason Reichert had brought them here was so somebody could shoot them. Then she thought about what he'd done to Shannon and decided it wasn't so impossible to believe after all.

They walked around the edge of the clearing, staying out of sight as much as they could, then found a path that led through another wooded area in the direction of the ranch house. They went a hundred yards or so before coming to a ten-foot chain-link fence with barbed wire on top.

"What do you make of this?" Val asked.

"We're approaching the house. It's probably a fence to keep the animals from getting too close."

Alex went to the gate. It wasn't locked, but a heavy bar attached to the gate was sunk into a metal tube in the ground, which would have kept just about anything locked inside. He lifted the bar, then swung the gate open. They went through it, and he clanged the bar back down into the ground.

They kept walking. The mesquite trees grew spottier as they descended the small incline of a rocky slope. As they neared the bottom, Val saw a dilapidated, low-roofed shed sitting in a cluster of trees that looked as if a good strong wind might blow it over. Ahead, she could just make out the roofline of the ranch house about a quarter of a mile away. Then she noticed something strange sitting between them and the house— yet another big chain-link fence topped by barbed wire.

"Another fence?" she asked. "What's the deal?"

Alex looked perplexed. "I don't know."

Nervousness crept through Val, which multiplied greatly when she saw Alex's eyes shift back and forth anxiously, scanning the area.

"Something's weird about this," she whispered.

"Val. We didn't just leave an animal enclosure. We entered one."

She felt a jolt of foreboding. "There's barbed wire on top of the fence," she whispered. "What do you suppose is in here?"

"I don't know, but I don't think we should hang around to find out."

Then Val heard the faint crunch of granite. She turned, and ten yards away on the rocky slope behind them was something she'd never expected to see in southwest Texas in this lifetime.

A Bengal tiger.

chapter eighteen

Val gasped, and Alex took hold of her arm to steady her. "Don't panic," he whispered. "And don't move."

Alex slid the gun he'd appropriated from Stanley out of the waistband of his jeans. "I can shoot," he whispered, "but it may take more than one shot to take him out. I don't want to draw that kind of attention in case there are people closer than we realize. There's a shed ten yards behind us. Back toward it very slowly."

He stepped aside, allowing her to ease in that direction, then began to step backward with her. Still the animal didn't move. It stayed in a low crouch, every muscle tense, clearly just waiting for a reason to start the chase.

"Just keep moving," Alex said softly.

He thought they were going to make it without incident, but when they got within twenty feet of the shed, the tiger began to creep forward. The cat took one stealthy step, then two, its gaze fixed on them intently.

Alex glanced back at Val. Her shoe landed on a rock and her ankle twisted slightly, knocking her off balance. Rock crunched beneath her foot. Alex spun back around to find the tiger at full alert.

Then the big cat began to run.

"Go!" Alex shouted.

In three strides, Val reached the shed and yanked the door open. Alex shoved her through the doorway, then followed her into the shed. He slammed the door hard and the latch caught, but the tiger slid its paw beneath the door, turned it over, and dug its claws into the aged wood, yanking the door back and forth, rattling it on its hinges.

"Alex?" Val said breathlessly. "Is that door going to hold?"

He stomped on the tiger's paw, once, twice, until finally the big cat pulled away. Alex stood there for a moment, waiting until he was sure the animal had retreated, then went to the wall of the shed. He peered out a slit between two of the boards to find the cat pacing up and down.

"What's he doing?" Val said.

"Still scoping us out. He looks a little hungry."

"And me without my kitty treats."

"Are you kidding? We *are* the kitty treats."

Alex wiped his brow with the sleeve of his T-shirt. "The barbed wire should have been a tip-off. I should have realized something dangerous was in here."

"Hey, it didn't ring the right bells with me, either." She blew out a breath. "Okay. What now?"

"If he'll get away from this shed and move on down the hill far enough, we can make a run for it."

"Until then?"

"We wait."

"If we don't get down to the house before the hunting party returns, we may have a harder time getting inside."

"We still have time. Let's play it this way for now."

Val turned around and sat down on the wooden slat floor. Alex joined her, both of them leaning against the wall.

"God, it's hot in here," Val said.

"I don't suppose you brought any water with you."

"Yeah. One bottle. Want some?"

"Let me get a little more desperate first. You go ahead."

"I'll wait, too."

Alex leaned his head back against the wall. The wood that composed the shed had grayed with age. Several of the boards had dried and shrunk from years in the Texas heat, with fissures throughout their lengths.

Val sighed. "Well. This sucks, doesn't it?"

"Just add it to the list."

"That list is getting pretty long."

"And now it's got a tiger on it. Unbelievable."

"I thought you told me Reichert could have any animal he wanted to out here except big cats."

"So he broke the law. He also murdered his wife."

"Good point."

Alex nodded toward Val's head. "You lost your bandage."

She put her hand to her temple. "Probably fell off on the way into the shed. I didn't notice. Guess I was a little distracted."

"When are you supposed to have the stitches taken out?"

"Tomorrow. Probably won't make that appointment, will I?" She sighed, touching her fingertips to the stitches again. "It'll probably leave an ugly scar."

"Nah. I've had some pretty nasty wounds stitched, and even those scars almost went away."

"When did you have stitches?"

"I fell out of a tree when I was six years old. Scraped my back on a limb coming down. It took twenty-seven stitches to close up three wounds, but now you can barely see the scars."

"You're lucky you didn't break your neck."

"That's what my father said as he was dragging me to the emergency room."

Val sighed, closing her eyes again. Her face was flushed red.

"Drink some water," he said.

"I'll wait."

"Drink."

Val sighed, then reached into her backpack. "Dave was right. You *are* bossy."

She pulled the cap up on the bottle, took a drink, then held it out to him. He put his palm up.

"Drink," she said. *"Now."*

He took the bottle and tipped it up, taking a single swallow. He smacked the top down again, then handed it back to her. "Now who's being bossy?"

She smiled. "A characteristic we actually have in common. And such a nice one at that. Did hell freeze over when I wasn't paying attention?"

"I'd be happy for anything to freeze over right about now."

She returned the bottle to her backpack, then leaned against the wall again.

Silence. And dirt and sweat. And a whole lot of heat.

Alex rose to his knees again and peered out another crack in the wall to see the cat still pacing up and down in front of the shed.

"Sure wish I could talk him into lying in the shade of that big tree about fifty yards down the hill."

"Nah. He's used to Africa. He doesn't mind the heat." Val sighed. "I, on the other hand, can do without it."

Alex settled back against the wall again. Half an hour passed. Then an hour. And through it all, the tiger seemed content to lounge right in front of the door to the shed. The later it progressed into the afternoon, the more the heat seemed to melt every minute into a sluggish, expanded unit of time that dragged way beyond sixty seconds. With the deathly still air inside the shed, even breathing became a chore.

"So," Val said, "if you could take your pick right now, would you be floating in a swimming pool, snow skiing in Switzerland, or sitting in front of a window air-conditioning unit turned on full blast?"

Alex grimaced. "Is there anything else you'd like to torture me with?"

"No. It's not torture. Really. It'll make you feel better to visualize something cold."

"Yeah. Right. It'll help to visualize an iceberg while I'm sitting in a furnace."

"Trust me. Close your eyes."

"What?"

"Will you just do it?"

He gave her a look that said "This is really dumb" then closed his eyes.

He heard her settle back against the wall. She took a deep breath and let it out slowly.

"Okay," she said. "Picture a place in the mountains where it's warm during the day. Not hot. Just warm. A place where there's not a speck of humidity in the air—just a nice, comfortable warmth that melts right into your bones."

He opened his eyes. "I can do without more heat."

"I'm getting to the cold part. Will you just be patient?"

He twisted his mouth with disgust, then closed his eyes again.

"Then evening comes," she said, her voice a near whisper. "The warmth starts to fade. At first you don't even notice it. But then you turn to the west and see the sun finally slip behind the mountains. A chill seeps into the air. A breeze stirs it up a little, swirling it around you until you feel a little shiver. Goose bumps pop out all over your arms."

Alex didn't feel the least bit cooler, but he had to admit he was enjoying every word Val spoke in that soft, mesmerizing voice.

"It was so warm during the day that you're wearing short sleeves," she went on, "but suddenly it's not enough to keep you warm. You go inside to grab a sweater. When you come back out, the last of the orange-and-red sunset is fading away and a narrow crescent moon appears. The night sky looks like a black velvet canvas, and stars pop out all over it like little chips of ice. The air is still. Totally still and quiet, as if the chill has slowed everything to a standstill."

Val paused. With his eyes still closed, Alex listened to the soft cadence of her breathing, waiting for her to continue.

"Finally it gets cold," she went on, "so cold that a sweater won't even keep you warm, so you slip inside, get a blanket, and put it around your shoulders. The moon turns from yellow to white, and your breath starts to fog the air. Pretty soon even the blanket isn't enough, but you don't care, because the cold feels so wonderful that you don't want to leave it. And now you know that there's a place where, no matter how hot it gets during the day, a little bit of winter comes at night to chase it all away." She paused. "A place you never want to leave as long as you live."

Then she was silent.

Alex kept his eyes closed, thinking about the place she'd described. And, miraculously, for those moments in time, the heat didn't feel quite so oppressive. But it had nothing to do with the wintry imagery and everything to do with the sound of Val's voice.

"Better?" she whispered.

Slowly he opened his eyes. With his head still resting against the wall of the shed, he turned to look at her.

"Yeah," he said softly. "It must be a beautiful place."

"The mountains of northern New Mexico. I spent a week there one summer. Best vacation I ever had."

"When you were a kid?"

She frowned. "No. Summers when I was a kid were spent in only one place. Cape Cod."

Alex knew that Cape Cod was hardly hell on earth. But clearly it held no fond memories for Val.

"You went there every year?" he asked.

"My stepfather had a house there. He had houses all over the place."

Ah. Her stepfather. The man she supposedly hated. "Cape Cod is nice."

"Yeah. I suppose it is. But he and my mother spent most of the summer entertaining business clients. And I spent most of the summer wishing I were anywhere else."

"So he had a lot of money."

"Oh, yeah."

Alex wanted to know more. But he had a feeling if he asked, she'd never tell him a thing.

Instead, he waited.

Val wiped her forehead on the shoulder of her T-shirt, and he wondered if she was going to continue. Finally she sighed softly and spoke again. But this time her voice was tight. Strained.

"See, William Hamilton was a very wealthy man. My mother worked for him. She had nothing growing up, and she wanted more. A lot more. They got married when I was nine years old."

"He married one of his employees?"

"Yes. Because she had something he wanted."

"Which was?"

"She was beautiful. I don't mean just a little. She was a knockout. Perfect hair, perfect teeth, perfect figure. Every spare dime she had went to manicurists, hairstylists, department stores. She worked hard at losing her accent, and finally went so far as to forbid me to speak Spanish, even though we'd spoken it almost exclusively until I was seven years old. My mother had me when she was seventeen, so she was only twenty-six when she married William Hamilton. He was forty-eight."

"Trophy wife."

"Yeah. And she lived in mortal fear that she wouldn't fit in. Actually, she fit in just fine. I was the one who didn't."

"How so?"

"We came to live with my stepfather in a house that made the Reichert house look like servants' quarters. My mother never spoke Spanish again. From that moment on, I had to talk right, sit right, walk right, act right. Appearances were everything. And when I didn't conform, my mother was horrified."

"Like when you dyed your hair orange."

"Yes. She spent every waking minute trying to keep me from doing something that might displease my stepfather, because, after all, he held the purse strings. She wanted me to dress like some little debutante and act like one, too. What I wanted was never taken into consideration if it clashed with her lifestyle."

Alex thought about where Val lived now, a cozy little apartment in a quirky neighborhood that fit her personality perfectly. He just couldn't see her in some big mansion with servants all over the place.

"Every time I changed my hair color, every time I got caught smoking pot at school, every time I got bad grades, my mother panicked just a little bit more. She hated the fact that I was such an embarrassment to her and her husband. She didn't give a damn about me. She saw me only as somebody who was systematically screwing up her life. The more rebellious I got, the more hateful she became, and I seriously got to thinking that she'd toss me aside in a heartbeat if it came down to me or William Hamilton's money. Then one day I found out—"

She stopped short.

"Found out what?"

She stared down at her hands, her face falling into a tight frown. "I found out how right I was. And just how sleazy a stepfather can be."

Alex felt his stomach clench. He glanced at her, hating to say the words. "Do you mean—"

"Never mind," she said quickly. "I have no idea why I told you that."

"Are you telling me your stepfather—"

"Don't jump to conclusions, Alex. It wasn't as bad as what you're thinking."

"Just how bad was it?"

"Bad enough. But you'll notice I survived just fine."

Alex couldn't imagine what she was talking about. He'd spent a lot of time wondering what made Val tick, but here was more evidence that he'd barely scratched the surface. She said she'd survived just fine. He wasn't so sure.

"And they're both dead now anyway," Val said. "So none of it really matters anymore."

"Dead? Your mother? You said she was pretty young."

"Never mind, Alex."

"Why don't you tell me about it?" he said gently.

She made a scoffing noise. "Because it's a sordid little story full of a lot of pathetic, tear-jerky stuff. And I *know* how you hate all that emotional crap. Believe me—you don't want to hear it."

"Maybe I do."

"Come on, Alex. Anyone with half a brain can see that you're not exactly overflowing with sensitivity. The last thing you want to hear about is my stepfather problems."

"Then why do you suppose I asked?"

"I told you before. Don't try to be sympathetic. It doesn't suit you."

With that, she dismissed him completely. She folded her arms and turned away, as if she wanted to get as far away from him as possible. Something had happened back then, but she wasn't going to talk about it.

At least not to him.

Alex told himself that he should be glad Val had refused to talk. Why had he even asked her any questions in the first place? He didn't need to know any of her deep, dark secrets. After all, she was right. Sympathy was not his strong suit. All his life he'd run the other way as soon as it looked as if he was going to get dragged down into somebody else's problems, because that was the last place he'd ever wanted to be.

Until now.

The moment that thought came into his mind, he shoved it aside. But the more Val huddled against the wall of the shed, refusing to look at him, the more he realized the truth.

He didn't want her to push him away. He wanted her to talk to him. He wanted to know everything about her, the good and the bad. Suddenly the idea of a woman's life becoming part of his didn't scare him in the least. In fact, he welcomed it.

This made no sense. None at all. Given the situation they'

were in, he knew he should be thanking his lucky stars that she'd chosen to keep her problems to herself. Instead, for the first time in his life he wanted to get close to a woman.

And she wouldn't let him.

"What are you so afraid of?" he asked.

She turned, a look of surprise in her eyes. "I'm not afraid of anything."

"I used to believe that. But it's not the truth, is it?" Moving slowly, he sat up, then turned to stare at her. "In fact, I think there are a lot of things you're afraid of. But you can scratch one off your list."

"What's that?"

"Me."

She blinked with surprise, but instead of denying it, she turned away, looking flustered. He pushed a strand of sweat-dampened hair away from her cheek, then coaxed her to look back at him again.

"I care about you, Val. How long is it going to take you to figure that out?"

For a moment she looked at him openly, her eyes wide. Then, slowly, her expression melted into distrust again. And all at once he knew that he wasn't the only one in her life who'd ever gotten that look. It was so sharp, so intense, so well practiced that it had become part of her, a weapon of defense she used when she sensed that one more person was going to let her down. It was her way of beating somebody to the punch.

But right now, something else was mingling with that expression, something she was trying very hard to hide: hope. One tiny glimmer of hope that he was telling her the truth. Christ, what in the world had happened to make her so cynical? To give her such a hard shell that he couldn't blast his way through it?

He could have told her again that he cared about her. He could have told her to trust him, that he wasn't going to hurt her ever again. He could have spoken a hundred different phrases of reassurance, but she was so adept at verbal side-stepping that he knew words just weren't going to cut it. He didn't know exactly what had happened to her in the past to make her so wary. He only knew that he never wanted to see that look on her face again.

Finally, out of sheer frustration, he did the only thing he could think of to do: he curled his hand around the back of her neck, pulled her toward him, and kissed her.

The moment his mouth fell against hers, he felt her surprise. Every muscle in her body tensed. He could feel her inclination to pull away, which told him that kissing her was probably a monumental mistake. But he didn't back off. Instead, he urged her lips apart with his, tangling his fingers in her hair and kissing her hard and deep, without restraint and without the slightest bit of mercy. He wanted the connection between them to hum through every cell in her body, until she knew for a fact that even when he stopped kissing her, something was still between them that wasn't going to go away.

Her initial resistance slowly subsided, but he didn't give an inch. He continued to kiss her until she went limp in his arms, surrendering completely. Only then did he finally pull away. She stared at him breathlessly, her eyes glazed and her cheeks flushed red, her voice as hot as the hill country of southwest Texas in the dead of summer.

"Alex?"

"Yes?"

"Don't stop."

chapter nineteen

The moment Val spoke those two words, Alex's mouth was on hers again. He tightened his hand against the back of her neck, his fingers spread, as he swept his tongue, hot and moist and insistent, deep into her mouth.

The relentless heat in this shed was making her mind so hazy she couldn't think straight, and everything Alex was doing to her was only making her hotter. She needed to push him away, to keep him at arm's length until she could get her bearings. Instead she went limp in his arms, giving in, letting him lower her to the hard plank floor of the shed. He pushed her sweat-soaked hair away from her left cheek and kissed her there, then moved downward to her neck, threading his fingers through her hair at the same time. She moaned softly and tilted her head back, allowing him to kiss all the way down her throat and back up again.

He moved to the tender spot just beneath her ear and teased it with a swirl of his tongue, then gave her a little nip on her earlobe that sent shivers all the way through her. He circled back around to recapture her lips in one more deep, all-encompassing kiss, until the heat they were generating together made the heat in the shed seem frigid by comparison.

She reached around to the small of his back and caught his T-shirt at the edge of his jeans. She yanked it up until it was free, then took a fistful of the hem and pulled it halfway up his back. She placed her palm flat against his bare skin, skimming over its sweat-slicked surface. That one skin-to-skin touch told her that she was never going to get enough of him. Never.

She slid both hands down his back, raking her nails all the way from his shoulders to his waist and back up again. He groaned softly, his lips humming against hers. Then she took a double handful of the back of his shirt and pulled it up toward his neck, urging him to take it off. He rose quickly to his knees. He pulled the gun out of the waistband of his jeans and laid it aside, then dragged his shirt off over his head and threw it down, the veins of his arms standing out in sharp relief every time his biceps flexed. He hovered over her for a moment, his chest and shoulders slick with sweat, and she didn't think she'd ever seen a more gorgeous man in her life. He was all bone and muscle, with dark hair across his chest that came together in a narrow band that ran down the hollow between his abdominals and swirled around his navel, before finally disappearing into the waistband of his jeans.

Still on his knees, he reached down, tugged the hem of her T-shirt free, then tucked his hands beneath it. He skimmed his hands up her sides, dragging her T-shirt along with them until it was bunched up under her arms, exposing her bra. She gasped.

"Alex—"

"My shirt, now yours."

"But—"

"You said don't stop. Did you mean it?"

He loomed over her, breathing hard, impatience running wild on his face. She tried to drag in a decent breath, but the thick, heat-soaked air in the shed made it impossible, netting her nothing but the scent of old wood and dust and sweat. The moment of lucidity she'd managed to find vanished again.

She reached up, grabbed him by the shoulders, and pulled him down, seeking his lips again. As his mouth fell against hers, she wrapped her arms around his neck, dragging him down to rest on one elbow beside her. She hooked her heel over the back of his calf and pulled him around until his leg was draped over both of hers, denim scraping against denim. She felt his erection against her thigh, straining against his jeans, pressing against her so hard that she knew she'd have a bruise in the morning and she couldn't have cared less.

He shoved her T-shirt out of the way again. He touched her breast through the thin fabric of her bra, circling its fullness, pressing, squeezing, moving tantalizingly close to her nipple, then moving away again. Her bra was so sweat-soaked that it felt like a second skin, offering virtually no barrier between her skin and his. She twisted, arched, until finally he caught her nipple between his thumb and forefinger and teased it gently. She felt a hard jolt of pleasure and squirmed beneath him, but he pressed his leg down harder against hers and continued to tease her nipple until she thought she'd go crazy. Finally he flicked her bra open and pushed the sweat-soaked fabric away. He took her hand, tangled his fingers with hers, then pressed it against the floor near her shoulder. At the same time, he leaned over her, lowering his mouth, brushing his tongue against first one nipple, then the other. She closed her eyes and threw her head back, her breathing harsh and irregular, as he continued the delicious torment with his tongue and lips. It was heaven and hell all at the same time, a pleasure so intense it was almost painful, making her want to scream at him to stop at the same time she wanted it to go on forever. But with his leg still draped over hers and her hand imprisoned in his, she was at his mercy.

Then she felt him shift. A moment later his breath, hot and ragged, skimmed the column of her throat, moving upward to the pulse point behind her ear. He kissed her there, sending warm shivers coursing through her. Then he whispered hotly into her ear, "If you really do want me to stop, say so now. This is your one and only chance."

Her throat was so tight with pure sexual arousal that she could barely get the words out. "No. Don't stop. Don't you *dare* stop."

He rose immediately, placing one knee on either side of her thighs, then reached for the button fly of her jeans. *Yes. Yes.* She wanted the damned things off, wanted to feel his hands on her there and everywhere. She wanted to do the same to him, to peel his jeans off until they were skin-to-skin with nothing in between them. She didn't give a damn where they were or what was happening. She only knew that she wanted Alex in every way there was for a woman to have a man, and when she ran out of those, she intended to invent a few more.

As she lay on the floor of the shed, barely able to catch a breath, Alex unbuttoned one button of her fly. The anticipation she felt was excruciating, and she wanted to shout at him to hurry, *please* hurry, because she couldn't take it anymore.

Instead, with one button hanging open, he placed his palms on her legs and skimmed his thumbs over her inner thighs, back and forth, over and over. She squeezed her eyes closed. Even through the heavy fabric of her jeans, it was just about more than she could stand. Now, right now, when she was desperate for him to move fast, he was slowing down. Driving her crazy. *Knowing* he was driving her crazy.

After a moment, he opened another button, then slid his hands to the sides of her waist, leaned over, and teased his tongue over the small opening he'd created in her jeans just above the edge of her panties.

"Alex, please . . ."

She squirmed against him, but her thighs were trapped between his knees. She put her hands against his shoulders, digging into them with her fingertips, but still it felt as if ages passed before he finally rose and reached for her jeans again.

Then, slowly, she became aware of something. A sound that was out of place. A creaking noise.

Alex unbuttoned the third button of her jeans, then took pity on her and moved right ahead to the fourth.

She heard it again: a plaintive creaking noise right above their heads.

She pressed her hand down on Alex's. "Alex?" she whispered. "What's that noise?"

By the way he stopped suddenly and tilted his head, she knew he heard it, too. He looked up at the ceiling of the shed.

"What the hell . . . ?"

Val glanced up, too, and through a crack between boards, she saw an unmistakable flash of black and orange. Her heart nearly stopped.

"Holy shit," Alex said. "He's on the roof!"

The boards creaked again. Alex grabbed Val by her upper arms, at the same time falling backward, rolling to the left and pulling her on top of him. He rolled again until he was shielding her body with his right up against the door of the shed. Val heard a huge crack. The roof caved in, and the tiger fell into the shed in a thunderous crash of splintered wood and a spray of dust.

As the animal squirmed wildly in the rubble, Alex leaped to his feet and hauled Val along with him.

"Let's go!"

She snagged her backpack at the last moment, right before Alex threw open the door and shoved her through it. He slammed the door behind him, grabbed Val's hand and took off running.

"He could still come back out through the roof," Alex said. "Let's move!"

They scrambled up the rocky hillside toward the gate. She slipped once, and Alex pulled her back to her feet and they kept on running. As they moved into the trees about twenty yards away from the gate, she glanced back to see the tiger scrambling through the opening in the top of the shed.

They reached the gate. Alex lifted the rod to open it, pushed Val through the opening, then followed her, clanging the gate shut behind them.

Val stumbled over to a tree, turned and leaned against it. Then she slid slowly down the trunk and rested her head back against it, her breath coming in sharp spurts.

"Oh, God," she said under her breath. "I don't think I've ever run that fast in my entire life."

Her hair was sweat-soaked, her face still hot and flushed. And her bra was unhooked, hanging open beneath her shirt. Her jeans were in a similar condition.

He'd wanted her. As insane as the situation had been, he wasn't about to say he didn't. Or that it had been a mistake. Or any of a hundred different things he could say right now to downplay it. Because he didn't want to downplay it. Not in the least.

He walked over to where she sat and offered her his hand. She stared up at him for a moment, then took it, and he pulled her to her feet. When their eyes met, she immediately looked away. She pulled her hand from his, turned away and buttoned the fly of her jeans.

"Val," he said. "What happened in that shed—"

"Was no big deal," she said, hooking her bra beneath her T-shirt. "I always get horny when I'm attacked by a tiger."

And with that, the wall came up. Just like that, she dismissed all of it. Every touch, every kiss, every moment they were on the verge of sexual explosion—gone. Meaningless. No big deal.

He stepped toward her. Her expression grew a little apprehensive as he advanced, and she was forced to take a step backward, bumping into the tree. Moving very slowly, he smoothed a tangle of hair away from her cheek, then took her face in his hands and stared down at her.

"Did what just happened between us really mean so little to you?"

For a full ten seconds she just looked at him, her eyes wide. She opened her mouth as if to say something, then closed it again. Finally she simply closed her eyes to avoid his insistent gaze.

"No," she whispered. "Of course not."

"Was that really so hard to say?"

"Yes."

He still didn't know why. Not completely. But he accepted the enormity of her tiny admission without pushing her for more. He pressed a gentle kiss to her lips, only to realize that she was trembling.

"Are you okay?"

"Of course."

"We have to get moving."

"I know."

There were a thousand things left to be said between them, but this certainly wasn't the time or the place to go into it. They eased apart, and Alex turned and surveyed the enclosure they'd just emerged from.

"Okay," he said. "Let's find a way to skirt this tiger cage so we can move closer to the house and see what's going on."

Alex turned and started down through the trees along the perimeter of the fence, whacking short saplings aside as he walked. Val leaned back against the tree for a moment, a wobbly sensation in her stomach, overcome by a feeling of sudden helplessness that made her knees weak.

When she didn't follow, Alex turned back and waited, his feet slightly spread and sweat glistening on his upper body. The harsh afternoon sun streaked through the treetops, highlighting every plane of muscle in his shoulders, his arms, his abdomen. He hadn't picked his shirt up on the way out of that shed, and now *she* was paying the price for it.

And it was her fault. She'd asked for it. Begged, practically. She felt a flush of embarrassment.

Now he knew. He knew just how important he was to her, and just how much she wanted him. She'd tipped her hand in every way possible.

I care about you. How long is it going to take you to figure that out?

She hadn't known what to say when she heard those words come out of Alex's mouth. How could the man she was certain had no heart have become so adept at seeing right into hers?

Her mind was a muddled mess, swimming with the memory of how he'd touched her and the words he'd spoken. But she couldn't stop to sort it all out now.

She pushed herself away from the tree, still feeling so hot and flushed that she could barely walk. But right now she had no choice. She pressed ahead, shoving aside the same saplings Alex had and following him through the trees.

Soon they realized that the tiger enclosure wasn't as large as it appeared, because the western boundary had been hidden by a thicket of trees. They skirted it, then headed south. Soon, down a long, brushy hillside, the ranch house came into view. They swung around until they were directly behind it, yet still under the cover of trees.

Northeast of the house stood a large horse barn with adjacent corrals and a hay barn with a pickup truck parked behind it. Northwest of the house were several small cabins backing up to a grove of trees. The cabins appeared to be made of actual logs, very rustic, clearly aimed at male guests.

But the action was happening on the east side of the house, where at least half a dozen men were erecting a large awning, while others prepared barbecue pits. And in the middle of it all stood a blond woman who, even at this distance, seemed to be in charge.

"Damn," Alex said. "The place looked deserted before. It's not deserted now."

Val pulled out her binoculars and zeroed in on the woman. She was tall and strikingly beautiful in the same oozingly sexual way that Shannon had been. She was maybe thirty. Maybe. She wore a pair of frayed denim shorts, a pink tube top, and sandals, and even in the short time Val watched her, it was pretty clear that the men working for her would be getting things done a lot faster if she went inside and put on a pair of baggy jeans and an old T-shirt.

"That must be Reichert's girlfriend," she said, handing Alex the binoculars.

Alex peered at her for a moment. "He's sure got a thing for younger women." He panned the binoculars around the area. "The men who are working are Mexican. Wonder if they're legal?"

"Knowing Reichert, probably not."

Alex lowered the binoculars. "There's no way to get in there now. Too many people around. We'll wait until tonight."

"But there will be even more people around then."

"We need the cover of darkness to get into that house. We'll wait until the party is in full swing, because by then everybody will be gathered on the patio or under that awning, not scattered around the cabins or the horse barn. We'll wait until the women show up, too. Another distraction. By then surely there will be a lot of alcohol flowing, too, which means that all those guys, including Reichert, will probably have their attention someplace besides the house and the barn. While you're monitoring what's going on out here, I'll go into the house."

"No," she said. "It would be better if I went in."

"No, it wouldn't. I don't want you anywhere near Reichert. He'd recognize you in a heartbeat."

"And he wouldn't recognize you?"

"If somebody's going to have to deal with him, I'd rather it be me."

"People will be in the back of the house, which means you'll need to go in the front door. What if it's locked? Can you pick a lock?"

Alex sighed with disgust.

"It appears, then, that you're not the man for the job."

Alex was silent for a moment, turning the situation over in his mind. "Okay. You said you had disguises. What kind of disguises?"

"Clothes, wigs, makeup . . ."

"Anything sleazy?"

"Oh, sure. I can do sleazy."

"I expect that the ladies who show up here tonight won't look like schoolteachers. If somebody spots you, maybe they'll be drunk enough to think you're one of them. You might even be able to fool Reichert if the need arises."

"So I'm going in?"

"You're going in. But I want you wearing one of the bugs right up to the time you plant it. I want to hear everything that's going on. Do you have something wireless you can wear that will let me talk to you?"

"Yeah. Fits right inside my ear."

"Good. But we have to come up with some kind of diversion I can use in case you get into trouble. Any ideas?"

Val scanned the area, her gaze falling on the hay barn. Through its large open doors, she saw bales of hay stacked nearly to the roof. In the middle of summer it would be dry as tinder.

"Sure would be a shame if that hay barn caught fire," she said.

Alex stared at her for a moment, and she expected him to tell her one more time what a goofy plan she'd just proposed. Instead, he got a calculating look on his face.

"Not a bad idea."

Val felt a rush of adrenaline. It was a hell of a good plan. Within hours they would have that ranch house loaded with listening devices, and before long Reichert would be on tape, possibly having hot sex with his girlfriend two days after his wife's murder. Eventually they'd say something to incriminate themselves. And if they were lucky enough to get the latter, then nobody—not even Henderson—could continue to accuse Alex of murder.

chapter twenty

At nine o'clock that night, Alex paced up and down outside the van, his boots scuffing through the dead leaves at his feet. Hot, humid, deathly still nights like this one made him tense. They always had. On nights like this, he had the uncanny sensation that danger was hovering just outside his line of sight, ready to attack. Tonight was no exception. And the disquiet he felt was fueled by the fact that Val was inside the van right now, getting herself ready for their undercover operation.

He wasn't at all sure about this. The plan was solid, but still he worried about the possibility of Val meeting Reichert head-on inside that house. He remembered the gut-wrenching feeling he had had when he thought that was what had happened at Reichert's house in Tolosa, and he had no desire to repeat the experience. But he didn't know a blessed thing about picking locks and he certainly couldn't learn now.

He reached for his cell phone he'd pulled out of the van earlier, knowing there was something he had to do before they left, and he couldn't put it off any longer. He wasn't looking forward to talking to Dave and getting the third degree, but he had to find out just what Henderson was up to after Stanley told him he'd spotted them in Tinsdale.

He dialed the number of Dave's cell phone. Four rings later, he heard his brother's voice.

"Hello?"

"Dave. It's me."

"Alex! For God's sake, where are you?"

"Just listen to me. We had a little run-in with a deputy sheriff this morning. Has he called Henderson?"

"What kind of run-in?"

"Just answer the question. Did he get in touch with Henderson to tell him he'd spotted us?"

"Us? Does that mean Val is with you?"

Damn. He hadn't intended to say that. "Yes. But don't let anyone know that. I know they suspect she's with me, but I don't want anyone to know it for sure."

"Okay."

"Now tell me—did a deputy sheriff contact Henderson, probably in the early afternoon?"

"Not that I know of. And I saw Henderson as I was leaving today. If he had any idea where you were, he'd have gloated about it."

So Stanley hadn't said a word. That didn't completely surprise Alex, but he was relieved just the same. Not that he couldn't still decide to say something eventually, but at least for now, no new law enforcement was on their tails.

"Alex?" Dave said. "What happened at Reichert's house? What the hell were you doing in there?"

"Don't ask."

"But—"

"I said don't ask."

"Why can't you tell me where you are?"

"Because the second you know where I am and you don't tell somebody, you're in deep shit right along with me. I have no intention of putting you in that position."

"Then at least tell me what you're up to."

Alex debated telling his brother anything, then relented. "I've got a lead on the real killer. I've got to pursue it."

"Reichert?"

"Don't ask me any more questions. I mean it, Dave."

"Okay. But this lead—what are you going to do if it doesn't pan out?"

For the first time, Alex truly felt the chasm that separated him from his brother, that separated him from everyone else on earth who was walking around free right now. The hard truth was that he might never be able to prove that Reichert was Shannon's killer. And if he couldn't, what would he do?

Only one thing was certain: under no circumstances would he allow somebody to slap a pair of handcuffs on him again, then throw him in a prison cell and slam the door shut behind him. No matter what he had to do, that was never going to happen.

"I'll worry about that if the time comes," he told Dave.

"Can I give you any help from here?"

"Not now. I'll let you know if I need anything. Just call me if anyone contacts Henderson, will you?"

"Yeah. I will."

Alex disconnected the call, then leaned against the van, the hot night air so thick he could barely breathe. For some reason, he found himself thinking about what he'd be telling Dave right now if their positions were reversed.

Get your ass back to Tolosa, damn it! Right now!

He wouldn't be sympathetic, and he wouldn't be listening to a lot his brother had to say. He'd just be telling him what a fool he was for the things he'd done, and to rectify the situation ASAP because it was the right thing to do.

But as he imagined saying all that to his brother, suddenly he didn't recognize himself. Suddenly he saw shades of gray where there was once only black and white. And suddenly he started to see that while Dave was trying to understand his position, understanding would have been the last thing he would have offered if he'd been in Dave's place.

The back door of the van opened. Alex swung his flashlight around, and when Val stepped out, he couldn't believe his eyes. How could she have gone into that van, only to have another woman come out?

"Holy *shit*."

"What?"

What did she mean, *what*? Val had never been one to play up her sexuality, but here she was wearing a denim skirt with a button front that clung to her like a sausage casing, rising so high on her thighs that if she bent over, nothing would remain a secret. Above that was a hot-pink blouse that plunged so low that he could clearly see that she'd foregone a bra. She'd added a wig with long, straight black hair that she'd swept forward to cover the stitches on her temple, and enough makeup to make a Vegas showgirl green with envy.

"Close your mouth, Alex."

He did.

"You said sleazy."

"Yeah, but—"

"I'm a private investigator. Think of it as a uniform."

Uniform, hell. Cops wore uniforms. So did janitors. And cleaning ladies. This was no uniform.

Well, one thing was good about it: he'd barely recognized her, so maybe Reichert wouldn't either, in case the two of them happened to meet. They'd talked about the importance of looking like one of the girls there tonight, who they assumed would be Mexican, so she'd used a darker makeup foundation. Since she was half-Mexican already, the look was complete. And because she swore she could fake the accent with the necessary broken English and sprinkle her speech with actual Spanish, he felt certain that she'd be able to pass herself off as one of the ladies of the evening.

"Wait a minute," he said. "You can't carry a weapon wearing that skirt."

"I have one in my purse."

"Where are the bugs?" he asked.

"In my purse, too. Along with the lock pick and a mini-flashlight."

"I want to be able to hear you when you go into the house."

"Don't worry. The bugs are plenty sensitive, even inside there."

"Did you get the hair spray?"

"It's in the backpack. Nonaerosol, so you can dump it all over a hay bale to get a fire going. The receivers are also in there, along with a camera with a nice telephoto lens, and a lighter."

He had to hand it to her: she did have the right equipment for the job.

"I talked to Dave while you were getting dressed," Alex said. "So far Stanley hasn't contacted Henderson."

"Really?"

"Looks that way. But if Stanley got that fax, so did a lot of other law enforcement agencies."

"Well, after tonight, maybe we won't have to worry about any of that."

They looked at each other a long time. Finally she turned away and put on her tennis shoes, then tossed her high heels into another pocket of her backpack. "Ready to go?"

They retraced the same path they'd taken that afternoon,

this time skirting the tiger enclosure. Alex knew they were approaching the house when he smelled barbecue. The twang of country-and-western music filled the air.

"Wow," Val said. "Those guys really know how to party."

That was an understatement. Alex glanced at the group gathered beneath the awning—about twenty men and at least half that many women, most of whom he could see, even at this distance, were dressed comparably to Val. There was a tremendous amount of activity, with everyone eating, laughing, dancing, and drinking, which meant they'd lucked out and hit the party at its high point. And the music was so loud that Alex breathed a little easier. Any sound Val made inside the house would never be heard outside.

"We need to get closer. We can move right to the edge of the clearing behind those cabins."

They moved through the trees, and a few minutes later they came up behind the cabins that sat northwest of the house. They were all dark—everyone was clearly at the party—making it a perfect position from which to operate. From here, looking between the cabins, they could see most of the action. When the time came, Alex could swing left to the hay barn that sat almost directly behind the house, and Val could swing right and circle the west side of the house, then move to the front door. Alex could monitor the movement of the party guests and inform Val if anyone made a move toward the house, keeping the lighter and the hair spray handy in case something went wrong.

Alex pulled the binoculars out of the backpack and handed them to Val. "Tell me which one is Reichert."

She took the binoculars and scanned the crowd. "There he is. The guy sitting to the right of the blond we saw this afternoon."

She handed them back to Alex. He zeroed in on Reichert—big man, cowboy hat, dark mustache, holding a cigar in one hand and a beer in the other. Sitting next to him was a bearded man, who leaned over and said something to him, and they both laughed.

"He's sure living it up for a guy who just buried his wife," Alex said.

"And I think we know why. Now tell me what that bus is doing here."

Alex turned his gaze to a small, rickety bus in the driveway. "It probably brought the women in. There are all kinds of brothels along the border towns. They recruit the Mexican women by telling them they'll get them across the border. Then they coerce them into prostitution to pay off the fee they charge. They'll leave here tonight as soon as Reichert's finished with them."

"He's disgusting."

"I think we've already determined that."

"Then let's get him, okay?"

Alex returned the binoculars to the backpack, while Val swapped her tennis shoes for black heels. She tossed her tennis shoes down beside a tree.

"All your hardware in place?" he asked.

Val fiddled with the receiver in her ear. "Yeah. How about you?"

He had her backpack over his shoulder, containing the receivers and recorders for the bugs. He clipped the transmitter to his belt and the microphone to his shirt so he could talk to Val. He turned on the receiver, then clicked the transmitter on. They tested communication in both directions and found it sufficient.

"When you get closer, get some shots of Reichert with his bimbo," Val said. "Unless they actually have sex on the patio, photos probably won't mean much, but get a few shots anyway."

Alex nodded. "Okay. You stay put until I'm in place behind the barn. Don't move until I give you the word, okay?"

"Of course. I always do what you tell me to."

"Now, Val. I hear you can go to hell for lying."

"Nah. I don't think just one sin would do it. I'd have to do at least a little coveting or something, too, wouldn't I?"

God, he loved her smart mouth, even when she was using it against him.

"Don't take any chances," he added. "If you can see you're going to get into trouble, just clear out and we'll go to plan B."

"Which is?"

"I have no idea. I'm counting on you for that."

She smiled, and even through all the makeup, she looked so beautiful that he wanted to kiss her.

"Be careful," he said, a smile curling his own mouth. "Don't make me come in there after you."

"I'll be okay. I'll see you back here in a minute."

But neither of them moved. They just stared at each other in the near-darkness, until finally Alex took a step toward her, rested his palm against the small of her back, and eased her against him. Val leaned into him, her arms circling his neck, and they fell together in a slow, deep, sensual kiss, wishing each other good luck and a whole lot of other things. Then she stared up at him in a way that made him want to forget this mission altogether and pick up where they'd left off earlier.

"I think you messed up my lipstick," she whispered.

"Which means I'm probably wearing it now."

She rested her fingertips against his cheek, then ran the pad of her thumb slowly across his lower lip.

"All gone."

She let her fingertips rest against his cheek for a moment more, before finally falling away from his face.

"Be careful," he said.

"You, too."

He slung the backpack over his shoulder and started to skirt north around the cabins and head for the hay barn, the taste of Val still hot on his lips. Looking over his shoulder, he saw her moving toward the back of one of the cabins, stepping lightly in those high heels. She reached the cabin and peered around it, and even at a distance he found his gaze sliding right down her body to those beautiful legs. God, she was something else.

Concentrate. You have things to do.

He slipped through the darkness, using his flashlight only when he had to, walking in a wide arc around the edge of the clearing to come up behind the hay barn. There were only two floodlights in the area, both of them at the horse barn, leaving the hay barn in near-darkness.

He slung the backpack onto the hood of the pickup truck behind the barn and pulled out one of the bug receivers, then the camera.

"Val? Can you hear me?"

"Yeah. Are you there yet?"

Her voice was a little muffled, but he could clearly make out her words coming through the receiver.

"Right behind the hay barn."

"What does the party look like close up?"

He peered around the corner of the barn. "Everybody's on their way to one hell of a drunk. They've got at least half a dozen coolers of beer and a margarita machine."

He swung the camera up and zoomed the telephoto lens, zeroing in on Reichert and his girlfriend. The man didn't seem to be one for public displays of affection, but Alex snapped the shutter a few times to document the two of them together, then put the camera back in the backpack.

"Okay, Val," he said. "Time to move in."

"Gotcha."

Suddenly a voice came through the receiver. A man's voice.

"What the hell are you doing back here?"

Every nerve ending in Alex's body jumped to attention. "Val?" he whispered. "What's up? Val? Talk to me!"

She whispered back, her voice shaky, "I've got trouble."

chapter twenty-one

Val had been so busy concentrating on what Alex was saying that she hadn't heard or seen the man come around the back of the cabin. But now he stood not ten feet away from her, a big, dark, bearded man who looked at her first with surprise, then wariness. Adrenaline flowed so wildly through her body that it was all she could do not to turn and run.

"Val?" Alex whispered in her ear. "What's going on?"

She couldn't answer him. The man was too close.

The man took a step closer. "I asked you what you're doing back here."

Val felt a jolt of apprehension. *He knows you don't belong here. He knows.*

"Just getting some air," she replied in Spanish-accented English.

He came closer, his expression filled with suspicion. She forced herself to move forward, to meet him halfway.

"Get your ass back to the party," he said. "That's what you're being paid for."

It was nearly dark behind the cabin, but still she could make out his face. He was handsome in a harsh, almost brutal way, the starkness of his features emphasized by a deep scar that ran from his right ear to his chin, an irregular slash through his beard that made him look even more dangerous than he already did.

Then she saw a flicker of confusion in his eyes. "Did I see you at the party earlier?"

"Play the part for now," Alex whispered. "It's all you can do."

"Now you've hurt my feelings," Val said. "I thought you'd been watching me all night."

The man's gaze traveled from her face to her breasts, then

slipped lower to her legs and came back up again. "Maybe I should have been."

Val's heart pounded unmercifully. She wanted to run, to scream, to do anything to get this hideous man away from her. But she couldn't blow her cover. The minute he knew something was up, he'd tell Reichert, and Reichert might realize who she really was. God only knew what would happen then.

"What's your name?" the man said.

She thought fast. "Elena."

"Elena. I'm Rick."

He moved right in front of her, and she smelled alcohol on his breath, along with the choking scent of cigarette smoke. With his fingertip, he brushed a strand of her phony hair back over her shoulder, staring at her as if it were dinnertime and she were the main course. "Yeah. Maybe I should have been paying more attention."

"Val," Alex said. "Tell him you have to go to the bathroom."

"The bathroom," she said. "Where is it again?"

He gave her a lecherous look. "Right off my bedroom."

Every nerve in Val's body came alive. "Your bedroom?"

"Let's go."

Rick took her arm in a rough, aggressive grip and started toward the house. Then she heard Alex's voice in her ear.

"Just take it easy," he said, his voice calm, controlled. "Go along with him so you don't blow your cover. I'll create a diversion. Trust me, sweetheart. I'll have you out of there in a minute."

Rick led her across the small clearing to a side door of the ranch house. Her heart was beating like a jackhammer.

"You live here?" she asked. "I thought Mr. Reichert—"

"Yeah, technically it's his house. But he only shows up during the hunts. Who do you think takes care of the place the rest of the time?"

So he was Reichert's right-hand man.

"I'm the one who really runs the show around here."

His arrogant right-hand man.

She had to stay calm. Alex was going to get her out of this. The moment he set the fire, this guy would let her go. Then she'd plant the listening devices and get the hell out of the house.

Rick unlocked the door, pulled her through it, and shut it

behind them. They were in the kitchen, and the only light in the room came from the floodlights outside.

"I've got the lighter and the hair spray," Alex whispered. "But it's going to take a minute. Stall him."

Rick backed her up against the wall, his gaze traveling leisurely over her again, stopping at her breasts.

"Nice tits, honey. Really nice."

Val thought she was going to be sick. She forced herself to stand motionless as he put his hand on her waist, slinked it downward to her hip, then curled it around the back of her thigh and pulled her closer to him.

"Of course, after where I've been for the past few years, any tits would look good to me."

He had her trapped against the wall, with no intention of letting her go. Suddenly she felt light-headed, and the music outside was so loud that even in here it pulsed through every nerve in her body.

Small talk. Keep it up.

"So . . . where you been the past few years?"

"Huntsville. Accommodations courtesy of the state of Texas."

Prison. Val's heart skittered wildly.

Alex wasn't talking to her. What was going on? *Please, please do something,* she begged silently. *Please.*

"I know there's a limit to what Lorena will let me do with her girls," Rick said. "But since I know she doesn't pay you much, there's no reason you and I can't work out a deal on the side. How would you like to earn a little extra money?"

She couldn't imagine what, in this man's estimation, would warrant a big tip, and she had a feeling she didn't want to know. "What do I have to do?"

He told her. In gross, disgusting detail. She swallowed hard, hoping she could maintain some kind of composure. Hoping she could keep from kicking him right in the balls so he'd associate that excruciating pain with the act he'd just described.

"I don't know—"

He reached into his pocket, pulled out a bill folded in half, then held it up between his index and third fingers. "A hundred bucks. Does that sweeten the pot?"

Val swallowed hard and didn't answer.

"Hey, I don't have to ask for it. I can take it, then deal with Lorena later. And I sure as hell don't have to pay you for it."

"No!" she said quickly. "I-I can use the money. I'll do whatever you want."

"Now, that's better," he crooned, slipping the hundred into the front pocket of her purse. "I like it better when a woman is willing, so I don't mind offering a little extra bonus. You'll find I'm a pretty generous guy when I get what I want. Let's go upstairs."

She heard a muffled curse through her earpiece. What was Alex doing?

She thought about the gun in her purse. But with Rick's hand clamped around her arm, dragging her toward the stairs, she couldn't reach it without his realizing something was up. And could she actually shoot him when he hadn't threatened her life? He thought she was a prostitute. He'd paid her. Of course he thought she should do whatever they'd agreed to. She knew she'd never be able to shoot a man under those circumstances, no matter how perverted he was.

Every step Val took was shaky, and she had to concentrate to keep from slipping on the stairs in her heels. By the time they reached the second-floor landing, she was trembling all over and prayed he didn't notice. He pulled her into the first bedroom on the right, then closed the door behind them.

"The bathroom?" she asked.

He made a sweeping motion with his hand toward a door. "Right through there. But don't keep me waiting long."

She went into the bathroom and closed the door behind her. The music outside was so loud that even standing in this upstairs bedroom Rick wouldn't be able to hear her if she whispered.

"Alex. I'm in the bathroom. What's going on?"

"The lighter won't work!"

Panic shot through her. "It was working earlier. Try it again!"

"I have been trying. It's no use."

"Shake it!"

"I tried everything. And I can't find another lighter in your backpack, and I can't find anything around here to start a fire with. Do whatever you have to do to get away from that guy, Val. Anything!"

"But I don't have the bugs planted yet!"

"Forget the damned bugs!"

"No! I'm not blowing this cover!"

"Then I'm coming in."

"No! Don't do anything! No matter what you hear, you stay put, do you hear me?"

"No way. I heard that bastard. I heard what he wants—"

"Do you want to get us killed?" Val whispered. "That's what's going to happen if you come blasting in here. There are men all over the place out there with all kinds of firepower, and all they'll know is that their buddy Reichert has a little intruder problem. Neither of us would stand a chance."

"Damn it, I don't want that degenerate to lay a finger on you!"

"He won't. I'll make sure of that."

"How? How can you make sure of that?"

She couldn't. But this might be their only chance to get the bugs in place, to get the information they needed to prove Alex's innocence, and nothing was going to stop her from doing it. *Nothing.*

"Val? Are you there?"

"He might find this earpiece," she told Alex, "so I'm taking it out. I won't be able to hear you anymore."

Over Alex's protests, Val pulled the earpiece out and dropped it into her purse. She squeezed her eyes closed. She had to do this. She had to.

"Don't worry about me," she said. "I mean it. I can handle this guy. Just go back to our rendezvous point and wait for me. I'll be out soon."

She was glad Alex could hear her but not see her, because he'd know just how much she was lying. She couldn't handle it. No matter what she'd told Alex, without blowing her cover, she couldn't stop Rick from doing whatever he wanted to do with her.

For a moment she felt so weak that she sat down on the edge of the bathtub, clasping her hands together to stop them from trembling. She blinked several times to ward off the tears that filled her eyes, then took a deep breath and stood up again.

You can do this.

She opened the door. Rick was standing across the room with his back to her. He turned around slowly and gave her yet another up-and-down look that said he couldn't wait to get on with it.

"Come on over here, honey."

Damned lighter!

Alex shook it again. Flicked it. No flame. He had a hair-sprayed bale of hay and not a damned thing to ignite it with. He'd even found a half-full can of gasoline, but without a spark to set it off, it was useless.

He ran out of the barn and grabbed the backpack off the hood of the pickup truck. He threw the dead lighter inside, then pulled out a flashlight. It was going to take him several minutes to approach that house and get inside unnoticed, then take Rick out and escape with Val. But he had to do it on the sly, because Val was right: if he stormed in there right out in the open, he could get them both killed.

He stopped for a moment and listened to the receiver, straining to hear what might be going on in that house.

Nothing.

What was that bastard doing to her?

The guy was an ex-con. In Alex's experience, prison generally made bad men into worse men. Val had told him she could handle the situation, but he knew better. Rick had already said he was willing to rape her to get what he wanted. What else might he be willing to do?

Nice tits, honey. Really nice.

Alex thought about the crude remarks he'd made to Val back in that motel room in Tinsdale, and he wanted to die. He wanted to beg her forgiveness, then swear to God in heaven that he'd never say anything like that to her ever again. And one thing was certain: if he went into that house and found that degenerate so much as breathing on Val, he was going to kill him with his bare hands.

Then he saw them.

On the dashboard of the pickup, scattered amid other debris, he saw a pack of Marlboros. A book of matches was stuck down inside the cellophane wrapper. With the bales of hay already drenched with hair spray, a single spark would be all it would take to send them up in flames. And he could get a fire going faster than he could make his way into the house.

He tossed the backpack down again, yanked on the handle of the driver's door, and found it locked. He ran back into the barn, grabbed a rake that was leaning against the wall, rushed back out to the pickup, and smacked it through the window. The glass shattered, and he hoped the music would drown out the sound. He threw the rake aside, reached inside, and opened the door. He grabbed the cigarettes, extracted the book of matches, then opened it.

Three matches. Only three.

They would have to be enough.

Val walked over and stood in front of Rick, nausea swirling through her stomach. As he reached for her blouse, she froze, trying her best not to back away. He unbuttoned one button, then two. He fumbled with the next one with no success.

"Damned buttons," he muttered, finally taking hold of her shirt and ripping the rest of them from their buttonholes, leaving it gaping open.

She gasped. "Y-you didn't have to—"

"Shut up. I'm paying you plenty. Buy another one."

She wished she'd worn a bra, but this shirt hadn't allowed for it. It wouldn't have mattered, though. It wouldn't have mattered at all, because he'd have ripped that right off her, too.

She stood there, teeth gritted, while he put his hands inside her shirt and curled them around her breasts, squeezing sharply. If a roach had crawled over her, she couldn't have been more disgusted. Tears filled her eyes, and she prayed he couldn't see them in the darkness of the bedroom.

He reached down, caught the hem of her skirt, and pulled it up all the way to her waist, insinuating his hand along her thigh. Val sucked in a sharp breath, but he seemed not to notice, concentrating instead on grabbing and groping her, turning an act that was supposed to be something beautiful into a horrible nightmare. She felt her mind becoming dark and blurry, and she willed herself to stay focused. If she faltered, he'd know she didn't belong here.

"We've got all night," she said breathlessly. "What's the rush?"

"That's right. We've got all night. And I intend to use every minute of it. You'll earn that hundred bucks, believe me."

And that was when she knew once wouldn't be enough. He would keep her here. He'd keep touching her, forcing her to breathe the god-awful smell of cigarettes and alcohol, doing things that sickened her to her very soul.

And she knew Alex could hear every word he spoke.

Please, Alex . . . stay where you are . . . please, please don't come in here. . . .

But she had the terrible feeling that he was going to come bursting through the door any minute, taking away any chance she had of planting those bugs and tapping the phone once she was free. She was so afraid he was going to risk himself to save her, and that was the last thing she wanted. She would survive this. But she knew what could happen to a cop in prison, and no matter what this man did to her now, she refused to risk Alex's life when she had the power not to.

Then, to her surprise, Rick backed away. She felt a jolt of hope, a momentary reprieve.

"Take your clothes off," he said. "Everything."

Oh, God.

In a minute, she would be naked. She tried to concentrate, to keep her wits about her. But she couldn't. Her mind went hazy again, and she felt herself slipping back into that subterranean depth that she'd fought so hard to claw her way out of all those years ago.

"Move it," Rick said.

Slowly she let her purse drop to the floor beside her. The air in the bedroom was hot and stagnant. She couldn't breathe. She was trembling so hard that she could barely take hold of her shirt, and suddenly all the memories she'd fought so hard to bury came back to her in a blinding rush—the violation, the defilement, then the god-awful disbelief she'd felt when she realized she really was alone in the world with nobody left to trust.

In a daze, she took off her shirt and let it fall to the floor.

His disgusting look of approval made her want to yank it right back up and cover herself again, but she couldn't. If she tried to take away what he'd already bought and paid for, there was no telling what he would do.

Then she heard the scream.

Outside where the party was going on, the country music fell silent. She heard another scream. Voices. People shouting.

What was going on?

Rick turned immediately and went to the window. He pushed the curtain aside.

"Shit! The barn's on fire!"

One match had done it. One match tossed onto that hair spray–doused hay bale had sent it up in flames. But Alex hadn't stopped there. He'd grabbed the half-full can of gasoline and heaved it onto the fire, causing the flames to spread quickly to other bales. Then he'd thrown open the back door of the barn, causing a huge influx of air, and the fire went wild.

The moment he heard the woman scream, he knew the fire had been spotted. He grabbed the backpack, threw it over his shoulder, then disappeared into the woods behind the burning barn.

Reichert raced to the barn, turned on a hose, and started spraying, but the fire was already too far gone, and he might as well have had a squirt gun for all the good it did.

As Alex moved through the trees, heading back to their rendezvous point, he kept glancing toward the back of the house.

"Come on, you asshole," he muttered. "Come on . . ."

Finally the door flew open and a bearded man rushed out, heading toward the burning barn. Alex almost collapsed with relief. *Thank God.* Thank God he wasn't in there with Val anymore. He just prayed that she was making a similar exit out another door.

He yanked the receiver off his belt and shoved it hard against his ear as he strode along.

"Talk to me, Val," he murmured, even though he was sure she wouldn't stop to put the earpiece back in so she could hear him. "Please talk to me. . . ."

He thought he heard her footsteps. A door opening, then

slamming. But there was so much commotion over the fire that he couldn't be sure.

Why wasn't she saying something?

His heart was beating frantically. He had a longer way to go than she did, and every step he took was filled with apprehension. He started to jog along the edge of the clearing, ducking some tree branches and swiping others aside.

She wasn't talking. *Why wasn't she talking?*

Moments later he saw her through the foliage, leaning against a tree trunk, breathing hard. Relief spilled through him.

"Val!" He strode up to her and took her by the shoulders, turning her around to face him. "I was going crazy wondering what was happening! Why didn't you tell me you were out of there?"

She just stared up at him. "I-I don't know. I—"

Then he realized that her face was tearstained. Looking down, he saw that her shirt was torn completely open.

"Val? Are you all right? Tell me you're all right. Tell me he didn't—"

"No," she said, sniffing. "Of course not. I'm okay."

"Look at your shirt! What did he do to you?"

She pulled the sides of her shirt together, then tied them in a knot at her waist to keep it closed. Her hands were trembling. "Nothing. It was really nothing."

"Val, clearly it was *something*. What did he do?"

"Alex, stop it. It doesn't matter. The worst thing is that I didn't—" She exhaled, refusing to meet his eyes. "I didn't get the bugs planted. Or the phone tap. I'm sorry. But by the time he finally left, I was so . . ." She paused, tears coming to her eyes again. "I guess I thought maybe he was going to come back in. He wouldn't have with the fire and all, so I shouldn't have run. I guess I just . . . you know. P-panicked a little."

"I don't give a damn about all that! Just tell me he didn't hurt you!"

"For God's sake, would you shut up about that?" She pulled away from him, wiping her eyes with her fingertips. "As you can see, I survived just fine."

I survived just fine. The same words she'd used when she'd talked about her mother and stepfather. He'd doubted them then, and he sure as hell doubted them now.

She turned away, kicked off her high heels, and picked up one of her tennis shoes. She brushed off her foot and slipped it on.

"Look at what a mess those shoes are now," she said, nodding toward the pumps. "Guess one more pair bites the dust." She put a foot against a tree to tie the tennis shoe. "And this shirt, too. Oh, well. At least they're deductible."

Her words were flippant, but her voice was tight. Strained. Christ, she must have been terrified. Why was she trying to make him believe that she hadn't been?

She put on the other shoe and tied it, too. "Well, I guess we'd better start looking for that elusive plan B. Any ideas?"

She looked up at him, and tears filled her eyes again.

"Val?" he said softly.

She stared at him a long time. Then her face contorted, and for a moment he thought she was going to cry.

"Don't, Alex," she whispered. "Don't look at me like that. *Please*. Just get me out of here."

He started to get an inkling of what was happening here, and he felt a tremor of foreboding. Right now she was refusing to talk about what had happened to her in that house. He just hoped it was because they were still so close to where everything had happened, and not because she was afraid to talk to him.

He had to find a place for her tonight. Someplace warm and protected, with a hot shower to wash it all away. He thought about some cabins for rent that they'd passed on the way here. They were relatively secluded, and at least twenty miles outside Tinsdale. Stanley hadn't talked, so nobody should recognize them if they stayed there tonight.

They started back through the trees. Alex took one last glance over his shoulder and saw that the barn was going to be a total loss. In the orange glow of the fire, he saw that the girls were hurrying back onto the bus, evidently in fear of law enforcement of some kind showing up. The men were still trying to get water on the flames, but it was clearly hopeless.

Then he looked back at Val, striding purposefully through the trees ahead of him. He had no idea how to deal with this, what to say, how to act. He only knew that before the night was out, he had to find a way to make her feel safe again.

*   *   *

Half an hour later, Alex was driving down the gravel road that ran through Lakeshore Village, the key to cabin sixteen in his pocket. The manager hadn't liked getting roused out of bed at nearly eleven o'clock at night, but she seemed to like the extra twenty dollars that Alex gave her for her trouble. He asked for the most secluded cabin she had, adding a little smile and a wink to make her think that they were just a couple who wanted to be alone.

Val hadn't spoken the whole way there. She merely sat in the passenger seat of the van, holding her shirt together with her hands, staring out the window. Several times he'd almost said something to her, but everything that came to mind sounded stupid or trite or completely useless, so in the end he'd just kept his mouth shut.

He pulled up to the cabin, parking the van beside it so the vehicle was only slightly visible from the road. He unlocked the door and they went inside. He flipped on a light, glad to see that while the place was rustic, it was comfortable, with a green-and-gold–plaid sofa in front of a fireplace, a small kitchen and dinette, and a bedroom with a double bed.

Val stood in the middle of the room, as if she didn't quite know what to do next.

"Why don't you take a shower?" he told her. "I'll bring our stuff inside and put some clean clothes outside the door for you."

She nodded wearily, then disappeared into the bathroom and closed the door behind her. Alex stood there for a moment, wishing he knew what to say, what to do. He'd been in more difficult situations over the years than he cared to count. Some of them threatening. Some of them *life*-threatening. He'd once stared down the barrel of a drug dealer's gun, and his life had literally flashed before his eyes.

But nothing he'd ever faced before—nothing—had made him feel as completely helpless as he did right now.

chapter twenty-two

Val clicked the bathroom door shut. Forcing back tears, she looked at her face in the mirror, at the wig and the makeup she wore that made her look like the prostitute that man had thought she was.

She yanked the wig off and tossed it on the floor, then grabbed a washcloth and soap and turned on the water and scrubbed her face until she'd annihilated every molecule of the makeup. She rinsed out the cloth, then threw it aside and turned toward the bathtub, desperate to wash the awful experience away, to scrub her skin right down to bone and muscle. She took a few steps, then felt the tears coming again.

She leaned against the wall, sobbing, then slowly slid down until she was sitting on the floor, her knees hugged to her chest. She squeezed her eyes closed, trying to block out the memory of the way that man had touched her, but she just couldn't. His face, his hands, his voice kept coming back to her, looming in her mind like some kind of monster, striking one horrific chord after another in her memory until everything she'd fought so hard to forget came rushing back in a torrent of fear and loathing.

But this time Alex had been there. *Just tell me he didn't hurt you. . . .*

She'd wanted so much to fall right into his arms, to hold on to him, to believe that he really did care about her, and that somehow he'd help the terrible feelings go away. But could she count on him? And if she could today, would she be able to tomorrow? That was always the question. What looked so real right now could just be an illusion. How many times in her life had the people she should have been able to trust left her out in the cold?

Five years ago she'd tossed Alex into that category of people who would betray her without so much as a backward glance. But now she saw something in his eyes when he looked at her, something that said he'd go to hell and back before he would ever hurt her again. So why couldn't she shake the feeling that the man she wanted so desperately to reach out to, the man who said he cared, would turn out to be just one more person who broke her heart?

Minutes later Alex carried a change of clothes to the door of the bathroom. He thought by now Val would be in the midst of a long, hot shower, but he didn't hear water running. He put his ear to the door. She was crying.

"Val?"

Silence.

"Val? Are you all right?"

"Of course. I-I'm fine."

He opened the door. She was sitting on the floor, her knees pulled up to her chest. The long black wig was lying on the floor, her own hair falling in a wild cascade down her back. She glanced up at him, then looked away again, wiping her eyes with the back of her hand.

"Please leave me alone."

"No. Not this time."

He put her clothes down on the counter, then turned and looked down at her.

"I-I took off that awful makeup," she said, her voice still choked with sobs. "Then I was—I was going to take a shower, but I guess I just . . ."

"Just what?"

"I-I don't know," she said with a weak shrug. "I just . . ."

He sat down on the edge of the bathtub. She shrank away from him.

"Talk to me, Val."

"There's nothing to say." She sniffed and wiped her eyes again, then started to rise. He took her arm and pulled her back down. She turned to face him, her chin quivering, and when she blinked, more tears slid down her cheek.

"What happened?" he asked. "You can tell me."

"It wasn't as bad as you're thinking," she said. "The fire was in . . . in time."

Alex froze at the echo of the words she'd spoken earlier that day. "But I guess it was bad enough, huh?"

She swallowed hard. Then her face crumpled. She bowed her head, her hand against her mouth, and a second later her shoulders jerked with silent sobs.

He slid down to the floor beside her and pulled her into his arms. She buried herself against his chest, wrapping her arms around his neck in a desperate hug. He whispered calming words to her that were probably all wrong, but it was all he knew to do. And through it all, his stomach was in turmoil because he felt so damned helpless to do anything but hold on to her and let her cry. A long time passed before her sobs wound down, and his shirt was wet with her tears.

"You said you wanted to hear about my stepfather," she said quietly. "Do you still?"

God, how he wanted to say no. He knew whatever words passed his lips in the next few minutes could either help or hurt, and he sure as hell didn't want to hurt her anymore.

"Don't worry," she murmured. "I promise not to cry anymore."

"I don't care if you cry all night long. Just tell me about it, okay?"

She sat up slowly and stared down at her lap. She took a deep breath, then let it out slowly. The longer she went without speaking, the worse he knew the story was going to be.

"When I was fourteen, I found photographs that he'd taken of me."

"Photographs? What kind of photographs?"

"The kind I didn't know he was taking."

"What do you mean?"

"When I was in my bathroom. I don't know how he did it, exactly. A hole somewhere in the wall, a hidden camera . . ."

Her voice trailed off. Slowly Alex understood, and his stomach twisted with disgust. "He took pictures of you? Nude pictures?"

She closed her eyes and nodded. He took a deep breath, trying to remain calm.

"How long had he been doing this?"

"Judging from the pictures, right after we came to live with him. I was nine."

"God, Val." The very thought revolted him. She'd said the man was sleazy. She hadn't said it strongly enough. "I hope you burned every one of them."

"No. He caught me. He came into the room when I was looking at the pictures. He told me that if I said a word, he'd make sure every pornographer in the world had copies of them, then reminded me that I'd never be able to prove that he was the one who took them. He was right."

Alex was trying very hard not to overreact, but it was a hard-won battle. *That son of a bitch.*

"Then he thought maybe it was time to have the real thing."

Alex felt as if the ground had dropped right out from under him. "He didn't. Val, don't tell me—"

"No, he didn't. But he tried. I went crazy. I kicked him. Hit him. Bloodied his nose. Scratched his face. Pictures were one thing. He'd already taken them, and I couldn't stop that. But he wasn't going to get away with anything else."

"And you were only fourteen?"

"Yes."

He felt a rush of admiration. She was tough. Damn, she was tough. How many girls that age would have the guts to fight back?

"I'd hated him from the beginning, I think because I could always feel what he was. I didn't know specifically. I was too young. But every time he looked at me, there was something about him that gave me the creeps. In a strange way, though, I was glad I found those pictures. I was sure that as soon as I told my mother, she would divorce him."

"What happened?"

Val swallowed hard. "The moment I opened my mouth and started telling her what he'd done, her face went stark white. At first I thought it was because she was horrified. I guess she was. Horrified that I'd found out."

"She *knew*?"

"Yes. She told me not to say another word. I started to cry. She shouted at me that I'd better not tell anyone anything, that if anyone found out, my stepfather would divorce her and she'd end up with nothing."

Alex felt every muscle in his body tighten, every nerve ending come alive with anger. "She knew, and she didn't protect you? Jesus, Val, what kind of a mother *was* she?"

"One who cared about her lifestyle more than she cared about her daughter."

Alex couldn't imagine such a thing. He couldn't imagine any parent abusing a child like that.

"I hope you told somebody else," he said hotly. "I hope you made that bastard pay for what he did to you."

"I thought about it. But who would I tell? I knew he'd win. No matter what I said, he was William Hamilton. All I'd get for my trouble would be humiliation. See, I was one of the bad kids. The ones who caused trouble. The ones nobody would believe in a million years."

"Did he try anything again?"

"He said crude things to me all the time, suggesting that he could have me anytime he wanted to, and there wasn't anything I could do about it." She paused. "But I swear I would have killed him if he'd actually laid a hand on me again."

"You said he died. When did that happen?"

"When I was fifteen. He had a heart attack."

"Good. I hope he's burning in hell."

"In the end, though," Val said, "my mother was the one who lost."

"What do you mean?"

"Not only had my mother signed a prenup, my stepfather had excluded her from his will. After he died, she was left with nothing. How's that for irony?"

"So what did she do?"

"She sold all of her jewelry and managed to get us an apartment and a car. She worked as the assistant manager at the apartment complex and brought in enough money to feed us. But I couldn't even look at her. School was terrible. Bad attitude. Bad grades. I barely remember those times. It seemed as if I was getting sucked down inside something dark I'd never be able to crawl out of, and there was nothing I could hang on to, to pull myself out."

She stopped for a moment, her eyes closed. "It gets worse before it gets better. Are you sure you want to hear it?"

No. He wasn't at all sure he wanted to hear it, but she

needed to tell it, so he intended to sit here all night if that was what it took.

"Of course. Go on."

She took a deep, ragged breath. "My mother couldn't handle having nothing. Being stripped of everything that was so important to her. And I think she realized just what a terrible thing she'd done to me, but she had no clue how to repair the damage. One day when I was sixteen, she took a handful of pills. I got home from school that day and found her dead."

"God, Val." His words came out on a choked breath.

"I tried to feel grief for her, but I couldn't. I just couldn't. I actually felt relieved she was gone, so I'd never have to look at her again. I know that's awful, but—"

"No, it's not. Not after what you'd been through."

Val paused for a moment, closing her eyes, and he could tell she was fighting tears.

"What did you do then?" he asked. "You were still a minor."

"I went to live with my grandfather. I hadn't seen him since I was seven years old. You've heard of parents disowning their children? Well, my mother disowned her parents. They were blue-collar Mexicans, and she wanted desperately to rise above that. By the time I was seven years old, she decided she didn't want anything to do with them. My grandmother died shortly after that, and my mother pretended she didn't even have a father."

Alex thought about his own family—brothers he'd fought with since he was old enough to throw a punch, and a sister who was so nosy and intrusive that sometimes he wanted to lock her in a closet. But he loved them, anyway. To disown his own family—he couldn't even imagine it.

"He persuaded me to come live with him in Austin," Val said. "To this day I don't know why I did it. Maybe because I had no place else to go. I hated him as much as I did her, just because he was her father. He was in his early sixties, so it was kind of a strange situation, me living with him when I was only sixteen. But it was the only real stability I'd ever known. He laid down the law and made me stick to it, which I fought like crazy. I gave him more crap than you can possibly imagine. But he took it. He took every bit of it, until one day I realized that he wasn't going to fight back like my mother had. He was just going to continue to tell me the rules and make me abide by them. And always—always—he told me he loved me. Why, I don't know, but he did. And pretty soon, I loved him, too. He died when I was twenty-one."

Her lips tightened, and her jaw began to tremble. "Okay. Maybe I lied. Maybe I am going to cry."

Alex put his arm around her and pulled her next to him. She tucked her head against his chest, sobbing softly. She'd been without love her whole life, and once she found somebody to love her, she'd lost him. How she'd managed to get through all that, he couldn't imagine.

"Did I mention that my grandfather was a cop?"

For several seconds, it was as if nothing in the room moved. Not a single molecule. And all at once Alex was transported back to Val's kitchen that night he'd brought her home from the emergency room. The photograph he'd seen on the shelf. The photograph of her with an older man in a police uniform.

Her grandfather.

"No," he said. "You never told me that."

"Yeah. Can you believe it? The rotten kid goes to live with a cop." She sighed, tears still lacing her voice. "It was the best thing that ever happened to me."

Suddenly it was as if all the pieces of Val's puzzle had fallen into place. Why she trusted no one. Why she wore armor an inch thick. Why she'd wanted to be a police officer when everything about her personality said she was better suited to any other profession on earth.

"I guess wanting to be a cop was my way of holding on to him," she said. "To the things he stood for. I don't know. Still, for a long time after he died, I didn't believe that there was anything in life that was permanent. Dependable. Trustworthy." She paused. "And then you came along."

His heart nearly stopped. "Me?"

"You were a rock, Alex. What you believed, you believed one hundred percent, and nothing on earth could sway you. Every move you made was grounded in some kind of principle. It went beyond doing what was right according to the law. It came from inside you. For somebody who'd grown up the way

I had, you seemed unbelievable to me. Almost untouchable. I'd never met anyone like you. In my mind, you were like my grandfather. Everything I thought a cop should be."

He'd had no idea. None at all. She'd spent so much time challenging him back then, trying to get under his skin, that he couldn't have imagined how she really felt. How important he'd been to her. And how much power he'd had to hurt her.

"Then you came to my apartment that night," Val went on, her head resting against his chest so she wasn't meeting his eyes. "I can't describe the feeling I had at that moment. I thought, '*He's here*. Oh, God, he's here. *Finally . . .*'" She took a deep, shaky breath. "It wasn't just because I was so attracted to you in a sexual way, although God knows there was plenty of that. It was so much more. Even though we fought all the time, still I thought you cared about me. And then you kissed me. I couldn't believe that you were even there, much less that you wanted me. And I had this crazy idea that . . ." She paused. "That if you ever decided you loved me, that nothing—I mean *nothing*—could ever make you stop."

Her words were astonishing. If he'd had any idea back then what was going through her mind, what would he have done? How would he have reacted? He honestly didn't know.

"Then I woke up to find you gone," she went on. "And then later that day—"

"I know." He let out a breath of frustration. "Val, I know I screwed up a lot of things back then. But please believe me. Dismissing you—I had to do it. I swear to God I had no other choice."

She was silent.

"You challenged everything I said. You wanted to do everything your way. Like shoot/don't shoot. You gave me crap when I told you that you couldn't open fire on a suspect in a crowd of bystanders, no matter how good a shot you were."

"Yeah. I did."

"You fought me every single step of the way. So what was I supposed to do?"

"Exactly what you did." She lifted her head and turned to look at him. Tears glistened in her eyes. "You never wavered, did you? Not once."

Alex stared at her a long time, the truth of the matter coming to him in small bits, until finally he understood. Every time she'd challenged him, it had been a test of sorts. She'd been searching for structure. For limits. For somebody to say the buck stopped here. She was trying to see if there was one more man on earth like her grandfather, the only person who'd ever made her feel safe.

And look what he'd done to her.

He'd slept with her. Then left her. Then kicked her out of the academy. And in the past few days, her flippant remarks, her sarcastic comments, her downplaying of everything that had happened between them—all of that had been designed to get him before he got her because she was so emotionally fragile that she couldn't withstand him hurting her one more time. And now it just wasn't enough to say he was sorry.

"You've told me how you felt that night," he said. "Now I want to tell you how I felt."

This was hard, so damned hard, because he'd denied it for so long that he didn't know the words to say to make it come out right.

"I've been with a lot of women, Val. But you were different. I knew that from the first day I met you. You challenged me. Made me work just to stay one step ahead of you. Yeah, you made me crazy, but there was something else. You made me feel . . . I don't know. Alive. I'd never met anyone like you, either. I swear to God that you're the only person outside of my family that I can't intimidate."

She gave him the briefest of smiles, ducking her head, her hair falling across her cheek. She reached up, tucked the strand behind her ear, and turned her eyes back to meet his again. She looked exactly as she had that night he'd come to her apartment—soft and sweet, without a hint of the cynicism that so often clouded her expression. *Damn.* He was so afraid of screwing this up.

"I know you think that the only reason I came to your apartment that night was because I wanted sex. But it wasn't anything like that. I cared about you, so much so that I couldn't stand the thought of you walking in there cold the next day. I wanted to prepare you. To break the news. To talk to you and make you understand how much I admired you, how capable I thought you were, and how just because it wasn't the right profession for you didn't mean I cared any less about you. I wouldn't have been able to say any of those things in front of the lieutenant. So I wanted to say them to you then."

"Why didn't you?"

"I don't know." He shook his head helplessly. "It was just . . . I don't know. Something had been happening between us for weeks, and you looked so damned beautiful, and I wanted you so much. And everything I came there to say just went right out of my mind. But what we did that night . . . it wasn't just sex. It was never just that. Never."

"You left in the middle of the night. What else was I to think?"

"I know," he said. "That was the most gutless thing I've ever done. And I've kicked myself for it ever since. But I couldn't face you. After what had happened between us, I knew how you'd look at me if I told you what was going to happen. Then after you left the lieutenant's office the next day, I wanted so badly to talk to you. To try to explain. You wouldn't let me, and I don't blame you. I deserved that slap across the face, and a whole lot more." He shook his head in frustration. "It was selfish. In every way. I was selfish for wanting you so much that I lost track of how much it would hurt you. But the truth is that I didn't want that night to be the end for us. I wanted it to be the beginning."

He couldn't look at her. He was so afraid of seeing something in her eyes that said, *Not good enough, Alex. Try again.* And if that happened, he had no idea what he was going to do. It was the only explanation he had, no matter how lame it sounded.

There was a long silence. Then, after a moment, he felt her fingertips against his chin. He turned, and for the first time he saw not one bit of doubt or suspicion in her eyes. It was the same way she'd looked at him that night so many years ago, right before he'd betrayed her in the worst way possible.

"Come closer," she whispered.

He eased toward her. She put her hands on his shoulders and brushed her lips against his in a tender, delicate kiss. Then she laid her head down on his shoulder again, exhaling softly, and he felt a swell of relief. They sat there for a long time like that, Val enveloped in his arms, and he realized that five years ago, even though he would have denied it to his dying breath, he'd left a part of himself with her. Tonight he was beginning to believe that he never wanted it back.

"Your grandfather took you on a vacation to the mountains once, didn't he?" Alex said.

Val sighed. "Three months before he died. It was so beautiful there."

Alex couldn't believe what had lain beneath Val's surface all this time. He'd always known that there had to be more to her than met the eye, but he'd never imagined this.

"You should take a shower," he said softly.

"I know. But I'm just so tired."

"Then it's a bath you need. Stay here."

He rose from the floor, plugged the tub, then turned on the water. After testing the temperature with his fingers, he held out his hands to her and pulled her to her feet. She teetered a little. He steadied her, then reached down to untie her blouse. She instantly recoiled.

"No." She took a deep breath. "I can't do that. Not now."

"You're not going to be doing anything. Just relax."

"No. It's not you, Alex. You know that. It's just—"

"Trust me," he whispered. "Just a bath. That's all."

Suddenly Val realized that all he intended to do was undress her so she could take a bath. It seemed so silly, as if she couldn't do it on her own, but suddenly she felt exhausted. So exhausted that when he reached again for her blouse, she let him untie it and slip it off her shoulders. Then he eased her around until her back was to him. He moved his hands around her hips and reached for the buttons of her skirt. Embarrassment flared again, and she caught his hands in hers.

"I can undress myself, Alex. I don't need you to—"

"I know you don't," he whispered against her ear. "But I want to help. Just lean against me."

Slowly she released his hands, exhaling softly, and leaned back against his chest. He felt strong and solid behind her, and she was glad he was there because just standing was starting to feel like a chore. He unfastened several buttons of her skirt, then slid it down, taking her panties along with it. She stepped out of them. He nudged them aside with his foot, then turned her back around to face him. She crossed her arms over her chest.

"Alex, this is kind of embarrassing. Please go. I'll be all right."

He reached over and turned out the bathroom light. The only illumination left was what was coming from the bedroom lamp through the half-open door. The darkness was soothing. Relaxing.

Alex took her hand and nodded for her to get into the tub. She stepped tentatively into the steamy water, then sank down into it, and she knew instantly that he'd been right. It felt wonderful.

He turned off the water, and silence fell over the bathroom except for the occasional drip of the faucet into the water below. He took a washcloth and a bar of soap from the sink and brought them to the edge of the tub. She reached for them, but instead of giving them to her, he knelt down beside her, dipped the washcloth into the water, and rubbed the bar of soap over it.

"Lie back," he said.

When Val realized what he intended to do, she couldn't believe it. "Alex, no. You really don't have to—"

"Just trust me, sweetheart. Lie back and relax."

After a moment, she slid farther down, resting her head against the back of the tub, the water pooling just beneath her breasts. She was totally open to him, totally naked, while he was fully clothed. She'd never felt so exposed to another human being in her life, and it was all she could do not to beg him to hand her the nearest towel.

"Relax," Alex whispered, taking her hand in his. "Just close your eyes and relax."

He placed the warm, soapy washcloth against her shoulder, then slowly dragged it all the way down her arm to her wrist. She watched his gaze in the dim light, following the path of the washcloth as it streaked tiny bubbles down her arm. As it neared her hand, he opened his palm beneath hers, bringing the washcloth all the way to her fingertips, then reversed the process and ran it back up her arm. He did it twice, three times, circling underneath to reach the tender skin on the inside of her upper arm.

Val had never felt anything like it.

He continued to stroke her with the cloth, until slowly her eyes drifted closed, until she was giving herself completely to him in a way she'd never expected.

He dragged the washcloth across her shoulder, then swirled it around her neck and upper chest. He found her other arm and gave it the same slow, gentle treatment. She breathed deeply, inhaling the steam, and it seemed to cleanse her from the inside out. Then she heard him dipping the cloth in the water and soaping it again. She waited, eyes closed, for where he would touch her next.

He placed the cloth against her upper chest, then swept it in a circle, moving toward her breasts. She tensed, but he merely swirled the washcloth in three or four cleansing circles, then moved down to her abdomen, then to her thigh. She sighed at his touch, melting further into the warm water.

He curled his hand around the back of her ankle, lifted it slightly from the water, then ran the washcloth up the length of her leg. Every move he made was so gentle, so giving, so unlike anything she'd ever believed Alex to be, that tears came to her eyes again. She thought about how she'd rebuffed him in that shed today when he'd asked about her stepfather, telling him how heartless he was, when all he'd done was ask her to tell him why she was hurting. And he knew she was hurting. In spite of all the smart-ass comments she tossed at him, in spite of all the accusations she threw his way, still he'd seen right inside her. And now tonight . . . tonight . . .

How could she have misread him so completely?

Because of what he did five years ago.

But somehow that memory had blurred, becoming impossible for her to grasp. All she saw was the man who was with her now, the man who was helping her wash away something awful and degrading, who understood enough about her to know what she needed when she didn't even know herself.

After soaping both of her legs, he rested the washcloth on her hip, then placed a gentle hand on the inside of her thigh.

"Open up a little for me, sweetheart."

By now she was so entranced by the wonderful feelings he was creating that she did as he asked without question. She let her left leg drift to one side, allowing him to dip the soapy cloth beneath the surface of the water and move it gently between her legs. Looking at him through heavy-lidded eyes, she saw that his gaze was intently focused on his task. She also saw that the whole time he was doing his best to comfort her, the man inside him wanted to touch her in a completely different way.

"Can you sit up?" he asked. "Need to get your back."

He took her hand and pulled her to a sitting position. He gathered her hair at the base of her neck and draped it over her shoulder. Soaping the cloth again, he bathed her back, rubbing in small circles, then moved the cloth up to squeeze soapy water over her neck. It slid in little rivers along her back and chest, sending warm shivers down her spine.

"Your hair," he said. "You're going to need the shower for that. Can you stand up?"

He unplugged the tub, then helped her to her feet. Every muscle felt limp, her skin warm and flushed. He turned the shower head straight down, then turned on the water, testing it, then adjusting it until it was the proper temperature. He reached over to the basket on the sink and handed her a little bottle of shampoo. He started to pull the curtain. She caught it with her hand.

"You could use a shower, too," she said.

"As soon as you're out."

"Now would be fine."

He stared at her a long time, both of them knowing what was at the heart of her invitation. She could feel his indecision, and she was astonished at how desperately she wanted him to say yes.

And how desperately she wanted him to say no.

Finally he took her face in his hands and kissed her gently. "No, sweetheart. You shower first, and then I'll take one."

With that, he flicked the light back on, then turned and left the bathroom, closing the door behind him.

chapter twenty-three

Alex stood outside the bathroom door, his back against the wall, his eyes closed, picturing Val in that shower right now, lathering her hair, then tilting her head back, her eyes closed, to let the water spill over it. He couldn't think of anything he wanted more than to duck under that warm spray of water with her. But keeping it platonic would have been a seriously difficult thing to do, even though the last thing she needed tonight was a man demanding sex from her.

The way he'd felt when Val had started to cry . . . *Damn*. He hadn't known *what* to do. The woman he thought was tough as nails was more fragile than he'd ever imagined. He couldn't stand to watch it. At that moment, he would have done anything to make her tears stop. But what he'd actually ended up doing—where had that come from? He had no idea. He'd never touched a woman like that in his life. Slowly. Soothingly. Reaching out to her instead of pulling back. Touching her because she needed comfort instead of touching her because it would eventually lead to sex.

Not that the thought hadn't crossed his mind. She'd looked so beautiful lying there in that water, her body covered with soap suds, that by the time she finally issued him an invitation to join her in the shower, it had been all he could do not to leap right in. Right now, though, he saw nothing in her eyes but total trust, and he had no intention of doing anything to lose that.

Even if it killed him.

He sat down on the bed and tortured himself with more thoughts of Val naked, until finally he heard her turn off the shower. After a moment he heard a blow-dryer, and soon after that the bathroom door opened and she stepped out.

He'd brought her jeans and a T-shirt, but she'd forgone the jeans, wearing only a pair of panties and the shirt, which grazed the tops of her thighs. Her hair was full and lustrous once again, her cheeks tinted pink from the hot water. He rose from the bed and started toward the bathroom. They stopped and stared at each other, and he prepared himself for her to say something flippant or sarcastic to ease any embarrassment she felt about what had happened between them in the bathroom.

Instead, she placed her hand against his shoulder and gave him a kiss on the cheek.

"Thank you," she whispered.

Her hand fell away from his shoulder, trailing down his chest. She turned and walked to the bed, leaving behind the soft scent of soap and shampoo, then slid beneath the covers. She rested her head against the pillow with a weary sigh, closed her eyes, and was still.

Alex grabbed some clean clothes, went inside the bathroom, and closed the door, thanking God in heaven that he'd been smart enough to do the right thing.

Ten minutes later, he came out of the shower wearing a pair of jeans. If he was going to be getting into bed with Val, that was as naked as he intended to get.

He turned out the light and slipped beneath the covers. He wondered if she was asleep already, but then she turned over to face him.

"Feel better?" she asked.

"Much."

She slid up next to him and laid her head on his shoulder. He put his hand on her hip and froze.

"You're naked."

"Yeah. I was hoping you'd get that way, too."

Right then Alex felt as if he were being handed the keys to paradise, only he wasn't at all sure that he should take them. For the past hour his mind and body had been at war with each other, and while his mind had been winning, right now he could feel the tide of that battle beginning to turn.

She rose on one elbow. The sheet fell away from her shoulder, exposing her breasts. She put her hand against his abdomen, skimming her thumb back and forth, and he knew now that the battle was all but lost.

"It's what I want, Alex. You. Tonight."

He closed his eyes. "God, Val—you don't know what you're doing to me."

"What?" she whispered. "What am I doing to you?"

He pulled her hand up and pressed it to his chest. *"That."*

Beneath her palm, Val felt his heart racing, and all at once her heart was pumping just as fast. She slid her palm away and placed a gentle kiss on the spot where it had been.

He exhaled. "Don't do that unless you mean it."

"Oh, I mean it."

She did. She'd never been so sure of anything. He was trying so hard to be considerate, turning down her invitation to join her in the shower because he was afraid of pushing her. And now every sweet, gentle word he spoke made her want him that much more. She kissed him in the same spot again, knowing she'd finally found the heart he tried so hard to hide.

"Just promise me something," he said.

"What?"

"If I touch you in any way that you don't like, you'll tell me."

She smiled softly. "I'm okay, Alex. I really am."

"I know. I just . . ."

"As long as you're the one touching me," she said, "anything goes."

"Oh, sweetheart—don't tell me that. I'll keep you awake all night."

"Right now, I don't need sleep. I need you."

Alex rose from the bed and pulled off his jeans and underwear all at once and kicked them aside. Even in the darkness of the bedroom, she could see that he was already fully aroused, and just the sight of him made it difficult for her to catch her breath. What had happened to her tonight, what had happened to her as a teenager—all of it disappeared from her consciousness. All she saw was Alex.

She expected him to lie down beside her again. Instead, he went to the foot of the bed, and she rolled to her back to watch what he was doing. He took hold of the sheet that covered her, and slowly, slowly he pulled it away. It swept over her breasts, then her abdomen, then her hips and legs and feet. He dropped it at the foot of the bed and stared down at her. For a moment she felt self-conscious, until she saw his expression of total appreciation.

"You're beautiful," he murmured. "I've always thought you were so damned beautiful."

She started to sit up.

"No. Lie still."

She relaxed back against the pillow. He knelt down at the end of the bed.

What was he doing?

He wrapped his hands around her legs just below her knees, then swept them downward along her calves, finally rubbing his thumbs against the arches of her feet, then sliding his hands back up again. He did it twice, three times, sending shivers all the way to the top of her head and back down again.

"I have a confession to make," he said, still stroking her legs.

"What?" she said.

"That night at your apartment after you were shot. I carried you to bed. I took off your ankle holster and stared at your legs. Just stood right there in your room and stared at them for I don't know how long. You wouldn't have liked it then. I hope you don't mind now."

"Of course not," she said, a little breathlessly. "I would have liked it then, too. I just wouldn't have told you so."

She saw a smile play across his lips. As far as she was concerned, he could look all he wanted to. Touch all he wanted to. Any *way* he wanted to.

Then, to her surprise, he took hold of her ankles and gently dragged her down toward the foot of the bed until her legs were dangling over it. Still on his knees, he nudged her legs apart, moved between them, and began to stroke her thighs. It surprised her a little, but she quickly gave in to the delicious feelings he was creating, his hands massaging her thighs, lightly at first, then more firmly, then lightly again. The sensation was incredible, but she couldn't say it was completely relaxing, because every movement of his hands seemed to set her more and more on edge. Her skin became flushed, her breasts hot and tingly.

And all he was doing was stroking her *legs*.

Then he curled his hands around the backs of her knees

and pulled her down some more, until just the tops of her thighs rested against the bed. He placed his hands gently against the junction of her hips and thighs, then moved his thumbs in the creases between them. Slowly. Gently.

"Last night in that motel room in Tinsdale, I said some terrible things to you," he said.

"It was my fault. I pushed you into it."

"No," he said, still stroking her with his thumbs. "I'll never talk to you that way again. For any reason. I'll never touch you like that again, either, as if I don't care about you at all."

He moved his thumbs closer to the most sensitive part of her, until she thought she'd go crazy for wanting him to touch her there. The moment he did, she moaned and moved against him, and immediately he dipped his fingers downward. She was wet—already so wet and swollen that every movement of his fingers felt like a thousand electric shocks.

"Yes," he said. "That's how I want you to be. Hot and wet."

"Alex . . ." she said, barely able to breathe. "Come here."

"Not yet."

He lowered his head and touched his tongue to her. The feeling was sudden and intense, so intense that she immediately shifted away, but he caught her hips in his hands, his forearms along the outsides of her thighs, trapping her in place.

"Easy, sweetheart," he said, his breath hot against her, then continued to tease her with his tongue. The feeling was astonishing—so incredibly personal, so invasive that she wanted to pull away, but so deeply arousing that she never wanted him to stop.

He didn't know what he was doing to *her*.

But she knew that wasn't true. He knew exactly what he was doing, and the very best way to do it. Soon, what had merely been a pleasurable sensation became a strongly focused need. Unconsciously, spontaneously, she began to move her hips against him until she felt something take hold, a spark of intense pleasure that caught fire and began to spread, slowly at first, and then faster. For a few mindless minutes, the world seemed to contract, until she knew nothing except Alex's touch and the sound of her own harsh breathing. She was getting close. So close . . .

And then he stopped.

Her body went limp with frustration. He turned his head to kiss her inner thigh, once, twice, teasing his lips over it. She dug her fingertips into his forearms, twisting in his grip, seeking his mouth again.

"Alex, *please* . . ."

She wasn't even sure her words were comprehensible, but then he touched her with his tongue again, this time tilting her hips up, opening her even more to him, and she thought she'd die from the feeling. He was moving exactly as she wanted him to—*needed* him to—and the fire flared again.

"Yes," she whispered. "Oh, *yes*. Like that."

Another buildup. Another sense of being positively insane with need. Another feeling that she was poised to plummet right over the edge. And once again he stopped. And once again she wanted to scream.

"Alex . . ."

He swirled his tongue against her thigh. "Yes?"

"I want you inside me. *Now*."

He froze, his fingers tightening against her thighs. She couldn't help smiling.

"Assuming you're ready to do that," she added.

"Ready? Sweetheart, I was ready the second I got into bed and found you naked."

"Show me," she said.

He stood up suddenly and moved her until she was lying fully on the bed again. He pressed her knees apart and stared down at her, his dark eyes full of hot anticipation. For a moment she thought he was going to tease her again before finally giving her what she wanted, so she wrapped her hand around him, stroking the length of him, back and forth, loving the fact that this particular part of him was just as impressive as the rest of his body. He squeezed his eyes closed, every muscle tensing.

"I'm warning you, Alex," she said, still caressing him. "In just a minute here I'm going to start to beg. It's not something I do well, and it won't be pretty. So please just spare us both the pain of that and—"

He lowered himself to his forearms and plunged inside her in one smooth, forceful stroke. The rest of her words caught in her throat, the feeling so intense that for a moment she couldn't catch a breath. He withdrew slowly, then thrust again, groaning with pleasure.

"Ah, Val, you feel so *good*. . . ."

Flames were already building inside her again, and his words were like a hot breeze, stirring them into a frenzy. With every stroke, she felt herself moving toward a climax again.

"Now I remember," he said, a note of wonder in his voice. "God, I remember. . . ."

She knew what he was talking about. Exactly. She knew he remembered what it had felt like to do this so many years ago. He remembered how incredible it had been. And all of it paled in comparison to what they were feeling now.

"This is better," she whispered. "So much better . . ."

"Yes."

Then she did start to beg—pleading with him to move harder, faster. . . .

"That's right, baby," he whispered against her ear. "Tell me what you want. Tell me."

She did. She told him with her voice and her hands and her legs wrapped tightly around him exactly what she wanted, and it all came down to him. Just him. Just having him falling into her with such blinding intensity, wanting her so much, needing her so much. The room began to blur around her, the pressure inside her building until she couldn't stand it any longer. She cried out his name, begging all over again.

Then all at once something contracted inside her, then exploded in a sunburst of sensation. She gasped, and Alex thrust harder, then fell forward and clung to her with a fierce groan. She wrapped her legs tightly around him, pulling him deep inside her, holding on as hot waves of pure ecstasy swept over both of them. And even as the sensations subsided, still she held on to him, relishing the weight of him against her, his hot breath against her neck, the brush of his hair against her cheek. God, how she loved every bit of it.

She kissed his shoulder, then slid her palms in long, sweeping strokes down his back. And when she finally found her breath again, she circled her arms around his neck, met his lips, and kissed him long and hard. When she finally pulled away and opened her eyes, she found him staring down at her.

"Thanks," she whispered. "I needed that."

He chuckled a little. "You and me both, sweetheart."

They smiled at each other a moment more. Then, slowly, his smile faded. "I was so afraid of doing the wrong thing. You don't know how much."

She brushed a lock of hair away from his forehead. "It couldn't have been more right."

He shifted over, lay down beside her, and pulled her into his arms. In that moment, she had a twinge of that frightening feeling she'd had every time in her life when she'd opened herself up to somebody else, that feeling that she was utterly exposed, utterly defenseless. Only now, as she lay in Alex's arms, that feeling died away, replaced by a sense of warmth. Of contentment. Of trust.

If she'd been tired before, she was exhausted now, but it was a pleasant kind of exhaustion that seeped all the way to her bones. Alex stroked her arm, her hip, her thigh, in slow, relaxing strokes.

"I want you to know something else," he said.

"Yes?"

"When you wake up in the morning . . ."

"Yes?"

"I'll be here."

chapter twenty-four

When Alex woke the next morning, Val was snuggled right up against his back, her hand draped over his hip, one of her legs tangled up between his. Her breasts were resting against his back and her warm breath fanned his neck. The room was fairly bright, and he wondered what time it was. Then he decided that he didn't care. He just lay there motionless, savoring the feeling of her body pressed so snugly against his, and after a while, her rhythmic breathing almost put him back to sleep again.

Then he heard his cell phone ringing.

He sat up and slid out of bed, leaving Val sleeping. He went into the kitchen, where he'd left his phone on the counter. He looked at the caller ID.

Dave.

He hit the talk button. "Dave? What's up?"

"I was just wondering what was going on there."

Alex sank onto one of the dinette chairs. "Did that deputy contact Henderson yet?"

"Not that I know of. What's happening on your end?"

"I'm still working on a lead. It may take a while longer. What does the investigation look like right now?"

"There's not much of one. Crime scene evidence, of course, but Henderson's not looking for any other suspects. Especially since you were found in Reichert's house."

"That couldn't be helped."

"I don't suppose you're ready to tell me the whole story."

"No, I'm not. The less you know, the better."

"Alex? How long is this going to go on?"

Alex rubbed his hand over his face, then exhaled. "As long as it needs to."

"There's got to be an end to this. Sooner or later you're going to have to—"

"Have to what? Hand myself over so they can go through the motions of a trial, then toss me in prison for the next twenty years?"

Dave was silent.

"If I don't find out the truth," Alex said, "nobody else is going to. I'm not stopping until I prove I didn't do this. I don't give a damn how long it takes."

"What do you mean? Days?"

Alex didn't respond.

"Weeks? Months?"

"I said I don't care how long it takes."

"And if you don't find the evidence you need? What then?"

"Dave. Get this straight. I'm not letting anyone throw me in a prison cell for a crime I didn't commit. *Ever.*"

There was a long silence. Then his brother's voice, touched with disbelief. "Are you telling me that you may not come back at all?"

When Alex said nothing, Dave let out a long breath. "I had no idea you were considering this."

"It's not my first choice."

"Millner. You know he's good. If it comes to it, I'm sure he can—"

"Will you shut the hell up about Millner? He's an attorney, not a goddamned miracle worker. Unless I can find more evidence, I'm a dead man."

There was a long silence, a silence that echoed the truth. Dave knew he was right. The enormity of the situation was starting to come down on both of them, and it was something that neither of them wanted to face.

"What about Val?" Dave asked.

Alex's heart skipped. "What about her?"

"She's accused of breaking and entering. With no priors, if she'd just stuck around and confessed to that charge, she probably would have gotten probation. That's all. So why is she with you?"

"Because she's a target. Reichert tried to shoot her once. He could very well do it again."

"I don't think he'll bother her anymore. Days have passed

and the authorities haven't come after him. He'll figure he's in the clear, that she hasn't told the cops anything to incriminate him. He won't risk adding another murder to the list if it's not necessary."

Alex hadn't considered that. What his brother was saying was probably true.

"She's better off here," Dave went on. "A good attorney might be able to work his way around the fact that she was with you in the Reichert house. But if you two are caught together now, the prosecution will go to the mat. Aiding and abetting a felon, accessory after the fact—all that. There's no telling what might happen to her."

Dave was right. Why hadn't he thought about that before?

"What's going on between you two?" Dave asked.

"It's none of your business, so don't even go there."

"I don't have to. You just did."

Alex dropped his head to his hand with a sigh of disgust.

"If the time comes," Dave said, "will you be able to let her go?"

Let her go? The very words made Alex sick. Until this minute, he hadn't even allowed himself to think about that.

"We're safe where we are right now," he told Dave. "And something could happen very soon to turn this all around."

"And if it doesn't?"

Alex was silent.

"If you don't find what you're looking for, what are you going to do? Run forever? And take Val with you?"

"Get off it, Dave."

"I know you're under a lot of pressure, and you probably haven't thought this through," Dave said carefully. "Otherwise I know you'd never even think of doing something like that to her."

Dave DeMarco. The voice of reason. *Damn it.*

Alex bowed his head, suddenly feeling like shit. With everything going on, he just hadn't stopped to think about all the implications of what he was doing. For the first time, he was starting to see the danger Val faced just by being with him.

"Dave?"

"Yeah?"

Alex cradled the phone against his shoulder and rubbed his temples. "I'm not saying this is going to happen, but if I send Val back, will you help her? Talk to Millner? Get him to defend her?"

"Of course I will."

"Tell him to pull out all the stops. I don't want her serving time. Not one minute of it."

"I'll take care of her, Alex. I promise."

"I still haven't decided what to do."

"I know. I'm here, though, if you need me."

All at once, Alex felt as if the phone he held was the only thing connecting him to the world as he used to know it. He thought about his job, his family, his life. All of that could be gone if he couldn't find a way to prove his innocence.

And Val would be gone, too.

"I don't know when I'll see you again," he told Dave. "Tell the family—" He stopped short, his throat suddenly tight. "Tell everybody that I love them."

He couldn't remember the last time he'd said that word, and he knew just how surprised his brother was to hear it.

"I'll tell them," Dave said. "Call me if anything's happening, will you?"

"Yeah. I will."

Alex hit the button to disconnect the call, then tossed the cell phone onto the table. He'd told Dave the truth. He wasn't going to stop until he found a way to prove his innocence. But had he made a mistake in letting Val become involved?

He went back to the bedroom, stopping at the doorway. Val was still asleep. Minutes ticked by as he stood there and watched her. He played the events of the past few days over in his mind, and slowly he realized that somewhere in the middle of all of it, something drastic had happened. It was more than just desire, more than just wanting her in his bed, more than just the physical pull he'd always felt whenever he was around her. Never in his life had he felt this overwhelming urge to hold a woman, to protect her, to be the one she depended on. He'd never envisioned his life taking such a fundamental turn, and the feeling staggered him. For the first time in his life, he could see a woman as part of his future.

Only he might not have a future to offer her.

When he hung up the phone with Dave, he thought he had a decision to make. There was no decision. She'd never be safe as long as she was with him, and if the worst happened and Reichert got away with murder, what kind of life could he offer her?

He walked to the bed and sat down beside Val. She stirred a little, then blinked her eyes open and smiled.

"Alex."

He took her hand in his.

"Did I hear the phone ring?" she asked.

"Yeah. Dave called."

Her eyes opened wider. "What did he want?"

"Just checking up."

"Anything new back in Tolosa?"

"No."

"The investigation?"

"Nothing new."

Alex stared down at her. Even with her hair mussed, her eyes heavy, and a pillow crease running across her left cheek, no woman on earth had ever looked more beautiful to him.

She rose up on one elbow. "Looks like we need to find another way to get that house bugged, doesn't it?"

"Val, listen to me. We have to be realistic about this. Getting into that house is going to be harder now, and it may take time. A lot of time. We may have to stake out the place for days before we get another opportunity to get inside. And Rick said Reichert comes to the ranch only for the hunts. If he leaves this time before we can get the place bugged, we may have a long wait before he shows up again."

"I know."

"No. I don't think you understand how long this could go on. And there's always the possibility that we may never get the evidence we're looking for."

"You're the one who doesn't understand," Val said softly, settling back against the pillow. "I don't care if it takes a lifetime."

Alex heard her words, but it was a moment before he understood the magnitude of what she was saying. She was telling him that she was willing to give up everything.

For him.

He thought about how she'd stood in the bedroom of that

ranch house last night and let that man touch her because she didn't want to blow her cover, because she thought it might be their only shot at getting those bugs planted. That she didn't get the job done only told him how horrified she'd been and how frantic she'd been to get out of that house when she finally had the opportunity.

Have you gotten it through your head yet, DeMarco? Did it have to come to this before you finally figured it out?

She could have stayed in Tolosa, faced the breaking-and-entering charge, and ended up with not much more than a slap on the wrist. Yes, at the time Reichert might still have been a danger to her, but she had her eyes open and she could have stayed out of his way. When it came right down to it, she was here for only one reason.

Because she wanted to help him.

But Dave was right. Every moment she spent with him dragged her deeper into a situation that was only going to hurt her. How could he let that happen?

Accessory after the fact. Aiding and abetting a felon.

This was his problem. Not hers. But if they were caught, those were exactly the charges she'd be facing.

"Let's go to the ranch right now," Val said, sitting up. "Find out if the hunting party is still there."

He put his hand against her shoulder and eased her back down. "Tonight. After dark."

"But—"

"It's too dangerous in broad daylight. We can check things out later tonight, see who's still there, then try to come up with a new plan to get into the house."

Val thought about that for a moment. "Maybe you're right." She smiled. "We'll go tonight."

Alex nodded, feeling a flood of guilt. He'd just lied to Val. She wasn't going to the ranch tonight. He was going. Alone.

From here on out, his neck was going to be the only one on the line. And Dave was right about where Val belonged. Once he told her that he was leaving, he intended to do everything in his power to persuade her to return to Tolosa. Then he'd move heaven and earth to prove his innocence so he could go home to her again. And if he couldn't . . .

If he couldn't, he'd lose her forever.

Val glanced at the bedside clock. "It's only ten-thirty now. We have a lot of time until tonight. What do you suggest we do in the meantime?"

Alex lowered his head and kissed her—a slow, deep, deliberate kiss that let her know exactly what he had in mind for the next several hours.

"Good suggestion," she murmured.

As he stretched out beside her and took her in his arms again, he tried to put the future out of his mind, but still Dave's words kept drifting around inside his head, refusing to go away.

If the time comes, will you be able to let her go?

He dreaded the very thought of it, because he knew the minute he told Val what he'd decided to do, she'd be hurt. Angry. She'd look at him as if he'd betrayed her, and there wouldn't be a damned thing he could do about it.

And he'd lied to her about something else. His decision to wait until tonight to return to the ranch had nothing to do with the danger involved. It had to do with buying time. Time to be with Val.

Just in case it was the last time he ever saw her.

Alex and Val spent the afternoon in the cabin, the hours passing in a hazy cloud of pure pleasure. Occasionally Alex would have a lucid moment when he thought about what was coming that night, but then Val would touch him and he'd drift back into oblivion all over again.

The day slipped away. Evening came.

"We've got a little while until we have to go to the ranch," Val said, tracing her fingertips over his chest. "Since it's nearly dark, let's get out of this cabin. Go down by the lake. Enjoy the oppressive heat. Sit on the dock and make out."

Alex smiled. "Sounds good."

They threw on some clothes, then left the cabin by the back door and headed down a short wooded path toward the lake. It was still again tonight. Not tranquil or calm, but a strained kind of stillness, as if something dark were on the verge of bursting right through it. Not a flutter of a breeze made its way through the trees, and the brutal heat of the day had barely melted away. It was one of those nights that seemed to ooze tension.

Or maybe the tension was coming from inside him.

They stood on the end of the dock, staring out over the lake. Val glanced up at him.

"You're frowning."

"Am I?"

"Yes."

"I didn't mean to be."

He forced himself to smile, even though he hardly felt like it. The closer it came to the time Val would expect to go to the ranch, the more stressed he felt.

"Suppose it could get any hotter out here?" Alex asked.

"Only if the sun went supernova."

"Nothing like summer in Texas."

"You said you didn't have a swim team at your school," Val said. "But can you swim?"

"Of course."

She put a hand against his shoulder and gave him a shove. He reached for the post of the dock and missed, and a second later he hit the water in a thunderous splash, holding his breath just in time to avoid getting a noseful of water. A few seconds later he came to the surface, slinging his hair back and swiping the water off his face.

Val was smiling. Of course she was. She was the one still standing on the dock. But he could remedy that in short order.

"Is it any cooler in there?" she asked.

"You'll know yourself in a minute," he said, treading water. "And you get to choose. You can get in, or I'm going to chase you down and throw you in."

She appeared to ponder that for a moment. Finally she shrugged. "Oh, what the hell."

She leaped off the dock right into Alex's arms. He swept her around in a circle, swishing the water in an orbit around them. He eased a little closer to the bank where his feet just touched bottom. They floated around for a moment, their arms encircling each other.

"Take off your shirt," Val said.

"Why?"

"Because I like what's under it."

He smiled. "We've been naked all day."

"Why stop now?"

He peeled his shirt off and tossed it onto the dock. "You, too."

"Can't. I'm a girl."

"I noticed. Now, off with it so I can notice some more."

"We're in a public place here."

"It's almost dark. And I don't see anyone else around."

She took off her T-shirt and tossed it onto the dock. He immediately reached down and flicked her bra open. She pulled it off, too, tossed it on top of her shirt, then slid back into his arms. They bobbed a little, chest to chest, the water sloshing between them.

"The lake," he said. "Good suggestion. Of course, I didn't expect to end up in it."

"Are you complaining?" she said, running her hands up and down his back.

"Nope. Not a bit."

"Oh, they're right there, aren't they?" she said, tracing her fingertips over a spot on his back.

"What?"

"The scars from your stitches."

"Oh, yeah."

"You say you fell out of a tree?"

"Uh-huh. Scraped my back all the way down."

"Must have been pretty deep. You said it took a lot of stitches."

"Twenty-seven in all."

He slid his hands around to her waist, then moved them upward to cradle her breasts in the spaces between his thumbs and forefingers. She blinked slowly, letting out a soft sigh.

"So what made you fall?" she murmured.

"I was climbing higher up in the tree to hide from my father. The last branch I stepped on wasn't strong enough, and I fell."

He moved closer and strummed his thumbs over her nipples. Her eyes drifted closed.

"Why were you hiding from your father?"

"Because I was late coming home. I knew he'd be mad."

"So it was better to continue to hide?"

Alex gave a humorless laugh. "Oh, hell, yes. Especially when he was coming after me. But then I fell right at his feet. Knocked the breath right out of me."

He ran his hands down to Val's hips and pulled her buoyant body against his, leaning in and kissing her neck at the same time.

"So was he mad?"

"No," Alex said between kisses. "Not really."

"So what did he do to you?"

"Nothing. I guess he was just glad I didn't kill myself. Or maybe he figured I'd hurt myself enough that any punishment was pretty much gratuitous. All he did was take me to the hospital."

Alex thought for a moment, wondering why that was. His father had never let any bad deed go unpunished. He remembered when John was nine and had practically drowned playing in the creek behind their house when he wasn't supposed to. John was still sputtering while his father was hauling out the belt.

Alex remembered being in the hospital. The stitches. The *number* of stitches. Telling how he'd cut himself on the tree limbs to the doctor, to his mother, to everybody who asked. But when he thought about the span of time between when he hit the ground and went to the emergency room, he realized he didn't remember a thing.

"You had cuts only on your back?" Val asked.

"Yeah," Alex said.

"That's kind of odd, isn't it?"

"It was just the way I fell."

Alex felt strange all of a sudden, as if his body temperature had suddenly shot up ten degrees. He leaned away from Val.

"What's wrong?" Val asked.

"Nothing."

No. Something. A memory. A hot, hazy memory of that night that he just couldn't seem to touch. But it was there, and slowly he began to realize that it was something that had hovered around the periphery of his mind for years, but he'd always shoved it aside, thinking he must have dreamed it, or made it up somehow. But there it was again. He swallowed hard, suddenly feeling as if he were being transported back twenty-eight years.

It had been a hot night. Like tonight. One of those hot, humid, deathly still nights that never really burned off the daytime sun because it had soaked into every blade of grass, every shrub, every tree.

He heard his father calling to him. Shouting at him. Threatening him.

Val took his hands in hers. "What is it?"

"I don't know."

He'd climbed farther up the tree. And then he saw his father, standing on the ground below. He took one more step up, and the branch gave way.

He remembered falling. It seemed to take forever, falling through those tree branches, like a parachute plunge from ten thousand feet. And then he hit the ground. The pain was incredible—all the air was smacked right out of his lungs, and for several seconds he couldn't breathe.

"I remember lying facedown on the ground," he told Val, his gaze turned away from her. "I heard my father's voice. He was angry." His voice came out in a hushed whisper. "So angry."

"You just said he wasn't angry."

Alex turned back. "I—" He stopped again, shaking his head. He'd always thought that he hadn't been. But that wasn't true. "I guess I just didn't remember."

All at once he realized how hard he was gripping Val's hands. He released them suddenly and moved away from her, sliding down into the water up to his neck.

"Alex? What's the matter?"

The sound of his father's angry shouts filled his mind.

What the hell do you think you're doing? I told you to be home before dark!

He remembered lying on his stomach, gasping for air. It hurt. Every attempt at taking a breath sent pain shooting all the way down into his lungs.

He heard a cracking noise. Then his father's footsteps.

Don't you ever disobey me again!

Pain suddenly shot down his back, a white-hot, searing pain unlike anything he'd ever felt before. It came again. And again. And again, until he nearly passed out. Then his father grasped him by the arm and hauled him to his feet, yanking him around to face him. And that was when he saw the tree branch the man held in his other hand.

"He hit me," Alex said, his voice so choked he could barely get the words out. "With a tree branch."

"What?"

Up to this moment, he'd always thought that it had just taken a moment for the pain to strike him. That each searing lash he felt was nothing more than his body waking up to the pain. But he hadn't had those cuts when he hit the ground.

He remembered crying, and his father's face had grown wild with rage. *Don't cry, goddamn it! Take it like a man!*

"He hit you?" Val said. "That's where you got the cuts?"

No. It couldn't have been as bad as he was remembering. His father couldn't possibly have done something like that to him.

"It was just discipline, Val," he said, his voice shaky. "That's all."

"Discipline? Twenty-seven stitches? Alex, for God's sake—what kind of man beats a child to a bloody pulp for staying out after dark?"

Alex swallowed hard, his mind feeling hot and hazy. No. That wasn't the way it had been. It couldn't have been.

Then suddenly he remembered what his father had said next, and his stomach twisted with the memory.

You got those cuts when you fell out of the tree. Understand?

And that was the story Alex had told. A lie. He'd told his father's version so many times that he'd actually come to believe it himself.

But now he knew. He knew the truth about that night, and it struck something buried so far inside him that he almost couldn't grasp it, something he knew on a subconscious level but had never been able to bring to light.

The ultimate knowledge of what his father really was.

As if a dam had burst, suddenly the memory of it came flowing out. He remembered every stroke of his father's arm, every scorching lash across his back. He felt every blow as if it were happening right now. Twenty-seven stitches. Christ, his father had ripped his back wide open. And then the man he'd always thought was above reproach in every way, who saw a chasm of difference between right and wrong, told him to lie about it.

"He told me to lie," Alex said breathlessly. "Told me to tell people I got the cuts when I fell from the tree. How in the hell could he have done that? And why didn't I remember?"

Val took his hands again, sliding down into the water until she was looking him right in the eye. "Because you were only six years old. You didn't want to believe that your father would do something like that to you."

And from that moment forward, Alex had learned to avoid his father's wrath by becoming just like him. By adhering to the same brand of mental toughness. No compassion. No extenuating circumstances. No bleeding heart. There was right and there was wrong, with absolutely nothing in between. Over time, Alex had learned his lesson well—the quickest way to draw his father's rage was to let emotion blur the line between the two.

Ruthless.

He'd heard that word so many times before in conjunction with his father, but he'd never believed it. Never.

Until now.

All this time he thought he understood the man as nobody else did, only to realize that he was the one who'd been so horribly misguided.

"My father," he said. "I'm just like him."

"What do you mean?"

Suddenly Alex was remembering things, so many things, so many times he'd made the decision his father would have deemed to be the right one, when it wasn't right at all.

"When I was in patrol," he told Val, "I remember dragging a guy to jail on Christmas Eve because he had an outstanding warrant for writing hot checks. I took him right out of his house while he was having dinner with his family. He had two kids. Little ones. They were crying as I dragged him away. My sister Sandy found out about it and let me have it. She said that all she could think about was how a couple of kids spent Christmas without their father. My father told Sandy to shut up. That I was right. That it was the guy's own fault for writing those bad checks in the first place, and that I had an obligation to bring him in. And I remember feeling so damned *proud* of myself."

Everything his father had beaten out of him that night in the woods was coming back in a torrent of emotion, so powerful it practically knocked him unconscious. He saw what his father had been. And then he saw what he'd been all these years. Good God—would he be the same if he had children of his own? Expect the impossible, then make them suffer if they didn't achieve it?

"The guy was hardly a threat," Alex went on. "I could have waited until the holidays were over. But I didn't. You'd have thought I'd have had pity for those kids. But I didn't feel a thing. I never let myself feel anything. It's one thing to be impersonal as a cop. It's another thing to be merciless."

Val shook her head. "No. That's not what you are."

"That isn't the only thing I ever did, Val. There's more. So much more." He closed his eyes. "Like what I did to you."

"No, Alex. If you were like your father, you never would have come to my apartment that night to try to break the news. You wouldn't have given a damn about me at all."

"And then I left you in the middle of the night. How cold was that?"

"No. You didn't leave because you felt nothing for me. You left because you felt too much."

And instantly he'd shoved those feelings aside because they made him feel weak and powerless and out of control, telling himself instead that what had happened between them was meaningless. An unfortunate mistake on his part. Bad timing. And then he'd systematically put Val out of his mind in a way that would have made his father proud—right up to the moment she showed up in his life again.

He and Val were the same in so many ways. They'd each locked themselves away from other people, Val because she was overflowing with emotion and only her grandfather had allowed her to get close enough to let it out, and Alex because he'd had all the emotion beaten out of him to the point that he didn't know how to let anyone in.

He glanced up at the sky. The pale orange light at the horizon had disappeared completely, revealing a half-moon and a sprinkling of stars.

He pushed a wet strand of hair away from Val's cheek with his fingertips, then kissed her. "Let's go back to the cabin."

She nodded. They got out of the lake. Val put her shirt on, while Alex merely slung his over his shoulder. Val slipped her hand inside his, and they walked back to the cabin.

They took a shower—a long, hot shower during which neither of them spoke at all, losing themselves in the water and the steam and the soap. Finally they stepped out and dried off.

"I need to dry my hair," Val said. "I'll be out in a minute."

Alex left the bathroom, knowing it was getting late, knowing it was time he got dressed and broke the news to Val. Instead, he lay down in bed and pulled the sheet up to his waist. He turned onto his side, his arm tucked under the pillow, staring ahead into the darkness of the bedroom. With Val—only with Val—he'd found more inside himself than a mirror image of a man he knew now that he never wanted to emulate. And now there was a possibility that he'd never see her again.

A few minutes later, he heard her come out of the bathroom. But as he was turning over, he felt her hand against his shoulder. She eased him back until he was lying on his stomach. Then, to his surprise, she straddled his sheet-covered hips and began to run her hands over his back and shoulders.

He started to rise, but she leaned into him, pressing with her palms, then moving her thumbs deep into his muscles, coaxing him to relax when he didn't think there was any way he could ever relax again. After a moment, he slipped his arms beneath the pillow and let his eyes drift closed. He absorbed every sweep of her hands, every nuance of her soothing touch, knowing there might come a time when he'd have only memories of moments like this.

Tell her. Right now. Tell her you're leaving.

Then he felt her lips on his back. A gentle kiss, right over the area where his scars were. A kiss to take away the old memory and put a new one in its place.

She leaned forward and slid her hands beneath the pillow on top of his. She kissed his neck, then brushed her bare breasts against his back. She was naked. He hadn't been completely sure of that, but there was no question about it now.

She sat back up and ran her hands down his rib cage, then brought them up to massage his shoulders with deep, satisfying strokes—soothing him and arousing him all at the same time. Then she slowly stretched out over him again, pressing her body against his, running her hands all the way down his arms and circling her fingers around his wrists. She kissed a spot beneath his right ear, then gently nipped his earlobe, sending warm shivers down his spine.

It's getting late. You have to tell her.

Finally he turned over, easing her off him, but the moment he was on his back she swept the sheet away and straddled him again. He felt a jolt of desire, which took a quantum leap when she slid herself over the length of his erection, moving back and forth, arousing him with heat and pressure without ever taking him inside. He stroked his hands along her thighs as she moved, amazed at how hot and wet she already was. Then she fell forward, dragging her nipples along his chest, still maintaining the smoothly cadenced motion that was driving him crazy.

Stopping was no longer an option.

He caught her face in his hands and kissed her, twining his tongue with hers in a slow, languid kiss. Still she moved against him, her hips shifting back and forth. Hot. Slick. He pressed his palms to her breasts, gently caressing them, and soon he felt a rising tension deep in his groin. He wanted to be inside her. *Needed* to be inside her. *Now.*

He skimmed his hands along her waist to her hips, guiding her, trying to move her in such a way that he could slide himself into her. But every time he was poised at her opening, she moved just enough to keep him at bay.

"Val," he said breathlessly, "I'm not any better at begging than you are, but here in a minute—"

She shifted her hips just slightly, and on the next stroke he got his wish. He groaned and clutched her hips, pulling her down until he was as deep inside her as he could get.

"Again," he said.

She rose, then thrust down on him again with a moan of satisfaction. Every muscle in his body contracted, poised to respond to her every move. Her fingertips bit into his shoulders as she repeated the motion, slowly at first, then faster, until she settled into a wild, hot rhythm.

He watched her, her eyes closed, her face flushed, that untamed hair of hers cascading over her shoulders, reaching for pleasure at the same time she gave it to him. He'd never seen a sexier sight in his life. The sounds she was making—tiny, breathless moans in the back of her throat—were almost enough to send him over the edge all by themselves. He tried to put his hands against her hips to slow her down, to keep this from being over before she was ready for it to be, but she persisted.

"Slow down, sweetheart."

She ignored him, continuing to ride him wildly, and he almost couldn't breathe for trying to hold back. He tightened his hands against her thighs.

"I'm close," he said under his breath. "So close. If you don't slow down—"

"No . . . I'm coming . . . oh, God, Alex . . ."

Yes.

She clamped down hard around him, and that was all it took to push him right over the top with her. Release hit him like lightning, sending jagged trails of ecstasy shooting through him. He pulled her down and wrapped his arms around her, hugging her against his chest, meeting every one of her downward thrusts with an upward thrust of his own, wringing every bit of pleasure out of the moment that he possibly could.

Val lay on top of him, glistening with sweat, breathing wildly. He loved holding on to her like this, her thighs surrounding his, her breasts pressed so tightly against his chest, the lean muscles of her back slowly relaxing beneath his hands. He'd wanted her for so long. Ages, it seemed. He'd deliberately tried to push her memory aside for five long years, but even when he'd been with other women, deep in the recesses of his mind, it was Val's face he saw, her legs wrapped around him, her voice crying out his name.

And he knew now why he'd never been able to forget her.

Slowly her breathing returned to normal. She slipped off and curled up next to him. He swept her hair away from her face and coaxed her to lay her head against his chest, wishing he could hold her just like this for the rest of his life.

Minutes ticked by. Val's eyes dropped closed, and he knew if they lay here much longer, she'd be asleep. For a crazy moment, he thought about slipping out of bed, getting dressed, and leaving, because he couldn't stand the thought of a last-minute confrontation as he was walking out the door. And it took him exactly three seconds to slap that thought right out of his head. He'd hurt her once by doing that, and he sure as hell didn't intend to do it again.

He took a deep breath, then moved away from her and sat up. He stretched to flip on the lamp. Sweeping the covers aside, he swung his legs over the edge of the bed.

"Alex?"

The mattress dipped behind him as she sat up and moved toward him. He put his elbows on his knees and dropped his head to his hands with a sigh of frustration.

Val put her hand against his shoulder. "Alex? What's the matter?"

Now. You have to go now, or you never will.

He rubbed his hand over his face, tension rising inside him. He stood up and walked to a chair in the corner of the room where he'd left his clothes.

"Is it time for us to go to the ranch?" she asked.

He put on his underwear, then slid into his jeans. Suddenly he felt as if the brutal heat outside the cabin had slithered inside, wrapping itself around him, putting him on edge all over again.

He turned to face her. She was poised on the edge of the bed, her legs tucked beneath her, the sheet pulled to her waist. Her golden-brown hair cascaded over her shoulders, curling intimately around her breasts, her head tilted questioningly.

"Alex?"

God, sweetheart, don't look at me like that.

"I'm going to the ranch alone."

She blinked. "What?"

"It's too dangerous for you to come with me."

"That's nonsense."

"No, it's not."

He pulled a T-shirt over his head, yanking it down over his

chest. He had to keep moving. If he slowed down, he'd stop altogether and climb right back into that bed with her.

"Wait a minute," she said. "I don't get this. Suddenly it's too dangerous for me? When did you reach that conclusion?"

"Last night when that bastard couldn't keep his hands off you. That's when."

"That's not going to happen again."

He buckled his belt, then grabbed his boots and sat down on the edge of the bed. Val's eyes narrowed. "Alex? What's going on here?"

"I told you. I'm going alone."

"So what do you expect me to do?" Val said. "Just sit here in this cabin twiddling my thumbs until you get back?"

He turned to look at her, his throat suddenly tight, wishing to God that it hadn't come to this.

"I'm not coming back."

chapter twenty-five

Val clutched the sheet to her chest, a sharp tingle of fore-boding prickling all the way down her spine.

"What do you mean, you're not coming back?"

"If you're found with me, you could face a whole lot more than a breaking-and-entering charge."

"What are you talking about?"

"Accessory to murder after the fact. Aiding and abetting a felon. If you're charged with those, you could end up in prison."

"But that's not going to happen," she said. "Not if we're careful. We're going to get Reichert, and then nobody will give a damn about any of the rest of that."

He pulled on his boots. "Getting something on Reichert is a long shot. You know that. We both knew it when we came here. And the longer this goes on, the more chance we have of being arrested. I don't want them to find you with me. I want you to go back to Tolosa."

Val blinked with surprise. For a moment she didn't under-stand exactly what he was saying. "Are you . . . are you telling me you want me to turn myself *in*?"

"Stanley didn't talk, so nobody can prove you were ever with me. One small breaking-and-entering charge. That's all they've got on you right now. Probation is the most you'll face."

Val couldn't believe this. He actually wanted her to return to Tolosa, as if everything between them had never been.

"Don't tell anyone that you were ever on the road with me," Alex went on. "Tell them I was the one behind the break-in. Blame it on me, Val. It'll help get you off the hook."

"No! I'm not going to say that! I'm the one who got you all tangled up in that break-in, not the other way around!"

"I've got a murder accusation hanging over my head. A little breaking and entering isn't going to matter. *Blame me.*"

"No! I'm not saying anything, because I'm not going back!"

"I can't make you do it. I can only tell you that I'm leaving tonight. And I'm leaving alone." He stood up. "I have to get some things together."

He grabbed the sack that contained his extra clothes, then left the bedroom. Val felt a tremor of panic. She climbed out of bed, sweeping the sheet along with her and wrapping herself in it. She found Alex in the kitchen, going through her backpack.

"Look," she said, "if it makes you feel any better, go to the ranch by yourself. I'll wait here. If you find something—"

"No. The longer you stay gone, the harder it will be for you to account for your whereabouts since the break-in. And every moment you stay away, you risk getting caught with me."

"But you need me," she said, desperation creeping into her voice. "I'm good at surveillance. You know that. I can help."

Alex didn't respond. He pulled her wallet out of the backpack and laid it on the table, along with the purse she'd carried last night.

"Your van," he said. "And your equipment. I may need them for a while. I'm sorry about taking them, but there's no other way."

"God, Alex—do you think I give a *damn* about my van right now?"

He opened the purse and took out the bugs and the flashlight, leaving her weapon behind. He stuffed them into the backpack and zipped it. Then he pulled the keys to the van off her key ring and put them into his pocket.

"Stop it!" Val shouted. "Will you just stop it?"

"Val—"

"No, damn it! What gives you the right to decide everything? Did you even think about talking to me? Ask me how I feel? For the record, Alex, I don't care about the risk. I care about . . ."

She paused, tears springing to her eyes.

"I care about being with you."

He shook his head, letting out a breath of frustration. Several seconds ticked by. He wouldn't look at her. Why wouldn't he just *look* at her?

"It's *my* decision," she said quietly.

"No, sweetheart. This is one decision I'm making for both of us."

He swung the backpack onto his shoulder and headed for the living room. All at once Val remembered what it had felt like all those years ago. She remembered how it felt to wake up and find him gone, every last excruciating moment of it. And now it was happening all over again.

She followed him, her desperation growing. She wasn't going to be able to talk him out of this. He was going to walk right out that door. He was going to leave her again, and there wasn't anything she could do to stop him.

He paused at the front door. "I'll get your van back to you soon, one way or the other."

"One way or the other?"

He took a deep, silent breath. "If I'm successful, I'll bring it back to you myself. If I'm not . . ."

Val felt a stab of foreboding. "What?"

"I'll leave it somewhere and then get word to you so you can pick it up."

"And then what?"

He didn't reply. What wasn't he saying?

"Alex?"

"They're not locking me up again, Val. No matter what."

Val felt her stomach take a sickening drop, as if the ground had fallen away beneath her feet.

"Are you telling me I may never see you again?"

He merely closed his eyes, his jaw tight, as if he couldn't bear to respond, and she had her answer.

Val felt as if her world had jerked to a complete standstill. She stared at him through tear-filled eyes, her voice a choked whisper. "No. You can't leave me again. Please. I can't take it if you leave me again."

"I don't want to leave you!" he said, frustration filling his voice. "Don't you know that? The last thing I want to do is walk out this door!"

"Then don't!"

He continued to stare at her, and for a moment it felt as if a chasm had suddenly opened up between them, one she'd never be able to cross. Then he held out his hand.

"Come here," he said softly.

She stepped forward and took his hand. He pulled her against him and hugged her tightly, enveloping her in his big, powerful arms, then pressed his cheek against hers and whispered in her ear, "I'm sorry it has to be like this. I'm so sorry."

"Take me with you," she said.

"I can't."

"We can go someplace where nobody will ever find us. People disappear all the time. How hard can it be?"

She knew she was talking nonsense, but she just couldn't seem to stop herself. She clung to him fiercely, trying not to cry, knowing all the while that it was a lost cause.

He stroked her hair, then gathered a handful of it in his fist and pressed it against her shoulder as he hugged her, burying his face in her neck.

"I'll find a way. I'll find a way to pin this on Reichert if it's the last thing I do."

"You can't promise that."

She felt his chest heave beneath her cheek in a silent breath of resignation.

"You're right. I can't."

Slowly he eased away from her and took her by the shoulders. "Val, I want you to listen to me. If days go by, weeks . . . you'll know, okay? You'll know I'm not coming back."

"Don't *say* that."

"Don't throw your life away waiting for me. I couldn't stand it if you did that."

She bowed her head, refusing to meet his eyes, refusing even to think about a future that didn't have him in it.

"Go back to Tolosa. Call Dave. He'll help you through the system. Do whatever he tells you to do. You can trust him."

She swiped at a tear that had started down her cheek, knowing a thousand more were right behind it and she wouldn't be able to stop any of them.

"I hate leaving you without transportation," Alex said.

"That's the least of my worries right now."

"And money." He reached toward his pocket, but she put her hand against his arm.

"No. You'll need it more than I will. I'll manage. I'm pretty resourceful, you know."

His mouth turned up in a brief smile. "I know."

"So you're going to the ranch tonight?"

"The sooner, the better."

"Be careful."

He nodded.

Tears suddenly began cascading down her face. Sobs choked her throat, so much so that she could barely speak. "I never stopped wanting you. All these years. I never stopped. And then you came back into my life again. . . ."

As her voice trailed off, he rested his palm against her cheek, then leaned in and pressed his lips to hers in a gentle kiss.

"I never stopped wanting you, either. And I never will."

He stared at her a moment more, his thumb stroking her cheek. Then he backed away, his hand falling away from her face. He turned and left the cabin, closing the door behind him with a gentle click.

And Val thought she was going to die.

She turned around and leaned against the door, tears streaming down her face. After a moment she heard the van's engine, then the sound of it disappearing up the road.

Then silence.

She went back into the kitchen and collapsed into a dinette chair, still sobbing. She was aching for him already. Aching for his hard, strong body pressed against hers. Aching for the promise of a shared future that might never be. Aching for the gentle words she'd never believed he had in him, words that had mitigated a lifetime of pain.

He'd told her that he'd wanted that night five years ago to be the beginning for them. She'd never imagined that this night might be the end.

No. He'll prove his innocence, and then he'll come home. I know he will.

But even as she told herself that, she had the most terrible feeling that Reichert was going to get away with murder, which meant she'd never see Alex again.

*   *   *

Alex drove down the highway toward the Reichert ranch, gripping the wheel with an intensity that just about ripped it out of the steering column. He felt a slow, seething anger, furious with Reichert for killing his own wife, furious that the crime had been pinned on him, and furious that he had to walk away from Val because of it. The memory of her tear-stained face as he left her in that cabin made him want to take the bastard by the throat, bypass the Texas legal system, and send him straight to hell.

He turned the van onto the dirt road that ran along the western perimeter of the ranch. Soon he reached the grove of trees where they'd hidden the van yesterday and buried it in the foliage again. He grabbed the backpack, then climbed the fence onto the Reichert ranch. He had no idea what he'd be able to accomplish tonight, but from here on out, every minute of his life was going to be spent pursuing one single-minded goal—to put Reichert behind bars and clear the way for him to go home again.

Alex made his way along the now-familiar path through the trees toward the ranch house. Fifteen minutes later he'd reached the shallow valley where the ranch house stood, and he was encouraged by what he saw. At ten o'clock, all the cabins were dark. He could only conclude that the hunting party had already left.

Good. Fewer people to get in the way.

The floodlights outside the horse barn were shining brightly, but the house looked deserted, with not a single window illuminated. It was entirely possible that if the hunting party had left, Reichert and his girlfriend had gone home, as well.

Then he scanned the driveway beside the house and was surprised to see no cars. Rick had said that he occupied the house even when Reichert didn't, but could it be that even he wasn't there?

The only vehicle in sight was the truck still parked behind where the hay barn had once stood, its driver's window blown out courtesy of the rake handle he'd smacked through it the night before. Right now the barn was nothing more than a few blackened embers and a concrete slab. The acrid odor of burned wood still filled the air.

One truck on the premises. Did it belong to Rick? He had no way of knowing.

Alex pulled out his cell phone along with the brochure Val had taken from Reichert's house in Tolosa. He called the ranch house. The phone rang six times before an answering machine came on. He dialed the number again and let it ring another six times, and still nobody answered.

This was good and bad. Good, because if the house was indeed vacant, he could easily get inside to plant surveillance equipment. Bad, because it might be days or weeks before Reichert returned and he could record anything that might implicate the man in his wife's murder.

That was okay. He could be patient. Very patient. He intended to haunt these woods, waiting, listening, until he nailed the bastard. And God help the man the moment he did. This was a death-penalty state. Alex hadn't always been able to ensure that the people he arrested for murder paid for it as completely as they should. Sometimes they pled to lesser charges; sometimes they walked. In this case, though, Reichert had made one mistake too many. He'd tried to kill Val. And that meant that Alex wasn't going to stop until he brought the full force of the law right down on Reichert's head.

Alex rang the house for a third confirmation that it was indeed unoccupied. It rang twice, and then he lost the signal. Out here in the middle of nowhere, he wasn't surprised. It didn't matter. The first two calls had already told him what he needed to know.

He tossed the cell phone into the backpack, slipped on a pair of gloves, then walked stealthily to the back of the house, surrounded by humid night air and the steady chirp of crickets. He eyed his surroundings vigilantly, but he saw no signs of life.

He edged up to the patio door, hoping he'd be able to pry it open. If not, he'd shatter the glass. In any event, after he planted the surveillance equipment, he intended to tear things up a little inside the house to simulate a burglary as a cover-up for the broken door. He reached for the handle.

The door was unlocked.

The skin prickled on the back of his neck, warning him that

he might have miscalculated. Could somebody have left the house and forgotten to lock this door?

Maybe.

He stood there a moment, debating what to do. He knew there was a possibility that somebody could be asleep upstairs, but because there had been no answer to his phone calls, that was unlikely.

He decided he'd just lucked out.

His senses on full alert, he eased the door open and stepped into the pitch-dark house. He pulled a flashlight out of the backpack, flipped it on, and saw that he'd entered a den of some kind. Sweeping the flashlight around the room, he saw a fireplace, then three animal-head trophies hanging on the paneled walls along with several pieces of western art. In front of the fireplace was a zebra-skin rug just like the one in Reichert's house in Tolosa. Then he panned the flashlight around to an overstuffed leather chair.

It was occupied.

Every muscle in Alex's body coiled instantly, instinct telling him to reach for his weapon. But it wouldn't have done any good. In the crook of the man's arm was a rifle, cocked and ready to fire.

"If you move," he said, "if you *breathe*, you're a dead man."

chapter twenty-six

Val sat at the dinette table in the cabin, the sheet still wrapped around her, rubbing her temples with her fingertips. There was nothing like a half-hour cry to make her head feel as if it were going to explode.

Her tears had finally stopped. Now she just felt numb.

Alex wanted her to go back to Tolosa. To call Dave. To have him help her through the legal mess that she was sure to encounter. Maybe she should do that.

Maybe she should think about it tomorrow.

She couldn't come to any conclusions tonight. She just couldn't. All she wanted to do was sit here and imagine that Alex might change his mind. She wanted to think that maybe he'd go to the ranch, do whatever he intended to do, then slip back through the cabin door and crawl right back into bed with her. She could hope, anyway, right up to the time she woke tomorrow morning and the bed was still empty beside her. Then she'd be forced to make a decision.

Until then, no.

She glanced at her wallet on the table. That, Shannon's laptop, and the clothes she'd bought at Wal-Mart on the way down here were about all Alex had left her with. And the purse she'd carried last night. She remembered now that it contained a hundred dollars, but the very thought of touching it disgusted her. Still, it was money, and before this was all over with, she'd probably end up needing it.

She pulled out the hundred, thinking back to what Rick had expected her to do to earn it. It had been a horrible experience, one that had brought back some of her most terrible memories. But then Alex had been there, making her feel warm and safe and cherished as no man ever had before, and suddenly everything had been all right.

The man with no heart. Could she have been more wrong about him?

Suddenly she was so tired she felt as if she could barely hold her head up. She started to put the hundred into her wallet. Then she paused. Stared at it. All at once she was wide-awake, every nerve ending humming with disbelief.

An address was written across the face of the bill.

Eighteen thirty-four Augusta Drive.

For the span of several seconds, Val didn't move. She just stared down at the hundred in rapt disbelief as the events of the past several days whizzed through her mind. Then, like a hurricane-force wind, everything spun around and circled back to the night Shannon had first approached Alex at the Blue Onion.

Now she knew. She knew who the real murderer was.

And it wasn't Jack Reichert.

"DeMarco. I had a feeling you'd be back. Damned if I wasn't right."

The man's cigarette-hardened voice slithered through the darkness of the den, a voice Alex had no trouble recognizing. He'd heard it last night through the receiver, telling Val the revolting things he expected her to do for the price he was willing to pay.

Rick.

Still dumbstruck at finding himself on the other end of a rifle, Alex let his thoughts race as he tried to get a handle on the situation. But it wasn't until Rick reached over and flipped on a lamp, then settled back in his chair again, that another jolt of recognition struck Alex.

He'd seen this man before. Years before.

Through a pair of binoculars last night, he hadn't recognized him. Rick was older now, and he'd grown a beard, probably to hide the long, irregular scar that went from his right ear to his chin. It was the kind of wound that came from the slash of a knife. The kind of wound a man could get in prison if he didn't watch his back.

Alex had known that Rick was an ex-con. What he hadn't

realized was that he'd been the one to put him in prison six years ago.

Richard Murdock.

Rick.

Alex still didn't grasp the whole picture. Reichert's right-hand man was somebody he'd arrested? Could it possibly be a coincidence?

Murdock lit a cigarette and took a long drag, then blew out the smoke. "So tell me, DeMarco. How did you know that I was the one who killed Shannon?"

For the span of several seconds, Alex didn't breathe. *Murdock* killed Shannon?

Holy shit.

Alex stared at the man with a calm demeanor, even though his thoughts were racing ninety to nothing. "I didn't know."

Every speck of color seemed to drain away from the man's face. "You didn't know—"

"I thought Reichert killed his wife."

Murdock's jaw twitched, a small, barely visible outward indication of the anger that was undoubtedly raging inside him right now. He'd just needlessly proclaimed his guilt, and was clearly displeased that he'd made such a blatant miscalculation.

"Well, now I guess you know the truth, don't you? That's your misfortune."

Alex didn't respond.

"Reichert told me you and that little PI had broken into his house in Tolosa, but I had no idea you'd made your way down here." His lips curled into a thin smile. "Until I got my hands on her last night."

Anger ignited inside Alex, burning so wildly that it was all he could do not to rush the bastard and take him out with his bare hands. But with his finger wrapped firmly around the trigger of that rifle, Alex didn't stand a chance. Rick had killed twice already. He wouldn't hesitate to kill again.

"I didn't know right away who she was. But then the barn went up in smoke, and she disappeared, and all at once I knew why she'd looked so familiar to me. And I figured if she was in the vicinity, you weren't far behind. I assume I have you to thank for the fireworks?"

Alex just stared at him, his jaw tight with anger.

"Well. I told you I'd get you one way or the other, DeMarco. I guess this just means my plans have changed a little."

It took a moment for everything to come together, for Alex finally to realize the truth. And the truth astonished him.

Suddenly Alex remembered Murdock screaming at him six years ago as he was being handcuffed and dragged out of the courtroom: *I'll get you for this, DeMarco. If it's the last thing I do.*

It had been such a dumb, empty threat, and such a cliché that the few times Alex had heard it uttered, he'd disregarded it. How could he have known that Murdock had meant what he said?

"Shannon wasn't the target, was she?" Alex said. "I was."

A tiny smile appeared on Murdock's lips. "You still are."

"You killed a woman just to frame me?"

"No great loss. She was really beginning to get on my nerves."

"So you were sleeping with her."

"Oh, yeah. She married Reichert when she was twenty-two, which didn't stop her from screwing around with me. When I got out of prison, I went back to working with Reichert, and Shannon wanted to pick up where we'd left off, too. Fortunately, she decided she was in love with me, which meant she'd do just about anything I told her to."

Alex knew this bastard was cold, but he would never have believed that anyone would do something like this.

"Shannon had no idea what she was involved in, did she?" Alex asked.

"She had a lot of assets. A brain wasn't one of them."

"How did you get her to bring me to her house?"

"Oh, she knew I was out to get you. I told her I wanted to take pictures of the two of you together to send to your wife. You know. Screw up your marriage."

"I'm not married."

"And I didn't take pictures, did I?"

Then he remembered what Shannon had said: *My husband's out of town. What he and your wife don't know won't hurt them.*

She'd been nothing but a pawn. An ignorant pawn who had no idea she was being roped into her own murder.

"How does Reichert feel about the fact that you killed his wife?"

"You kidding? He and Angela are ecstatic. He was going to have to pay big bucks to get rid of Shannon in a divorce."

"Then Reichert knows—"

"No. He still thinks you did it. It just so happens that I got to do him a favor at the same time I framed you."

"How did you drug me?"

"Tranquilizer. The one we use on the big cats. I wasn't sure of the dosage, but I managed to get it just about right."

"I assume you were the one who shot Val back in Tolosa."

"Can't believe I missed. Six years in prison really screwed up my aim. They don't let you take a lot of target practice in there."

"Why did you do it? She didn't see anyone but me in Reichert's house the night of the murder."

"I had no idea Reichert had hired a PI to tail Shannon. I didn't think she saw me leave the house, but I couldn't take any chances. And then the two of you broke into Reichert's house. I figured that meant you suspected him, so I relaxed a little, drove down here, took care of the hunt. But after last night, when I realized you were in the vicinity, I got to thinking that you were on to me."

He flicked the end of the rifle. "Toss me that backpack. Nice and easy."

Alex slid it off his shoulder, knowing he had no way to get to the weapon inside without getting shot. He lobbed the backpack to Murdock. He opened it and looked inside.

"Hmm. Looks like you were planning a little surveillance. Blew it last night, so you thought you'd try again?"

He located Alex's gun, pulled the magazine out of the handgrip, then tossed the empty weapon aside. He put the magazine in his pocket, then settled back in his chair.

"I figured you'd be back, so I thought I'd wait and see. You called here tonight, what? Three times? Checking to see if anyone was home?" He smiled knowingly. "And now here you are. The bastard of a cop who put me in prison."

"What am I going to do, Murdock? You kill somebody; I put you away. It's my job."

"Well, in just a little while, there's going to be one less cop on the payroll. And, sooner or later, one less PI getting in the middle of things she shouldn't. Where is she?"

Alex felt a jolt of apprehension. "She has no idea you're guilty. She still thinks Reichert did it."

"Now, I can't be sure of that, can I?"

"Leave her alone, Murdock."

"Tell me where she is."

Alex was silent.

"Never mind. I'll catch up to her sooner or later. And maybe this time I'll get to finish what I started last night. Right before I kill her."

The raging anger Alex felt was eclipsed only by his fear for Val's life. At this moment, Murdock had no idea where to find her. But since Alex had insisted she return to Tolosa, it wouldn't be long before he'd have his hands on her again. She'd be looking over her shoulder for Reichert, when Murdock was the real threat.

Goddamn it. He had to find a way to stop this man.

Murdock put a booted foot up on the coffee table. "Tell me. If a couple of bodies were buried out here on this big old ranch, how long do you think it would take for somebody to find them?"

Alex knew the truth. No one would ever find them.

"Okay, DeMarco. Time to get out of the house. This is bound to get a little messy, and I wouldn't want to get any stains on Reichert's rugs."

Alex had to think fast. He could try to overpower Murdock, but the man was nearly as big as he was, with a rifle that he was obviously well versed in the use of. If he ended up dead, he couldn't do a thing to help Val. But he had to do something soon, or Murdock would kill him.

And Val would be next.

Val stared at the hundred-dollar bill, still unable to believe what she was looking at.

That hundred-dollar bill from the pool game. Did you see her give it to me?

Did you see me give it right back to her?

She'd written her address on it. Her subtle way of suggesting I come home with her.

Val had seen Alex give that hundred back to Shannon. Whoever had it after that had to have taken it from Shannon's purse the night of the murder.

Then Val remembered the letters.

I can't wait until you're free. That was what Shannon had written. Free. As in released. But not from a marriage.

From prison.

Rick.

He was an ex-con. Just released. He could use the same kinds of rifles Reichert did. And tranquilizers, too.

He was Shannon's killer.

Val had no idea what his motive was, but right now, it didn't matter. She could tell the Tolosa police that Rick had given her this hundred-dollar bill, which would surely make him a suspect. If the authorities searched the ranch, they might be able to find the animal tranquilizer that matched what had been in Alex's system the night of the murder, and maybe even the rifle she'd been shot with. Rick would be arrested, and Alex would go free.

Unfortunately, she had nothing that would persuade the local authorities to arrest Rick tonight. She knew it would take getting right into Henderson's face with the evidence she was holding in her hand before he'd be forced to consider anyone but Alex a suspect.

But right now, Alex could very well be in danger. If he went to that ranch thinking he was going after one man when the real murderer was somebody else, he could make a tactical mistake that could cost him his life.

She yanked up her cell phone and dialed Alex's number. It went immediately to voice mail.

Damn it. His phone was turned off.

She closed her eyes, willing herself to remain calm. She had to get out to that ranch. But how? Alex had taken her van, and she had no other transportation. She knew nobody within four hundred miles.

Wait a minute. Yes, she did.

She paused only a moment before picking up the phone again and calling information. She asked for a phone number, then dialed it. The phone rang four times. She heard the telltale stutter of the ring as it forwarded to another number, and a moment later a very sleepy man answered.

"Hello?"

Val took a deep breath, wishing she had more time to think about this. But she had no time. She just had to hope that she wasn't making a monumental mistake.

"Stanley. This is Valerie Parker. And I really, *really* need your help."

chapter twenty-seven

As Stanley drove into the Lakeshore Cabin complex, his hands were shaking. They'd started shaking the moment he hung up the phone after talking to Val, and he didn't expect them to stop shaking anytime soon.

Damn it. Get a grip, will you?

Val had woken him from a dead sleep and told him some wild story about Alex DeMarco and a hundred-dollar bill and a man on a big ranch west of here who'd really killed the woman DeMarco was accused of killing. Stanley hadn't exactly followed everything—Val had talked way too fast—but he did hear the part about it maybe being a matter of life and death. And then Val had asked him—no, *begged* him—to drive her out to the ranch.

Stanley steered the squad car along the narrow road through the trees, counting off the cabin numbers as he went. He knew a prudent lawman wouldn't automatically take the word of a known fugitive, and he was pretty damned sure that for the umpteenth time in his life he was getting ready to make a huge mistake. But Val had sounded so desperate that he just hadn't been able to ignore her.

That's because you're a gullible moron.

That was probably true. History would certainly bear that out. But then he'd thought about how she'd brought that water to him before he started that long walk back to town. He'd thought about how she'd told him not to worry, that he wasn't going to get hurt, and she'd been right. And then he'd thought about how she'd encouraged him to ask Glenda to dance at the celebration, and sure enough, Glenda had said yes. All very nice things.

And so he'd come.

Still, a little voice was whispering to him—that same little voice he often heard right before he screwed something up in a major way. It was telling him that this had to be a setup. That somehow DeMarco would get the better of him, and he'd end up looking like a fool one more time. But he couldn't think of any scenario under the sun where a fugitive would be dumb enough to call a law enforcement officer and ask him to come pick her up, so surely Val was telling him the truth.

Wasn't she?

He brought the squad car to a halt two doors down from number sixteen and cut his headlights. Lights were on inside the cabin. He could just make out the form of a woman near the window.

Okay. It wasn't as if he had to go rushing blindly into the situation. He could hang back. Play it smart. Scope out the cabin. See what was up. Move in slowly. Do everything a sensible officer of the law should do in order to keep control of a situation.

But he hadn't counted on what happened next.

All at once, the door to the cabin burst open and Val came running out. As she raced toward his car, Stanley was sure that he'd made a deadly mistake. Even though DeMarco wasn't in sight, he had the terrible feeling that he'd just walked into an ambush. For some reason, DeMarco had put Val up to calling him with that preposterous story, and now he was going to pay for being dumb enough to believe it.

By the time Val reached his car, his heart was whacking his chest like machine-gun fire. Before it occurred to him that maybe he should lock the door until he assessed the situation more completely, she yanked it open and leaped into the passenger seat. He recoiled, pressing himself against the driver's door, mentally crossing himself and hoping what came next would only make him look stupid and not dead.

"Stanley!" Val said. "I thought you'd never get here!"

In one smooth swoop, she reached over, took his face in her hands, and gave him a smack right on the lips.

"Thank you," she said. "Thank you for coming. I don't know what I'd have done without you." She settled back and reached for her seat belt. "Take a left as you leave the cabins and go west. The ranch is about ten miles from here."

For a few seconds, Stanley just stared at her. He didn't understand everything that was going on here. The only thing he knew for certain was that real fugitives didn't kiss deputy sheriffs.

"I still don't get it," he said, still a little wary. "Where are we going? And why?"

"I'll fill you in on the way. But remember, Stanley. Even though Alex acted like a jerk out on the highway yesterday, if he'd been the murderer you thought he was, he wouldn't have let you go at all. He'd have shot you and left you for dead. You know that, don't you?"

Stanley had definitely wondered why a heartless murderer like DeMarco had let him live. And how a nice lady like Val had ended up with a guy like him. It didn't make sense. From the way she and DeMarco had gone at it on the dance floor at the Founder's Day Celebration, he knew just what kind of relationship they had. Hell, the whole town knew. And he had to think that a nice, smart lady like Val couldn't possibly make such a big mistake when it came to picking a man as to end up in the company of a killer.

"Yes," he told her. "I know. I believe you."

"Okay, then. Step on it!"

Stanley did a turnabout, then gunned the engine and roared up the main road of the cabin complex. When he reached the exit, he did a tire-squealing turn onto Highway 4.

"What about backup?" Stanley said. "Do we need reinforcements?"

"Not yet. I haven't got enough for you to arrest this guy right now. The most important thing is to get to Alex and warn him. Tell him who the real killer is. Then we can go from there."

Stanley floored the gas pedal and reached sixty in record time, feeling like Dirty Harry, James Bond, and Mad Max all rolled into one. For once in his dull, boring life, his body hummed with excitement. There was nothing like driving hard to really get a man's blood rushing.

"I don't know what's going on out there," Val said, a worried note in her voice. "It could get dangerous."

Stanley's blood slowed considerably. He liked feeling danger, but he wasn't completely sure he liked living it.

Tonight it didn't look as if he was going to have a choice.

Alex stood in the breezeway of the horse barn, absolutely certain that Murdock intended to make this his last night on earth.

The man had bound his wrists, tied them with a long rope, then thrown that rope over one of the rafters of the horse barn and yanked his arms over his head. Then he secured the end of the rope before leaving the barn and walking back to the house.

What in God's name was he up to?

Alex leaned back against the wall of the barn, the rope cutting into his wrists, his arms aching as if they were being ripped from their sockets. The night was unforgivably hot and humid, and the odor of the incinerated hay barn still filled the air. Sweat poured down his forehead, and he had to swipe his face against his arm to keep it out of his eyes. Down the breezeway of the barn, he heard the steady swish of a horse's tail, swatting at flies.

The barn was dark, with only the light from the floodlights outside to provide illumination. He had no idea why Murdock hadn't turned on the lights. Maybe because even though they were miles away from the rest of humanity, he thought it best to commit murder under the cover of darkness.

He heard the glass door of the ranch house open and close. He leaned over and could see Murdock making his way up the path. He came inside the barn, sat down on a bale of hay near Alex, and cracked open a beer. That was what he'd gone back to the house for?

He took a long drink, then rested his back against a stall door, holding the beer in one hand and a rifle in the crook of his other arm.

"Man, there is nothing like a cold beer on a hot night," he said. "It's one of those things you miss the most when you're in prison. Drugs you can get. But a cold one? Nope."

Alex couldn't believe this. The man was sipping a beer as if he were watching a ball game.

"What are you waiting for, Murdock? Why don't you just shoot me and get it over with?"

"You know, that's what I'd planned to do, at least for the first couple of years I was in prison. But as time went on, I pictured putting a bullet through your head, and I thought, you know, one shot and it's over. Oh, there might be a split second in there when you think, 'Shit, I'm done for now,' but all in all it's a pretty quick and painless way to go. Nothing like six years of hell in a shitty prison cell. Then one day I thought to myself, if that son of a bitch could only be living my life right now, he'd regret the day he put me in here. So I decided I wanted to make that happen. But now you've cheated me out of the pleasure of picturing you in prison: watching your back twenty-four hours a day and praying you don't catch the eye of some sicko who decides to make you his girl-friend." He took another long swig of beer. "Yeah, I'm definitely going to have to kill you, but I'll be damned if I'm going to make it quick and painless. I just haven't quite figured out the best way to make it slow and excruciating."

He settled back against the wall of the barn, resting the beer against his knee.

"But it'll come to me," he said. "Believe me. It'll come."

Val led Stanley along the dark path through the Reichert ranch, holding his flashlight low as they drew closer to the house. She'd been both elated and apprehensive that they'd found her van in the same place where she and Alex had hidden it yesterday. It meant he was somewhere on the ranch, but where?

She wished she could have gotten Alex to answer his phone. She'd tried three times since they'd left the cabin and gotten his voice mail every time. And by the time they got to the ranch, she was having trouble even picking up a signal.

They reached the tiger enclosure, and Val led Stanley west around it. The tiger greeted them along the fence with a throaty growl, and Val thought Stanley was going to jump right out of his skin.

"That's a tiger!" he exclaimed. "What the hell . . . ?"

"It's a long story," Val said. "I'll fill you in later."

Stanley gave her a panicked "What have I gotten myself

into?" look, and she wondered if she'd done the right thing by bringing him along. Maybe she should have left him in his car until she returned with Alex. As much as she liked Stanley, she had to admit that his policing skills left a little bit to be desired.

Soon they reached the clearing where the ranch house stood. Val scanned the area. The cabins were dark. Evidently the hunting party had gone home. She saw only one light on in the back of the house. Looking at the driveway, she saw no cars. The only vehicle in the vicinity was a pickup truck behind where the hay barn used to be, its driver's-side window missing.

Was Reichert still here? Rick? She didn't know.

"Look at that," Stanley said, pointing to the burned-out hay barn. "What do you suppose happened there?"

"Another long story," Val said, looking around nervously. "I don't see Alex. But he has to be here somewhere."

Val's anxiety escalated with every breath she took. It was so quiet here tonight that she imagined she'd be able to hear Alex's footsteps if he was anywhere around, but she heard nothing. Saw nothing.

Where was he?

Then she glanced across the clearing to the breezeway of the horse barn, and what she saw made her heart stop.

Alex. Oh, God. No.

For a moment she just stood there, paralyzed. The floodlights outside the barn were shining just brightly enough that she could see the outline of his body, his arms tied over his head.

"Stanley," she whispered. "There he is! There's Alex!"

Stanley whipped around, his eyes growing wide. "Oh, my God." He swallowed hard. "Where's the bad guy?"

"I don't see him. But that doesn't mean he isn't in that barn." Forcing back a swell of panic, she grabbed Stanley's arm. "Go back to your car. Radio for help."

"What are you going to do?"

"I'm going to get closer. Try to free Alex."

"No! I c-can't let you do that!"

"What?"

"That's—" He took a deep, shaky breath. "That's my job."

Maybe, but given the way he was trembling right now, she knew he'd be more of a hindrance than a help, and she certainly couldn't afford that now.

"Stanley, please go radio for backup. *Please.*"

"Only if you promise to stay right here."

"I can't! He's going to kill Alex!"

"And if that guy gets ahold of you, he'll kill you, too!"

Val opened her mouth to argue again, then thought better of it. "Okay, Stanley. Maybe you're right. It would be too dangerous for me to go in there by myself. I'll stay right here and keep an eye on the situation. Just get somebody out here. Anyone with a badge and a gun. And hurry!"

Stanley gave her a quick nod, then ran back through the trees. Val glanced back at Alex. She couldn't imagine what Rick must have done to get the drop on him, but from the way he was bound right now, it was clear the man had no intention of letting him walk away alive.

The barn was dark. Was Rick in there? Or had he left Alex there and returned to the house? She had no way of knowing.

If the hay barn were still there, she could have used it for cover to get closer. As it was now, she'd have to circle the edge of the clearing, come up beside the ranch house, and use that as a vantage point to get a better view inside the breezeway of the barn. If she didn't see Rick, she could check out the house to see if he was inside. What she'd do after that, she didn't know.

A wild flurry of emotions raced through her. Love for Alex. Hatred for Rick. Fear that she wasn't going to do the right thing. She put a hand against her chest, wishing she could slow her racing heart. Nothing was certain here. She'd have to play it by ear. And the thought of that scared her to death.

She'd lived her whole adult life that way—taking chances, playing the odds, tossing out the rule book and just winging it—and usually she came out on top. But the stakes had never been this high. The actions she took in the next few minutes could determine whether the man she loved lived or died.

She took a deep breath, pulled out her weapon, and started toward the house.

*   *   *

Murdock ground out yet one more cigarette on the barn floor, then turned his gaze up to Alex.

"Got a question for you, DeMarco. Do you like cats?"

"Fuck you, Murdock."

"I'll take that as a no." He took another swig of beer. "You know, I've been sitting here racking my brain trying to arrive at a really creative way to kill you. Then all of a sudden I thought, 'Uh-oh. I forgot to feed the tiger.' "

Alex's blood ran cold.

"That's right, DeMarco. A tiger. A big old Bengal tiger with a very bad attitude. It'll be just you and him. You're a big guy, but I gotta tell you—my money's on the tiger. And what a hell of a spectator sport. Those Romans really knew what they were doing." Murdock started to take another drink of beer. Then he froze, glancing out the door of the barn in the direction of the house. Slowly he lowered his beer again.

"Well, I'll be damned."

Alex turned his head, trying to see out the door. What was he looking at?

Murdock picked up his rifle. "So she's here after all."

Alex lurched forward as far as the ropes would allow and looked toward the house.

Val. Oh, God. No.

She had her weapon drawn and was peering carefully around the side of the house. Alex felt a flood of panic. He'd left her in that cabin so she'd be safe from all this. How had she gotten here? How?

"You know that slow and excruciating thing?" Murdock said, raising his rifle until he had Val in his sights. "I think we can start it off right now."

"Val!" Alex shouted. "Look out!"

She spun around at the sound of his voice. Murdock pulled the trigger. The bullet struck her, and Alex watched in horror as she crumpled to the ground.

"Bull's-eye," Murdock said.

chapter twenty-eight

"Goddamn you!" Alex shouted. "You son of a bitch! You goddamned fucking *son of a bitch*!"

"We don't tolerate trespassers around here."

Murdock strode out of the barn, his rifle in the crook of his elbow.

"Val!" Alex shouted. *"Val!"*

His scream was strangled, pleading, filled with agony, willing her to get up. He kept screaming. She didn't move. She lay on the ground on her side, her arms sprawled in front of her, the light of the floodlights casting a harsh shadow along her back. Her hair was fanned out on the ground around her head, and blood had formed a huge crimson stain on her chest.

She lay still. Deathly still.

Alex gritted his teeth and jerked madly on the rope that held his arms over his head. The rope ripped into his wrists, but still he tried to pull them free, yanking with every ounce of his strength.

Why hadn't she stayed away? *Why?*

Murdock stopped and picked something up off the ground, and Alex realized he'd grabbed Val's weapon. Then he walked over to where she lay. He stared down at her a moment, then pushed a booted foot against her back.

Still Val didn't move.

Murdock shoved Val's gun into the waistband of his jeans, then pulled his cigarettes from his pocket. He casually lit one, took a long drag, then started back toward the barn.

Tears sprang to Alex's eyes, and he bowed his head, pain and regret ripping through him. He yanked on the rope again, ignoring the ache in his wrists and the blood oozing down his arms, wanting desperately to get free so he could put his hands around that bastard's neck and kill him, just as he'd killed Val.

Murdock came back into the barn, tossed Val's gun aside, then sat back down on the bale of hay again. "Well. It doesn't look like she'll be going anywhere anytime soon."

"You sadistic motherfucking *bastard*! God*damn* you!"

Murdock took a long drag off his cigarette and blew out the smoke.

"She knew something was up," Alex said hotly. "Cops will be out here any minute!"

"Nah. I don't think so. If she had backup on the way, she wouldn't have been poking around by herself."

Alex had a horrible feeling that he was right. *Damn it.* She couldn't have known that he was in trouble. So what was she doing here?

"In fact, with the two of you being fugitives and all, I'm betting nobody even knows you're in this part of the state." Murdock chuckled a little. "Murder doesn't get much easier than this."

Alex narrowed his eyes, his vision growing blurry with sheer, hot anger. He wasn't going down without a fight. He was going to take any opening, no matter how minuscule, to get his hands on Murdock. And he was going to kill him—as brutally as he'd killed Val, and with no remorse. Until this moment, he wasn't sure he believed in a place where somebody would burn throughout eternity, but now he knew beyond a shadow of a doubt that hell had to exist. Because nothing a mere mortal could do to this cold-blooded bastard would begin to make him pay for what he'd done to Val.

Murdock took one last drag off his cigarette, then stood up, giving Alex a wicked smile. "It's showtime."

He tossed the butt down and ground it out with the heel of his boot, then glanced out the doorway of the barn. Suddenly his body tensed, his eyes widening with surprise.

"What the—" His gaze shifted back and forth. "Where the hell did she go?"

Alex yanked against the ropes, leaning out to look toward the house.

Val was gone.

He couldn't believe his eyes. It couldn't be. Hope raced through him. She was alive. *Alive.*

"There was blood everywhere," Murdock said, panic edging into his voice. "I thought I got her square in the chest."

His gaze panned back and forth along the back of the house. Then Alex saw a shadow moving by a window, and he could barely breathe for the relief he felt. This game wasn't over. Not yet.

"She's inside the house!" Murdock said.

Alex knew if she could stay conscious long enough, she could get to a phone and call for help. But he knew he had to buy her some time. He had to keep Murdock out of there long enough for her to make a phone call.

Hold on, sweetheart. Just hold on.

"Hey, Murdock," Alex said. "Any weapons inside that house?"

Murdock whipped around, giving him a look that said there were.

"I gotta tell you," Alex went on. "She's one hell of a shot."

"Then it's time I finished her off, isn't it?"

"If you go into that house," Alex said, "you'd better be prepared to get your head blown off."

Murdock paced to the door of the barn, tension lacing every stride. "She's half-dead already. Even if she can find a gun, she won't be able to pick it up, much less fire it."

"Don't bank on it. I don't care if she's bleeding all over the floor, she's still a crack shot. You, on the other hand, appear to need a little more time at the shooting range."

"Shit!" Murdock shouted. "The phone!"

Damn.

He ran back, grabbed his rifle, spun around, and raced back to the door of the barn. He aimed at the house and squeezed off four shots in quick succession. Alex heard the bullets hit a metal mark. Murdock lowered his rifle with a satisfied sigh.

"Got the box on the back of the house where the phone lines come in. She won't be calling anybody now."

Then his expression grew worried again. He turned to Alex. "Does she have a cell phone?"

Alex didn't respond.

Murdock tossed the rifle aside and pulled a knife out of his pocket, then he picked up a semiautomatic pistol that had been sitting beside him on the hay bale. He flipped open the blade of the knife and walked around behind Alex. Murdock put the gun right at the back of his neck, and for a moment Alex thought he intended to make his a quick death after all.

To his surprise, though, Murdock sawed through the rope several inches above where his hands were bound. The sudden release, when his arms had been stretched over his head for so long, sent pain rocketing through Alex's arms and shoulders. Murdock shoved him from behind and sent him sprawling onto the ground.

"You're going in there with me," he said. "She might shoot at me, but not if you're in the way. Now get up."

Alex came to his feet, breathing hard, his wrists still bound in front of him.

"Turn around."

Alex did, and Murdock grabbed him by the back of his collar and shoved him out the barn door, pressing the gun into his back at the same time.

"Don't want her deciding to take potshots out the window, now, do we? If she does, you'll be the one she hits first."

"She's got the upper hand. You have no idea where she's hiding in that house."

"Yeah, but once she thinks I'm going to blow your head off, I'll just bet you she'll come running."

They walked across the yard and reached the spot where Val had fallen. Alex looked down at the pool of blood. She'd managed to get up and get into the house. But had she managed anything else?

"Open the door," Murdock said.

Alex pushed the sliding door open and Murdock shoved him inside. Val wasn't in the den. *Thank God.*

"Val!" Alex shouted. "Wherever you are, stay put!"

"Don't think you want to do that, Val," Murdock called out. "Not when I've got a gun pointed right at his head. Now get your ass out here, or he's history."

Murdock pushed Alex ahead of him through the den to a doorway leading down a hall and peered around it. Then he dragged him to the kitchen doorway and did the same.

Alex listened. Nothing. Either she was staying put as he'd told her to, or she didn't have the strength to move.

Or she was dead.

No. He refused even to think it.

He looked down at the carpet near the sofa and saw blood drops, then spotted a blood smear on the doorway leading out of the room about shoulder height. That gave him hope. At least she'd been walking.

"What now, Murdock?" Alex said. "You've got a hell of a murder scene in progress here. Blood everywhere. Try explaining that to Reichert."

"He won't be back here until next month. Got plenty of time to clean things up."

"This is a big house. She could be hiding anywhere."

Murdock shoved Alex down to the sofa. "Get out here, Val!" Murdock shouted. "If you don't, I'm going to blow his head off!"

Suddenly Alex heard the sound of the door sliding in its tracks again, and a loud *whap* as it smacked all the way open. A man in uniform stepped inside, his weapon drawn.

"Police!" the man shouted. "Put your hands up!"

It couldn't be. *Stanley?*

Murdock whipped around. The deputy squeezed off a shot, echoed by a shot from Murdock's gun. Stanley missed.

Murdock didn't.

Stanley took a hit in the upper leg. His weapon went flying, and he fell to his knees in the pile of broken glass just inside the door, clutching his thigh.

Alex leaped off the sofa and rushed Murdock, but he was a stride too far away. The man whipped his gun back around and Alex slid to a halt. Then Murdock edged over, picked up Stanley's gun, and stuffed it into his pants.

"Aw, *shit!*" Stanley shouted, clutching his leg. "I did it again!"

Murdock looked at him with confusion. "Did what?"

"Screwed up," he said, gritting his teeth with pain. "I should have waited. Damn it, I should have waited until they got here!"

"Until who got here?"

"The cops from Ruston and Wendover. They're going to be

beating down that door any minute, and what are they going to find? Me bleeding all over the floor." He closed his eyes and shook his head painfully. "I'll never live this down. Never!"

"Cops are coming?" Murdock said. "How many?"

"I don't know. Seven, maybe eight. And every one of them is going to laugh his head off and tell me what a fuckup I am. *Again.*"

Murdock shot Alex a nervous glance. "Call the woman. Get her in here right now!"

"Just once I wanted to pull something off myself," Stanley went on. "A big arrest. Something important. Hell, right about now I'd have just settled for not getting shot!"

"You're going to get shot again if you don't shut your mouth!"

Murdock was starting to get a little agitated, a little out of control, and for good reason. The seven or eight cops on the way could throw a serious wrench into his plans. Alex inched closer. If the guy really lost it, he just might get a little careless, and Alex had no intention of missing even the smallest window of opportunity.

Then, out of the corner of his eye, he saw Val sitting on the floor, peering around the doorway of the hall that led to the front entry. His heart leaped, only to clench in fear when he saw her bloodsoaked clothes, her ashen face.

No! Go, sweetheart! Get out of here!

She slipped back around the door. He wondered if she'd found a weapon, then wondered if she'd have the strength to use it even if she had.

She was alive. She was still alive.

A moment later, he heard a sound toward the front of the house. Murdock evidently heard it, too, because he turned in that direction.

"Hey!" Stanley shouted.

Murdock whipped back around.

"Why don't you do it, you son of a bitch? Just shoot me! I really don't give a damn. Not anymore. I'm sick to death of being the brunt of everybody's jokes. I've had it! When they come beating on that door, I'd just as soon be dead!"

Alex inched closer to Murdock. He'd known that Stanley was incompetent, but he didn't figure him for crazy. The last thing he should be doing was baiting a guy like Murdock, especially with his backup on the way.

All at once Alex heard a loud whack coming from the direction of the front entry of the house, followed by four more whacks that sounded like a battering ram was plowing right through the door.

"They're here!" Stanley shouted.

Murdock whipped around when Stanley shouted, pointing his gun away from them. Alex lunged for Murdock, smacking him in the chest with his bound hands. Murdock stumbled backward and Alex fell on top of him. His gun tripped across the carpet. Alex rolled to his left, slapped one of his hands down onto the gun, then rolled again and rose to his knees. Murdock sat up and pulled out Stanley's gun that he'd shoved into his waistband.

"Drop it!" Alex shouted. "Drop it right now or I'll blow your fucking brains out!"

Murdock dropped it.

"Back away!"

He did. Alex came to his feet, anger surging through him. With his hands tied, he couldn't get hold of Murdock's gun, so he gave it a kick and sent it sliding on the carpet back toward Stanley, who picked it up.

"Facedown on the ground!" Alex shouted. "Hands behind your head!"

Murdock complied.

Still Alex stood over him, breathing hard, the gun pointed at the back of his head. He thought about what Murdock had done to Val. How he'd put her through hell last night, then tried again to kill her today. Hatred and disgust for everything this animal had done surged inside him, blinding him to everything except the desire to see him dead.

"I ought to blow your fucking head off," he said through clenched teeth, his mind growing dark. "Save the state the cost of throwing you back in prison."

"Alex!" Stanley said.

"I could do the world a favor and just blow you away right here," he said, shaking with rage. "Nobody would ever know the difference. Nobody would ever know that it wasn't self-defense."

"Alex, don't!"

"I could splatter your brains all over this floor, and you'd just be one more fucking slimebag who got what was coming to him. How does that sound? Are you ready to die, Murdock? *Are you?*"

"Alex!" Stanley said. "He's a murderer! *You're not!*"

Still tense with fury, his body shaking with anger, Alex continued to hold the gun on Murdock. Somewhere in the back of his mind, Stanley's words started to take hold, but it was several seconds before rationality finally crept in again. He lowered his weapon, his hands still trembling.

He'd almost killed Murdock.

He felt light-headed for a moment, unable to believe just how close he'd come to pulling that trigger. Never in his life had that kind of feeling come over him, a feeling that had nearly driven him to kill somebody in cold blood. Now he knew what it felt like to love a woman—to love her so much that he'd kill anybody who tried to hurt her.

He knelt down beside Stanley and held out his hands. "Get me untied."

The deputy tried to untie the rope that bound Alex's hands, but it was pulled too tight. He slipped his hand into his pocket, pulled out a pocketknife, and eventually managed to saw through it.

"Okay, Stanley," Alex said, yanking Murdock's hands behind his back and using a piece of the rope to bind them. "Where's your backup?"

Stanley looked at him with a shaky expression. "Uh . . . no backup."

Alex blinked. "But you said—"

"It's just me. I was going to call for backup when I heard shots. I didn't have time to call anyone. I just . . . I just turned around and came back."

Alex blinked with disbelief. "So all that crap about the cops beating down the door . . . ?"

"I was b-bluffing."

Alex just stared at him. "Bluffing?"

"It was what you told me to do, wasn't it? I saw Val peeking around the corner, and I could tell she caught on because she knew I hadn't had time to call anyone. I just hoped she could distract him somehow. Pretend to be the cops storming the place."

"You told this bastard to shoot you! Are you nuts?"

"I was afraid he'd heard Val. I was afraid he was going to go to the front door. I had to do something."

He pulled the knot tight around Murdock's wrists, then stood up. "Watch him."

Stanley raised his weapon again. "I will."

"How's the leg?"

"Okay. I don't think it's that bad."

Alex raced into the kitchen and yanked open drawers until he found dish towels. He ran back out and tossed one to Stanley.

"Fold it up. Hold it against the wound. Hard. And don't move it."

Then he dashed to the front door and found Val slumped against the wall, a fireplace poker still clutched in her hand. His heart hit his chest with a painful thud.

Blood. There was so much blood.

"Alex? Oh, Alex, oh, God—" She reached out and clasped his hand. "You got him, right?"

He knelt beside her. "Yeah, sweetheart. We got him."

He pulled the fireplace poker from her hand, trying not to panic. Blood covered the front of her shirt, her arm, her palm where she'd held it against the wound. No wonder Murdock had been fooled into thinking she was dead.

He put his arm behind her back, pulled her around, and laid her down on the tile floor. He pulled up her shirt and saw the wound. Fortunately, the rifle Murdock had used was a smaller-caliber weapon than the one he'd used in Tolosa. It was a clean bullet hole four inches below the top of her shoulder—too high to have hit her heart, too lateral to have hit her lung. Alex felt a small flush of relief. Then her eyes drifted closed.

"Val?"

She stirred a little, but didn't answer, and Alex felt a tremor of panic. She'd lost blood. A lot of it. He had to stop the bleeding and get her to a hospital.

He just prayed he did both those things in time.

chapter twenty-nine

The next two hours were pure agony for Alex.

Stanley told him that the nearest hospital was nearly fifty miles away in Wendover and would take at least an hour to reach. That was too long.

After packing and wrapping Val's wound to stop the bleeding, Alex called for help. He finally reached a trauma center in San Antonio, and they dispatched an AirLife flight. Then Alex gave the phone to Stanley, who called the cops from Ruston to come pick up Murdock and haul him to jail.

For the next thirty minutes, Alex put pressure against Val's wound. He managed to stop the flow of blood, but she'd lost so much already that he knew she was in danger. She drifted in and out of consciousness, and he was helpless to do anything but hold her and pray.

The cops from Ruston arrived to take Murdock away just before the AirLife flight arrived, and Stanley filled them in on the situation. Then the paramedics took both Val and Stanley aboard, telling Alex that because it was a trauma situation and not merely a transport, he couldn't accompany them. When the emergency personnel hooked Val up to fluids and monitors and God knew what else, he could see the worried looks on their faces. He kissed her good-bye even though he wasn't completely sure she knew he was there. Then watched the helicopter climb into the night, its lights eventually disappearing in the distance, and he prayed that it wouldn't be the last time he'd see her alive.

He ran back to Val's van to make the trip to San Antonio. As he drove down the highway, it seemed as if he were moving into an endless darkness that he might never emerge from. And through it all, images of Val's face as she lay on that gurney, pale and unconscious, filled his mind. The very thought that he might have lost her ripped his heart in two. His *heart*. Up until a few days ago, there hadn't been enough evidence anywhere to convict him of having one of those.

He counted every mile he put behind him, until finally he saw the city lights of San Antonio in the distance. Twenty minutes later he was pulling into the hospital parking lot, his stomach knotted with a sickening mixture of anticipation and dread.

As he entered the hospital, he couldn't get the worst-case scenario out of his mind. What if Val had lost her life to save his? How could he ever live with that?

He went to the front desk of the emergency room. "Valerie Parker," he said to the woman behind the desk. "They brought her in on an AirLife flight. Can you tell me her condition?"

The woman stood up. "Are you a family member?"

Alex's heart lurched. "No, just a friend. Please tell me—"

"Is your name Alex?"

He stopped, startled. "Yes."

"She was asking for someone named Alex."

For a moment Alex couldn't move, couldn't breathe. "Where is she?"

"They've taken her to surgery. Now that they've got her stabilized, it's just a matter of repairing the damage from the bullet wound."

Alex felt such a flush of relief that he thought for a minute that his legs weren't going to hold him up. He put his palms against the counter until the feeling passed. Val was alive. He took a deep breath and let it out slowly, feeling a tremendous amount of tension slip away. She was going to be okay.

"But you don't look so good," the nurse said.

"No. I'm fine. Believe me. Can you tell me about the deputy sheriff they brought in with her?"

"Gunshot wound to the leg. All they had to do was extract the bullet and debride the wound. He's in a room now, probably sleeping."

"Good. I'll see him in the morning."

"You can go up to surgery and wait for her there, if you want to. Third floor."

Alex headed upstairs, stopping only to phone Dave to tell

him that the real killer was in custody. The relief he heard in his brother's voice almost matched his own. Then he told Dave about Val and let him know that he'd probably be staying in San Antonio for several more days.

Then Dave warned him that until Murdock was in custody in Tolosa, Alex was still suspect number one, and that he still had a legal mess to work out when he came back to town with the bail-jumping and the breaking-and-entering charges. In light of the identity of the real murderer, though, he told Alex that he didn't think Reichert would be gung-ho to press charges on the latter. Alex didn't give a damn about any of that. Those problems seemed so petty compared to what he'd gone through in the past few hours that he merely told Dave to boot Millner into action. Then he hung up the phone and concentrated on the only thing that mattered right now.

Val.

An hour and a half later, a doctor came out to the waiting room to tell Alex that everything had gone just fine, and that he could come in to see her. He stood up, relief washing over him. But he wasn't going to relax completely until he'd touched her again. Held her hand. Kissed her. Told her how crazy she was for trying to save his life.

And how much he loved her for doing it.

Val opened her eyes, but it was a minute before she realized where she was. In a hospital. In a very ugly gown. Hooked up to about a thousand tubes and needles. Her shoulder was bandaged and her hair was stuck up inside some weird paper cap that rubbed against her forehead.

Then she turned and saw Alex. For a moment she thought he must be a dream, but then she reached out her hand, and he enveloped it in both of his. He felt strong. Steady. In control. Which meant that she didn't have to be.

"Alex," she said weakly. "You're finally here."

"I had a long way to drive. By the time I got here, they'd already taken you to surgery."

"Tell me it's over. Tell me we can go home soon."

"It's over," he said, smiling softly. "Murdock is in custody."

"Murdock?"

"Rick. I have a lot to tell you about that."

"Stanley?"

"He's going to be fine, too."

"He took a bullet."

"You both did."

"Yeah. I'm kinda tired of getting shot."

"That's not going to happen again, sweetheart. Not on my watch, anyway."

She smiled. "I have a lot to tell you, too, about what happened tonight."

"There'll be plenty of time for that tomorrow. But for now . . ."

His voice trailed off. He just stood there, staring down at her, as if he wanted to say something, but couldn't find the words.

"The whole time I was at that ranch," he said finally, "when I was sure I was going to die . . ." He looked away, bowing his head, his voice suddenly choked. "I kept thinking about you. And I thought, if I ever got the chance to see you again, just one more chance . . ."

He paused again, and she was surprised to see tears fill his eyes. He blinked quickly, then let out a breath of frustration.

"I'm not very good at this."

She smiled. "I don't think either of us is very good at it. We're kind of short on experience."

He nodded. "I just wanted to tell you . . ."

"What?"

"I love you, Val. And nothing will *ever* make me stop."

He stared at her with such warmth, such tenderness, that she felt her heart suddenly laid bare—totally open, totally vulnerable, totally belonging to him. And for once in her life, it wasn't something to be afraid of. It was something to cherish.

"I love you, too, Alex."

He leaned over and gave her a gentle but lingering kiss, making her feel so warm and safe and secure that she nearly drifted right off to sleep again.

The nurses insisted she stay in recovery for another hour. Alex refused to leave her side, watching over her as she drifted in and out of sleep. Finally, at about four A.M., they wheeled her into a regular room. Since the other bed in the double room was unoccupied, the nurses took pity on Alex and told him he could sleep there. He made certain Val was comfortable, then pulled off his boots and lay down, his size-fourteen feet hanging off the end of the bed. Within seconds of his head hitting the pillow, he was asleep.

Val closed her eyes, too, secure in the fact that when she opened them again, he would be there.

At a little after seven o'clock the next morning, Stanley phoned his aunt Thelma to tell her what had happened the night before, only to discover that she'd found out herself not five minutes before. One of the cops from Ruston had apparently told his girlfriend about the incident at the Reichert ranch, and her brother worked for Odell, so of course the news got to Raydine, which meant that within thirty minutes the whole town knew, including his aunt. He assured her that he was just fine, but she told him that she'd be the judge of that when she got there in a couple of hours to bring him home.

An hour and a half later, as Stanley was watching an *Adam-12* rerun, he glanced over to see Alex at the door of his hospital room. In spite of everything, just the sight of the man intimidated him. He flipped off the TV and sat up a little, trying not to look stupid in his dumb hospital gown, trying not to wince at the pain in his leg. And then he saw who was with Alex, and he felt even more self-conscious.

Glenda.

Suddenly he couldn't breathe, and it had nothing to do with his injury. She looked as beautiful as she always did, soft and delicate as a dandelion. She was holding a yellow pad and a pen.

"Stanley?" Alex said. "How you doing?"

"Uh . . . okay. How's Val?"

"She's doing just fine."

Stanley turned to Glenda. "I guess you heard."

"The whole town knows. Mr. Grimstead says it's the biggest story they've ever had down at the paper, so the minute he heard, he sent me here to talk to you." She smiled. "Hope you don't mind."

"Uh—no. No, of course not."

"I saw Alex on the way in and interviewed him already. He filled me in on everything."

Stanley turned his gaze to Alex, swallowing hard. "Everything?"

"Yes," Alex said. "I told her exactly what happened."

Stanley closed his eyes. He thought about how he'd lain at that murderer's feet, sniveling, begging, practically wetting his pants, praying that he could get the guy to believe what he was telling him before he killed all of them.

"I told her how you took the situation into your own hands," Alex said. "I told her how you took a bullet. And I told her that while you were laying there bleeding, you still had the guts to hold it together long enough so that you could bluff Murdock into thinking that you had an entire army on the way."

Stanley blinked with surprise. He swallowed hard, shifting his gaze back and forth between Alex and Glenda. *That* was what he'd told her?

"I didn't exactly, you know, overpower the guy," Stanley said.

"I know. You played it exactly right."

"Huh?"

"Murdock had the upper hand. If you'd acted like a tough guy, he would have seen you as a threat, and he wouldn't have let his guard down. You set up the scenario, Val provided the distraction, and I took him out. We were a hell of a team."

A team?

"It was a brilliant plan, Stanley. And you pulled it off."

He stuck out his hand, and Stanley shook it. "I don't forget a favor. If there's anything you ever need, you just let me know."

Stanley nodded.

"And something else."

"Yeah?"

Alex came closer, lowering his voice. "When I got angry back there, thanks for pulling me back. You had a better handle on the situation than I did right about then. You know what I mean?"

Stanley nodded, knowing that from now on, that was going to be something just between the two of them. "Yeah. I know."

"I'll drop by again later," Alex told Stanley. "If there's anything you need, though, I'll be with Val."

"She's a nice lady. You take care of her, okay?"

Alex smiled. "No problem. Hang in there, Stanley."

As Alex turned and walked out the door, Stanley couldn't

believe it. The man had been so sincere that he almost believed every word he'd spoken. Almost.

Glenda pulled a chair up close to his bed and sat down, still holding that pad and pen.

"Alex told me everything," she said, a note of excitement in her voice. "He told me who they really are, about his murder accusation, all of it. And he went on and on about how you saved their lives." She smiled. "So I guess this means you're a hero."

Hero?

Just the word sent shivers running down his spine. He'd dreamed of this moment since the day he'd first seen Glenda walking down Cedar Street. He'd dreamed of her looking at him in awe and admiration because he'd stopped a holdup or rescued a hostage or something equally life-threatening. He'd dreamed of being called a hero. And that was what she'd done. She'd called him a hero.

Hell, he hadn't been a hero at all. An officer of the law should be able to look danger right in the eye and never blink. Not him. He'd been terrified.

"You outwitted a murderer," Glenda went on, her eyes alive with interest. "What were you thinking? Right at that moment?"

She looked at him intently, her pen poised over her pad, waiting to capture the very next words he spoke. He started to tell her how it was no big deal, really. All in a day's work for a lawman like him, that he and danger went hand in hand. But she was staring at him as if she saw right through him, and for the first time every bit of the bravado he'd tried so hard all these years to make a part of himself slipped away. As he stared back at Glenda, he felt more exposed than if he were walking down a country road minus his pants. And suddenly all he could do was tell the truth.

"I was scared," he murmured. "Every minute. From the time I got to that house to the time Alex finally took the guy out, I was scared. I've never been so scared in all my life."

He looked away, unable to believe that he'd spoken the words, knowing he'd just lived up to everything everybody had been saying about him all these years. And now he'd gone and confessed it to the one person he fervently hoped would never know.

"So. I guess I'm not the hero you think I am."

Silence fell over the room. He waited for her to get up and walk out, to put as much distance between herself and a coward as possible. Instead, she set her pen and pad down on the chair and came to his bedside. She sat down beside him. She put her hand against his arm. It was warm and soft, just as he'd always imagined it would be.

"It doesn't take much to be a hero if you're not afraid," she told him. "Seems to me that the brave man is the one who's scared and does what needs to be done, anyway."

For a moment, her words paralyzed him, because he'd never in his life thought about courage that way. Could it be that guys like Alex were afraid, too, only they took action anyway?

Glenda continued to stare at him with an odd but pleasant look on her face, like maybe she knew something he didn't, though he couldn't imagine what.

Then she leaned in closer. He smelled her perfume, the sweetest, most inviting scent he'd ever experienced, and like every other time he'd ever laid eyes on her, she was so beautiful that just the sight of her made him dizzy. Then she drew closer and did the unthinkable.

She touched her lips to his.

In that moment the whole world seemed to tunnel down to this one moment, this one place in time where Glenda McMurray was kissing him. And he knew that if he left this earth in his next heartbeat, he'd die a happy man.

Later that day, Alex was sitting by Val's bed, listening with disbelief as she related the story about the hundred-dollar bill, and how she'd figured out that Murdock was guilty. Then it was Val's turn to be surprised when Alex told her that he'd been Murdock's target all along, not Shannon.

Alex heard a knock on the hospital room door. The door opened, and Dave poked his head inside. Alex couldn't believe it. He had no idea his brother was coming to San Antonio.

"Can I come in?" Dave asked.

"Sure."

Dave winced a little. "Can I bring Brenda with me?"

Oh, boy. Alex had hoped to be able to shield Val as long as possible from some of the more fringe members of his family, but she was feeling quite a bit better now, and he supposed it was as good a time as any for an initial exposure.

"Come on in," he said. "Both of you."

Alex stood up and hugged his brother, feeling as if he'd left Tolosa a lifetime ago. Brenda actually gave him a heartfelt hug, too, and Alex had to admit that there was indeed a first time for everything.

"How did you two get here?" he asked.

"We drove to Dallas and caught a Southwest flight out of Love Field this morning," Dave said.

"Why didn't you tell me you were coming?"

"Because we were afraid you'd tell us it wasn't necessary," Brenda said, "to which I would have said, 'Bullshit,' and then you would have said, 'No, it's *not* bullshit,' and it would have turned into a nasty argument, and . . . well, you can see how this was a much better way to handle the situation."

Dave turned to Val. "You'll have to forgive Brenda. She tends to state things a little differently than the rest of the human race."

Val smiled, looking not the least bit distressed.

"Millner's on the case for both of you," Dave said. "He says he's cleared up far worse problems during a coffee break."

Alex grinned. "You know, I've always liked that guy."

Dave rolled his eyes, then turned to Val. "So how are you feeling?"

"Much better now."

"Is my brother taking care of you?"

"Every minute."

Brenda stepped over to Val's bedside, wearing her usual uniform of black jeans, black T-shirt, black boots, and black sunglasses, with that look on her face that said she could bite the bumper off a Buick and spit out scrap metal. She swept her sunglasses off and gave Val a once-over.

"So," she said to Alex. "This is Valerie Parker. The one who saved your ass."

"Yeah, Brenda," Alex said. "The one who saved my ass."

Brenda nodded toward Alex. "Six four, two-twenty, and it

takes a shot of estrogen to save the day. It's like I've always told him: never underestimate the power of a pissed-off woman."

Val turned to Alex with a big smile. "Oooh. I like her."

Alex shook his head sadly. He was in for it. He couldn't have fallen in love with a nice, normal woman who would help him counter some of the insanity that ran in his family. No. He had to find one who fueled the fire. For the rest of his life, he was going to be tormented by his family, and his wife would think it was funny.

Wife? Where had *that* come from?

He banished the thought, but still the word kept popping into his head. He waited for it to give him hives, or fry his brain, or maybe just float away on the same crazy cloud it had floated in on.

It didn't. And he knew why.

Because Val was the one.

She was the one who made him think. Made him feel. Made him not want to let another moment pass when he wasn't touching her. Holding her. Kissing her. The one he wanted to fight with, make up with, make love with, grow old with. He thought he'd even known it five years ago, too. They'd just had to go to hell and back before he finally realized it.

Dave turned to Alex. "I suppose you've been yelling at her."

Alex smiled. "All the time."

"Good," Dave said. "That's good."

Val looked perplexed. "What's that supposed to mean?"

"It means," Alex said, sitting down on the bed and taking her hand, "that my brother is a know-it-all."

"Who knows more than Alex wants to admit," Dave added.

Alex brushed a strand of hair from Val's cheek and tucked it behind her ear. Then he leaned in and gave her a kiss. It went on a little longer than he'd anticipated, but he just couldn't seem to stop himself.

"Hey!" Brenda said, making a face of total disgust. "You two want to get a room?"

"They have a room," Dave said.

She looked around. "Oh. Yeah."

"And we're leaving it." He took Brenda by the arm. "We'll get the whole story later. We just wanted to see for ourselves that you two were all right. We'll take Val's van back later and you two can fly home as soon as she's feeling better."

"Thanks," Alex said. "That'd be great."

"And when you get back, you can come have lunch with the family."

Alex closed his eyes with a weary sigh.

"Sounds wonderful," Val said. "I can't wait to meet everyone."

"They can't wait to meet you, either. We'll see you two later."

Dave and Brenda left the room, pulling the door closed behind them.

"My family," Alex said, sighing with resignation. "Oh, well. If you survived Brenda, everything's downhill from there." He smiled. "You're going to fit right in."

Val's brow crinkled. "Is that a compliment?"

"Of course it is. Oh—and I have a question for you."

"Yes?"

"Will you marry me?"

For a full ten seconds, Val stared at him, her expression completely dumbfounded. Her mouth hung open as if there were something she wanted to say, but she just couldn't find the words.

"Wh-what did you say?"

He leaned closer and spoke very slowly. "I said, 'Will you marry me?' "

She continued to stare at him as if his words simply wouldn't compute. Then she turned away suddenly, waving her hand.

"No, Alex. No. You're getting all caught up in the moment here. You didn't mean to say that, and I'm perfectly willing to forget that you did."

"Val?"

She turned back slowly. "Yes?"

"Have you ever known me to say something I didn't mean?"

She blinked. "Uh . . . no."

"Then why in the world would you believe that I don't mean this?"

"I-I don't know. It's just so . . . so . . ."

"Look, I know it sounds like it's coming out of nowhere, but is it really? I'm thirty-four years old. I've never even come close to feeling about a woman the way I feel about you. It was there five years ago, and it's here now. Do you really want to wait around another five years to see where we stand then?"

She smiled. "That's not a bad argument."

"Coming from the master, I'll take that as a compliment. Can I also take it as a yes?"

"Yes. You can take it as a yes."

He exhaled. "Well, thank God. I really needed to win this one."

"Don't think they're all going to be that easy."

He smiled. "I may be in love, but I'm not delusional."

Her expression grew solemn. She put her hand against his face, stroking his cheek with her thumb. "I can barely remember a time when I didn't love you."

Alex knew exactly how she felt. But why hadn't he seen it until now? Why hadn't he understood that unsteady, breathless feeling he had when he was around her, that unaccustomed feeling of being totally out of control, that feeling that somebody else had stolen away a piece of him that he might never get back? Why hadn't he recognized those things for what they were?

Love.

He leaned down and gave Val a gentle kiss to seal his proposal, still astonished at everything that had happened since she came back into his life. How could he have known that the wild, willful woman he thought he should avoid at all costs was the one he would end up loving forever?

Don't miss this irresistible novel
by Jane Graves!

I GOT YOU, BABE

On the run for a robbery she didn't commit, Renee
Esterhaus is stuck in the middle of Texas with a
broken car and a sadistic bounty hunter hot on her
trail. Desperate for a way out, Renee decides to
make a promise she never intends to keep—offer
the first man she meets a night of unforgettable
pleasure in return for a ride. A night to remember,
all right, since the handsome guy turns out to be a
cop with a pair of handcuffs and zero tolerance
for sweet-talking criminals.

John DeMarco was supposed to be on vacation.
But even with his guard down, he doesn't expect to
be duped—especially by a beautiful blonde con
artist whose claims of innocence and tempting
curves are nearly impossible to resist. Renee is
not a woman he can trust . . . so why does he
feel himself falling in love?

Subscribe to the new Pillow Talk e-newsletter—and receive all these fabulous online features directly in your e-mail inbox:

♥ Exclusive essays and other features by major romance writers like Linda Howard, Kristin Hannah, Julie Garwood, and Suzanne Brockmann

♥ Exciting behind-the-scenes news from our romance editors

♥ Special offers, including contests to win signed romance books and other prizes

♥ Author tour information, and monthly announcements about the newest books on sale

♥ A *Pillow Talk* readers forum, featuring feedback from romance fans...like you!

Two easy ways to subscribe:
Go to **www.ballantinebooks.com/PillowTalk**
to sign up, or send a blank e-mail to
join-PillowTalk@list.randomhouse.com.

Pillow Talk—
the romance e-newsletter brought to you by
Ballantine Books